Magus Draconum

A Novel of the Road of Legends

Robert B. Marks

Published by Legacy Books Press
RPO Princess, Box 21031
445 Princess Street
Kingston, Ontario, K7L 5P5
Canada

www.legacybookspress.com

This edition first published in 2023 by Legacy Books Press in
association with Nuada Press
1

Printed and bound in Canada, the United States of America and Great
Britain.

Serialized on Tapas between April 5, 2022, and January 10, 2023.

This book is typeset in a Times New Roman 11-point font.

Cover art by Art_Dabdab, adapted from *Abandoned in the Arctic Ice
Fields*, by William Bradford (1823-1892).
(https://dabdab.carrd.co/)

Library and Archives Canada Cataloguing in Publication

Title: Magus Draconum : a novel of the Road of Legends / Robert B.
    Marks.
Names: Marks, Robert B., 1976- author.
Identifiers: Canadiana (print) 20190240946 | Canadiana (ebook)
    20190240962 | ISBN 9781927537435 (softcover) | ISBN
    9781927537442 (Kindle)
Classification: LCC PS8626.A75417 M34 2020 | DDC
    C813/.6—dc23

This book is not responsible for any mishaps that may occur to the
reader while attempting to pet dragons.

To Dennis L. McKiernan,
And the Dragons of alt.fan.dragons,
(wherever you may now be).

Introduction

Believe it or not, even though this book has a wizard university, it has nothing to do with *Harry Potter*.

I wrote *Magus Draconum* in the last years of the 1990s. It was my first novel as an adult (not my first novel, though – that was *Demon's Vengeance*, and it reads like it was written by a teenager...which it was). It was where I broke away from the more cliched stories of an ancient evil rising, and instead decided to tell the story of an immortal – or at least the formative years of one.

Most of the inspiration came from *Magic: the Gathering* and my experience as an undergraduate during my first degree at Queen's University, with a dash of *Highlander* thrown in for good measure. The main character, Delgar Dragonmage (originally Delric Dragonmage), first appeared in a short story based on the the illustration from the Nalathni Dragon *Magic* card that I tried to sell to Wizards of the Coast's magazine, the Duelist. They turned down the story, but it and the character stuck with me. That story became one of the events of Delgar's life, and appears in Part I, nearly unaltered, as Chapter XIII ("The Beginning of Wyrd").

So why is this book only now, over twenty years later, seeing the light of day? The answer has everything to do with Peter Jackson's *The Lord of the Rings* trilogy. Or, more specifically, how the major publishers reacted to it.

The Lord of the Rings trilogy was a phenomenon unlike most others. I remember when *The Fellowship of the Ring* was released to home video – for over a week you could walk down the street and overhear parts of the movie playing from the houses as you passed by. Fantasy was suddenly hotter than it had ever been, and the publishers glutted themselves on it. For a few months, there was a window in which it became very easy to sell a fantasy novel to a major publisher. If you missed that window, however, the waiting time for a reply to any submission went from a few months to years.

I missed that window.

By the time my e-book *Diablo Demonsbane* was published, I had two publishable fantasy novels ready to go – *Magus Draconum* and *War of Succession*, both of which were standalone novels. My agent at the time and I figured that of the two, *Magus Draconum* would be the harder sell (its sub-genre could best be described as biographical apocalyptic mythical fantasy). So, we went all-in on *War of Succession*, figuring that *Magus Draconum* would be the follow-up once I'd proven myself.

What happened instead killed my fiction career.

Here's the thing about writing novels: to the writer, a novel is a marathon. It is an endurance run, and momentum is key. Rejection letters do not really make a difference – finding a publisher is a numbers game, and when you've got an agent, much of that gets taken out of your hands anyway. I didn't run into the problem of my book being rejected. The problem was that *War of Succession* didn't get any answer at all.

Despite being an agented (and solicited!) submission, the novel sat on the desk of one publisher for years, before being moved to sit on the desk of another publisher for years. I finally lost faith in the entire world of the big publishing houses when I had to ask my agent "how many decades must I wait for a reply?" Since the book that would launch my fiction career outside of what was, at the time, the very small world of e-books, had been stuck in limbo, the momentum for my other novel projects failed.

After all, what was the point of writing a novel if nobody would ever see it anyway?

It hit particularly hard because I came up as an author before the proper rise of the self-publishing world, before authors like Hugh Howey broke the mold with books like *Wool*. This was (and remains) a major psychological barrier to publishing it through my own publishing company. It took over two decades to overcome it (in fact, *The Eternity Quartet* with Ed Greenwood was an attempt to test the waters while giving me an opportunity to write some fiction that somebody might actually read).

But here we are – and *Magus Draconum* is finally in your hands.

It's a story told by a much younger storyteller than I am now. That makes it rougher than my writing today, but also a bit more daring, I think. And besides, where else will you read about thousands of dragons attacking a magical glacier?

Enjoy!

Robert B. Marks
September 25, 2022

Prologue: A Man Alone

The figure watched the light snow kick up at his boots as the wind howled around him, icy and biting. The blue-white glacier beneath his feet still radiated some of its former evil, but it no longer tried to drink his life.

He could remember when it had.

Looking around the frozen landscape with his haunted blue eyes, the man ignored the chill biting through his leather boots. He wore a heavy woolen cloak and robes, and he rubbed his leather-gloved hands together, a paltry defense against the all-consuming cold.

"My world," he muttered with a sad, soft voice. "This was once my world." It had been called Mideorth, a land filled with life and beauty. But the name was meaningless now; all the joy had fled from it. For a moment he felt a tear coming, but he pushed it down. He had wept too often for his fallen homeland, and one more tear would be an admission of utter defeat.

He remembered so much. He remembered when the

world was green and full of life. He remembered the times when his spirit was filled with joy. He remembered the thousands of years...

He blinked in shock. Had it really been six thousand years? Had it all passed so quickly?

Forcing back another tear, he watched the sun begin to set over the luminous ice. Somewhere to the south he knew the ice ended for a short distance, but that little, free stretch was a wasteland of snow for most of the year. He had been back so often, seen the small settlements that remained of what had once been a great and noble people, watched as they tried to fend off starvation with what little they could grow in the mere four months they had before the harsh winter swept down upon them again.

Even now, the source of the glacier remained a mystery. It had simply come and destroyed all that he knew, transforming a fertile world into a wasteland. And no matter how hard he tried, there had been nothing he could do to stop it.

"I am Delgar, Magus Draconum!" the man shouted at the top of his lungs, listening as his words echoed for an eternity and then faded. "You will not destroy me!" he shouted again.

The echoes surrounded him, a mocking reply to his challenge, and then all he heard was the empty howling of the bitter wind.

Delgar gazed at the sun, watching it finally sink beneath the horizon, cloaking the world in luminescent darkness, the night lit by the stars and the glacier. How deep was the ice now? He seemed to remember it being two thousand feet deep. Or maybe it was three thousand; for some reason that memory eluded him.

He drew his cloak closer around him and began to walk, the rough ice only slightly slippery under his feet. As he strode forward, he remembered.

Six thousand years. It had been that long. And he recalled so much...

Part I
Delgar Dragonfriend

Chapter I: An Innocent Youth

There was something special about the boy, Daegar decided, and he had a feeling it wasn't just a father's pride speaking.

Resting for a moment, hoe at his side, Daegar looked at his son. The boy, short, gaunt, sandy haired, and full of energy, was playing in the garden again. Daegar grinned; he was only twenty-nine, and the ten-year old bundle of joy would probably kill him from exhaustion within two years.

"Delgar!" he called, striding over.

The little boy, his bright blue eyes gleaming with excitement, looked up. Daegar's heart soared; if there was anybody who gave his life more meaning than Delgar, he didn't know who it could be.

"What are you doing now, little one?" Daegar asked, rubbing his grubby hand through his shoulder length blond hair. Long hair was the custom of his people, the Nordlanders, short hair only reserved for the monks who serviced the spiritual needs of the people.

"I'm a Dragon!" Delgar declared happily, and spread his hands out in a strange imitation of wings. Daegar noted that Delgar's hair was already beginning to darken; a sign that he would take after his mother's side of the family. Oh well, there were plenty of ways that he took after his father too.

"I don't see you breathing fire," Daegar challenged playfully.

"I'm just not doing it now."

Daegar nodded sagely, delighted by the innocent logic. "I see."

"Will you tell me a story, Dada?" Delgar asked, stopping in the middle of the field, his arms falling awkwardly to his side.

"I'm working right now," Daegar pointed out. "I told you a story this morning."

"But I want another story," Delgar pouted.

Glancing back at the field, Daegar decided he didn't want to return to his toils quite yet. Smiling at Delgar, he deftly changed the subject. "Why are you a Dragon?"

Delgar's face lit up, eyes filled with excitement. "They're big and powerful and they fly so high! They live forever and..."

Daegar frowned melodramatically. "And what would happen to your dada if you became big and powerful and immortal and flew so high?"

"You'd be a Dragon too," Delgar said confidently, hands on his hips.

"And why would you want to be big and powerful?" Daegar asked. "Look at you! You're ten winters old. If you get any bigger, you'll be able to beat any Dragon that ever comes at you."

Delgar grinned widely.

Suddenly, a brief movement in the high grasses

surrounding the field caught Daegar's eye. Putting his finger to his lips, he motioned Delgar to him. The little boy crept up, and looked where Daegar pointed.

"Now be very, very quiet, and move very, very slowly," Daegar hissed, his heart fluttering. Careful not to make a move, lest he send the creature into flight, he pointed again. "You see that?"

Delgar's eyes widened. A tiny green serpentine head gazed at him evenly from the grass, its beady eyes blinking occasionally. A long forked tongue flickered out, and the drake stretched out its snaking neck. Twin wings flapped for a moment, almost as if the little creature meant to take off, but then it glanced at Delgar and calmed down.

"It's a grass drake," Daegar whispered. "You see how it's perched on that blade of grass? That's how they sit."

"Can I keep him?" Delgar asked loudly, and then put his hands over his mouth, his eyes wide with fear that he would scare it away. The grass drake only looked at him, completely unperturbed.

"It's a wild animal," Daegar explained softly, smiling at the innocence of the question. "You can't keep it as a pet. It's not right."

"Why not?"

"Because it's not. You'll understand when you get older."

Delgar pouted. "I want to understand now."

Daegar smiled and hugged his son. "Some things come with age. Don't worry about it. If you're very still and you're really lucky, he may come closer."

Come closer it did. Delgar held out his hand, stepping slowly forward, and the grass drake leapt into the air, landing on his arm. Delgar startled as it turned and looked at him, but the little creature only flicked its tongue at him and settled down contentedly.

Daegar's eyes widened in disbelief as he knelt down

slowly beside his son. "Keep very still," he cautioned.

Grinning, the boy looked the grass drake in the eyes. The little creature cooed softly and looked around.

"Can I keep him?" Delgar asked again, adding quickly: "I'll take good care of him, and I promise he won't burn the house down."

Daegar shook his head, torn between amusement and wonder. "Remember this moment, but you will have to let him go. It is the way of things."

Delgar frowned for a moment, almost heartbreaking disappointment in his eyes. "I don't like that."

"I can't do anything about it. Wyrd is wyrd."

Leaping into the air, the grass drake flew over the fields, every stroke of its wings graceful and stately. Finally, the small creature disappeared back into the tall grasses.

Daegar hugged his son and smiled, the wondrous moment forever impressed in his memory. "I'll bet that was better than any story."

Delgar nodded eagerly. "Can I do it again?"

"We'll see," Daegar mused. "Now, go inside and help mama."

As Delgar meandered to the thatched cottage by the fields, waving his arms in the air as though he might take flight like the grass drake, Daegar looked towards the grasses. Incredible, he thought. It was absolutely incredible; not even in the legends had there been an event even remotely like it.

It was also getting late, he reflected, and he still had a lot of work to do. Returning to his hoe, he plucked the weeds from his crop with the precision of a man who had been a farmer all his life, wondering if even now a grass drake gazed at his son.

Helyna had invited Thorgar and Bessa to dinner that night, and Daegar couldn't fault her: Thorgar was one of his childhood friends, and he often came bearing the meat of a freshly downed deer, a welcome addition to Daegar's simple diet.

After a delightful meal of roasted venison cooked by Helyna, the candles were lit, Delgar sat down to play, and Bessa joined Helyna in cleaning the plates, knives and cooking spit in the kitchen. Daegar glanced out the window at the starry night, collecting his thoughts and musing on the day's events with the contentment that only a full stomach can provide.

He gazed at the tall, muscular warrior sitting beside him at the rough wooden table and grinned. Thorgar had decided to leave his farming roots and joined with some reavers ten years ago. Since then, he had become a warrior of increasing fame all over Nordland, and the village considered him to be a protector.

"How does battle suit you?" Daegar asked.

"About as well as farming suits you," Thorgar replied with a wide grin, a sparkle in his eyes. "The Dragon's winning this time."

Daegar looked to where Delgar sat on the ground, playing with his wooden animals. He had gone to Wigmund a couple of years ago, asking the carpenter to make him some animals for his son. Wigmund had quickly delivered a wooden Dragon, unicorn, cow, horse, rabbit and eagle, each exquisitely crafted. Delgar had liked the Dragon and unicorn the most, and the others were soon forgotten.

Making whooshing sounds, Delgar sat, the Dragon in one hand and the unicorn in the other, banging the two together, the mock battle fast and furious.

"You keep track?" Daegar asked his friend, raising an eyebrow.

11

"Yes," Thorgar replied, a sudden twinge of sadness in his voice. "Gives me something to do while I pine for a child of my own."

Daegar grimaced. Thorgar had taken a bride from a raid, only to have her perish in labor. To make matters worse, the child was stillborn as well. It seemed as though something had died in his friend that day.

"I think Delgar's special," Daegar said quietly, cursing himself for his timing. But the incident in the field was strange and wondrous, and he had to tell *somebody*. "Something happened today."

Thorgar laughed, the sadness not quite replaced by a sparkle in his eyes. "Of course Delgar is something special to you! He's your son!"

"I mean something out of the ordinary," Daegar said. "Something that doesn't exist in other children."

Suddenly, very interested, Thorgar leaned forward, his brown moustache bristling. "What happened today?"

"We came across a grass drake when I was farming."

"This is Nordland. Every summer the grasses are full of those timid things. You can't walk for more than ten feet without running into one."

"This one perched on Delgar's arm."

Thorgar leaned back thoughtfully, his gaze impassive. It was a look Daegar had seen in his friend before, usually when the warrior was considering something of great import. "Are you sure?"

"Of course I'm sure. I was two feet away at the time."

There was a moment of silence, and then Thorgar shrugged. "Perhaps it is a portent."

"Of what? Is it good or bad?"

"The monk would know."

Daegar shook his head. "I don't trust him."

Helyna's plump form bustled out of the kitchen, followed by Bessa. Helyna's dark hair was ruffled, but her blue eyes sparkled with a passion Daegar loved with all his heart. When Delgar had been born, he did not know if he could ever share his love, but now he couldn't imagine his life without both of them to complete his spirit.

Nodding to Daegar, she turned to Delgar. "Come on, love. It's time to go to bed."

"I don't want to go to bed," Delgar whined, putting down his toys. "I want dada to tell me a story."

"Dada will be up shortly to tell you a story," Helyna promised. "Now say goodnight to Uncle Thorgar."

"Goodnight Uncle Thorgar."

Grudgingly, Delgar allowed Helyna to lead him off into the hallways of the cottage.

"What were you two talking about?" Bessa inquired. She was Thorgar's new wife, a thin woman from the south who the warrior had captured on a raid and promptly fallen for. Daegar only hoped that she would rekindle what was lost in his friend, and at times it appeared that his prayers would be answered.

"Delgar," Thorgar replied, then turned back to his friend. "Why don't you trust the monk? He is a holy man."

"His mind is too closed," Daegar explained. "Anything he can't understand is the work of the Damned One, and I don't want to bring Delgar before a man like that."

"I will respect your wishes," Thorgar promised, pursing his lips. "By the way, I will be bringing you a sword when we meet next."

Daegar blinked, startled. "Why?"

"The goblin raiders struck Garson's Peak last season," the warrior explained. "In a couple of years, they could work their way inland to here. I want you to learn how to use it, my friend."

"You know how I hate weapons," Daegar said, unwilling to give Thorgar's fears any substance. "I'm a farmer, not a warrior."

Thorgar leaned forward, his eyes eager and serious. "Weapons are a necessary evil. Remember, the Damned One holds as much sway on Mideorth as the Eternal One. I want you to be protected, so Delgar will grow up in safety."

"I will consider it," Daegar said, holding up his hand as his friend began to protest. "But that is all I will promise. After all, protecting us farmers is what you warriors are here for."

"We should go," Bessa told her new husband, her voice becoming husky. "There are some things I want to do."

Thorgar grinned as he allowed her to pull him from the table. "Duty calls," he joked, making his way to the door. "I fear we must take our leave of you. Where is Helyna?"

"I'm here!" Helyna called, rushing towards them. She gave both Bessa and Thorgar a kiss on the cheek, and they watched the two newlyweds walk off into the night, a torch in the warrior's hand.

"You have an early morning tomorrow," Helyna pointed out.

Daegar nodded. "I know. But I have to tell Delgar a story first."

Helyna slid up to her husband and pressed herself against him, her hands on his rear. "And I want you too."

Daegar smiled and kissed her, one of his hands cupping her breast. "Delgar first."

Making his way down the hall, he turned into Delgar's room to find the boy humming a nameless tune as he sat in bed, the candle burning low on the table beside him.

"Hello little one," he said softly.

"Is it time for my story?" Delgar asked eagerly, his eyes afire.

"Oh yes," Daegar said, sitting down on the bed. "What do you want to hear about?"

"I want to hear about Dragons!"

Daegar chuckled; somehow, he knew *that* was coming. "Okay, I'll tell you a story about Dragons. I'll tell you about the Dragon and the wizard."

"I've already heard that one," Delgar pouted. "Tell me a new story about Dragons."

"Okay, I'll tell you about the Dragon and the maiden," Daegar conceded, remembering a story from his youth. Somehow, it seemed fitting right now. "Once, a long time ago, when the world was young, there was a great Dragon, the greatest of them all. He had seen the last of the Dragon Masters fall in the great rebellion of Dragons where fire fell to Mideorth and civilization began. This Dragon was named 'Garasus.'"

"Why was he named Garasus?" Delgar asked, leaning forward eagerly.

Daegar didn't even pause. "Garasus is a name of great importance to the Dragons, and he was proud to bear that name. And, for thousands of years Garasus guided the mortals who came to him with wisdom and honor. But, the years were not kind to him, and as his wealth grew, so did his greed. And soon he became a creature of great evil, and he began to demand tribute from the kingdoms around him.

"At first the kingdoms did not obey, thinking that Garasus would not harm them, for they had all been grateful to receive his wise counsel. But when the tribute did not arrive Garasus took flight, and he burnt many of the cities of Bethara to the ground, killing thousands."

Delgar nodded, staring at Daegar in rapt attention.

"So the kingdoms began to give Garasus tribute in gold and gems, and soon his hoard became enormous," Daegar continued. "But there are only so many riches in the world, and the time came when the kingdoms could not give Garasus any more gold or jewels. So they sent representatives to the Dragon, asking what they could give to sate his hunger.

"Garasus thought long and hard, for he had lived for many thousands of years and had experienced much. But he had always been denied one forbidden pleasure. So, he told the kingdoms that he would accept maiden sacrifices to sate his hunger.

"The kings were horrified, but they had no choice. So, they began a lottery, where the names of all the unmarried maidens were placed in a great pot and a name was selected, and every year the maiden selected was fed to the Dragon, who consumed them and only left their bones for any to know they had ever been.

"Many years passed, and then one day the princess of Harboria, Emilye, was selected to be sacrificed, and the king wept with sorrow. But, he was a man of duty, and his daughter understood it too. So, she was tied up to the great stake, and taken to the field where the Dragon feasted, a field filled with the bones of his victims.

"Two warriors were in love with the maiden, and they were named Tarwyth and Idan. Tarwyth was a cruel man who tortured his slaves, and he wanted to have Emilye for his own so that he could kill her father and take the kingdom. Idan, however, was a good, honorable man, who loved Emilye for what she was, and had no ambitions to rule. Both lived in the countryside of Harboria, and both raced to Emilye's rescue."

"Does Idan win?" Delgar interrupted.

Daegar smiled. "You'll have to wait and see."

The boy frowned. "I don't like stories where the bad guy wins."

A grin on his face, Daegar continued. "The two warriors met on the road as Emilye was being tied up on the stake, and they decided to eat together. Tarwyth decided to find out who Idan was, and asked Idan where he was going. Idan was an honest soul, and replied that he was going to save Princess Emilye and marry her. Tarwyth did not say who he was, but began to scheme against the good warrior. Finally, he decided to kill Idan while he slept, so that he would not have to fight him.

"But Idan had a magical shield, and in his sleep the shield warned him in his dreams. The shield could become invisible, and Idan awoke to see Tarwyth standing over him with a sword. Tarwyth said that he had heard something, and Idan nodded and pretended to go back to sleep. He rolled over, though, and grasped his shield, which became invisible.

"Tarwyth decided to strike, but Idan was faster, and placed the shield between himself and his enemy. The sword bounced off Idan, and Idan pretended to wake, asking what was wrong. Tarwyth only said that a branch had fallen on him, and that it was nothing to worry about. Once again, Idan pretended to go to sleep, his magic shield in his hand.

"Tarwyth moved to Idan's other side and struck with his sword, but again Idan was faster, and he placed the shield in the way so that the blade bounced off. Tarwyth growled in fury and struck again, as hard as he could, but his fury undid him, for the sword bounced back so hard that it cleft his own skull. And thus Tarwyth was sent to the realm of the Damned One, the underworld wherein lie the horrors of the damned."

"I'm glad Tarwyth didn't get the maiden," Delgar declared. "I thought he was stupid, though."

Daegar raised an eyebrow. "Really?"

"I wouldn't have been fooled by that trick."

"You probably wouldn't," Daegar said, taking up his tale again. "With Tarwyth dead, Idan took his steed and rode as fast as he could to save Emilye. When he got to the field where the Dragon feasted, he found Emilye struggling as the Dragon came closer, preparing to eat her.

"Idan charged, striking the Dragon with all his might. Garasus only laughed, though, and breathed fire at the warrior. But, Idan had his magical shield, and as he hid behind it, enveloped by flame, he saw the one place that Garasus was vulnerable: the eye.

"Idan charged again, driving his sword into the Dragon's eye. Garasus howled in pain and fury, but the blow was mortal, and finally he sunk to the ground, his soul sent to the realm of the Damned One. But the Dragon's blood fell on Idan, and it burned his face, but with that wound came knowledge that the Dragon had.

"Then Idan knew that Emilye could never return home, for she would be considered a traitor and killed. And so Idan freed Emilye, and then took his sword and cut out the Dragon's teeth and planted them in the ground. From the teeth grew a hundred warriors to protect the two, and they went off to get married. Finally, they founded the kingdom of Idonia, but that is another tale."

Delgar yawned. "Can I have one more story?"

"Not tonight, little one," Daegar said, beginning to wonder what pleasures Helyna had in mind. "I have to go to bed too."

"Why was the Dragon so evil?" Delgar asked. "Aren't there any good Dragons? The grass drake was good. I could feel it."

"I don't know," Daegar answered, musing on Delgar's words. What if he actually could sense the intentions of a grass drake? He put it out of his mind; it was idle speculation, anyway. "Perhaps some day you'll find out. After all, perhaps there are Dragons like the grass drakes; they aren't evil at all. Remember the grass drake."

Delgar yawned. "I will."

"Goodnight little one," Daegar said softly.

"Goodnight dada," Delgar replied.

Leaning over, Daegar gave Delgar a kiss on the cheek, and then snuffed out the candle, leaving the boy to dream of great heroes and Dragons.

Chapter II: The Visitor

For Delgar's twelfth birthday, Daegar was at a loss for what to get his son. He considered more wooden toys, but Delgar's collection of Dragons and unicorns had grown steadily until it was threatening to take over his small room. Then Daegar thought about giving Delgar a bigger room, but the harvest hadn't been as kind that year, and he had to spend all his time trying to make up the shortfall.

Then he asked Helyna what she thought, but the conversation was less than productive.

"How about some more wooden Dragons?" she asked, washing some tomatoes for market.

Daegar shook his head. "He already has too many of those, and Wigmund told me that if I ask for another Dragon, he'll burn the house down."

"That sounds like Wigmund," Helyna commented, placing a plump, ripe tomato carefully into a wicker basket. "Have you ever known him to be anything other than gruff?"

"Never," Daegar replied. "He thinks he was born to be a reaver."

Another tomato came out of the water bucket and was placed in the basket. "Did he ever try?"

"Oh yes," Daegar chuckled. "His heart was in the right place, but he couldn't hit the side of a castle with a sword."

Helyna handed him the basket. "That is for market today; we'll keep the rest. What about a horse?"

"He's a big lad, but not that big. Are we selling those lettuces?"

She shook her head. "Just the tomatoes. How about a dog?"

Daegar pulled a black cloak over his grey tunic and fastened it. "Too expensive. We need to spend the money on meat, remember?"

"Take Delgar with you to market," Helyna said. "Maybe you'll see something there. Besides, I don't need his help today."

Daegar took the basket and kissed her. "I think Delgar is already there with Thorgar. I'll be back by sundown." With that, he was out the door.

He loaded the basket on his wagon and set off, the morning sun at his back. The ride was pleasant and peaceful, and several times he passed neighbors on their way back, bundles of supplies in their hands. He just hoped he could sell what he had; they only had two thirds of last year's harvest, and he still needed to buy as much meat as last year.

The village market was always a sight to see. All of the merchants were out, calling their wares from their small booths. Daegar grinned as he saw Wigmund holding a wooden Dragon up to some children.

"No more Dragons, huh?" he called.

"They pay more than you do," Wigmund retorted with a playful smile.

Daegar stopped the cart just behind his booth and began to unload his wares. Oddly, there was no sign of Delgar. Daegar looked around for a moment, then shook his head; it was, after all, a small village, and everybody knew everybody else. No doubt the boy had just wandered off to the far side of the market.

As he finished putting out the tomatoes and started on the cucumbers, he heard Delgar behind him.

"Dada, dada!" Delgar said, leaping up and hugging him. "Thorgar told me an incredible story, and showed me some big swords, and he..."

Daegar silenced him with a kiss on the cheek. "Wait, little one, wait! I only just got here, after all."

"Hello, farmer," Thorgar said. Daegar looked up from his son to see the warrior wearing his shining coat of mail and a flowing blue cloak.

"The season was good to you, Thorgar," Daegar said. The warrior grinned.

"And was it as good to you?"

Daegar shook his head. "A storm destroyed one of our fields, but we'll survive. We always have."

"If you have any trouble, just ask," the warrior offered. "The raids were very rich this year."

"Just a moment," Daegar said, turning to his son. "It's your birthday today, and I want you to take this," he dropped a couple of silver coins into Delgar's hand, "and get yourself something really nice. No weapons, though."

Delgar's eyes filled with glee. "I'm going to buy a Dragon!"

Daegar chuckled. "Well, if you ask Wigmund kindly enough..."

The boy shook his head. "Not a wooden Dragon. A real one!"

Daegar gave Thorgar a harsh look as the warrior stiffled his laughter. "You might have some trouble finding a real one. But if you can find a *real* Dragon, be very careful."

Delgar hugged his dada and wandered off into the crowd.

Thorgar took out a long, sheathed sword and placed it on the table by the tomatoes. "I told you I would bring you this."

"You know I don't want it."

"Daegar, the goblins raided Torant this summer," Thorgar pointed out. "They're getting farther inland, and in a couple of winters they could be here."

"Haven't you warriors been able to find them?" the farmer asked.

Thorgar shook his head. "They move too fast. By the time we arrive they've gone, and covered their tracks."

"Well, if it will take them a couple of winters to get this far inland, then I won't need this until then," Daegar asserted.

The warrior only shook his head. "Daegar, you can't just swing a sword with skill the first time. You have to be trained."

"And who will train me?" the farmer snorted. "Wigmund?"

"Wigmund couldn't hit the side of a longship with help. Edgewulf or Wigfrith could teach you, though."

"I was joking."

"I wasn't."

Daegar sighed, lifting the sword in his hand and finding it surprisingly light. "I'll see what I can do. No promises, though."

"You'll have to do better."

Daegar nodded. "I'll see what I can do."

"That blade is named 'Warrior's Bane,' and is quite ancient," Thorgar said. "It will serve its bearer well."

Daegar held the sword up to the sunlight, drawing it

partially out of its sheath. The wavy pattern shone in the light, writing as if alive, but Daegar shook his head. In the end, it was only a piece of steel that could have been used for something better.

Delgar wandered the market, fingering the money in his hand. He wasn't that good at reading and counting yet, but he figured he had just over half a crown. He wondered if it would be enough to buy him a grass drake.

He glanced at Wigmund, who had a line of wooden Dragons on his table. For a moment he was tempted, but he already had four wooden Dragons, and the thought of a living Dragon made his heart flutter with joy. Passing the table by, he headed towards a small animal merchant.

"What do you want?" rasped the man, a scarred, gangly figure. "I can sell you a lovely puppy."

"I don't want a puppy," Delgar said. "I want a grass drake."

The man chuckled. "I don't sell those. Nobody does."

"Why?" Delgar asked, scratching his dark sandy hair.

"They're taboo," the merchant said. "Nobody's allowed to touch them."

"Why are they taboo?"

The merchant shrugged. "Maybe they have powerful friends?"

"I touched one," Delgar declared. "It sat on my arm."

The merchant smiled. "Of course you did."

"It sat on your arm?" came a new voice.

Delgar turned to see a girl his own age staring at him. She had long blonde hair, and she held a grass doll in her hands. She wore a rough dress, not unlike what the rest of the village women wore.

Delgar nodded. "It sat on my arm for almost five minutes!"

The girl smiled, eyes wide. "Wow! You actually touched one!"

Delgar stuck out his hand. "I'm Delgar."

"I'm Lera," the girl said, taking it. "My family just moved here."

"Who's your dada?"

"Wulfgar. Who's yours?"

"Daegar."

"I like you," Lera said, sticking her hands behind her. "You're neat."

"I like you," Delgar replied. "You're pretty."

Lera blushed.

"Lera!" a deep voice called. "I need your help, honey!"

"I've got to go," Lera said, dashing off. "I'll see you later!"

"Goodbye!" Delgar called.

"She's certainly a pretty one," a voice said behind Delgar. "Do you like her?"

Delgar turned to see a tall, strange man. He had the purest long, blond hair the boy had ever seen, and he wore a grey tunic and a grey cloak. Even standing, he had a catlike grace. In his hand he held a wide brimmed, floppy hat, and at his belt was buckled a strange, curved sword.

"I like her," Delgar said. "Who are you?"

"I'm Daelyn," the stranger said. "And what's your name?"

"Delgar."

Daelyn kneeled, the action more graceful than anything Delgar had ever seen. "You should be careful about who you give your name to. Names are very powerful, you know. Only give your name if somebody has given theirs first."

Delgar nodded. "What do you do?"

"I wander," Daelyn replied. "I go here, and there, and

everywhere."

"You move funny."

Daelyn smiled. "I guess I do. I'll tell you a secret, though. Do you want to hear a secret?"

Delgar nodded enthusiastically.

"I'm a Tuatha de Danaan," Daelyn whispered.

"What's a...Tuatha de Danan?"

"An Elf, child, an Elf."

"Your ears aren't pointy."

"An Elf doesn't have to have pointy ears."

Delgar's face split in a wide grin. "Can you do magic?"

Daelyn smiled. "Absolutely. All Elves can."

"Can you tell the future?"

Daelyn nodded. "Sometimes."

"Can you tell mine?"

"Be very careful what you ask for," Daelyn said. "The future is a very dangerous thing to know."

"I'm not afraid."

"I'll tell you a bit, how's that?"

Delgar nodded.

Daelyn held his hand close to the boy's forehead and closed his eyes. For a moment, Delgar felt strange, invisible forces acting around him, swirling like a cyclone, bearing him off into infinity. In that moment, he felt a great love, a great sadness, the chill wind of an everlasting winter, and the brief kiss of a strange mist.

Daelyn opened his eyes, and then he and Delgar stood in the market again, surrounded by people.

"That felt neat!" Delgar declared.

"You actually felt something?" Daelyn asked. When Delgar looked up, he saw an odd expression on the Tuatha de Danaan's face.

"It was...it was...indescribable," Delgar said, frowning for a moment at the big word he had just used.

"You have great potential," Daelyn said. "Very few

could feel the magic I just used."

"Did you see my future?"

Daelyn nodded. "I see greatness and incredible sorrow. I will not tell you more, except to say that we will meet again."

"Why not?"

"Sorry?"

"Why won't you tell me more?"

Daelyn pursed his lips. "Because the future is not set. Even those who are heavily touched by Wyrd can set their own fates, but to do so they must live life in the present. Living solely in the future is a form of death."

Delgar frowned. "Well, can you tell me where I can get a grass drake?"

"No," Daelyn said. "But I will give you this for your birthday." He took a small stone out of the pouch at his belt and put it in Delgar's hand. "That is a luckstone, and if you keep it with you always, it will protect you. Now, use your money to get a chain for it. Well met, and fare well."

With that, Daelyn stood up and disappeared into the crowd. Gazing at the stone in his hand, Delgar's eyes widened. The stone was colorless and translucent, and in the middle of the perfectly rounded stone was a hole, just large enough for a small chain.

Delgar wandered the market, looking for a chain for his new stone. Finally, he found one at the southern part of the market, where he ran into Thorgar again.

"What did you get yourself?" the big warrior asked.

Delgar held up the stone and grinned.

Thorgar's eyes widened. "A luckstone! Where did you get it?"

"Daelyn gave it to me!"

"Who's Daelyn?"

"He's a wanderer," Delgar replied. "He told me I'd be

great in the future!"

"If you've found a luckstone, than you just may be. Put that around your neck and take it back to your Dada. He'll want to see it."

"And where are you going, uncle Thorgar?"

"I have to go home now," Thorgar replied. "I'm setting out on an expedition tomorrow, and I have to prepare. Being a warrior isn't all fun and games, you know."

"Bye Uncle Thorgar," Delgar said, and ran off into the crowd. He pushed his way through the throng of people until he came to his fathers stall, where most of the tomatoes had sold.

"Dada! Look what I've got!" Delgar called, holding up the luckstone.

Daegar's eyes widened. "Now that is remarkable! How much did it cost you?"

"It was given to me by Daelyn. The chain cost me a silver. And I met this beautiful girl named Lera, and I-"

Daegar silenced him with a hug. "Not so fast, little one. You're growing up, though. Just look at the way you're talking."

And, for a moment, Daegar noted how Delgar seemed to be just a bit taller, just a bit more mature, and a bit more confident.

But then Daegar's gaze dropped to the luckstone, his mind reeling with the ancient tales of Elf-kind. If Delgar had been given one, then he was special indeed. He would get his son books, he decided. He would teach Delgar to read properly and perhaps his son would be far more than just a farmer.

But then some customers arrived, and he pushed the thoughts to the back of his mind.

Chapter III: Signs and Portents

Daegar wasn't sure where the time went. It seemed like only yesterday that Delgar had turned twelve, but then the winter came and Daegar had Brother Guthwulf teach Delgar how to read during the cold nights.

And then the planting season arrived, and books came for Delgar with the spring market, brought by Guthwulf, who no doubt hoped that Delgar would join him in the holy calling. If Guthwulf had noticed the luckstone, he never mentioned it. Delgar had little time to read, however. With the planting came work, and the boy was now old enough to help his father. The spring turned to summer, and the summer turned to the harvest, and more books came with the market. Soon Delgar was spending his evening hours with a book in his hands, reading the sagas of Idan and Belathus, and other stories that Daegar had never even heard of.

As the winters passed, Delgar also began to spend more and more time with Lera, and soon the only time that

Daegar could see his son was during the workday and the occasional meal; Delgar's world had become Lera and his books.

Delgar turned fifteen, and Daegar had to marvel. His son was still tall and gaunt, but the blue eyes held a keen intelligence. His hair had turned dark brown, just as Daegar had expected, and he thought it would become darker still. The winter began, and as the snow fell, Daegar felt a sense of dread with every day.

Delgar was growing up, and soon he would have to leave the nest. Almost every hour, he wondered if this was how his father had felt so many years ago. But turning the hourglass back was an impossibility; Delgar would leave the nest, and he would probably do it soon.

Daegar dreaded that moment, but there was nothing he could do about it. He had seen Delgar and Lera kissing during one sunset, and he knew the inevitable would occur.

Marriage. Delgar would be old enough in another year, and so would Lera. And then the couple would be off on their own, either farming or smithing or whatever else they chose to do.

Daegar frowned. At least Thorgar was back. He had been on a campaign against the goblins for the last three winters, hunting them through the woods, but the campaign had ended as the warriors involved pressed to return to their families for the winter.

They sat at the table with cups of warm mead one cloudy afternoon in heavy cloaks, looking out the window as the snow blew around the open shutters. At the other end of the room, the fire blazed in the hearth, sending smoke curling up the chimney.

"Thorgar, do I have any grey in my hair?" Daegar asked, gazing at his friend in the flickering light..

The warrior laughed, pounding his hand on the table.

"No grey hairs, Daegar! Do you think you're getting old?"

"Delgar's growing up too fast," Daegar complained. "I feel like an old man."

"Daegar, you don't even have thirty five winters yet," Thorgar said, leaning forward. "You have another ten winters of life to you, at least. I'm the one with the dangerous job, remember?"

Daegar nodded. "How was your campaign, anyway?"

The warrior snorted. "A great waste of time. We spent three winters running down tracks, but we were always too late. We should have spent time fortifying the villages, but the king wanted a glorious battle. You're ready for the goblins if they should come, aren't you?"

"Aren't you going to be here?" the farmer asked.

Thorgar shook his head. "The campaign is only over for the winter. Daegar, you haven't been learning the sword, have you?"

Daegar shook his head. "Been spending my time farming. It's what I do."

"I'll teach you what I can this winter," Thorgar offered.

Daegar only shook his head.

"Daegar, they raided a village not more than five miles away from here during harvest. They could be here this spring."

"We have nothing they want," Daegar pointed out. "Why would they come?"

"We don't know what they want. For all we know they want blood."

"Fine, you can teach me what you can," Daegar conceded. "But don't go turning me into a reaver, or I'll never hear the end of it."

Thorgar chuckled. "You'll probably be worse than Wigmund. He tried to join the campaign, did you know?"

"Really? How did he fare?"

"Well, he ended up accidentally throwing his sword into the lake during a swing, and we wondered for a moment whether we should give him to the goblins, but in the end we let him go back to his woodcarving."

Daegar laughed. "Amazing how somebody who works in a precision craft can't hit the side of a castle with a sword."

Thorgar looked around. "As a matter of interest, where is Delgar?"

"He's off with Lera," Daegar replied. "Wandering through the forest, I think."

"I hope he's armed."

"It's Delgar," Daegar pointed out. "He can take care of himself. Besides, he has the luckstone." Daegar frowned, suddenly wondering why that would be any comfort at all.

Delgar sighed inwardly as he looked at the tall, slim beauty beside him. Lera had blossomed into the pride of the village, with almost every boy in the village pining for the blonde beauty. But her heart belonged to Delgar, and his heart belonged to her. And the village knew it.

The other boys envied Delgar as they envied no other, but there was nothing they could do about it. Any time one of them had ever approached Lera, she had let them know exactly how she felt, and the chastised boy had slinked off home, cursing Delgar under his breath.

Perhaps it was the luckstone, but the girls felt the same way about Delgar. More than once he had been forced to fend off their advances, some of them offering themselves in what he considered a most wanton manner. But he always turned them aside gently, and they went home cursing Lera under their breath.

In the end, the entire village could see that the two were meant for each other. The village elders had begun to plot to bring Delgar among them, as he was quickly becoming known as a man wise beyond his years. However, Delgar managed to hold them off as deftly as he did the amorous girls. As he had once told Lera: "Maybe I'll be ready for a seat in a few years, but not yet."

"It's beautiful," Lera breathed, her voice a high contralto. Delgar snapped back to the present. She had dressed in a blue woolen cloak which complimented her crystal eyes perfectly.

"Yes," Delgar agreed, looking around the forest. The snow had tapered off to a light fall, and it gave the woods an air of magic. They stood on a tree covered hill looking over a great valley which stretched to the horizon. Through the forest wound a rocky path, barely visible in the snow.

"Okay, Delgar, when are we going to do it?" Lera demanded.

Delgar blinked. "Do what?"

"Get married, you silly," Lera said, hugging him. "All the village is talking about us, and we'll be old enough next harvest."

"Oh, that," Delgar gulped. "I hadn't really thought of it. Not next harvest, though."

"Why not? I want to spend the winter giving you children."

He grinned. "It doesn't sound like that much fun."

She hit him. "You big oaf! You've heard how fun it is, just as I have. We should settle down into a little love nest."

"Don't you want to travel a bit first, Lera?" Delgar asked. "There's a great big world out there, with lots to see, and as soon as we get married we have to start our farm, and then we're stuck in the village until we either die or get rich enough to move."

She fingered his luckstone, drawing it out of his tunic.

"I just want to be with you, wherever you go."

He held her close again and kissed her. "Then right after the harvest we'll hire a ship and go south for a winter or two. And then we'll see the great deserts of Barsh, and the lovely forests of Taerraland, and perhaps go to Pakaria."

She kissed him back. "And perhaps see some Dragons?"

He smiled. "Of course. And then we'll come back here," he kissed her again, "and get married."

"And we'll have lots of kids," she said.

"Hundreds."

She made a show of hitting him. "Not THAT many! You'd kill me!"

He kissed her. "Fifty, then?"

"Try twelve."

"Twelve's okay."

"What's that?"

Delgar blinked. "Sorry?"

Lera pointed across the valley. "That. Do you see it?"

Delgar squinted, looking to the horizon. The valley passes were blocked with snow and the trees looked like small, spiky, snow covered hills. Just over the horizon, though, he made out a small, dark column of smoke rising to the heavens in the light breeze.

"Could be a funeral pyre," Delgar suggested. "You remember how high the smoke rose when Wigfrith passed to the Eternal One."

"But visible from that far away?" Lera asked. "It has to be bigger than just a funeral pyre."

"A forest fire?"

"In the winter?"

"I hate to suggest it, but what about raiders?" Delgar finally said. "Uncle Thorgar keeps saying that the goblins are getting closer."

Lera pressed herself to him for comfort. "Could they be coming for us?"

"Not this winter," Delgar declared. "You see there? The pass is snowed in. If they come at us, it will be in the spring, and the warriors will be ready."

"Are you sure?"

Delgar nodded. "Of course I'm sure." *I think I'm sure*, he added silently.

Lera looked around, marking how the sun was sinking into the horizon. "We should get back. Dada will be expecting me soon."

"And I should tell father and uncle Thorgar," Delgar agreed. He offered his arm. "Shall we away?"

"Yes," she smiled, taking his arm. "We shall."

Delgar returned at the setting sun to find Thorgar still visiting. He and Daegar stood out in the snow, Thorgar showing his father how to use his wavy patterned sword.

"Don't overextend," Thorgar instructed. "Always stay balanced."

Daegar swung high and then low, Thorgar parrying each blow with his own blade. "I think I can hit the side of a castle," the farmer declared.

"Only barely," Thorgar stated. "You still have to learn how to size up opponents. If you press the attack on a strong opponent, like me, then you'll be skewered before you ever have a chance to hit."

"If it's a strong opponent, block him first, and then attack," Daegar said. "And if it's a weak opponent press the attack."

Thorgar lowered his sword. "Good! And how will you know if your opponent is strong or weak?"

"Look in the eyes."

"Not bad, but also look at the stance. Well met,

Delgar."

Delgar nodded. "Hello Uncle Thorgar."

"Your father needs practice, Delgar," Thorgar declared. "Make sure he gets it."

"Uncle, Lera and I saw something."

Thorgar chuckled. "I'll bet you saw many things."

"We saw a column of smoke."

The warrior paused, scratching his beard. "Now that could be important. Where was it?"

"Just outside the pass," Delgar replied. "Towards the sea."

Thorgar grunted. "I was afraid of that. The goblins are getting closer. They could be here in the spring." He turned to Daegar. "Now do you see why I have you practice?" He turned back to Delgar. "Boy, I'm going to start teaching you this autumn. You'll be old enough to bear arms then."

"And old enough to get married," Daegar pointed out, sheathing his sword. "Speaking of which, do you have any plans regarding Lera?"

"We'll travel a bit first," Delgar said. "And then we'll get married and start our farm."

"We'll see if you can afford that after the harvest," Daegar decided. "If you aren't starting your own farm, your mother and I may well need you here."

Delgar nodded and turned to Thorgar. "Uncle, I've always wondered why the customs only allow a man to bear arms once he's reached a marriageable age."

Thorgar chuckled. "How do you think most warriors get married, boy?"

"The sagas have them winning their wives through great deeds."

Thorgar nodded. "Right! Don't you think it would be embarrassing to a warrior to win his bride but not be old enough to claim her?"

"I suppose it would," Delgar said.

"And what would be the point of gaining honor if you can't use it to marry?"

"Not much, I guess," Delgar conceded.

"Now you know. Daegar, you've taught your son well!"

Daegar smiled. "He always was an exceptional boy."

"With an exceptional father. But, my wife is expecting me, and I must be home."

Daegar raised his hand. "Farewell!"

"I will be here at noon to continue your instruction," the warrior declared. "By the time we've finished, you'll know enough to survive a small swordfight." With that, Thorgar trudged into the snow.

Daegar opened the door of the cottage for his son. "Delgar, what are you doing tomorrow?"

"Lera and I are going to the winter fair," Delgar replied. "Are you coming?"

"I think Thorgar would kill me if I did," Daegar chuckled. "Perhaps I can drag him out to it after my lesson. Before Lera and you go out, I need you to chop some more firewood. We're beginning to run out."

"Can it wait until the afternoon?"

Daegar shook his head. "I know young love, and if you're left to you're own devices, I'll be lucky to see more firewood next winter. In the morning, and Lera can help out. I've seen her help you, and I know she isn't as delicate as she looks."

Delgar stared at the floor. "Yes, father."

The meal that night was a quiet one, with Helyna busy in the kitchen cleaning some old pans, Delgar brooding over having to cut firewood before he could go to the fair with his beloved, and Daegar thinking about the threat of goblins. Well, he decided, if they did come he'd be ready for them.

37

For Delgar's part, the goblins didn't bother him at all. After the meal, he retired to his room where he lost himself reading an old saga. Finally, he could no longer keep his eyes open, so he put the book down, snuffed out the candle, and went to sleep.

For the last three years, his dreams had been filled with Lera, but this one was different. He found himself standing in the wreckage of a village, and he feared that it was his own. Some wooden Dragons lay in a smouldering heap, blackening in the last of the fire.

And then he was soaring high into the sky, the village vanishing as he was surrounded by clouds. He looked to the side to find himself with the body of a great Dragon, wings flapping as though he had been a Dragon all his life. He reveled in the feeling of the wind over his draconic body, and he tried to glide upwards, away from the mundane world.

Suddenly, he saw the face of a woman, slim and raven haired, and he reveled in it, the greatest of joys filling his heart. For a moment he felt the cyclone of fate around him, spinning him away from the beautiful face, and his heart knew the greatest of sorrow. And then he was in his Dragon body again, soaring across a great desert.

He tried to turn, but he couldn't, and fate drove him onwards despite his every attempt to break free. He saw a huge glacier cover the desert in a great icy deluge, and in it he felt death. And then he felt the kiss of an ethereal mist and the world below him vanished to his eyes.

He walked through the mist that surrounded him, but he could find nothing. For a moment, he heard somebody speak in an alien tongue, but then he was plunged into darkness.

He opened his eyes and sat up in his bed, his sheets soaked with sweat. The golden rays of the dawn seeped in through his shutters, and he blinked in the light, dim as it was.

But the words he heard kept going through his mind, even as the rest of the dream began to fade from his memory. A shiver went down his spine as he tried to work out what they could possibly mean.

Magus Draconum.

Chapter IV: A Random Act of Violence

Delgar found that the winter passed very quickly, no doubt because Lera almost never left his side. Every day he watched his father take sword lessons from Thorgar, who declared him an apt, but unwilling student. Daegar was quite happy with the distinction, declaring several times that war and weapons were the tools of the Damned One, and that he was only learning how to use one to protect his wife and child.

Delgar's mother, however, had enjoyed watching her husband train, and often provided encouragement as Daegar tried to overcome the seemingly indomitable Thorgar. She also seemed to have fallen as much in love with Lera as Delgar had, and made a point of providing a packed lunch for whenever the two went out. Delgar never had the heart to tell her that Lera's mother was doing the same and half the food packed was never eaten.

Still, Delgar was bothered by the words from his dream. No matter what books he consulted, he couldn't work out what language "Magus Draconum" was, and neither could anybody he talked to. Not even Brother Guthwulf, who knew seven languages, could tell him what they meant, although the monk did take time to bless the romance between Delgar and his beloved.

And then the winter turned to spring, and the news began to come in of raids. The nearby villages had been pillaged and destroyed, inspiring Daegar to bear his sword whenever he went outside. Rather than take up steel, Delgar cut himself a staff, and spent a couple of days swinging it around to get the feel of it.

But, regardless of the threats of raiding, the crops were planted on time, and foreign merchants in the spring market were reported to be on their way. For a few weeks, life appeared to be normal. Delgar and Daegar worked in the fields while Helyna prepared the goods for the coming market.

Even before the merchants arrived the market was a feast for the eyes. Multi-colored stalls filled the town square, drawing the eye away from the dull thatched cottages that surrounded it. The Raging Boar Inn began to showcase foreign bards and skalds in the evenings, and as more visitors arrived the atmosphere in general became jovial.

As the market began in earnest, Delgar found himself dividing his time between Lera, his father's stall, and Wigmund's shop. Wigmund was still as abrasive as ever, but tried to help Delgar to find a fitting gift for Lera.

"I can carve you a flute," Wigmund offered. "Any woman would love a man with a flute."

"I can't play a flute," Delgar pointed out.

"Then learn! I can't do anything more for you."

"What about a wooden Dragon?" Delgar suggested. "She likes those."

"Do you know how long it will take me to carve one

of those?"

"I'll pay you well."

"I'm sure you will," Wigmund grunted. "But it will still be a lot of trouble."

Delgar grinned. "She's worth it."

Wigmund shook his head. "I don't know why I keep letting you and your father talk me into this. Maybe your family just has silver tongues. First your father with the Dragons, and now you. Fine, I'll carve your beloved a Dragon. The Eternal One only knows that I've gotten enough practice at it!"

Delgar laughed. "I won't ever forget this. Neither will she!"

"You'd better not," Wigmund grumbled.

Whistling a happy tune, Delgar made his way through the small crowd to his father's stall.

"Delgar!" Daegar called. "Lera is looking for you."

Delgar cursed under his breath. "I forgot! I was supposed to meet her, but I was overlong at Wigmund's."

Daegar chuckled. "Whenever I forget something for your mother, I always greet her with a kiss."

"Does that work?"

Daegar frowned. "Not really. But, it can't hurt. Also, I need you to get more grain from your mother. Just a basket will do. Take Lera with you if you wish. I don't think your mother would mind."

Delgar nodded. "I'll see to it." He began to weave his way through the square, avoiding the venders trying to sell their grain and old fruit. Finally, he saw the lovely head of golden hair he was looking for.

"Lera!" he called. She turned and ran into his arms, pressing herself close to him.

"Where were you?" Lera asked. "I was waiting."

"Getting you a surprise," Delgar replied, kissing her. "It will be ready in a couple of weeks."

She fingered the luckstone around his neck. "I asked my father about our marriage, and he said yes! I'm going to give you a great big dowry when we join."

He kissed her. "We travel first, remember."

"I remember," she said, an impish grin on her face. "And don't think those kisses are going to make me forget you were late. I'm not *that* much of a pushover."

"I have to go and get more grain from the farm," Delgar laughed. "Do you want to come?"

She crossed her arms. "Have I ever said no?"

He smiled and kissed her. "Never."

"Well, what are we waiting for?"

Delgar offered his arm, and they made their way out of the village into the fields and valleys beyond. Delgar looked up at the clear sky, and then at Lera, and sighed.

Lera looked at him. "What is it, Delgar?"

"If this was more perfect, it would have to be a dream. I just wish this moment would stay in my memory forever."

She leaned closer to him. "I'm sure it will."

Then he spotted the smoke. A billowing pillar rising just over the horizon, dark and angry.

"Delgar, what is it?" Lera asked.

"My home is burning!" Delgar cried. "Quickly!"

He pounded up the road, Lera struggling behind him. He came to the top of a hill overlooking his farm and gasped.

Small, crooked figures danced around the burning wreck of the cottage. A portly form lay on the ground, covered in blood. All at once, the small shapes raised their arms, and Delgar saw the glint of metal.

At that moment, Lera came puffing up the slope. When she saw the sight before her, her jaw fell.

"The goblins are here!" Delgar said. "We have to warn the village."

"But we're unarmed!" Lera protested. "If they find us, they'll kill us!"

"They'll kill everybody if we don't warn the others," Delgar said, tears already running down his cheeks. "I have to find my father." He raced back down the hill, Lera in close pursuit.

Delgar felt like he had run for hours. Every minute stretched out to infinity as he ran, racing towards the village and praying with every step that he wouldn't be too late. As he came over one of the hills looking over the village, he sighed in relief, only to have Lera barrel into him.

"We're not too late," Delgar panted.

"I haven't run this hard in years," Lera breathed.

"We just have to get to my father, and he'll warn the others," Delgar decided. "Then we can rest."

He began to run down the hill, pounding towards the bright tents. Finally, he burst into the village square, startling a good portion of the crowd, Lera right behind him.

"Delgar," Daegar said. "What's wrong? Why are you back so quickly?"

"The goblins are here," Delgar panted. "They burnt the farm and killed mother."

There was a mumble from the crowd. Daegar leaned against the wall of his stall, his hand falling to his sword hilt. "Oh, by the Eternal One," he wept. "Helyna!"

"Father, we have to do something," Delgar insisted. "They'll be here soon!"

At that moment, a high pitched warcry sounded from all around the square. A short, swarthy form leapt out from a couple of stalls, bringing his crimson axe down on one of the villager's head. The man went down, blood and brains streaming from the wound.

Daegar shook his head and drew his sword. "Defend

yourselves!" he screamed, and he jumped out from behind his stall. A goblin attacked him, but Daegar parried and took off the creature's head with a single stroke.

The crowd erupted into chaos as the shrill battle-cry became louder, and dozens of small, ugly forms jumped out to attack. Delgar saw Wigmund swing a sword at one of the goblins, but the monster ducked and struck with his axe. Wigmund went down, screaming in pain as his intestines slid out from his belly.

"My Dada!" Lera cried. "I have to see him!" She rushed into the confusion.

Delgar ran after her. "Lera! No! Don't go alone!"

Somehow he made his way through the crowd, avoiding the notice of the raiders as he ran. His heart pounded so loudly he feared the noise alone would give him away, bringing one of the goblins All around him the stench of blood and death filled the air.

One of the goblins shrieked with joy and tossed a torch into the air. The torch landed on the roof of one of the cottages, setting it ablaze. The smoke fell heavily on the village, filling the air with a suffocating odor.

Delgar tore his eyes from the scene and looked around desperately, blinking as the smoke obscured his vision. He had to find Lera. He couldn't let her die.

Then he heard Lera's scream, and he broke into a run. He crashed through the melee to find Lera held on the ground by two goblins, her chest covered in blood, her skirts pulled up past her hips, a third goblin about to enter her with his throbbing member. Delgar screamed in rage, and *something* welled up inside him.

He felt power flow through his veins, a forceful, painful energy begging for release. It surged through him and surrounded him, became one with him. For a brief moment he understood the whole of creation, all with that strange power he did not know he had.

As the goblins turned to look at him, Delgar felt the power raising his hand for him. A burst of white hot energy tore through him and escaped, striking the half-naked goblin full in the chest. The goblin screamed in pain as the hole began to burn, turning the creature into a living torch. Delgar turned to the other two creatures, the white hot power flowing through him and escaping once more.

The second goblin never had a chance to scream. A bolt of energy took it in the head, blowing it into a fine mist. The burning body fell to the ground. The third goblin turned to run, screaming, but the power blew its leg off. As it grasped at its truncated limb, the fire consumed the creature, its screams of agony lost in the greater cry of the crowd.

Delgar knelt by Lera, wincing as he saw the bloody, oozing gash across her chest. "You'll be all right," he sobbed. "I'll find you some help. You'll be all right."

"Get me out of here," Lera gasped, tears of pain and sorrow in her eyes. "My dada's dead. I saw him die! By the Eternal One, why do I feel so numb..."

Delgar nodded. "I'll take you into the woods. We should be safe there."

He knelt down and picked up her frail form, holding her to him as though she might break. As quickly as he could, he carried her out of the village and past the tree-line. The musky scent of the woods forced out the smell of death as he laid her gently on the ground, out of sight of the village.

"I'll be back soon," he promised. "I've got to see if my father's all right. I'll be back."

He thought he saw her nod, and he raced through the trees, mentally marking her makeshift nest. As he came within sight of the village, he fell to his knees and began to weep.

The collection of cottages had been set alight, and the

fire blazed high into the sky. He saw a couple of people still fighting in the charred ruins, and for a moment thought he saw his father's blade glint in the fire-light, but then the figure holding the sword was cut down, and the last of the villagers fell. The goblins danced around the burning village, bundles of loot in their arms, singing a horrible song in a guttural tongue.

Delgar made his way quietly back into the forest to the site where he left Lera. He found her breathing shallow, her face pale and eyes beginning to glaze.

"Delgar," Lera stammered. "I'm so cold."

"You'll be all right," Delgar tried to say, but the words stuck in his throat. Instead, he picked her up and began to walk into the woods, trying to escape from the horrors behind them.

He walked forever, her quivering, frail form in his arms. Each step took him farther away from the reality of what had occurred, and he fled it gladly The sun began to set before him, and he looked back to see a column of smoke over the horizon.

With a start he realized he was heading towards the sea, where those few villages that survived the goblin raids would barely be able to help him. He wondered why, but the question was fleeting, almost as if something hidden deeply inside him already knew the answer.

"We're coming close to some villages," Delgar said, turning down to look at the wounded maiden in his arms. "They'll be able to help us."

But there was no reply. Delgar looked down to see Lera's glazed eyes staring up at him sightlessly, her pale skin cold to his touch.

Delgar sat down, placing her gently on the ground. For a long moment he stared at her, thinking of all the joy he had once seen in those eyes.

For a moment, her voice came to him, clearer than he

could ever recall hearing it in life. *"I just want to be with you, wherever you go."*

"We should have gone traveling," Delgar murmured. "Seen the world together. Been with my mother and father..." But then his voice cracked, and the tears began to flow down his cheeks. In a crystal moment, he saw his father standing beside him, cooing softly to a grass drake. His mother helping in the kitchen, always ready with a smile for her little boy. But his father couldn't help him any more. He had passed on, lost to his son forever. His mother's joyous gaze was forever stilled. His home had been destroyed, and was lost to him for all eternity.

And then he looked at Lera's still form, and he wept even harder. All the joy in her eyes had vanished, her soul sent swiftly to the Eternal One's bosom. The power in his breast that his love for her had summoned stirred for a moment, but then vanished, lost in his sorrow.

He lay on the ground beside her, wracked with sobs. All the loss, all the pain he had suffered came back to him in a single instant. He tried to hold her in his arms once more, but her body had become stiff and cold.

Delgar never would be sure of how long he had wept, but when he arose, his heart drained, the moon was high in the sky. He no longer felt alive inside, but he did know a painful purpose. He knelt to the ground and dug with his hands, working until a large enough hole lay before him, illuminated by the soft moonlight.

He gently picked Lera's still form up in his arms and laid her to rest in the hole, kissing her once more as he had done so often in life. For just a moment, he thought he felt her stirring beneath him, but when he looked he found that he had only been holding her closer in his grief, and her eyes still stared sightlessly ahead.

"Goodbye, Lera," Delgar whispered. "I wish you could have given me all the children you wanted. I wish I could be with you right now. I wish..." But then he was wracked with sobs again, and when he could speak again the sun was beginning to rise. "You'll always travel with me in my heart," he finally said.

Then he began to cover her with dirt, his hands becoming grubby as he piled handful after handful over her. Several times he had to stop to weep, and the tears watered her grave. Then he composed himself and began to bury her again, until the next bout of weeping began.

Finally, Lera's grave stood unmarked in the forest, and the grove he sat in seemed to have become magical. He felt her spirit around him, in the grass and the trees, and for a moment he wept, not in mourning, but in the joy of laying a loved one to rest where she would always know true peace.

His vision blurred as the tears came, and once again the sorrow poured out of his heart. Lera would never again come to him, and he would never again lay his eyes on her beautiful face in life.

Finally, as the sun set, he lay down in his exhaustion and fell into a deep sleep, thankfully devoid of any dreams.

Chapter V: An Escape to a Dragon

It seemed to Delgar that he staggered through the woods for weeks, seeking some solace or purpose. He felt empty and dead, Lera's pale and lifeless face staring at him every time he closed his eyes. But he could no longer cry; he had no tears left.

At first he tried to keep count of the days he wandered, but after three days passed he no longer bothered. He began his trek heading towards the western seas, but then he turned to the north, and then he turned to the east, and then back to the south.

He wished he could be certain of what he sought. Perhaps there was a man he needed to see. For a while he thought he should join the reavers, but the idea fled as his trek became longer. The heat of the days plastered his garments to him, sweat mingling with dried blood. Lera's blood.

For a moment he stopped, listening to the forest around him, trying to find some semblance of feeling in his inner self, but there was nothing. Then he began to walk again, the noon sun beating down on his brow.

As the afternoon turned into evening, Delgar came upon the burnt remains of a village. Blackened frames were all that remained of thatched cottages, and the fecid stench of death made him gag. Undaunted, he began to walk towards what would have once been the village square.

His eyes widened as he saw the remains of the great pyre in the center of the village. Around the charred pile of wood and ashes lay several coats of mail and weapons. He had seen that sort of pyre once before, when Thorgar sent one of his war-band to the Eternal's realm. The smoke had risen straight up that day, and that was always a good sign; it meant the warrior's soul had sped to its destination quickly and without obstruction.

For a moment Delgar blinked at the memory, Thorgar's face clear in his mind, but then it faded, and try as he might, he could not remember the visage of the warrior. He tried to remember his father's face, but he couldn't. His mother's face was also a blank. For a horrible moment, he thought he would forget Lera's face, but then he closed his eyes, and her dead gaze stared at him once more.

He opened his eyes and looked at the ring of weapons and armor around the pyre once more. *Thorgar and his warriors must have been here,* he realized. Had they killed the goblins, or retreated? How many men did they lose? Or did they simply burn the dead that they found? The questions circled in Delgar's mind, but he could find no answers. The remains of the pyre merely stared at him, an enigma to his mind.

I could take one of the weapons, Delgar thought. *Nobody would ever know.* He reached out to one of the swords, but then stopped short. If he took a blade, then what? By tradition, the soul of the warrior whose blade it was would come to destroy him for not taking it in combat, returning from the Eternal One's realm to send him to the Damned One's Kingdom under the earth. So it was with all weapons of war: they had to be earned in war or given freely.

He stepped away from the pyre and glanced around. Not even a crow called to break the silence. The only inhabitants of the village were the souls of those dead who had not made their way to either realm, and waited for the night to fall. Delgar swallowed. It would be better for nighttime to find him in the forest, where the ghosts would not seek him out.

Delgar walked calmly out of the village and into the forest, watching the sun as it began to set. He plucked some fruit from the branches of a nearby tree, sating some of his hunger. Then he sat against the trunk of a tree at the edge of a small clearing, and watched as the sunset slowly cloaked him in darkness. Finally, he drifted into a blissfully dreamless sleep.

He woke to the twittering of birds and the morning sun on his brow. The soft light illuminated the clearing before him, the large trees offering a natural temple to the Eternal One. Delgar leaned back, lazily delighting in the beauty before him.

For a moment, he thought he could make sense of the gentle calls of the birds.

"There sits Magus Draconum," one sang.

"He does not know the greatness of his wyrd," another called out.

"He will," a third sang. "Soon his destiny will be upon him."

Delgar blinked at the strangeness of it all, and leaned forward to listen closer. The words faded away to meaningless song, and he shook his head. He had to get out of the woods; he was becoming mad, like an old hermit in one of the sagas.

He stood up and lumbered out of the clearing, trying to clear the drowsiness from his mind. Finally, he began to stride purposely forward. If he headed east, perhaps he could find an inland village untouched by the raiders. For the first time, his head was clear: he had a purpose.

The woods began to thin around him, and he noticed some mountains rising before him on the distant horizon. As he walked, the shadows shortened and lengthened, until he was at last forced to stop again and forage for food, hoping to find some before it was too dark to see.

As he settled down against a tree, a strange fruit in his hand, the sun began to set before him. He wondered idly where he was, for he had never seen the mountains before. He thought of how Lera would love to see all this, and then felt a hollow pain in the soul he had believed so dead.

And then night fell, and he drifted into sleep. He dreamed of a land of ice and a sky filled with Dragons, and as he looked up to the draconic sky, he felt joy.

And then the morning sun shone down on him, and he startled awake. He looked around the clearing, listening as small animals rustled in the woodlands around him.As he stood, he prayed that madness wouldn't take him before he found what he was looking for. Then he began heading eastwards.

He walked until he could go no farther, and then he sat and rested under the afternoon sun. The heat beat down on him, and for a moment he wondered what month it was. Had the summer began already? He plucked a green apple from a tree, wincing at the raw taste as he bit into it. If the summer had begun, then some of the summer fairs might have started, and he would be able to get some supplies.

He got up and walked again, trying to put his hunger out of his mind. For a moment he wished he could just return home, where there was always enough to eat and he could be with Lera and...

But home no longer existed. The harsh reality of the situation pounded on his mind, forcing him forward. He staggered onwards, the hunger beginning to consume him. Soon he would have to rest, and then he would continue to walk, until he either perished or came to a village.

"You there!" came a voice. "Stop where you are!"

Delgar halted and turned. A tall woodsman stood before him, his axe in one hand and a bow in the other. His dark hair was streaked with grey, and he wore beaten old leathers. "Who are you?" the man asked.

Delgar swallowed, suddenly at a loss for words. "I am Delgar, son of Daegar," he finally replied. "My village was destroyed by goblins, and I am the only survivor."

The woodsman's eyes narrowed. "Where was you village, boy?"

"It was by the western pass," Delgar replied.

The man blinked. "How long have you been wandering?"

Delgar shrugged. "A long time."

The woodsman laughed, a hearty sound that nearly made Delgar bolt in fear. "I would say that! It would take me two weeks to ride there, much less walk. But the goblins have managed to make their way near us anyway. Do you have any idea of where you are?"

Delgar shook his head.

"You're almost at the North Sea. Come! My village is only a day away from here."

Delgar nodded and began to follow the man. They walked to the south until the sun began to set, and then they set camp. Delgar watched as the woodsman deftly gathered kindling to make a fire. Finally, as the sun set, the two were illuminated by the flickering flames.

"You haven't asked me my name yet, boy," the woodsman said.

Delgar shrugged. "I've been out here a while."

"I'm Frithgar, son of Daegwulf. What did your father do?"

"He was a farmer," Delgar replied. "But I think Thorgar tried to make a warrior out of him in the end. All for my sake."

"I have heard of Thorgar," Frithgar said, scratching his beard. "That man is well sung of by the skalds."

"Is he still alive?" Delgar asked. "He'll know me."

Frithgar shook his head. "I have no idea, boy. The goblin raids have cut us off from the rest of the world. Worst raiding I've ever seen. It's almost as if something is driving them out of their homes in the far north."

"What could cause that?"

"More goblin tribes, famine, could be anything. This sort of thing has happened before, just never this severe."

The woodsman held out some dried meat. "Eat this, boy. You look like you haven't been properly fed in weeks."

Delgar grabbed the morsel and wolfed it down, ignoring Frithgar's chuckles. For a moment the horrible hunger subsided a bit, and a thought began to form.

"I want vengeance," Delgar muttered.

Frithgar shook his head sadly. "They all look alike to me, and even if you could find the tribe that killed your father, I doubt the leader now is the same as the leader then. Rather cut-throat lot, boy. Best you can do is try to live with it."

"Can I get a message to Thorgar once I get into your village?" Delgar asked.

Frithgar scratched his beard, pulling a grey hair out and glancing at it. "We'll see, boy. The village elders will have to decide what to do with you. You'll probably have to work to earn your keep. What can you do?"

"I can farm," Delgar replied. "I can also read and

write."

"Reading and writing is impressive," Frithgar said. "Perhaps we could send you to the royal court as a scribe."

"I don't think I want to be a scribe," Delgar said. "I'm not sure what I want to be." For a moment a shadowly memory surfaced of the burning power that surged through his veins as he tried to save Lera, but the it faded the moment he tried to put his finger on it.

"Wyrd probably hasn't left you much choice," Frithgar pointed out. "In the end the elders will decide, boy. You have something about you, though. No matter now. Get to sleep, boy. We have a long walk tomorrow, and I want you rested."

Delgar lay down on the ground near the fire and closed his eyes. That night, he didn't dream.

He woke at sunrise, watching the fiery orb rise majestically over the great mountains, bathing the world in a gentle orange light. Beside him, Frithgar yawned and stretched. The old ranger turned to Delgar and grinned.

"Today you see the village elders," he said. "Get up, boy. We have a long walk ahead of us."

That day, they walked until the sun was directly above them, and then they came to the village. The little collection of thatched cottages reminded Delgar painfully of home, but Frithgar motioned to him to follow, cutting off any reminiscences.

"Frithgar!" a loud voice called. "What do you have here?"

Frithgar turned and embraced the large, burly man who approached him. "Brother! It is so good to see you! I have a boy here who wandered from the western pass. I've brought him to see the elders."

"You're back just in time," Frithgar's brother said. "The goblins were spotted approaching from the west. We'll have a fight on our hands soon enough, that's for sure." He turned to Delgar. "Who are you, boy?"

"Delgar, son of Daegar," Delgar replied.

"You'll have to help fight, Delgar Daegar's son," the man said.

"He'll first need some proper clothes," Frithgar said. "You don't expect him to meet the elders in those rags, do you?" He turned to Delgar. "Come with me, boy."

At that moment, the horrifying familiar war cry sounded all around the village, and Delgar cringed.

"Goblins!" came a cry, and the villagers rushed to their weapons. The goblins broke out of the tree-line, murder in their eyes. Delgar backed up, watching as Frithgar and his brother pulled out their weapons to face the raiders. A goblin leapt on Frithgar, and the woodsman cut the creature down with his axe, but then four more attacked him, and Delgar saw the man go down under the horde.

All around him, the chaos of battle began again. The villagers attacked the goblins, at first seeming to drive them away, but then more poured out of the trees, and the defenders were forced back. The stench of death began to rise around him.

Everywhere Delgar looked, there was horror. One man went down, clutching desperately at his slashed throat. Another died when a goblin cleft his skull with an axe. One villager lay on the ground, trying to gather his spilled intestines, a shocked look on his face.

Delgar ran as fast as he could towards the tree-line, praying he wouldn't be spotted. His prayers were not answered: a shrill cry sounded behind him, and he heard noises of pursuit. He pounded into the forest, heading towards the mountains.

He needed a cave. If he could just find a cave, then he could hide in the darkness there and the goblins would never find him. The mountains rose high and snowy above him, and he skirted along the rising slope.

He had to rest. He heard his pursuers coming closer, but he just couldn't run any farther. He staggered past an outcropping of rock and then stopped.

A huge cave lay before him, its open mouth inviting him in. Without hesitation, he staggered into the cave, gasping for breath. He saw two tunnels before him, both of them leading into darkness, one wider than the other. As he tried to choose, he found himself attracted to the wider passage, but the attraction was joined by a sense of dread.

He heard the goblins behind him, and his hesitation vanished. He walked into the larger passage, his hands on the mossy walls as he was cloaked in darkness. The cave headed downwards into the mountain, and Delgar thought he could hear something breathing all around him as he walked for what seemed like hours.

For a moment he heard the clanging of hammers, but then there was silence. He stopped for a moment, listening in the darkness. He heard his pursuers behind him, muttering and grumbling. Then he pressed on, determined to hide.

He felt as though he walked for hours, his hands first on moss and then on rough bare stone, praying for some light to guide him. The stone was cold to the touch, and he swallowed. If he could see his hand, what would it look like? Would it be blistered and cut from the rough rock.

Suddenly, he was bathed in light, and he saw short forms running in the tunnel before him. All around him the ringing of hammers on metal sounded, and then a cry of alarm.

Fleotdraca! Wigendes, ofsloh thone Fleotdraca!

Then there was a roaring and a rushing of flame, a searing heat, and then there was darkness.

Delgar paused, staggered by the vision. For a moment he took his hand off the rock, rubbing the raw flesh. In amazement, he found himself unburned. The only pain came from the scrapes and blisters he had earned in the cave. Then he heard the breathing and muttering behind him.

Were they still the goblins, pursuing him because they had become lost in the darkness themselves and had nothing else to do, or were they ghosts? Delgar paused, but caution won over curiosity. If they were goblins, as soon as they found him they would kill him. He put his hand back onto the tunnel wall and began to make his way downwards again.

He found the wall arching away from him, and reached out with his other hand, only to find empty air. *I must be in a room*, Delgar decided. He traced his way along the wall, seeking another passage. To his amazement, the stone became smooth, as if it had been carefully carved.

Once again he was bathed in ethereal light. He saw the small men, standing around a broken body in strange leather armor. One of the small men spoke, his rough voice echoing through the cavern.

Mathmas. Miccel Mathmas!

The small figure held a gold bracelet up to the light, watching as it shone. The bracelet had a serpent design, and radiated a strange sort of power. Delgar gazed at it in awe, transfixed, for it was finer than anything he had ever seen. Then the room went dark, and his last impression was of two passages on the far wall, the one to the left larger than the other.

Once again, Delgar felt the strange attraction to the larger passage, and he heard the calls of the goblins as they made their way towards the room. Without hesitation, Delgar struck out to where he remembered the large tunnel being, and breathed a sigh of relief as his hands met the carved stone at the edge of the passage. Slowly and carefully, hyperaware of every sound, he made his way down the passage.

The echoes of the ancient tongue arose to haunt him once more, breaking the silence. *Fleotdraca!* Delgar only shook his head, willing the ghosts to go away. Behind him he heard the goblins getting closer, and he began to move as fast as he could down the tunnel. As he walked, the walls became rough again, as if the delicate carving had been destroyed.

For a moment Delgar blinked, unable to believe his eyes. At the end of the tunnel was a soft glow, illuminating the broken walls and darkness around him. For a moment Delgar wondered if he would be silhouetted against the light for the goblins to see, but he found himself drawn towards the light, moving surely among the battered rock. As he approached the end of the tunnel, the light became brighter, until he finally had to shield his eyes.

He came to a large cavern, and the illumination blinded him. Finally, his eyes adapted to the brilliance, and he gaped in amazement.

The cavern was filled with treasure, and the hoard itself glowed with an unearthly light. Looking at the ground, Delgar saw that much of the treasure was old, ancient beyond his understanding. Old, unreadable ruins decorated one sword, which was slowly rusting away. He looked closely at an old cup, decorated with images and pictograms he could not fathom.

He heard the ringing of metal on metal, and gasped in horror as he saw a great, serpentine head rise above him out of the gold. The huge eyes regarded him for a moment, glowing slightly against the midnight black scales. A single word came to mind: *Fleotdraca*.

The Dragon's head reared above him, looking far into the tunnel. Delgar heard the shrill war cry of the goblins, and then a great roaring as the Dragon called out in anger.

He threw himself to the side of the hoard as the goblins charged, only to stop short as they came to see the great wyrm.

As Delgar scrambled in the hoard, he looked back to see the goblins glance behind them, and then charge. First there was a great light, then a burning heat, and then Delgar saw only darkness.

Chapter VI: The Dragon

Delgar awoke to the soft glow of the hoard. As he sat up, the Dragon's huge head turned to regard him, gazing at him with deep green eyes.

"You are not of the Tuatha de Danaan," the Dragon stated.

Delgar gulped and glanced around, looking for some way to escape. "No sir, I am not."

"I have been here for millennia, but I have never seen one like you," the Dragon said. "What are you?"

"I am a human," Delgar answered. "A poor farmer from far away."

The Dragon shook its mighty head. "You are far more than that. I can see wyrd cloaked around you. What did you see as you came here?"

"I saw ghosts," Delgar replied, standing up slowly. "I saw small men with treasure, and I heard them say things in a language I do not understand."

Delgar heard a deep grunting, and then realized the

Dragon was laughing. "You are not yet a wizard, and you can see the ghosts of this place and hear their speech. Truly you are special. I will exchange names with you. I am Fleot'heortan the ancient one."

"I am Delgar, son of Daegar. Why did you not kill me?"

"I could sense what you will be," Fleot'heortan replied. "I could feel the corruption in those that wished to harm you. And I was told you would come."

Delgar blinked. "Told? Who told you?"

"You will meet him soon enough," the Dragon said. "He will come to collect you when the time is right. Until then, I will nourish and teach you."

"Teach me? What must I learn?"

"You must learn what we are," Fleot'heortan stated. "You must learn what has come before. You must learn of the great Road. But now, you must rest. Sleep and be healed, Delgar of Nordland."

Delgar opened his mouth to protest, but only a yawn came out. He found himself falling slowly onto the hoard, and then he dreamed.

He dreamt of a great mist covering all he could see. Then there was a great thought, loud and clarion, and the mist parted to reveal a strange world. Delgar found himself swooping down on the world, its strange vegetation a blur beneath him. Creatures beyond his imagination reared up to see him, and then he was flying away, high above the world into the great mist.

Another thought sounded, great and all powerful. The fog parted yet again, and another world came into being. Delgar looked down on the world, seeing Dragons and other creatures bowing to some great figure. Then another figure came to be, and the attention of the lesser creatures was divided.

Then the Dragons and other creatures attacked one

another, and in the chaos the majority fled, and as they ran more thoughts sounded in the mist, each forming a world from the ether.

Delgar startled awake, sitting up on the hoard. As he moved, gold coins rang as they knocked together. Fleot'heortan looked down on him, a merry glow in his eyes.

"You slept so long, little mortal! I feared you would never awaken!"

Delgar rubbed his eyes in amazement. His hunger had fled entirely, and when he moved his aches and pains were gone. "How long did I sleep."

"The sun has risen and set ten times since while you slept," the Dragon replied. "What did you dream of?"

"A great mist," Delgar replied. "And there were worlds in the mist, and powerful figures. I don't remember much more."

Fleot'heortan nodded sagely. "You dreamt of the beginning."

"The beginning of what?"

"The beginning of all, many eons ago."

"Why did I dream of this?"

Fleot'heortan glanced around. "This mountain is special. Millennia ago, before the rise of the kingdoms of man, this was a place of the Dragon Masters. After the Great Rebellion, this palace was abandoned, but many of the creatures of that time remembered it was there, even if they did not remember what it was.

"Soon this mountain became known only as a place of power, and all who found it coveted it. The first to find it were the Tuatha de Danaan, who fought many wars over it. They were driven out by the Dwarves, who used the power of this palace to make many trinkets and steal from those around them without mercy or pity.

"And then I came, scattering the Dwarves and

claiming this mountain until the end of the great cycle. Because they had changed this place, their spirits were linked to it, and thus their ghosts remain, even though it has been seven thousand winters since they fled elsewhere.

"I claimed this place and made it my own, and thus my spirit is chained here as well. But, I, like all Dragons, am a creature of power, and I have worked my magic here. Now, only the oldest peoples even remember that this place exists."

"What is the Great Cycle?" Delgar asked.

"The Great Cycle is time itself," the Dragon explained. "Everything is a cycle. When a mortal dies, they only complete part of the cycle. When a mortal is reborn, the cycle is continued. Even worlds are subject to the cycle. When the world dies, it is reborn as the new cycle begins."

Delgar shook his head. His mind reeled with the new, strange concepts, and he found himself longing to talk about something more mundane. "What happened to the goblins?"

"The fire consumed them."

Delgar frowned. "Then what do you eat?"

The Dragon chuckled. "I have no need to eat. This place will sustain me until the end of the world."

Delgar was silent for a moment, and then he ventured another question. "What does 'Magus Draconum' mean?"

Fleot'heortan's head rose above Delgar, the serpentine eyes filled with what Delgar could swear was alarm. "You do not need to know. How did you learn those words?"

"I dreamed them," Delgar replied, stepping back towards the darkness of the tunnel. "When I was younger."

The Dragon's head lowered. "Now I am beginning to understand. Great events truly are coming."

"What events?" Delgar inquired. "What are you talking about?"

"You do not need to know that now," Fleot'heortan stated. "You must now learn of Dragons. There are different kinds of Dragons in the world.

"I am a Great Dragon, and I am a creature of power. Like any creature of power, if another Great Dragon is near, I will sense it. Any creature of power can sense another. There are many Great Dragons in the world, but I am one of the oldest: I remember the Dragon Masters.

"There are also lesser Dragons. The Teraeni Dragons are some of the most powerful lesser Dragons, but they will never be equal in power to the Great Dragons. They are exceptional, as they have the intelligence of the Great Dragons. Other Dragons, such as the grass drakes, are not as intelligent, but are still Dragons. The grass drakes are the least of the Dragons, for they do not have the power of speech, and they do not have the intelligence of the other Dragons."

"Who were the Dragon Masters?" Delgar asked.

"You will discover that later," the Dragon replied. "I will only say that they were second in power only to the gods themselves."

"Why are you teaching me all this?" Delgar inquired.

"Your wyrd is already written on the Great Road," Fleot'heortan replied. "You are near to becoming a Dragonfriend, and then you will become much more. It is difficult to decide what to tell you at this early time."

Delgar blinked. "What is a Dragonfriend?"

The great head lowered to look Delgar in the eyes. "A Dragonfriend is a mortal or immortal who has rendered a great service to Dragonkind. A Dragonfriend has earned the protection of the Dragons, and is watched carefully so that he will never want. No Dragon has ever harmed another, and no Dragon has ever harmed a Dragonfriend."

Delgar frowned. "So am I a Dragonfriend now?"

Fleot'heortan shook his head. "Now you are in my

debt. Some day, perhaps I will be in yours. But you must let wyrd work as it will; to fight it or try to control it is futile, and will only cause problems."

"I want to command my destiny," Delgar stated. "I do not want to be a puppet of fate."

"Nobody can ever truly command their destiny," Fleot'heortan said. "One can only ever be certain of their destiny once they have met it; until then, they must travel in the eddies of life and wyrd, uncertain of where they will finally end."

"And what is the Great Road?" Delgar asked.

"I don't think you need to know that," a new voice said, lyrical to Delgar's ears. Delgar turned to find himself facing a tall man with the purest long blond hair he had ever seen. The man's slightly slanted grey eyes gazed at him with a piercing stare, and he stepped forward with an inhuman grace, reminding Delgar of something almost feline. The stranger wore a grey cloak over a grey tunic, and on his head was a dark, wide brimmed floppy hat.

The Dragon bowed. "Then you do not think he is ready?"

The stranger shook his head. "He is still a child, no matter how his fate hangs on him."

"I will resign myself to your wisdom," Fleot'heortan said, sliding back.

Delgar stared at the stranger for a moment, trying to place him Then his hand closed on the luckstone, and he knew who the man was.

"Well met, Daelyn," Delgar said.

Daelyn nodded. "It is good to see you, Delgar. You seem to have grown well. Are you ready to face your destiny?"

Chapter VII: Daelyn

Delgar frowned at Daelyn's question, looking the Tuatha de Danaan in the eye, but failing to match his gaze. Finally, he spoke. "What is my destiny?"

Daelyn smiled. "A clever answer," he said. "But I cannot reveal your wyrd to you now. I'm not even entirely sure what it is. But I do know what you can do."

"What will you do with him?" Fleot'heortan asked, head arching upwards.

"I will take him to place where he can learn," Daelyn stated. "Surely you sensed his command of magic?"

The Dragon nodded. "I had thought him an apprentice. I had expected a Tuatha de Danaan from your description."

"He is not an immortal," Daelyn said. "But he can be a wizard." He turned to Delgar. "Your time here is over. Some day you may return, but for now you must come with me."

"Where will you take me?" Delgar asked.

"To the south," Daelyn answered. "There is a very good school there."

"You want me to learn magic."

Daelyn nodded. "Yes."

"But what if I don't want to learn?"

"What will you do? Go home?"

Delgar looked down, a tear rolling down his cheek. "That wasn't fair."

"Life is not fair," Daelyn said. "You have potential, Delgar, and I will take you somewhere you can make use of it. Will you come, or do you want to sit here and talk to an old Dragon for the rest of your years?"

Delgar glanced at Fleot'heortan, but the Dragon only lowered its head. "I would go if I were you, Delgar. We may meet again some time."

Delgar nodded. "Then I will go with you, Daelyn. Farewell, Fleot'heortan."

"Farewell, Delgar."

Daelyn motioned to the tunnel connected to the hoard cavern. "The exit is this way."

"You know the way out?"

"I got in, didn't I?"

"But how will we see? You didn't bring a torch."

The Tuatha de Danaan only smiled.

Delgar shook his head and stepped into the tunnel, watching as his shadow grew long in the light of the hoard. He suddenly felt a strange heat, and when he looked back, Daelyn was there, hand raised. Delgar's eyes widened as he saw Daelyn's hand glow with a soft white light.

"Follow me, Delgar," Daelyn said. He led Delgar along the long hallway. In the gentle glow Delgar noticed the rough walls bore the faded remains of murals. While he couldn't make out any faces, he saw small forms holding court, surrounded by riches. For a moment he stopped, wondering who the ancient Dwarf-king was, now all but forgotten. Then Daelyn tapped him on the shoulder, and they continued on their way.

They came to a large room, and Delgar looked up to see the ceiling high above him. On the walls he saw more murals. On the left side a great battle was depicted, where Dragons and Dwarves fought together against what appeared to be an extremely powerful mage.

"The last battle," Daelyn explained. "All the elder races remember the struggle for freedom against the Dragon Masters. It was the only time that Dwarves, Tuatha de Danaan, Cyclops, Dragons, Fir Bolgs and Formorians fought together for a common goal. After that, the elder races went their separate ways. The Tuatha de Danaan and the Dragons, however, have always kept their close ties."

"Where was mankind then?" Delgar asked.

"Humankind had not risen then," Daelyn replied. "Nobody is certain where your people came from, but they rose out of the ashes of the war after the final battle. At least, that is what I heard."

"So you didn't see this war?"

Daelyn shook his head. "I am only around three thousand years old, Delgar, and I have only been a soldier for a thousand of those years. The Great Rebellion was over two hundred millennia ago."

"Do know what this room was used for?" Delgar said.

Daelyn shook his head. "Fleot'heortan has been the master of these caverns for longer than I have been alive. He may know, but I do not. This way, Delgar."

Again Daelyn led him into a large passage to the right, and Delgar marveled at the intricate carvings and decorations, most of which had not seen any light in millennia. To the left several passages branched off, and Delgar swallowed, a chill running down his spine. If he had used his right hand on the way down to guide himself, he would have been lost in a maze of tunnels.

They walked for what seemed like hours, Daelyn tirelessly holding his hand out in front to provide light. Delgar noticed that the light seemed to frighten away the ghosts which had appeared to him when he had come down, and the tunnels were silent except for his and Daelyn's footsteps.

Suddenly, Delgar felt a blast of warm air, and sunlight shone on his face. Beside him, Daelyn sighed with relief.

"At last," the Tuatha de Danaan said. "I have always preferred the open air to underground tunnels. I find caves stifling."

"For a while I thought I would never see sunlight again," Delgar said, shielding his eyes and wincing as he gazed at the afternoon sun as it dipped behind some clouds.

"We must head south," Daelyn stated. "We will walk to Taerraland."

With that, the two travelers began to trek through the forest, each lost in thought. The woods were filled with the sounds of birds and small animals, and Delgar felt strangely at home with Daelyn, as though the Tuatha de Danaan's ties to nature made Delgar belong as well.

They finally made camp as the sun began to set, Daelyn finding a pleasant clearing to rest in. They spent half an hour gathering deadwood, and then Daelyn used a tinderbox to make a fire.

As they sat by the fire, warming themselves, Daelyn leaned over to Delgar. "What do you know of magic?"

Delgar blinked. "I know nothing. How do you know I have potential for magic?"

Daelyn sat back. "I felt it the moment I first saw you. And, when I sought you later, in the ruins of your village I could sense that you had used some."

Delgar shook his head, trying to push away his memories of that horrible moment. "I had no idea what I was doing. It acted all on its own."

"You will learn control," Daelyn said. "They will teach you in Taerraland. Uncontrolled magic is very dangerous."

"I noticed that you have magic," Delgar said.

Daelyn nodded. "I am a Tuatha de Danaan. My people have a gift for what you call magic."

"What kind of magic is it?"

"I suppose it is best described as a sort of nature magic," Daelyn stated.

Delgar blinked. "Does this mean you can command nature?"

Daelyn shook his head. "Most magic can influence things, but can never command them. I cannot control nature, but I can influence it to do things. However, I cannot make something do what is contrary to its nature. I cannot make the wind choke somebody to death, nor can I make a tree form a mountain. I cannot make a deer eat meat, either."

"Is there a magic which can? Control things, I mean," Delgar asked.

Daelyn nodded. "There is, but it is used mainly by those who wish to perform evil. Shaping and influencing is one thing, but controlling something is another. You should rest now; we have a long day ahead of us."

"Don't you have to rest?"

"I'm a Tuatha de Danaan. I don't need as much rest as you mortals do."

Delgar nodded and lay back. As he heard the fire hiss and crackle, he drifted into a gentle sleep.

As they traveled through the woodlands, Delgar began to understand just how vast they were. For days they headed southwards, making their way gently through the thicket,

Daelyn somehow always finding the easiest possible path. Towards the end of the day they would forage for food, as Daelyn's supplies were limited to what he could carry.

Sometimes the Tuatha de Danaan would stop and look around the forest, almost as if he felt something coming, and then change the route. Delgar heard and felt nothing, and he wondered what Daelyn was sensing.

On the fifth day, they came to the ruins of a village. The cottages were blackened and burnt, and a large pyre lay in the center of the hamlet.

Daelyn looked around the village square for a moment, and then he looked at the pyre. "This happened some time ago."

"Are we far inland?" Delgar asked.

Daelyn shook his head. "We'll actually see the coast as we head southwards."

Delgar looked at the pyre and back to the devastation, and then he cursed. "Those damned goblins. Will this ever end?"

"It will," Daelyn asserted. "This happens every six hundred years or so. And the last time it happened they got just as far inland before they were stopped."

"How do you know?"

"I fought in that campaign," Daelyn replied. "I am a soldier, after all."

But Daelyn would say no more about it, and they returned to the woods, continuing their journey to Taerraland.

Two days later, Delgar brought the subject up again as they sat by the fire, waves crashing to the west. Clouds hid most of the stars, but the moon broke through, bathing the clearing in a soft glow.

"So you're a soldier?" Delgar asked. "When did you start fighting?"

"I answered the call to battle against the Formorians

73

just like everybody else did," Daelyn stated. "The war was long and brutal. After that I swore I would never fight again unless I absolutely had to."

"But you are still a soldier," Delgar pointed out.

Daelyn nodded. "Of course. Once an immortal becomes a soldier, he can never stop being one. Just as I am still a bard, as I was three thousand years ago."

"Can you sing for me, then?" Delgar asked.

Daelyn smiled. "Perhaps later. I do not feel the mood for singing right now."

"So what do you do right now?"

"Right now I wander," Daelyn replied. "I want to see as much as possible."

"It's a large world," Delgar said. "How long have you wandered it?"

Daelyn grinned. "Every world is a large world. And I have all eternity."

"Is there more than one world?"

"There are an infinite number of worlds, all different."

"How do you go from one world to another?"

Daelyn smiled. "You will learn that when you are ready for it. Until then, rest and be glad that you have such a large and wonderful world of your own."

Delgar groaned. "When will I be ready?"

Daelyn shrugged. "Before you can learn to run you must learn to walk. The knowledge will come, be assured of that. But, now you should rest."

Delgar put his head to the ground and closed his eyes, the sound of the campfire filling his ears. He dreamed of a great and vast world, and in a clarion moment, realized that he watched his own, until the vision faded.

Then, he thought he heard Daelyn singing, a sad and beautiful song that touched his very soul. In the song he felt himself journeying over the vast emerald fields of an ancient land, his heart strangely light and carefree. But, he could not be sure of if it had been real or only a beautiful dream.

And then the sun was shining in his face and Daelyn was offering a friendly hand, the Elven features a joy to behold.

"I have already broken our camp," Daelyn stated. "I was just waiting for you."

Delgar stood and stretched, inhaling the pleasant air. "I heard singing last night."

Daelyn raised an eyebrow. "Did you? How interesting."

But, despite Delgar's nudging, the Tuatha de Danaan would say nothing more.

For another week they traveled, and the forest gave way to the crystal blue sea. Delgar looked out in awe, watching the waves crash against the shore. Beside him, he heard Daelyn take in a deep breath.

"By the Eternal One," Delgar breathed. "I had no idea it was this beautiful."

Daelyn held up his hand. "Be blessed, bringer of life and creature of the Road." He turned to Delgar. "My people came to our homeland through the sea-roads. For all time the Tuatha de Danaan will be linked to the sea."

"Nordland also has such a link," Delgar said. "The tales tell how our people came from the sea and settled here."

"The sea is the hope and bane of all peoples," Daelyn stated.

"Bane?"

"All good things are also banes," Daelyn said, turning to the young northerner. "A wonderful thing in excess can be a great curse. Did you not know?"

Delgar did not answer then, but as the day wore on and they walked close to the shoreline, he considered what he had seen and learned. That night they made their campfire just behind a hill, so that they could not be seen from the coast. Somehow, Daelyn was able to quickly find and kill some rabbits, which cooked and sizzled on the fire.

"I had thought myself learned," Delgar said between bites. "But I am finding that I did not know all that I had thought.

Daelyn smiled. "Good. Soon you will be ready to learn."

"What will I learn?" Delgar asked.

"Only what you are willing to open your mind to. You cannot learn that which you do not believe in."

"And you are taking me to learn magic?" Delgar asked.

Daelyn nodded. "It is both your talent and your fate, but I cannot say any more on the latter."

"Can all men do magic?"

Daelyn shook his head. "Not all. Some simply do not have the aptitude, but they are rare. Many simply never open their minds to the learning of it. You, however, have a sort of wild magic, and can be a great magician."

"Why are you helping me?" Delgar asked.

"In many ways, I am as bound by fate as you are. Right now, this is my fate. Also, I see a very good man before me, and I wish to see him reach his full potential."

Delgar nodded and turned back to his thoughts and roasted rabbit.

For another week they traveled south, and the heat of summer began to set in, despite the earliness of the season. The coastline gave way to forests, and Delgar suddenly noticed that the mountains had vanished from sight. They passed through another great forest, coming out onto a vast plain.

"We are now at the northern border of Taerraland," Daelyn said. "To the east is Pakaria, and the warlords of Pakaria have never held a lasting peace with the noble castes of Taerra. We are only a couple of weeks journey from Pakaria, so we must be cautious."

"Will we see any battles?" Delgar asked, his eyes suddenly alight.

Daelyn frowned. "If we are unfortunate, yes."

But, as they headed south towards the heartland of Taerraland, Daelyn would not say any more about the subject. Delgar soon found the subject fleeing his mind as he journeyed on the gravel roads that crossed the country. After another two days of travel, they came to a small village.

"We'll stay in an inn tonight," Daelyn decided. "I long for a feather bed, and I have no doubt you do as well."

Delgar nodded his assent, and they strode along the main street of the village, watching as the people bustled past merchant's stalls in a summer fair.

Delgar stopped, staring at the thatched roofs and the colorful stalls, and wiped away a tear. Daelyn stopped in front of him.

"What is the matter?" the Tuatha de Danaan asked.

"A fair was the last place that Lera and I saw each other alive," Delgar said, his voice breaking slightly. "I still miss her so much."

Daelyn stepped close to Delgar and put his hand on the young man's shoulder. "Never forget her," he said. "But rejoice in her life rather than mourn her death. If one mourns forever, than one cannot live, and you must live."

Delgar nodded, tears streaming down his cheeks. "I'll never forget her," he vowed.

Gently and kindly, Daelyn led Delgar into a nearby inn. Smoke rose into the air from a hearth in the middle of the common room, causing Delgar to cough. After a couple of minutes, though, the young man felt better. He watched Daelyn talking with the bartender for a moment, and then the Tuatha de Danaan motioned towards the stairs. The bartender nodded, and Daelyn walked back over to Delgar.

"We have a room for the night," Daelyn said. "We'll leave tomorrow morning."

That night, Delgar's sleep was blissfully free of dreams.

Daelyn woke Delgar the next morning, and the two set off just after the sunrise across the now hilly landscape. The voyage was pleasant in the morning, but as noon approached, stormclouds formed overhead. Daelyn looked up at the dark, ominous sky and shook his head.

"We'll have to find some shelter tonight," he said. "This storm will be brutal."

"Is there another village nearby?" Delgar asked.

Daelyn shook his head. "We'll have to find a cave or something of the sort. Even a barrow will do."

Thunder rumbled overhead.

The two walked swiftly up one of the hills and looked down. Delgar pointed at a feature in the distance.

"Is that a barrow we can use?" he asked.

Daelyn nodded. "We had best hurry." As he spoke, the ground was illuminated by lightning. The two broke into a run, pounding towards the small mound on the landscape. For a moment, Delgar feared he would collapse from exhaustion, but somehow he found the strength to go on.

Finally, as the rain began to pour down upon them and the ground was cloaked in darkness, they made their way to the barrow. Delgar looked up in awe. The entrance was carved out of three massive stones, each grey monolithic rock covered in runes older than any of the civilizations he had ever read about. Inside, an unworldly light shone, illuminating the doorway as though it was a gate to the underworld itself.

Daelyn shook his head. "This could be a dangerous place, but we will have to use it." He winced as a hailstone caught him on the cheek. "Delgar, inside!"

Dashing into the barrow, Delgar found himself in a large circular cavern. The walls were smooth grey stone, bare of any decorations. A small hoard of treasure lay at the end of the room, glowing with a light Delgar had only seen before in the cave of Fleot'heortan. On the top of the treasure was a golden throne.

Delgar gasped in shock as he gazed upon the throne. An ancient skeleton in golden armor sat before him. The bones were covered with dust, but the skull's hollow eyes gazed forward so intently that Delgar found himself looking away.

"Where are we?" Delgar asked.

"The gateway to the world of the dead," Daelyn replied. "This is a place where the dead and the living can cross at certain times. That thing there is the guardian."

Delgar shook his head. "I don't like this place." Even as he said it, curiosity overcame his fear. If the guardian did speak, what would it say? What secrets would it impart?

"We'll stay by the entrance until the storm passes," Daelyn said, sitting down. But Delgar noticed the Tuatha de Danaan's eyes remained fixed on the ancient skeleton.

Delgar sat down and stretched, watching the storm outside. Lightning shot from cloud to cloud, and both rain and hail fell to the earth. As the lightning flashed, the crashing thunder became deafening, as though some great giant had just fallen.

He wasn't sure what brought his eyes back to the skeleton. A chill began to run down his spine, and he slowly looked back into the cavern, his eyes falling upon the ancient corpse.

The skeleton was staring directly at him.

Delgar shook his head and looked to Daelyn, but the Tuatha de Danaan stared silently back at the ancient warrior. Delgar nudged Daelyn softly, but Daelyn did not move.

The guardian motioned to the young man, dust falling from the ancient bones. "I have already spoken to him," it rasped, its voice both hollow and infinite. "Why are you here, Magus Draconum?"

Delgar swallowed. "I am Delgar. What is a Magus Draconum?"

"You were Magus Draconum," the guardian said. "You will be Magus Draconum. You are Magus Draconum."

"I don't understand," Delgar said. "Are you trying to tell me my future?"

"There is no future. There is no past. There is no present."

Delgar shook his head and swallowed again. "I don't understand."

"You will," the skeleton stated. "All will join the dead."

"Not now," Delgar said. "Why have you come here?"

"I am the guardian of the dead," the corpse said. "My spirit was summoned by you. I cannot resist the pull of a creature of power."

"But I am not a creature of power," Delgar protested.

"You are wyrd's creature. You were wyrd's creature. You will be wyrd's creature. I am subject to the call of Magus Draconum."

"Why do you say I am wyrd's creature?" Delgar asked.

"You are the sign of the end of the world. You are the savior of the world. You are the one who will bridge the many worlds. You are the unwilling immortal."

Delgar shook his head. "I am only a boy," he muttered.

The skeleton gazed at him, and Delgar felt as though it examined every part of his soul. Then the ancient head bowed.

"Time has spoken. Wyrd has spoken. You are not ready for my counsel. Forget my words, for they are not for you." And then the guardian was silent.

Delgar watched the skeleton for what seemed like hours, but the strange life he had seen in it earlier had fled. All that was left was Daelyn's still form and the storm.

Chapter VIII: Journey's End

Delgar jumped as lightning struck a nearby tree, shattering the branches and blinding him. As the crash of thunder faded, Delgar blinked several times, trying to get the white-hot image out of his eyes. Finally, he looked across the barrow to see Daelyn staring at him.

"The guardian spoke to you, didn't he?" the Tuatha de Danaan said.

Delgar nodded.

Daelyn gazed at the lifeless skeleton. "He spoke to me as well. What did he say to you?"

Delgar opened his mouth, but then closed it. The memory had already grown fuzzy; half formed images and words flowed through his mind, but nothing clear arose. Finally, Delgar shook his head. "I don't remember."

Daelyn nodded. "Probably for the better. The dead do not see things as the living do. Time, space, the great Road, all of it is meaningless to them. At least, we would say it is meaningless to them." He looked out at the storm.

"It is very hard to say what the dead would think."

"Do you remember what he said to you?" Delgar asked.

Daelyn nodded. "It isn't your concern."

"Did you see him speak to me?"

Daelyn shook his head. "When you speak to the dead, you are half in their world. Even a Tuatha de Danaan druid cannot affect others when she is inside that world."

"But why did he come?" Delgar asked. "Who summoned him?"

Daelyn smiled. "Both of us, I think. When the elements are out of balance, such as they are now," he motioned to the storm, "the pathway between the realm of the living and the realm of the dead is more easily opened."

Delgar frowned for a moment. "I wish I could have remembered what he said to me," he muttered.

Daelyn blinked.

"It might have been news of Lera."

"I don't think that would be likely," Daelyn said, looking outside. The roaring of the storm had begun to cease, and a couple of stars poked out of the clouds. The Tuatha de Danaan turned back to Delgar. "The dead are not subject to the living, and rarely answer questions. You should get some sleep. The pathways between worlds have been shut, and you will need your rest."

Delgar nodded, leaned against the wall, and closed his eyes. His dreams were filled with phantasmagoric images of the talking dead, but a single phrase returned to his mind: *Magus Draconum*.

He startled awake to harsh sunlight on his face. He blinked and looked around, but Daelyn was nowhere to be seen. Finally, he stood up and stretched.

Leaning against the cold stone wall and yawning, he looked around the barrow. The morning sun cast its light through the door, illuminating the small pile of treasure. Delgar blinked. The hoard no longer seemed luminous, but old and rusted instead. The once intimidating skeletal guardian was reduced to a dusty pile of bones. Delgar frowned, suddenly regretting losing the fearsome wonder of the night.

"I had wondered when you would get up!" came a familiar voice, and Delgar turned to see Daelyn in the doorway, an apple in his hand. "You've slept for some time; it is past mid-morning."

"Are we leaving now?" Delgar asked.

Daelyn tossed him the apple. "Eat that first, and then we'll be off."

Delgar happily bit into the apple. For a moment he wondered how he could feel so refreshed with so little food. But then Daelyn was calling him, and emerging from the barrow, they began to walk to the southwest.

In the first day of travel after the barrow, they came to a small forest, where Daelyn led Delgar to an ancient grove. The afternoon sunlight shone down in warm waves, and for a brief moment Delgar felt completely safe.

"This is a Tuatha de Danaan holy place," Daelyn explained. "Here we can commune with the essence of the natural world. You'll need to learn to recognize such places, as they are part of the magic of the world around you."

Delgar nodded. "Is this part of being a wizard?"

"It can be," Daelyn said. "If you follow the true path."

Then Daelyn muttered something in his musical native tongue, and they were off. That evening they camped on a hillside, Daelyn standing a silent vigil all night.

The next morning, he told Delgar that they were near Pakaria and its warlords.

That day, they drew near some small mountains, but turned west instead of trying to pass through them. It rained lightly in the afternoon, and Delgar found himself wrapping his cloak around his body as the rain pattered down. If Daelyn was disturbed by the rain, he gave no sign of it.

It was on the third day that they saw the battle. They spent the morning climbing up a long rise, and as the sun bore directly overhead, Daelyn stiffened.

"What is it?" Delgar asked.

"Two forces are fighting," Daelyn stated. "They're in our path. We'll have to wait until they finish and pass."

"A battle?"

Daelyn grimaced and nodded. "People are dying this day."

They spent another hour cresting the ridge. As they walked, Delgar heard clashing metal and the faint screaming of men. Finally, they reached the top of the ridge and gazed down at the conflict. Two small armies were battling in a valley. The first wore red cloaks, and the second wore blue cloaks. As Delgar watched, the red-cloaks began to press back the blue-cloaked army.

"Who is who?" Delgar asked.

"The people in blue cloaks are soldiers of Taerraland," Daelyn said. "The others must be from Pakaria."

Delgar shook his head. "It doesn't look too bad."

"It is an exercise in terror," Daelyn stated. "When you fight, all you can think about is surviving to the next moment. As soon as you lose concentration, you die. As soon as your luck runs out, you die."

Shouting erupted within the blue ranks, and the army surged forward, pushing the red-cloaked fighters back. For a moment Delgar saw one of the soldiers clearly, waving the other red troops on, but then the man was surrounded, and something pale and bloody flew into the air.

"They've killed the Pakarian commander," Daelyn said. "We should be able to go through soon."

"Should we go down and help?" Delgar asked.

Daelyn shook his head. "That would only get you killed. The only time you should ever fight is when there are no other options. We will wait, and then we will go to Taerra."

"What is Taerra?" Delgar asked. "Is it this entire land, or is it just a city?"

"A city. It holds the throne of the castes, and it holds the Mageschool."

"Won't I have to pay to learn magic?" Delgar asked.

"Money is not an issue," Daelyn said. "After all, right now you are my charge."

Delgar looked back to the battlefield to see the red troops fleeing from the field. The Taerran soldiers cheered for a moment, and then began to gather their dead. Delgar fiddled, every now and then glancing at the position of the sun. Finally, after what seemed like hours, the army quit the field.

Daelyn nodded. "Right. Now we may go down."

The two travelers made their way down the crest and onto the battlefield. As they came within sight of the corpses, Delgar gagged. The stench of death filled the air, a combination of blood and excrement. Around them blood-flies hovered over the corpses, beginning their horrible feast.

Daelyn stopped at one corpse and called Delgar over. Once the young man had made his way there, Daelyn motioned at the dead soldier.

"This is the face of war," the Tuatha de Danaan said. "No glory, no great victory, only death."

Delgar nodded sadly. "I think I have seen too much of it now."

"Then hopefully you will never forget."

They made their way off the blood-soaked field, and Delgar finally managed to calm his nauseous stomach. Once they left the battlefield behind, they came to a large hill near the mountains. Behind them, the sun began to set.

Daelyn nodded. "Just over that rise you will see Taerra."

Delgar started up the hill. "What are we waiting for, then?"

He came to the summit and looked out. Far away in the southwest lay a small jumble of towers. Even with the great distance, Delgar's mouth fell open in shock.

The towers seemed to reach towards the sky, and there were so many of them! Thousands of people could live in that city. All around the settlement lay vast tracts of farmland, small communities dotting the landscape, barely visible.

"Your first city," Daelyn said. "And for the next few years, your home."

"I had never dreamed..." Delgar stammered.

"We are but two days away," the Tuatha de Danaan stated. "Until then, you will have to admire its beauty from a distance."

"Let's waste no time!" Delgar whooped, starting down the hill.

"Stop!" Daelyn barked, and before he could think about it, Delgar staggered to a halt. "Come back up here and rest for the night first. You'll do no good at the Mageschool if you arrive there dead from exhaustion."

Delgar sheepishly climbed back up the hill.

The next two days Delgar spent in a state of excitement. Every second moment he pressed Daelyn about what the city would be like, but the soldier only shrugged off his questions.

"Will there be books there?"

"Probably," Daelyn said.

"Will there be food there?"

"You'll see."

"What about scholars? Will there be scholars?"

"You'll find out when you get there."

"Can't you tell me anything?"

"You'll have to work very hard."

"But what else?"

"Delgar, you'll find out when you get there."

Later, Delgar thought he had been unfair to Daelyn, but then, in the prime of his youth, all of his burdens fled with his new excitement. A city full of things for him to discover!

For his part, Daelyn spent the majority of the time with a small smile on his face, as though he was reminded of a pleasant time. Finally, on a bright, sunny afternoon, they came to the gates of the city.

Delgar followed Daelyn around the city in a state of glee. The streets were filled with people, and there were pubs on almost every second corner. The high towers stretched to the sky, and a grand castle dominated the northern end of town. Merchants hocked their wares from corners of city streets. It was almost as if every dream of the small village he had grown up in had been realized by this magical place.

Finally, they came to the gates of the Mageschool. The Mageschool itself was a small walled town inside Taerra, with a robed, heavy-set guard sitting just inside the open gate reading a book. Daelyn walked up to the guard and smiled.

"Still buried in the pages of Yuliman, Corant?" the Tuatha de Danaan asked, grinning at the bearded, middle-aged man.

The guard looked up in shock. "Daelyn! It's been decades!" he said in a deep, rumbling voice.

Daelyn nodded. "True. Is Berran still the chancellor?"

Corant nodded. "There have been one or two Archmages who have tried to take the chair away from him, but they've never been able to get the popular support. Berran still runs things well, although he has said that if Vertanus ever wants the chair, he'll have it."

"Could you send a message to him? I have a new student here, and I am in a hurry. I think he'll see me."

Corant nodded and stood up. He walked inside the gatehouse for a moment, and then a young student mage, wearing red robes, burst from the gatehouse and ran into the small town.

"I trust you know your way?" Corant said.

Daelyn nodded. "Of course I do. Come along, Delgar."

Delgar followed the Tuatha de Danaan through the quiet streets of the Mageschool, glancing in awe at the ancient buildings. The streets were paved with small stones, and robed figures wandered the streets, usually carrying books or satchels.

"When you meet the chancellor, you will be meeting one of the most powerful Archmages in all of Mideorth," Daelyn said. "Be polite, follow my lead, and speak only when you are spoken to."

"Won't it look good if I seem enthusiastic?" Delgar asked.

"It will appear far better if you are respectful. Your future is at stake here."

Delgar nodded. "I understand."

They came to a large building built almost like a cathedral, and Daelyn motioned the young man inside. Delgar stepped into a small, stone hallway with a high ceiling.

"The chancellor's office is this way," Daelyn said, leading Delgar through a labyrinth of corridors. Finally, they went through a door into a large office where a thin, clean shaven, silver haired man sat at an ancient desk.

Around the desk were four padded wooden chairs.

Daelyn bowed politely. "Chancellor Berran."

Berran nodded. "It is good to see you Daelyn. I understand you have a student for me."

Daelyn motioned for Delgar to take a seat and sat down. "As usual, you get to the point."

"Both of us are in a hurry," Berran stated. "Is this your student?"

Daelyn nodded. "His name is Delgar Daegar's son."

Berran turned to face Delgar. "Are you from Nordland, boy?"

Delgar nodded. "Yes, sir."

"Can you read, boy?"

"Yes, sir."

"Can you write, boy?"

"Yes, sir."

"How old are you, boy?"

Delgar gulped, counting for a moment. "Fifteen winters, sir."

Berran nodded. "A bit young, but I think you will manage."

The chancellor turned back to Daelyn. "He's polite. I'm impressed. Usually the rich come in with these spoiled brats who want to look good for some tavern wench."

"He has incredible promise," Daelyn stated. "Fleot'heortan and I are in agreement about it."

Berran nodded. "That is impressive." He took a closer look at Delgar. "I can see the wyrd surrounding him."

"Look closely," Daelyn said.

Berran's eyes widened. "Could this be true?"

"I have never seen anybody with such potential in my life, Berran. This is where he needs to be."

Berran leaned back in his chair. "And who will sponsor him?"

Daelyn dropped a small pouch on the table. "I will.

His tuition and allowance, to be added to any scholarships he earns."

"You know our payment schedule?"

Daelyn nodded. "Payment is not an issue."

"And his supplies?"

"I would prefer that the Mageschool supply them," Daelyn said.

"We used to include that in our scholarships," Berran said. "But we have not done that in some time."

"Then I will pay for his supplies as well. Take the money out of the first installment."

Berran took a parchment and quill pen out of his desk. "What program do you want him in?"

Daelyn leaned forward. "An Archmage program in a natural magic concentration, with some general theory and control magic. The best program you can offer."

"That would be our eight year program."

Daelyn nodded. "That will do."

Berran turned back to Delgar. "Boy, I won't finish signing you up unless you actually want to be here. Do you want to be here?"

Delgar nodded. "Yes, sir."

"It is going to be eight years of very hard work. After your fourth year you will be a Mage, and then you will be allowed to decide on your main concentration for Archmage training. Then you will train for another four years, and then you will be an Archmage. If you do not keep a high academic standard, you will be re-evaluated and then perhaps expelled. You are answerable to myself, your tutors, and your sponsor; in your case, Daelyn. Are you still certain you want to go through with this?"

Delgar swallowed, his throat suddenly dry. The realization of the vast importance of his decision washed over him. What if he said no? He could be a mercenary, wander the world, find lots of books...

But the thought of all that knowledge, all that learning, pulled at him. As he thought about it, he realized all that he could accomplish through his training, and he could still see the world afterwards.

Finally, he shook his head. "Yes, sir. I am still certain."

Berran smiled and shook Delgar's hand. "Welcome to the Mageschool of Taerra. I will have a novice come and take arrange for your lodgings. Your timing is wonderful, and the new term starts in two weeks. You'll probably need that time to settle in, anyway. I'm sure you'll make Daelyn proud."

Delgar just nodded and prayed to the Eternal One he had made the right choice.

Chapter IX: Lessons in Theory

As the early afternoon sunlight streamed in through the large elegant windows, Delgar sat back in his chair and tried to look as small as possible. The classroom was filled with students, all of whom looked richer, older, and smarter than he did. He glanced around the lecture theater again, taking note of the locations of the exits. The wilderness had been bad enough, but at least Daelyn had been there. Here he was all alone.

The last he had seen of Daelyn had been in the Chancellor's office two weeks ago. He had been shown to his room, and shortly afterwards a note had been delivered to him, with instructions on where to get supplies and what to get. He remembered his throat drying up at that moment as the reality of his situation hit him.

But, he had swallowed down his fear and homesickness, and begun to explore the Mageschool. The school was huge, a fortress in itself. The majesty of it all had left him breathless; where his room was a small cell, the school was fit for royalty. The lecture halls were huge and eldritch, the banquet halls were vast and well stocked with food, and the study rooms were quiet and comfortable. No matter how often Delgar tried to feel at home, the alienness of his situation overpowered him: he was alone and without family in a strange place.

But he had to trust in Daelyn; the Tuatha de Danaan had never sent him down the wrong path.

So, he had spent his two weeks gathering supplies and trying to keep himself as busy as possible. Somehow, though, he often found himself sitting forelorn in his cell. It was odd, he reflected one day, that he had only really began to realize how much he had lost when he was safe and sound again.

The entrance of a short but powerful man with short grey hair and a close cropped beard brought Delgar's attention back to the present. The newcomer turned to gaze at the class with confident brown eyes, and then he placed the papers in his hands on the desk before him.

"Well," he said with a soft, aristocratic accent. "Welcome to basic magical theory. I see by the looks of terror on your faces that you are the new class. Let me assure you now that you have every reason to be terrified."

The wizard took a deep breath. "I am Archmage Velnan, and I will be your instructor for the next eight months. Rest assured that less than half of you will survive your first year, and only half of those that remain will actually graduate. Those that manage to complete their education here will be those students who are here to learn. None of us care how nice you are, who your sponsor is, or how much money you have. All that we care about is how well you can work, and how much you manage to learn. If you are here to pass time for four years, or because your parents want you here, then you may as well leave now; you are wasting your time staying here."

Velnan paused for a moment, looking over the class. For a minute he made eye contact with Delgar, and his eyes narrowed slightly, but then his gaze moved on.

But nobody stood up and moved towards the door. The class simply sat and watched their instructor.

Velnan nodded. "Very well. I will be teaching you magical theory. You will not be tossing fireballs at one another; in fact you will not be casting any magic at all this year. What you will be learning is how magic works and what ethics lie behind it." He pointed to somebody to the right and behind Delgar. "What is your name, boy?"

"Teranus, sir," came the reply.

"Very well, Teranus, do you know what magic is?"

There was a moment of silence, and then Teranus' voice called out. "Power."

Velnan shook his head. "Wrong." He glanced around the class again, and finally pointed to Delgar. "You, child, what is your name?"

"Delgar, sir."

"Delgar, do you know what magic is?"

Delgar thought for a moment. Daelyn had told him what some magic was, but did that apply to all magic? Was that the real question he was being asked, or was there more to it?

He finally swallowed and spoke. "I don't really know, sir, but I think that it has something to do with making things do what is in their nature."

Velnan nodded. "Well said, and partially right." He turned to the rest of the class. "Magic is the application of natural and unnatural forces upon any given object or situation. Magic is not 'power', and never has been. One cannot force an object to do one's will. Magic is the use of mental energies not to force, but to influence. One uses natural forces to make an object do what is in its nature, and unnatural forces to make an object do what is outside

95

of its nature."

The Archmage stared at the class. "I do hope you are writing all of this down."

With a start Delgar realized that he had only been listening to the Archmage, and began to furiously write down what he was being told.

Before he knew it, the class had finished, and the sun was beginning to set. Velnan concluded what he had been telling the class about what they would be studying, and looked at the papers in front of him.

"Right," the Archmage said. "I want you all to read the first four chapters of Telemon's *The Magician*, and be prepared to write a quiz on them. I will see you all tomorrow. Have a good evening, and enjoy your dinner. Delgar, will you stay a moment, please?"

Delgar swallowed hard and watched as the students around him filed out of the exits. Velnan put his papers in order, waiting until the lecture hall was empty, and then leaned against one of the chairs.

"Have you ever had any formal training, Delgar?" he asked.

Delgar shook his head. A drop of sweat ran down his forehead.

"Have you ever used any magic?"

Delgar nodded. "Once, when my village was raided by goblins."

"Wild magic," Velnan muttered. "That's rare enough." He looked up at the young student. "Will you relax? I'm not going to murder and eat you. Do you know how you cast your magic in that raid?"

Delgar shook his head. "No sir."

Velnan nodded. "Very well. I don't want you to cast any magic until the faculty sanctions it. What you have is called 'wild magic', and can be very dangerous. Am I clear?"

"Yes sir."

"Good. Now, go and enjoy your dinner, and don't tell anybody what we discussed."

Delgar nodded and left, sighing in relief as he went.

Delgar sat quietly in the feast hall, chewing on some fresh bread. The great room was filled with conversation, but the young man remained quiet. All he wanted to think about was his food and the reading he would have to do for the next day of class. The last thing he wanted to deal with was what Archmage Velnan had told him about wild magic.

"Do you mind if I join you?" a soft voice said. Delgar looked up to see a young man who looked just a bit older than himself.

Delgar smiled. "Not at all."

The young man placed a plate of food on the table and sat down. He had sandy hair and a thin face, with sparkling blue eyes.

"You must have made quite the impression on Archmage Velnan," the young man said.

Delgar grunted. "I hope to never make that kind of impression again."

The sandy haired youth laughed. "Sounds familiar. My name's Tomlin." He held out his hand.

Delgar took it. "Delgar Daegar's son."

"Your accent is a bit odd. Where are you from?"

"Nordland," Delgar said. "Where do you come from?"

"Silvia," Tomlin replied. "It's on the western coast of Taerraland. Nordland's pretty far away."

Delgar swallowed a mouthful of beef. "I didn't have much choice in the matter."

"Father made you do it, then?"

Delgar shook his head. "I prefer not to talk about it."

Tomlin stuffed some vegetables into his mouth and swallowed. "Me, I'm a special case. My father is very rich, and he wanted me to learn how to manage the estate. I'm not cut out for lordship though, so I came here. Grabbed some money, took a boat up the Great River, and here I am. Came right through the docks at Taerra." He sat back with a satisfied grin. "Not too many people with that story."

Delgar nodded. "True enough."

Tomlin leaned forward, picking his teeth. "Really, what's your story?"

"I prefer not to talk about it."

"Tell me a bit then. Who's your sponsor?"

Delgar looked up and swallowed. "Daelyn."

Tomlin shook his head. "You're joking, right?"

"No."

"By the Eternal One," Tomlin breathed. "You actually know Daelyn? Wow! What's he like?"

"Quiet."

"Unlike me," Tomlin said with a chuckle.

Delgar laughed.

"Thought I could get a smile out of you," Tomlin said. "I don't think I've ever met anybody as quiet or depressed-looking as you, do you know that? Your story must be really sad."

Delgar nodded. "My parents and fiancé were killed. Daelyn brought me here and enrolled me."

Tomlin sat back, eyes wide. "I'm sorry. I had no idea."

Delgar poked at some of the leftover meat on his plate. "As I said, I prefer not to talk about it."

"Maybe some beauty would cheer you up," Tomlin suggested. At Delgar's black look, he added: "Natural beauty, I mean. Just south of Silvia there is a huge forest, and every season the leaves are a different color. Well, except for winter, but in the spring and summer the leaves

98

are this radiant green, and in the fall you can't count the number of hues on both hands, there are so many."

"We have pine forests up in Nordland," Delgar said. "And every winter the snow falls on them and it is the most magnificent thing any mortal man could ever see. I fear your southern forests cannot hold a candle to our northern trees."

Tomlin pounded the table. "We shall have to see! Once we're mages, you will come to my home in Silvia and I will show you our wonderful forests, and then you will take me to Nordland and show me your great woods."

Delgar grinned. "That sounds fair enough."

Tomlin held up his hand and fingered an ornate gold ring on his ring-finger. "I swear by my family signet I'll take you to see the forests of Silvia."

Delgar nodded. "And I swear by the Eternal One that I will take you to see the forests of Nordland."

Tomlin sat back. "Well, that's settled, then. What are you doing this evening, friend?"

Delgar chuckled. "Working."

"I mean after that."

"Sleeping."

"Surely you can spend some time with old Tomlin," Tomlin said. "Maybe on the weekends, at least?"

"I think I can manage weekends."

Tomlin grinned. "You'll love this city, Delgar. There are theaters with great plays, ale-houses, inns, and if you really want them, lots of women."

"I don't think I'll be interested in the last one for a while," Delgar said.

Tomlin shrugged. "I understand, but I think I can bring you around."

"We'll see."

It was the beginning of a routine that Delgar would never regret. Every weekend he and Tomlin would meet and visit a theater or ale-house, and soon he found himself looking forward to the end of the working week and the beginning of the weekend.

The first term passed quickly, and he found that he had a natural grasp of the material. So, when the first term examination was returned with a ninety percent, neither Delgar nor his teachers were surprised. However, Delgar was one of the lucky ones.

On the first day of class in the winter term, Delgar sat down beside Tomlin and looked around the classroom. A quarter of the chairs were empty.

"Where is everybody?" Delgar said, removing his woolen cloak and taking out his notebook.

Tomlin shrugged. "Maybe Archmage Velnan wasn't kidding when he said half of us wouldn't pass."

"But only a quarter of us are gone."

The class became quiet as Velnan strode into the room, casting off his blue cloak and placing his usual pile of papers on his table. He sat down on the table and glanced at the students.

"Well," the Archmage said. "I'm pleased that so many of you passed your first term. Don't worry about those comrades of yours who didn't; the Mageschool gives a hearty letter of referral to all of its students when they leave, no matter what their grades. The class average was unexpectedly high: over seventy percent." He folded his arms. "Now you're ready to learn, and I think I can call you novices now.

"Last term we talked about basic magical theory. We talked about what magic is and how it is used. We discussed sources of power, and the gifts of various peoples on Mideorth. Let's begin by recounting those. Novice Tomlin, what is the gift of the Tuatha de Danaan?"

Tomlin paused and gazed at the ceiling. "They can travel from world to world, and they have a special connection with nature."

Velnan nodded. "Very good. Novice Beltan, what is the gift of the Dwarves?"

A young, dark haired novice stirred from the back of the class. "They can work the living stone, and they are great warriors."

Velnan nodded. "Excellent. Glad to see you were paying attention back there." He turned to face Delgar. "Magus Draconum, what is the gift of the Dragons?"

Delgar blinked. "What did you call me?"

Velnan crossed his arms. "I called you Novice Delgar. What did you think I called you?"

"Magus Draconum, sir," Delgar replied, trying to appear as small as possible.

"Now why would I call you a couple of nonsense words?" Velnan asked. "No matter. Novice Delgar, will you please tell me what the gift of the Dragons is?"

"Profound wisdom and power," Delgar replied.

"Very good," Velnan said, and turned to face another student. "Novice Melina, what is the gift of the Faeries?"

Tomlin tapped Delgar on the shoulder. "I like her," he whispered.

"Does she like you?" Delgar hissed.

"I'll find out this Friday," Tomlin replied, a sly smile on his rough face. Over the winter Tomlin had decided to grow a beard, and was so far having very little success.

"The gift of mystery," Melina said, bringing Delgar's attention back to the class. Come to think of it, she did have a melodic voice, Delgar thought.

Velnan nodded. "Very good. Everybody was paying attention; quite a change from last term. Each of these gifts is a kind of magic, even if these races do not understand it themselves. So, we are going to begin this term by discussing these magical powers, and then we are going to learn how the sources of magic actually work. We are going to learn what a spell is and how it is influenced by verbal and mental preparations. You will be prepared to begin your practical magical training when it comes next year."

The Archmage took a breath and leaned forward. "And, if you thought that last term was easy, this term you will find to be incredibly difficult. There will be a major test each Monday, and if you fail three tests during the term, you will fail the year and be rejected as a student here."

Delgar swallowed. It was going to be a long term.

Delgar was still exhausted when he was called from his room to the chancellor's office. He had just finished putting his books in order after writing his final examinations, a hard and grueling time when he had spent more nighttime hours awake than he had ever wanted to think about. He had no choice in the matter: if he failed the examination, he would fail school. But, despite his fatigue, there was no refusing the call of the chancellor, so Delgar put down the books and headed out of his residence.

He found four people sitting in Chancellor Berran's office, three of whom he recognized. Daelyn gave him a sage nod, as did Archmage Velnan. The fourth man was tall and dark haired, but with a fair complexion and almost green eyes.

Delgar swallowed when Berran looked up and motioned to the only empty chair in the office. "Please sit, Novice Delgar."

Delgar sat down carefully, trying to make himself seem as small as possible.

"Your sponsor, Archmage Velnan, Vice-Chancellor Vertanus and I have been reviewing your record for this year, now that your examination results are in," Berran said. "We have all been quite amazed."

"Sir, I can explain," Delgar began. "I didn't get a lot of sleep the night before, and-"

"And your results are exemplary," Berran stated. "I don't think the Mageschool has ever had a student as apt at theory as yourself. Be proud, Master Delgar; you have lived up to your sponsor's expectations, and my own."

"I'm a Master?" Delgar stammered, hardly believing his ears.

Velnan nodded. "Any novice who passes his first year becomes a master of magical theory. Be thankful, young Delgar; half of your class didn't make it."

"Before we admit you to your first year of practical magic, Vice-Chancellor Vertanus has some questions for you," Berran said. "Vertanus?"

The tall man turned in his chair to face Delgar. "Master Delgar," he said with a deep, aristocratic voice. "I understand that you have performed some wild magic. Is this true?"

Delgar nodded. "Yes sir."

"Will you please tell me exactly what happened?"

Delgar took a deep breath. Finally, he began to talk. As he told the Archmages what had happened, the tears began to flow out of him, until he faced the wizards, tired and drained.

Vertanus nodded and turned to Berran. "I don't see any hazard here. Obviously the wild magic only arose when Master Delgar's life and family were threatened. I don't believe he will accidentally destroy one of the laboratories."

Berran nodded and turned to Delgar. "I'm sorry for putting you through that, but it was necessary. Welcome to your second year, Master Delgar. Archmage Velnan has requested you as his student, so he will be your tutor next year. Also, Daelyn has arranged for us to provide you with employment over the summer in our libraries. You will be working with several of your classmates; this arrangement is very common for students whose sponsors live far from Taerra, and our students come from all over Mideorth. Do you have any questions?"

"Just one, sir," Delgar said. "I have a friend named Tomlin, and I was wondering if he passed."

"I really shouldn't release that information," Berran said.

Velnan held up his hand. "I don't see a problem. His marks were not as high as yours, but he certainly passed. I believe his tutor will be Archmage Lydia; she specializes in earth magic."

"Thank you sir."

"Well, I don't believe that we have any more business with you today, Master Delgar," Berran said. "You may go."

As Delgar got up, Daelyn put his hand on his shoulder. "Delgar, could you please wait outside for a moment? I want to talk to you after this."

Delgar nodded and walked out of the office. Just outside the door he collapsed in relief. He had passed. As he listened to the muffled voices of his sponsor and the Archmages, he had the unshakable feeling that he had only taken the first steps on a long journey.

Chapter X: Lessons in Reality

For Delgar, the summer passed too quickly. He enjoyed his job in the library, but it ended with the coming of autumn, and it was time to begin his studies again.

However, between the end of his job and the beginning of class, he had two weeks to prepare himself. Vclnan had come to him at the beginning of those two weeks and told him what he needed to purchase, where to find it, and how much it would cost. He had also told Delgar to relax while he could; the second year of schooling would be twice as hard as the first one.

And so, it was on a sunny and pleasant day that Delgar saw her. He was sitting with Tomlin in front of one of the large, limestone halls of the Mageschool, a bag of books beside him, watching the new students arrive. They filled the courtyard, so thick they almost hid the large trees. Around them the other buildings bustled with activity. Delgar smiled; he remembered all too well what it was like when he was one of the pre-novices.

"I think he's from Barsh," Tomlin said, pointing at one dark skinned student following a master. "I've heard that the desert nomads have skin like that."

"He could also come from the mountains of southern Pakaria," Delgar suggested. "That's pretty close to Barsh."

"Look at him, though," Tomlin said. "He walks like a nomad. I'll bet he even talks like one. Some of those nomad Amirs can be pretty rich. He's probably a prince of some sort."

Suddenly, Tomlin's eyes lit up, and he stood and waved. "Jenara! Over here!"

Delgar looked around. "Who?"

A slim, raven haired beauty jogged over from the other side of the crowd to join them. She had deep, grey eyes and a pleasant smile on her face. She grinned at Tomlin, and then looked at Delgar. For a moment they stared at each other, Delgar lost in the depths of her eyes.

"I never thought you'd actually be able to make it," Tomlin said, a huge smile on his face. "Parents finally say yes?"

Jenara tore herself away and laughed, a musical sound that had Delgar grinning in delight. "They did, but I think at the behest of your father. He said something about me talking some sense into you."

Tomlin shook his head. "I'll surprise him yet! I'll talk the sense into him, once I graduate. Jenara, I want you to meet Delgar Daegar's son, from Nordland. He had the gall to get a better mark than me last year. Delgar, this is my cousin, Jenara."

Delgar took her hand and kissed it. "It is a pleasure and an honor."

Jenara smiled graciously. "Likewise."

"Delgar is one of those rare students who comes here at an early age," Tomlin said. "Got in two years early. He's only sixteen; a young pup!"

Jenara sat beside Delgar and chuckled. "Then I guess I am rare too. I'm also sixteen."

Tomlin did his best to try to look old and decrepit. "And I'm special too: I'm ancient. These young whippersnapper Archmages, why, in my day..."

As Delgar laughed, his heart seemed strangely lighter, but there was an odd familiarity about the conversation. He gazed at Jenara's supple features, yet he couldn't place where he had seen her before. Finally, he shook his head, a grin on his face. No matter; it was probably nothing more than a dream anyway.

"I have to go, Tomlin," she said, giving him a quick kiss on the cheek. "I still have to unpack." With that, she skipped off into the crowd.

Tomlin looked at Delgar, a wide grin on his face. "You like her."

"She's nice," Delgar conceded.

"You should go for her."

Delgar blinked. "What?"

Tomlin frowned. "Look, you can't stay dead inside forever."

"I'm just biding my time."

"Until what? Lera comes back from the grave?"

Delgar stood silent for a moment.

Tomlin shook his head. "I'm sorry; I shouldn't have said that. Regardless, I saw the way she looked at you and you looked at her. It won't hurt, and I'm sure if Lera could look down on you she would approve."

"Maybe," Delgar finally said.

Tomlin patted him on the shoulder. "Good man. Just don't wait long. Girls like her don't stay available for too long."

"Concentrate, Delgar," Velnan said, staring at the potted plant.

Delgar focused on the green leaves, but Jenara's image kept appearing in his mind. The small fern fluttered quietly as his concentration slipped away.

"You're distracted."

Delgar nodded sadly. "Yes sir."

"Look, we're only half a term away from the winter examinations. You have to be able to do all of this."

Delgar nodded.

Velnan sat back and crossed his arms. He glanced out the window of the laboratory, watching the clouds scud across the sky.

"I'm sorry, sir," Delgar said. "I just can't get Jenara out of my mind."

"Love is a wonderful thing, Master Delgar," Velnan said. "But only in small doses. Now, review: what are the three principles of magic?"

"Harmony, concentration, and discipline," Delgar stated.

Velnan nodded. "Excellent. And what is the most important?"

"Discipline."

"Correct. So, clear your mind."

Delgar closed his eyes, forcing Jenara's face from his mind. He forgot the date last night, the bounce in her step, and the other young man who was making eyes at her.

He opened his eyes. Velnan and the potted plant lay before him.

"Now," Velnan said. "How do you influence natural forces?"

"First, become one with the object," Delgar replied.

"Good. Become one with the fern."

Delgar reached out with his mind, sensing the plant's life. He felt the warm heat of the sunlight on the leaves, bringing more life into the slight veins. As he felt the very essence of the plant, a warmth flooded through him. He gasped in ecstacy; he felt so wonderfully *alive*.

Velnan grinned. "Excellent! Now, what do you do next?"

"Examine the forces," Delgar said, mentally reaching out again. He opened his eyes, and saw the life forces winding around the stem of the fern, spreading over the leaves like a silky spiderweb. The connection to the sunlight and the earth stretched out before him, reaching up to the heavens and down into the ground. In a crystal moment, he realized how easily he could shape them.

"And then what?" Velnan asked.

"Manipulate them," Delgar answered, beginning to strengthen the life forces around the plant. He extended the force deeper into the ground, and then reached into the heavens and intensified the sunlight. The fern began to grow before him, sprouting new leaves and basking in the nourishment provided by his power.

Delgar blinked. "I did it!"

Velnan nodded, a slight smile on his face. "Yes, and it only took you two months. Not bad for a beginner, but you must become much better. What else should you have done?"

Delgar shook his head, stifling a yawn. "I don't know. I feel...tired."

"Not surprising," Velnan said. "This was the first time you ever actually used your powers under controlled circumstances. Now, you did not keep a steady control on the growth of the fern. I had told you two inches, and you gave it four. The leaves are not nice and orderly, which I also asked for. You need more practice."

"Yes sir."

Velnan sighed. "Look, I really mean it. Just because you did well in theory does not mean you can coast through your practical studies. Spend less time with your girlfriend-"

"She's not my girlfriend," Delgar interrupted.

"-whatever she is, and practice. Two hours a day, at least."

Delgar nodded. "Yes sir," he said unhappily.

"Master Delgar, there is a place for love," Velnan said. "Don't let it out of its place. Now go; you have practicing to do."

Delgar gathered his books and walked out of the room. As he strode down the tall, limestone hallways, he reviewed his triumph in his mind. He had done it! He had made the plant grow! He couldn't wait to tell Jenara.

Jenara's face popped into Delgar's mind, and all thoughts of studying vanished like smoke. She had time this evening, and they could spend the entire evening together. Practice could wait, after all; the plant wasn't going anywhere, was it?

Delgar and Jenara sat on the hill just outside of the Mageschool walls, staring at the full moon. He gazed at her wonderful face, watching her grey eyes dance in the moonlight.

Delgar wondered what she was thinking. She had sat with some boy in her theory class for dinner, and he hadn't felt it right to intrude. But he had wanted to walk over and declare her for himself and himself alone. Instead he watched her laugh at the boy's jokes, every chuckle making him feel ill.

Could he tell her what was on his mind? Did he dare? What about that boy, whatever his name was? Delgar shook his head. What was she thinking? Was it anything like what he was?

"Bastion asked me to the Taerra Farmer's dance," Jenara said. "I don't know if I'll go or not."

Delgar blinked. Was it his imagination, or did she

sound uncertain as she spoke? Suddenly, something Tomlin had said came to mind: *Just don't wait long. Girls like her don't stay available for too long.*

For a chilling moment, he knew what Tomlin was talking about. If he didn't act, he would lose her. She wouldn't wait around forever, and that Bastion boy was bigger and more handsome than he was. Bile rose in his throat. He swallowed, forced it down, then began to speak.

"Um, Jenara, don't go. I, um..." He cut off, cursing himself silently. Why was it so damned hard to say what he meant, especially when it was this important?

"I'm listening," Jenara said. Delgar found himself lost in her intense eyes.

Just say what you mean, Delgar told himself. He took a deep breath. "Look, I'm afraid of losing you. You are so wonderful that I don't want to be without you. And this is really hard to say, so please don't go out with him. Go out with me instead."

Delgar turned away, blinking back tears. *You damned, awkward fool!*

Suddenly, Jenara was there, holding him closely, her eyes brimming with tears of her own. For a wonderful moment they held on to each other as though they were a solitary island in the great river of the world.

Finally they disengaged and walked arm in arm back into the Mageschool. Delgar whistled a happy tune; for the first time since he had left Nordland he felt whole again.

Daelyn read the report card with interest, and then handed it back to Chancellor Berran. The Tuatha de Danaan leaned back in his chair, gazing at the stone ceiling.

"As you can see," Velnan said, "your charge nearly failed this term. And, if he continues like this, he won't survive the end of the year."

111

"I am at a loss," Berran said, leaning forward. "Delgar is such a fine student, but this reversal in his fortunes, why, it is almost as if he has stopped trying."

Daelyn opened his eyes and glanced around. Chancellor Berran, Vice-Chancellor Vertanus and Archmage Velnan stared back at him.

"Did you see his wyrd," Daelyn said. "This was part of it."

"I haven't see it," Berran said.

"I have," Daelyn stated. "I do have some druidic training, after all. The question is how do we get him out of this rut. Could his wild magic be interfering with his studies?"

Vertanus shook his head. "The only time a student has ever been retarded by wild magic is when he keeps using it; Delgar's case is the reverse."

"What about living conditions?"

"You know better than to ask about those," Berran said. "We have always had a high standard of student living."

"Study time?"

"Plenty," Velnan said. "If only he wouldn't spend it all with that Jenara girl, he would be fine."

Daelyn blinked. "Jenara girl?"

"A novice student," Velnan stated. "Average grades, but gifted."

"And Delgar is spending all of his time with her?" Daelyn pressed.

"Yes."

Daelyn began to laugh, and then he laughed harder when the three Archmages looked at him in mystification.

The Tuatha de Danaan shook his head. "Both the problem and solution are perfectly obvious. You are all too old for your own good; you've forgotten how to be young. Delgar, my dear Archmages, is in love."

"So should we remove this impediment?" Berran asked.

Daelyn shook his head. "It is no impediment, my dear Berran. If Delgar is as deeply in love as I think he is, he will do anything this 'Jenara' asks him to." He paused for effect. "Even study."

Vertanus pounded his forehead with his fist. "I've been so blind!"

Daelyn looked at him. "Sorry?"

"I'm getting married in three years," Vertanus explained. "I should have seen this immediately."

Berran blinked. "That's a long engagement. Who's the lucky girl?"

"Her name is Marissa," Vertanus said. "She's a diplomat in Barsh; we're having the wedding once she returns from her assignment."

Daelyn stood and took up his cloak. "Well, I think you have the situation in hand now. I believe you will find the route to Delgar's heart is through Jenara, and I suggest you use it. Good day."

Daelyn chuckled as he walked through the hallowed halls of the Mageschool. These mortals could be so blind at times, but it was endearing. He just hoped that his advice would help; Delgar's wyrd had predicted great events, and the young man needed to be ready when they arrived.

Time was short, and it was growing shorter.

Chapter XI: Temptation and Redemption

"Concentrate, Master Delgar," Velnan said. "I want it to grow by two inches, with orderly leaves, and then I want it to shrink by three inches." He sat back in the winter sunlight and looked at the fern.

Delgar stared at the plant, focusing. The life forces wound around the leaves and stem, pulling him in. With a flicker of his mind, he touched one of the strands of energy, carefully nourishing and directing it.

As he watched, the fern flourished in front of him, until he had it exactly where he wanted it. Then, he began to shrink the fern, cutting off its lines to the earth and sun, depriving it of its nourishment. The fern shrunk, almost dying, but Delgar restored some of the connecting life forces and the plant blossomed to life again.

Velnan smiled. "Excellent! You're finally getting good at this."

"I'm getting as much practice in as I can," Delgar said.

Velnan nodded. "It shows. Your natural talents are beginning to show themselves."

Delgar chuckled. "Well, it was either that or have Jenara put scorpions in my bed, and I decided I didn't really want to sleep with scorpions."

Velnan smiled. "So that's the cause of the change. Good for her. Now that you are becoming proficient with plants, it is time to move into another element: the air. Then, I think you'll be caught up with the others."

Delgar nodded.

"Now, Master Delgar, what forces lie in the element of air?"

Delgar thought for a moment. "Wind, fire and light."

"And fire is also linked with?"

"The element of earth."

"Correct. And which of these forces can you influence?"

"Fire and light?"

Velnan shook his head. "You're forgetting your theory. If there is a force, a magician can influence it."

"All."

"Right. We will begin with wind. Concentrate, and tell me what you see in the air."

Delgar closed his eyes and reached out with his mind. The forces of wind and light intertwined before him, delicate as a spider's web. There was a gentle breeze, and the lines of force wavered, almost breaking.

"I see glowing lines of force," Delgar said, opening his eyes. The weave of energy faded until it was nearly transparent. "They're so delicate."

"They are also very easy to manipulate," Velnan stated. "And they are very powerful. With the wind you can create cyclones, and with fire you can create balls of flame. The air is the source of almost all battle-magic, and you must learn some."

"Why?" Delgar asked. "I don't plan to get into any fights."

Velnan shook his head. "The world does not respect your plans and wishes, Master Delgar. You may not intend to fight with magic, but you may have to. And you must be prepared. I am now going to teach you magic of destruction. Remember, it must always be used as a last resort."

Delgar shook his head gravely, lost in thought. The force lines disappeared before his eyes.

"Now," Velnan said, bringing out a candle. "Are you feeling up to lighting this candle, or have you used too much power today?"

"I feel fine," Delgar said. "How do I light the candle?"

"You have to-"

A deafening explosion sounded, causing both Delgar and Velnan to flinch. As they recovered their wits, the smell of sulphur filled the air.

"Ignar!" Velnan cursed. "Excuse me, Delgar."

Velnan stalked out of the laboratory, leaving Delgar alone with his candle. Delgar glanced at the candle, and with a burst of focus brought the force lines of the air back into sight.

To light a candle requires fire, Delgar thought. *And to make fire you need heat. To make heat you need light.* Delgar leaned forward, reaching out to the strands of sunlight, stretching them until they lit upon the candle's wick.

The candle did nothing. Delgar sat back for a moment, scratching his chin. Theoretically, it shouldn't be difficult. It shouldn't require arcane words, merely focus. He already knew how to manipulate some forces, so the others couldn't be too hard. So why wasn't it working?

Velnan shouting something down the corridor, and another voice replied calmly but loudly. Delgar shook his head and turned back to the candle, bringing up the lines of force. Several of the lines of sunlight still lay on the candle.

The knowledge came to him as though he had always known it. It was his power that manipulated the forces, not the forces themselves. They were merely tools. He felt the harmony washing though his body like a blissful wave, and he focused his mind on the candle, reinforcing the silky lines of sunlight with his own strength.

The wick burst into flame.

Delgar sat back, gazing out the window at the snowy park below. He had done it, without any help. He looked back at the candle, and with a quick manipulation of the wind currents, snuffed it out.

A grin lighted up his face. He could do it. He extended his will, and the candle lit with the greatest of ease. Suddenly, he felt some other power swirling around him. He blinked, startled, but then a long-forgotten word came to mind.

Wyrd.

He was plunged into a vision of ice and death. A great wall of ice crushed through a forest, driving all the forest dwellers out of the living woods, drinking the very life energies themselves. And the sky was filled with Dragons.

Delgar blinked, and then he was back, staring at a lit candle on a wooden table. For a moment he closed his eyes, taking a deep breath. Could he have tapped into some unknown resource? He looked at the candle again, watching the silky forces around it. A quick manipulation of wind snuffed it out.

"Very good!" Delgar heard, and he turned around to see Velnan standing behind him. "Now do it again."

Delgar turned back to the candle, focusing on the forces around it. As he felt the harmony swirl through him, he reached out with his mind and began to manipulate the silky lines of sunlight.

Nothing happened.

Delgar frowned and tried again. The candle's wick remained free of flame.

"Do you remember what you did, Master Delgar?" Velnan asked.

Delgar tried to remember the harmony flowing through him, the knowledge he had possessed, but instead of the earlier revelation the image of the glacier burst into his thoughts. He forced it down, but to no avail; his mind remained a blank as far as the candle was concerned.

Finally, he shook his head. "I can't remember."

Velnan sat down opposite the candle. "Well, I saw you light it, so I know you can. Now we just have to remember how you did it. Do you want me to guide you through it?"

Delgar nodded.

"Very well," Velnan said. "The forces of the wind must be carefully but firmly manipulated. You must encourage them with your own strength. Although they are more fragile, they are also harder to manipulate. But, above all else, take care. Let Ignar's mistake serve as an example."

Delgar blinked. "Who is Ignar and what did he do?"

"Ignar is the fool that created that explosion a moment ago," Velnan said. "He is an Archmage, but just barely. He majored in battle and control magic, and has recently been experimenting with summoning spells."

"Summoning spells?" Delgar interrupted. "What are those?"

"They allow you to summon the image of a creature from the forces in an element and give it some life," Velnan said. "So, you could create a creature of water and have it perform a task for you."

"Could you summon a living creature?" Delgar asked.

Velnan nodded. "In theory, yes. However, that is

forbidden, for it is the worst kind of control magic. I fear that some day an Archmage will cross that line, but none have yet.

"Now, to return to the lesson, Ignar is very reckless and does not exercise proper control. Just now, he nearly destroyed the laboratory he was working in. I fear that if he continues like this, he will be expelled from his position in the Mageschool."

Somehow, Delgar didn't think Velnan sounded too dismayed at the prospect.

"Let him serve as an example to you," Velnan continued. "Discipline above all else. Otherwise you are dangerous to yourself and the people around you."

Velnan smiled. "Now that I've finished my sermon, shall we continue with the lesson?"

Delgar sat on the hill in the center of the courtyard, his arm around Jenara. The two rested, sharing each other's warmth in the cold night. Above them, the stars progressed slowly through their eternal course.

"There's the Great Dragon," Delgar said, pointing. "It just looks like a snake to me."

Jenara laughed, the music in her voice bringing a blissful smile to Delgar's lips. "And how do you know that Dragons don't look like that?"

"The only Dragon I've ever met didn't look like that. It had wings."

Jenara slapped him playfully. "Oh, come on! You haven't met a Dragon."

Delgar chuckled. "Sure I have. I told you about how Daelyn found me after my village was destroyed, didn't I?"

Jenara nodded. "And you wandered through most of Nordland and saw a battle."

"Yes, well, I didn't tell you where he found me."

Jenara looked at him sternly. "You aren't really going to tell me he found you in the cave of a Dragon?"

Delgar nodded. "In the cave of the oldest Dragon. His name was Fleot'heortan."

Jenara sat up and turned around to face him, her hands on her hips. "Okay, so what did this Dragon look like?"

"Well, he was big," Delgar recalled. "And he had black scales, and huge wings. I didn't see that much of him; he spent most of his time buried in his treasure."

Jenara blinked. "You aren't making this up, are you?"

Delgar shook his head, and then looked up. Some clouds obscured one of the constellations, and a chill wind blew between the buildings.

"I think it's going to snow," Delgar said, wrapping his cloak around him. "The season is right for it. And we both have work to do."

"You said you'd help me with making the fern grow," Jenara stated. "We'll do that first, mister big-time third year student."

Delgar groaned. "Do you have any idea how many times Archmage Velnan had me practice on that fern last year? Even while I was learning how to manipulate air forces last year, he was making me play with the fern."

"Well, you can do it one more time for me," Jenara said, an impish grin on her face.

Delgar shook his head. "Very well. Fun with the fern." He stood, offered Jenara his hand, and helped her up.

"Master Delgar!" a harsh aristocratic voice called. "Might I have a word with you?"

Delgar turned to find a thin, tall, clean shaven man regarding him. "Do I know you?"

"Perhaps by a poorly earned reputation," the man said. "But we have never met in person. May I have a word?"

"I can meet you in the residence," Jenara offered.

"Right in the ante-room."

Delgar nodded and turned to the strange man. "I guess I have a couple of minutes." Behind him, Delgar saw Jenara making her way towards one of the ivied buildings.

The man nodded, and the torchlight from the nearby buildings reflected off his jet-black hair. "Master Delgar, I am Archmage Ignar, of the combat magic faculty."

Delgar drew in a deep breath. "I have heard of you."

Ignar smiled. "No doubt you have. People tend to see me as rather out of control; my students tend to have a great deal of fun around me. No doubt that is why the rest of the faculty dislikes me; can't be having fun in school."

Delgar chuckled. "True. What do you want?"

"I have heard of you, Master Delgar," Ignar said. "You are becoming the talk of the faculty, do you know that? Sadly, they don't tell you everything you need to know."

"What do you mean?"

"Haven't you ever wondered why you are being taught by the most prestigious Archmage in the school? Not even Vice-Chancellor Vertanus is as renowned as Velnan. And they are keeping you very carefully placed in natural magic. Almost as if they are afraid of you."

Delgar nodded. "Go on."

"Master Delgar, I teach combat and control magic," Ignar said. "Control magic deals with summoning, and occasionally actual power. If an exceptionally gifted student came through the school in such a powerful discipline, the Mageschool might consider that very dangerous. Now, you are allowed to transfer into another field before your final year, and I would be happy to instruct as gifted a student as yourself."

"You want me to transfer into combat and control magic," Delgar stated.

Ignar nodded. "I can teach you things they won't dare to."

Delgar shook his head. "I don't think I'm interested."

"Think of what you can do, Delgar," Ignar said. "The world can be yours."

"I don't want the world," Delgar pointed out. "I already have the little part I want."

Ignar shook his head. "What a shame," he said, and began to walk off. Then he turned. "Master Delgar, have they ever told you about your wyrd?"

"I've heard it mentioned."

"Anybody who knows how to look can see it quite clearly," Ignar said. "Have they told you what it is?"

"No."

"It's in the shape of a Dragon," Ignar stated. "If you want to transfer, my office is in Deltran Tower." With that, he disappeared into the darkness.

Delgar stood in the pale torchlight for a moment, at a loss. His wyrd was in the shape of a Dragon. For a moment, the vision he had seen last year came back to him with crystal clarity.

A glacier destroying all before it, and a sky filled with Dragons.

The summer sun shone down on the Mageschool courtyard as Delgar, Jenara, and Melina walked into the city of Taerra. The bustle of the town rose around them, and they finally made their way into one of the local taverns, The Farmer's Lot.

The Farmer's Lot was a small tavern, but popular with the students. It showed in many ways: on the wall was a large sign forbidding fireballs, and on the roof there were several scorch marks. Tomlin stood up from a table close to the back, calling them over.

As the three students sat at the table, a barmaid brought them their usual drinks. Tomlin raised his glass and shouted out: "To surviving a third year!"

Delgar, Jenara and Melina raised their glasses and drank deeply. Around them, Delgar could feel some of the other patrons stare at them for a moment and then return to their drinks.

"Tomlin, you started early, didn't you?" Delgar asked, a smile on his face.

Tomlin raised his glass. "My father sent word: he's proud of me. So, I had to celebrate. Had to start early, so that I could be warmed up. Now I'll be able to get really drunk!"

Delgar laughed and looked at his companions. "That's Tomlin."

"Now watch," Tomlin began. "You see that fly on the ceiling? I can burn it right up."

Melina shook her head. "Dear, don't do that. Last time we got thrown out."

Tomlin held up his hand, displaying a second ring on his finger. "But you see this? I have to show off now. Otherwise the engagement is off."

Delgar grinned. "So that's what the mysterious ring is all about. When were you going to tell us?"

"Later," Melina said. She looked at Tomlin. "Much later."

Tomlin called for another drink. "It'll be great. I'll freelance, she'll do...whatever she does, and we'll do it every night."

Jenara blinked. "How much of a head start do you have?"

"A couple of hours?" Melina said. "Tomlin, how long *have* you been here?"

Tomlin leaned forward, his half full drink in his hands. "Do you and Jenara do it every night?"

Delgar shook his head as Jenara turned beet red. "We're nice and proper."

Tomlin swallowed the remains of his drink and called for another one. "Shame. Less fun that way."

"So, where are you working this summer, Tomlin?" Jenara asked.

"Not," Tomlin replied, waving for another drink. "Getting married and traveling instead. You two?"

"We're both at the library this year," Jenara said.

Delgar leaned back and put his arm around Jenara. He had one more year to go, and then he would be a Mage. He rolled the idea around in his head. And then he would have another four years of training, but he'd be where he wanted to be. The woman he loved was beside him, his friends were around him, and he felt at home.

Delgar raised his glass. "To another great summer, and one more year!"

Chapter XII: Graduation

Velnan gazed at Delgar with a fatherly smile. The young man sat by the window, enjoying the autumn air. Outside, the park trees were filled with all the colors of the rainbow.

"Well, Master Delgar," Velnan said. "Are you ready to begin your final year of Mage training?"

Delgar nodded. "Almost unbelievable that I made it."

Velnan chuckled. "I knew you would."

"My wyrd?"

"Something like that," Velnan said. "But also pure potential. I think you will be one of the best Mages to come out of the Mageschool. So, shall we begin?"

Delgar nodded.

"Master Delgar," Velnan began. "I have taught you to influence and manipulate the elements, and I have taught you basic magical theory, but there are other types of spells that you may learn. They are not easy, nor are they simple manipulations of the elemental forces. They are often hard to remember. So, when Mages and Archmages discover these spells, they write them down."

"You're going to teach me how to read spellbooks," Delgar realized.

Velnan nodded. "It is the last thing I need to teach you, and it will take all year. After you have this knowledge, you will truly be a Mage."

"So what comes after Mage training?" Delgar asked.

"You have been taught simple magic," Velnan replied. "In your Archmage training you will learn complex magic, how to create forces, access higher planes, and other such arcane knowledge. However, this must come in good time."

Velnan handed Delgar a large leather-bound book. On the cover was Delgar's name, and Delgar flipped open the book to find some of the early pages covered with odd runes.

"This is your spellbook," Velnan said. "I am giving it to you. I have included some higher spells that will help you, but the rest is for you to fill in."

Delgar ran his fingers along the cover with care. "I don't know what to say."

Velnan smiled. "'Thank you' would be a good start. Now Master Delgar, shall we begin with the first spell?"

Delgar nodded, and began his final year of Mage schooling.

The spring larks sang in the trees as Chancellor Berran and Vice-Chancellor Vertanus stepped up to the podium. The graduating class was assembled in the park, with the usual crowd of onlookers.

Delgar tried not to scratch in his new woolen Mage's robe. He glanced around the crowd, trying to find Jenara's face. Finally, he saw her, leaning against a tree, a wide smile on her face. He smiled back, and began to look for Daelyn. The Tuatha de Danaan was nowhere to be seen.

Delgar shook his head. He was certain that Daelyn would be there somewhere, even if he was late. He heard the Chancellor clear his throat, and turned to face the podium.

"Four years ago," Chancellor Berran began, "I welcomed a class of four hundred to this institution of higher learning. Of those, one hundred and eighty four left after their first year, and another hundred and twelve left in the three consecutive years. This is the way it usually is.

"Those of you who stand here today, new members of the Order of Mages, are the best of that class. You are the most responsible, the most adept, and the most intelligent of your class. You are a credit to your families, your sponsors, and your nations. Never forget that.

"For those who are going into the world to work through the Mageschool or freelance, this is the end of your schooling. For others it is not. However, for everybody it is merely the beginning of your journey in the magical arts. We have taught you the tools you need to be ready to learn and survive. And, I believe that you are all well qualified to do both.

"For some, those who are going into Archmage training, you stand at the beginning of a far deeper journey of discovery, from which you will grow and learn more than you could imagine. You will enjoy it immensely, I assure you.

"So, as the Chancellor of the Mageschool of Taerra, I wish to welcome you all to the order of Mages."

There was a smattering of applause, and then Vertanus stepped up to the podium.

"It is customary to appoint a valedictorian to speak for the graduating class," he said. "We have thought long and hard about the selection, and finally we came to a decision.

127

Would Delgar, Daegar's son, please step up to the podium."

Delgar took a deep breath and walked forward. They had told him a week ago that he would be speaking, and he had nearly strained himself trying to think of what he would say.

He stepped up to the podium and cleared his throat. "I'm not much of a speaker," he said. "But I am told that I have done just about everything a student can do. Get drunk, nearly fail, pass with honors, and accidentally blow up a fern."

There was a smattering of laughter, and then Delgar continued. "But I learned something very important while I was here. I came here as a poor farmer's son, and the only means I had was through my sponsor. My home had been destroyed in a raid, and so I had nothing to fall back on. However, here I was able to flourish and become more than I had ever imagined.

"I think I truly grew up here, and learned the most important lessons of my life. Never forget the past, always cherish those around you, and look forward to the future. You will always take out of life what you put into it, for it is truly the journey that matters.

"On behalf of the graduating class of Common Year twenty four hundred and twelve, I want to thank the Archmages for giving us all the opportunity to learn these things. Thank you."

There was a standing ovation as Delgar returned to his place in the class. A smiling Vice-Chancellor Vertanus stepped up to the Podium. "Mages, if you will please come up when called, Chancellor Berran and I shall give you your degrees and rings of office."

When Delgar was called, he felt on top of the world. But there was still something else he had to do.

"'Mage Tomlin'," Tomlin said for the umpteenth time, his arm around Melina. "It has a wonderful ring to it, doesn't it Delgar?"

Delgar shook his head. "I think it suits you. Now stop saying it."

Tomlin laughed. "You're just jealous! 'Mage Tomlin' sounds much better than 'Mage Delgar'."

"And what about 'Mage Melina'?" Melina asked her husband. "How does that sound?"

"It...it...," Tomlin struggled, "it alliterates."

Delgar and Jenara laughed as Melina hit her spouse.

"Delgar!" Velnan said, walking over. "Congratulations!"

Delgar shook his mentor's hand. "Thank you! Will you be teaching me in the Archmage training."

Velnan nodded. "It still has to be set, but I believe so."

"Thank you, Archmage Velnan," Delgar said.

"You're welcome. I should leave you to your friends." With that, the Archmage made his way back through the crowd.

"I wonder if anybody has seen Daelyn," Delgar wondered.

"I have," said a familiar voice, and Delgar turned to embrace his sponsor.

"Where were you?" Delgar asked.

Daelyn pointed. "Way at the back. I was delayed by something, and arrived a bit late."

"Now what?" Delgar asked.

"Now I'm going to leave you here to become an Archmage and make a life for yourself," Daelyn stated. "You don't need me any more, and I've already paid your Archmage tuition in full. You have your own wyrd to fulfill, and you'll do it best on your own."

"So this is goodbye," Delgar said.

Daelyn nodded. "For now. Our paths will cross again,

but not soon."

As Daelyn began to walk away, Delgar called out. "Daelyn! My wyrd is in the shape of a Dragon."

Daelyn stopped, but did not turn. "Yes, it is."

"What does that mean?"

"None of us are certain," Daelyn replied. "But wyrd will work as it will. You will have a powerful destiny, but you must let it happen. Otherwise, you will destroy yourself. Farewell Delgar."

With that, the Tuatha de Danaan vanished into the crowd.

"Was that an Elf?" Jenara asked, her eyes wide.

Delgar nodded. "They prefer to call themselves the Tuatha de Danaan."

"And what did he mean about your destiny?" Jenara demanded.

Delgar shook his head. "I don't know; I don't think he knows either. Nothing to worry about, I think. Jenara, I want to ask you something."

Jenara nodded. "Go ahead."

Delgar began to speak, and faltered. He thought for a moment. *Say what you mean*, he thought.

"Jenara, I love you," Delgar said.

"I love you too."

"I want you to spend the rest of your life with me," Delgar finally said, his voice as uncertain as it had ever been. "Will you marry me?"

She was silent for a moment, her eyes downcast.

"Look, I know I can't offer you too much, but I can-"

She put a finger over his lips and then kissed him full on the mouth. "Of course I will," she said as he caught his breath. "But not yet. I want to graduate first."

"Why wait that long?" Delgar asked. "We could-"

"Because I want to finish this first."

Delgar nodded. "Next spring, then."

130

"Yes, my love," Jenara said. "And then I'll be yours forever."

They kissed again, but even as they kissed, the image of an all-destroying glacier and a sky filled with Dragons invaded Delgar's mind.

Chapter XIII: The Beginning of Wyrd

In midsummer, Delgar had to bid a tearful goodbye to Jenara. His fiancé was on her way home to explain to her father how she was going to be getting married and try to see to a dowry. Delgar was left working in the library and wishing that the love of his life would return.

After a couple of weeks, he found himself in a state of boredom. So, he began to change things about himself. First he tried to change his clothes, but he found that the usual style of the Mages was more comfortable. Then, he decided to grow long hair, and did so using some of the magic Velnan had taught him, but that turned out to be a pain after a month. Finally, he decided to grow a beard.

And still Jenara did not return.

For a few days, he tried to grow a full beard, but the sides refused to grow in. Then he thought of using magic, but it would be a waste of magic, particularly after the look Velnan had given him when he had seen the young Mage's hair a month ago. So, he decided to grow a goatee, and to do so naturally.

It was a week after he made this decision that Delgar awoke to the sound of faint breathing. Swallowing, he glanced around his chambers for an intruder. He half hoped it was Jenara playing some prank, but his eyes finally set upon two shapes blocking his open window.

On closer examination, they seemed to be two foot tall featherless birds, one asleep and nuzzled to the other, who was watching him wearily.

"We need help," one of the birds said. Delgar leapt out of bed, pressing himself against the wall. The other bird woke up, and turned its head to face him.

"Who are you?" Delgar finally stammered.

"I am Relara, and this is my lifemate Gelra," the bird said. "We are Teraeni Dragons."

Delgar blinked and stretched casually, or what he hoped looked casually. "I thought Dragons were supposed to be larger," he stated. "At least the Dragon I met was larger. His name was Fleot'heortan."

"Are there not small mammals and large mammals?" Relara responded.

"We are smaller cousins of the big Dragons," Gelra said. "But that is beside the point."

"So what can a newly graduated Mage do for you?" Delgar asked. He stroked his chin, wondering what Jenara would make of this, or if it was all some strange dream.

"Somebody created a spell that summons our kind from our homeland in Pakaria," Relara said. "We need to find the person who had done this and destroy the spell somehow."

"That's not possible," Delgar said. "To actually summon any living creature is nearly impossible to all but the highest Archmages, and even to them there is an injunction against that sort of magic."

"Our people have been disappearing," Gelra protested,

puffing up his wings. "We cannot afford to lose our kin to a magician who does not want to follow an injunction."

Delgar examined the dragons carefully. The stared back at him, pleading looks in their eyes. They didn't seem to be lying, or mean any harm at all. They didn't seem capable of inflicting any, either.

"I'll see what I can do," Delgar said, pulling on his tunic. Velnan was preparing for a sabbatical, so it was possible he hadn't left yet. Perhaps he might know something. It was a start, at least.

As Delgar walked down the hall, he could tell that the Dragons were following him. A faint flapping sounded behind him as they flew from perch to perch, sometimes settling on the hafts of torches.

When he turned a corner, Delgar noticed a familiar figure, wearing a light blue robe. He rushed up to overtake the man.

"Velnan!" Delgar called, startling the older magician. Velnan turned and looked behind him. As his gaze fell on the two tiny Dragons, a bemused look crept into his eyes.

"Greetings, Mage Delgar. Who are your guests?" Velnan asked.

"Dragons," Delgar replied. "I've told them I'll help them. Do you know of anybody who has been making illegal spells? Specifically summoning spells."

"Somebody has been summoning us from our homeland," Relara added.

Velnan stroked his beard. "Archmage Ignar was finally expelled for not taking proper precautions in his spellcasting; about time, too. He's the only person I can think of who might try something like that. He is powerful enough to do it, sad to say. The school should have expelled him years ago."

"Where can we find him?" Gelra asked.

Delgar glared at the Dragon. "Will you please let me ask the questions?"

Gelra started to speak, but Relara put a hand on the base of his wing. In front of them, Velnan chuckled and shook his head.

"You might want to look for him in the ruins of Idonia," the Archmage said. "He always wanted to search the place for artifacts, but nobody ever let him."

"He's pretty close, then."

"Possibly. It is difficult to say."

Delgar turned around and began to walk back to his chambers, the small Dragons in tow. "Delgar! One thing," Velnan called behind him. Delgar turned.

"Be careful," the older mage cautioned. "You may be a promising student, but Ignar is very powerful. Do you want me to fetch help?"

Delgar shook his head. "I don't even know if he'll be there. Besides, I can handle myself."

"I know you can handle yourself. The question is whether you can handle Ignar?"

Delgar smiled. "I'll be okay. Look, can you leave a message for Jenara?"

Velnan nodded. "What do you need me to tell her?"

"Tell her I've gone on an errand and I should be back in a month or so," Delgar said. "I will definitely be back for the beginning of classes.

"Okay," Velnan said. "I'll tell her. And Delgar, if you find him, send back for help. Do not, under any circumstances, engage him in battle. You are not ready."

Delgar nodded, then began to make his way back to his room.

Gelra looked worriedly at Relara. The two Dragons began to follow Delgar once again. Behind them, Velnan stroked his beard in thought, and then walked down the passage.

The packing for the trip was rushed, the Teraeni Dragons urging him on. Still, they had a maddening inconsistency. At times the Dragons were unwilling to wait, and at other times unwilling to hurry. Delgar finally told them that he would take as long as he needed, but he did need to pack certain human essentials.

At last, they made their way out of Taerra into the countryside. The kind weather sped them out of the Great River valley, and they made good time to the border; it only took them two weeks. He was quickly questioned by the border guard at the great wall, and then the young Mage entered the land of Pakaria, the Dragons fluttering over the fortifications. After a few hours, he looked back at the thin white line of the wall, a stone ribbon disappearing over the horizon. And the Dragons were still as cryptic as ever.

They walked until the sun began to set, and then Delgar made camp. He sat in silence, staring out into the distance as his small fire flickered.

"Where is Idonia?" Gelra asked, breaking the silence.

Delgar blinked. "Sorry?"

"Your friend mentioned it back at the Mageschool," Relara added.

"Ah, I see," Delgar said. "A better question would be: where was Idonia? Idonia fell to the Goblin armies almost a thousand years ago; at least, that is what the chronicles say. The raiders were so thorough that only a couple of ruins survive. One is Stataria, which was ransacked a long time ago. The other is Idona, which is where we are going."

He glanced at the countryside. The horizon was filled with the great plains, the tall grasses bearing a reddish tint in the light of the dusk, and the wall had passed beyond human sight into the distance. "We should be in Idona by tomorrow afternoon," Delgar said. The two Dragons took flight and began to circle.

"We are going to hunt for food," Relara declared. "We will not be long." The two Dragons flew into the distance.

As Delgar rested by the campfire he further contemplated the Dragons. Fleot'heortan had told him about the Teraeni Dragons, but now he had found them to be far stranger then he had ever expected. As the stars rose overhead the young Mage began to wonder which rumors of Dragons were true and which were fiction.

Delgar woke at the crack of dawn. He looked in surprise at the two Teraeni Dragons. They had seemed so much like birds that he had expected them to sleep like birds. Instead they had curled up on the ground together.

"Good morning," Delgar said, trying to seem cheerful. From the look on the Dragons' faces he was either being unconvincing or overly successful.

One of the Dragons stretched, and huddled over the fire pit, warming itself on the last embers. "I'll sleep on the cold side tomorrow, Relara," the other Dragon said. Delgar watched in fascination as Relara rubbed tiny hands over the ember, her wings wrapped around her like a cloak.

"We intrigue you, don't we?" said Gelra. The tiny Dragon went to join his mate, cuddling her with his wings.

"I know very little about you," Delgar said. "There are so many myths and legends it is hard to sort out the truth."

"Did the Ancient One not tell you of us?" Gelra asked.

Delgar shook his head. "He told me very little."

"Most of the myths are wrong," Relara said outright. "We do not vanish into thin air and we do not have

137

powerful magic."

Delgar flinched, surprised by the Dragon's curtness.

"We are, however, immortal," Gelra added. "We were both born over three thousand years ago. You must understand, when a race is immortal there is not much need for reproduction. Therefore we do not have young ones often. This also means our numbers are very small, so we cannot spare one Dragon to an upstart Archmage with a summoning spell."

"Why didn't you ask a Great Dragon for help?" Delgar asked. "Surely they could do more than me."

"We were told to seek you out, Mage Delgar," Relara stated. "And now that we can see your wyrd, we know that Fleot'heortan was right to send us to you."

Delgar blinked. "Fleot'heortan sent you?"

Gelra nodded.

"Did he say anything else about me?"

Relara shook her head. "Nothing we can tell you."

Delgar stood and put out the fire. "This is amazing," he said, shaking his head. "I would love to learn much more about you." He looked at the eastern horizon, watching as the sun began to rise high in the sky. "But we must be going."

The ruins of Idona looked a great deal like the ruins of Stataria to Delgar. He had been there once two summers ago with Archmage Agron, the librarian. After several days of digging, they had found some ancient books, and returned to add them to the Mageschool library. The decrepit stone walls encircled a network of cobbled streets and the crumbling remains of what had once been the great buildings of a vast civilization.

They entered the ruins cautiously, the afternoon sun casting deep shadows around them. The Dragons flew from perch to perch in the ruins, keeping a careful watch as Delgar began to cast. He laid a couple of spells of protection on himself, weaving the forces of the air around him; unlike the Teraenis, he could not easily take off and fly away if he was attacked. He cast two more spells, warding both of the Dragons from magical harm. Relara looked at herself in interest as a brief sparkling came over her, disappearing as the spell took hold.

"There is nobody here," Gelra announced, flapping over to rest beside his mate, who was perched on the cracked remains of an arch. "Not in this area, anyway."

There was a shimmering behind Delgar and a form walked out into the open. Delgar spun. A tall, thin, clean-shaven man in black robes regarded him with deep grey eyes.

"Ignar," Delgar said. "Fancy meeting you here."

"At your service, Mage Delgar," the magician said, bowing pleasantly. "What brings you into the ruins of Idona?"

"Some minor business for the archives," Delgar replied. "Yourself?"

"I was just exploring these ruins for some sign of ancient magic," Ignar said. "You can join me if you wish. Have you reconsidered my offer?"

Relara looked at Gelra for a minute. The two Dragons flew to a perch just behind Delgar.

Delgar glanced back at the Dragons, and then turned to face Ignar. "I'm afraid not; I'll stay with Archmage Velnan."

Ignar shook his head. "Pity. I must compliment you on your companions. They are rather interesting, especially for a mission of minor importance for the archives."

Delgar took a deep breath. "I hate to bother you, but have you created a summoning spell of some sort?" Delgar asked. The two Dragons looked at Ignar intently.

"Like this?" Ignar asked with a smile, waving his gloved hand. A forty foot long crimson Great Dragon appeared behind him, shaking its serpentine head back and forth and spreading its great wings. "I do believe that I have. The actual creatures are much more helpful than a magical representation."

"We must ask you to stop casting these spells," Relara said. "You have endangered our race and very likely many more."

"Oh dear," Ignar said. "I can't do that. Especially not for a couple of weak Dragons like yourselves. The last ones I summoned died so easily. Delgar, you look angry. Are you going to try to stand against me? It would be far more entertaining than just killing you outright. You don't really think I'm going to let you leave this place alive, knowing what you know, do you?"

Gritting his teeth, Delgar stepped forward and focused his power, preparing to manipulate the energy of the air and land. "I will stop you," he said, holding up his hand.

"Not when you are dead," Ignar stated, gesturing to the Great Dragon. The Dragon took flight. Ignar waved his hand, and a ball of fire sped towards Delgar's head. With a quick motion, Delgar created a shield in the air, but the splash of the fireball still threw him to the dusty cobblestones. Shaking his head clear, Delgar placed his hand on the ground and manipulated one of the strands of energy. The earth exploded under Ignar, the Archmage stumbling back.

"Now I am angry," Ignar stated as he dusted himself off, cold malice in his eyes.

"We'll take care of our cousin," said Gelra. "You deal with Ignar." The two Teraeni Dragons took flight.

Ignar grinned. "You should have listened to me. I'll be sure to make good use of your corpse." He waved his hand, and a wall of wind forced Delgar back against a pillar. With a supreme effort, Delgar redirected the spell, but just barely.

Delgar took a deep breath and focused his power. It was time to try to take the offensive.

High above Delgar and Ignar, the Great Dragon glided gracefully to an attack posture, glaring down at the two Mages on the ground. The Dragon stopped cold upon seeing the two Teraeni Dragons before him.

"We cannot let you attack," Relara said, flapping her wings to stay in place.

"Out of the way, little ones," the Great Dragon growled. "You must not be hurt here."

"One of the mortals is under our protection," Gelra said. "The young one."

The Great Dragon shook its head. "The wizard is trying to take control, and I cannot stop him! You must move out of the way!"

"Fight it!" Relara cried. "Fight it for the sake of all of us!"

With an earth-shattering roar, the Great Dragon spewed white-hot fire towards the two Teraeni Dragons. Even as Gelra pushed Relara out of harm's way, he was engulfed by the incinerating heat. Gelra fell towards the earth, smoking, with Relara following. On the ground Ignar smiled in exultation.

Delgar continued to cast spells, trying to blast the evil mage with everything he had, only to have them easily countered by Ignar. As Delgar came to the end of his power, sweat flowing down his brow, Ignar smiled.

"You really are ambitious, but it has now cost you your life," the Archmage said. "However, you have caused me difficulty, and for that you will suffer." He waved his hand, and Delgar was thrown to the ground, held down by an invisible vice-like grasp. "Watch your little friends die, Mage Delgar!"

As Delgar watched in horror, the Great Dragon began a dive towards the Teraeni Dragons, flame beginning to form in its mouth. At the sight of the Teraenis on the ground it stopped dead in its tracks.

Relara was bent over the charred body of her lifemate, weeping. The Great Dragon hovered in the air, just above Relara; the little Dragon was reduced to sobs, unable to defend herself. At that moment Delgar realized what was going to happen. All he could do was watch, watch as Ignar stared at him and gloated, watch as the Great Dragon turned to the Archmage with rage in its eyes.

Never before on Mideorth had Dragonkind killed Dragonkind.

The Great Dragon began to fly towards Ignar, gathering all of the flame that it could muster into its mouth. Ignar didn't see the Dragon until it was too late.

The wyrm released its flame, incinerating Ignar. The magician didn't even have a chance to scream before he was reduced to ashes. The Dragon landed near Delgar, who weakly put his hand up in warding.

Tears ran down the Dragon's face as he roared in rage. "I have killed my own kind," the Great Dragon said, voice surprisingly soft. "What has he done to me?"

Delgar got up and staggered forward. "Where are the Teraenis?" he asked in alarm. The Dragon waved its hand. Delgar scrambled toward them, praying that things were not as bad as he suspected.

What he saw made him weep. The body of the tiny Dragon was damaged beyond repair. No magic in the world could help her lifemate. Sobbing, Delgar fell to his knees.

"I'm sorry," he said, his voice cracking. A thump behind him marked the arrival of the Great Dragon.

"There was a doom on us all," the Dragon said. "Dragonkind has now killed Dragonkind, and our world will never be the same again. Magician, I have your enemy's spell book here, and the spells in it are yours by right of conquest."

Delgar took the magical book from the Great Dragon. He looked at it for a minute, and then dropped it on the ground. "Will you please destroy this?" he asked. "I am drained of my power, and cannot."

The Great Dragon nodded. A minute later a white-hot fire destroyed the spellbook.

Relara left for her home in mourning, flying out of the ring of ruins where her lifemate had died. As her form became dwindled on the horizon, the Great Dragon turned to Delgar.

"All of our kind are feared by mortals," it stated. "They hunt us out of fear, the fear born of ignorance. The result is that when in need, few mortals will help our kind."

Delgar gazed at the setting sun. Relara was just a speck against the sunset. "I did what was right," the young mage said. *And it killed Gelra*, he added silently.

"Remember this," the Great Dragon said softly. "We immortals have long memories. Relara will always remember her lifemate, and the love they shared. And she will always remember that you helped our kind, as will the rest of the Teraenae." Delgar turned to look at the Dragon.

"As will I remember," the Great Dragon continued. "As will all of Dragonkind. Great events are coming, and we will need a protector. Perhaps you are the one; your wyrd is strong. I name you Dragonfriend, Delgar of Nordland. Should you ever be in need, all you need do is call upon us."

"How?" asked Delgar.

"The way you would call on any of your friends," the Dragon replied. "We will be listening and watching."

With that the Great Dragon took flight, leaving Delgar alone with his thoughts. Delgar finally shook his head and began to pick his way out of the ruins, trying to keep his balance. As the last of the adrenaline left his system, Delgar was sent reeling, the world spinning around him. He finally collapsed just outside of the ruins.

He tried to move, but couldn't. All he could do was stare up at the sky, watching the sun set.

He saw a shadowy figure rise over him, and then all went dark.

Chapter XIV: Homecomings

Delgar awoke to the crackling of a fire. He opened his eyes slowly, wincing at the bright flames. He made out the outline of a figure sitting on a nearby stone, but not much else.

"At last," the man said. "I feared the worst. How do you feel, Mage Delgar?"

Delgar winced, trying to see out who was speaking. He propped himself up on his elbow, but even as he did, the world began to spin. Finally, he sunk back to the ground. "I feel awful. Velnan?"

Velnan stepped closer to the fire. "Yes, it's me, boy. I decided to follow you and make sure you didn't run into problems. I see I arrived too late."

"When did you leave?"

"About a day after you did," Velnan said. "I would have caught up to you, but my horse went lame on the journey. The Damned One's luck. You, however, seem to have made quite a mess of yourself."

Delgar nodded weakly.

"I told you that if you found Ignar, you were not to fight him!" Velnan shouted. "You were to send for help! What were you thinking, boy?"

"I didn't have time," Delgar mumbled. "It all happened so fast."

"What happened?" Velnan asked.

"Ignar's dead," Delgar said. "His spellbook was destroyed. One of the Teraeni Dragons was killed."

Velnan shook his head. "Unfortunate. Those are very rare and magical creatures, Delgar. When one of them dies the entire world suffers a loss."

Delgar looked around, but he could only see some stones outside the fire's light. "Where are we?"

"Just outside the ruins of Idona," Velnan said, "close to where I found you."

"What about Jenara," Delgar asked.

"You'll see her soon," Velnan said. "I left a message for her. She'll be expecting us in the next couple of weeks, although I don't know how we can possibly make it on time while you're in this condition."

"I'll be better soon," Delgar said, again struggling to rise.

Velnan shook his head as the young Mage slumped back to the earth. "You've overextended yourself almost to the point of death, boy. It will take you weeks to recover from this. I fear that I will not be able to give you your research assignment."

"Research assignment?"

"I'm going on sabbatical, remember?" Velnan said. "You didn't really think you were going to have those two months off, did you? But, considering this, you just might."

Delgar grunted. "So what will I get now?"

"While I am away, you are to rest and recover,"

Velnan instructed. "But, first I have to get you back to Taerra."

"They'll know me at the border," Delgar said.

Velnan shook his head. "It is much easier to leave Taerraland than to enter it. Another war has just broken out."

Delgar blinked. "What do you mean?"

"I mean that one of the warlords of Pakaria has declared that he will take part of Taerraland, and the army is now moving."

"How will we get in, then?"

Velnan stroked his beard. "I have papers verifying who we are, so that will get us past the great wall. Unfortunately, we still have to avoid the Pakarian warlords as we travel there. However, we can deal with that in the morning. You need rest."

Delgar nodded. He closed his eyes, but then opened them again. "Velnan, how did you know a war had started?"

"I found out at the wall," Velnan replied. "Now go to sleep."

Delgar closed his eyes and swiftly fell into a sleep filled with dreams of Dragons.

Delgar awoke to the chirping of birds and looked around. Velnan sat on the stone he had occupied last night, and was whittling down a large branch with his knife.

Rubbing his temples, Delgar sat up. "I have the most horrible headache," he moaned. "Good morning."

Velnan shook his head. "Afternoon. Look at the sun."

Delgar glanced up, shielding his eyes. "Why did you let me sleep so late?"

"You had to," Velnan said. "You need to be able to travel." He brandished the newly-carved staff. "This will help you walk. Let me help you up there."

Velnan pulled Delgar to his feet, the young Mage reeling as the world spun around him. Velnan grabbed Delgar's chin and stared into his eyes.

"Look at me," Velnan commanded. "Look at my eyes. Focus on me. You can still do it."

Delgar blinked several times, and the world finally began to settle down. He took an unsteady step forward, righting himself with the staff.

"That's good," Velnan said. "One step at a time. Come on, you can do it."

They walked for a bit, Delgar teetering at times, but recovering after a while. Finally Delgar looked around and turned to Velnan.

"Velnan, why are you taking me south?" he asked. "Shouldn't we be headed west?"

Velnan shook his head. "You're in no shape to walk to the great wall. A bit farther and we'll come to a small village. There we'll get some soup for you and buy some horses. Then, I can lead you to Taerra with some ease."

Delgar nodded. "Let's waste no time."

Velnan gazed at him with concern. "Don't strain yourself, boy. You still have a lot of recovering to do.""

Delgar waved him off. "I'll be fine. Just don't walk too fast."

They reached the village just after nightfall, passing the first ring of thatched huts to find the village inn. Velnan and Delgar stood at the door of the inn, watching the patrons and innkeeper carefully. Finally, Velnan nodded his head and said: "I think it's safe. You find a table and I'll get what we need."

Delgar nodded and slowly made his way to one of the tables, staggering for a moment but righting himself. He tried to shake his head clear, but that only made the headache worse. He heard a couple of the patrons say something about him and laugh, but he didn't care.

Finally, Velnan came over to the table with a large bowl of soup, a thin chicken broth with a touch of lemon juice. Delgar's mouth watered at the sweet scent of the broth, and as Velnan watched, he began to drink.

"Your friend drinks like a starving man," the innkeeper said, bringing some chicken to Velnan.

"He's had a long day, and he is unwell," Velnan said. He pressed a golden coin into the man's hand. "Thank you again for your kindness, sir."

The innkeeper nodded. "Any time, master, any time." With that, he went off to serve his other customers.

"I have arranged for our good innkeeper to purchase horses for us," Velnan said, biting into the first chicken leg. He chewed and swallowed. "If you can manage it, we'll be at the border by late afternoon."

Delgar nodded. "I think I can make it."

"How's your head?"

"Still pounding, but I can manage."

"I hate to say it, but you'll feel worse before you get better," Velnan said. "I know from experience."

Delgar finished his soup. "What happened?"

Velnan waved to the innkeeper for more soup, and then turned back to Delgar. "I was a young Mage, just like you, and just as foolish. I had fallen for a girl named Tamarline, and her affections were split between myself and another Mage named Vargas. So, full of myself and feeling all-powerful, I challenged him to a duel."

The innkeeper placed another bowl of broth before Delgar, and as Velnan tipped the man again, the young Mage began to drink hungrily.

"Did you lose?" Delgar asked between sips.

Velnan shook his head. "I won, but just barely. I was ill for over a month, and in that time Tamarline met somebody else and married him." He stroked his beard

149

sadly. "Actually, I think in the end she wasn't worth it, but I'll never know."

"I'm sorry," Delgar said.

"Don't be. It happened a long time ago."

Delgar finished his second bowl of soup and sat back, trying to keep the pounding out of his head. Velnan looked at him for a moment, and then began to help him up.

"Come now, young Delgar," the Archmage said. "A bed is prepared for you, and you need your rest. We'll be leaving first thing in the morning."

Delgar could only nod as the headache began to consume him.

Velnan shook his head as he looked over the ridge. "This isn't good."

"How many men?" Delgar asked.

"Too many," Velnan replied, looking up at the early afternoon sun. "We'll have to go around."

Delgar would have shaken his head, but it was too painful. He had finally managed to fall into a half-decent slumber when Velnan woke him. And then they were off, making their way to the border on their new horses, the Archmage leading him as though Delgar rode a pony.

And then they had begun to run into armies.

The first army they came across in the late morning, and they watched it march towards the border for a few minutes. Finally, Velnan declared that they would have to go around them, and they were off, the Archmage leading Delgar's horse as quickly as he could in a wide circle around the army.

Around noon they came over a hill only to see another army marching westwards, and once again they had to detour. Then they had to stop for a bit as Delgar struggled to stay in the saddle. Finally, they began to move again,

150

making wide arcs around the Pakarian soldiers. And then, another rise had left them behind another army.

"Are they all from the same warlord?" Delgar asked.

Velnan nodded. "It may be Lord Gwynan. He is one of the warlords powerful enough to act on his own."

"Maybe we should try to ride right through them."

Velnan shook his head. "I doubt they'll have a great deal of respect for the Mageschool at a time of war, Delgar. No, we'll go around. Don't worry; we'll be at the border by dark."

They began to move again, and the headache grew worse. Finally, Delgar felt as though he was riding through a dream: Velnan occasionally saying something important but mostly unheard, as they progressed towards the great wall in the distance.

Delgar was ready to collapse by the time they actually got there. The walls were dark before the setting sun, and Velnan answered the challenge of the guard with words and the waving of papers. There seemed to be a bit more, but Delgar was in too much of a daze to remember exactly what. Something about a wagon or carriage?

And then Delgar's world went dark again.

Delgar awoke to bright sunlight in his eyes. He glanced around to find himself lying in a wagon, with a soldier driving while Velnan rode his mare in front of the cart.

"He's awake, Master Archmage," the soldier called.

Velnan fell back to ride beside Delgar. "How are you feeling?"

"Horrible," Delgar rasped. "Where are we?"

"A week and a half from Taerra," Velnan said. "You've slept for three days. I've sent messengers ahead to inform Vice-Chancellor Vertanus and Jenara about your situation. Somebody should be meeting us en route."

"So we're safe?"

Velnan nodded. "We are." He rode closer and placed his hand on Delgar's forehead. "You don't have the fever yet, but it will come. That will be the worst of it."

Delgar groaned. "There's more?"

Velnan nodded sadly. "You may have learned to do great things, but there is also a great price when you overextend yourself. This will serve as a lesson."

"I'm thirsty."

Velnan pointed to a large canteen next to Delgar's cot. "There is cold soup there. Take what you need; it's all for you. Then get some more sleep."

Delgar tried to rise, but he was too weak. "I don't want to sleep."

Velnan shook his head. "The illness won't give you a choice. The best thing you can do for yourself right now is to get as much sleep as possible."

Delgar took the canteen and drew a long drink out of it. The cold chicken soup swirled in his mouth as he swallowed, then he took another drink. Finally, he put the canteen down and propped himself up.

"I feel slightly stronger now," he said.

Velnan nodded. "No doubt because you've just eaten for the first time in days. You need to rest."

"What's the fever you mentioned?" Delgar asked.

"The worst part of the sickness," Velnan stated grimly. "As your power returns to you, your body will overcompensate for it. Your temperature will rise until you are burning hot, you will suffer hallucinations, you will be unable to take food, and you will suffer pain. Once it is over, though, you will be almost recovered."

"How long will I suffer?"

"Weeks," Velnan said. "If you aren't properly cared for, you may yet die from it. Now sleep: you'll need all of your strength soon enough."

Delgar wanted to ask another question, but his fatigue overcame him once more and he fell into a deep sleep.

Delgar awoke with a pounding headache. For a moment he wanted to scream, for he felt as if he had been lit on fire. As his vision swam before him, he saw a grey haired shape and a beautiful, dark form sitting by him. Creaking wheels sounded around and under him.

"Jenara?" he croaked. "Is that you?"

"Yes love," the dark shape said. "You'll be all right. I'm here."

Delgar shuddered, waves of heat and a deathly chill washing over him. "I'm burning, love, I'm burning."

"It's the fever," he heard Velnan say. "It will only grow worse. Mistress Jenara, see to him. He needs liquids regularly, but no solid food. He also needs to sleep as often as possible."

He felt an icy hand on his forehead, and he shuddered uncontrollably.

"He's burning up!" Jenara gasped. "Is there anything else we can do?"

"The fever must run its course," he heard Velnan state. "Happily, we only have another week to go before we reach Taerra. Then some healers can look at him."

Only have another week, he thought, the words echoing in his mind. *How long will I sleep? What is happening to me?*

Darkness answered his questions.

Chapter XV: Recoveries and Portents

Delgar's world was a farrago of color and sound. Every now and then he tried to focus on a shade or shape before him, but as soon as he tried the thing became so blurry that it melded into several other shapes. Sometimes he had a lucid moment where he could almost make out something solid; his father's face before him in what could only have been a dream. But then it was gone, and Delgar was lost in the menagerie of images.

Eventually he began to become aware of some things. A cold hand pressing against his forehead and a nozzle of some wineskin or canteen against his lips. Cold or warm liquid passing down his throat.

Somebody's feeding me, the rational part of his mind thought. *Could it be Jenara?*

But then the sensations passed, and he was left to his living nightmare. A wave of pain swept over him, destroying whatever rationality he had left. The images and sounds swept him away, and his rational mind was drowning.

Drowning!

Drowning...

He stood on a field of ice, a chill wind blowing his robe against his skin. Above him, the harsh sun glared down, but no heat came from it.

"Am I dreaming?" he wondered out loud.

"No and yes," a voice said. Delgar turned to find himself facing his father's sage form.

"You're dead," Delgar breathed, shivering in the cold. Snow kicked up around him.

Daegar nodded. "You have passed into the point between death and life. You are in the living dream."

"I don't understand."

"You aren't supposed to."

Delgar began to sob. "I'm so sorry I was too late. I wish I had..."

Daegar held him softly. "It's all right," he said. "I have fulfilled my wyrd. And I am proud of you! None of our family has ever managed to become as great as you!"

"I'm just a Mage," Delgar protested. "I've done very little."

Daegar shook his head in confusion. "You have done incredible things. You will do incredible things. It is so hard for me; time used to mean so much, but here..."

Delgar embraced his father. "I missed you. But where are we? Is this merely an illusion, or is it in my future?"

"Your future, I think," Daegar answered softly. "Or perhaps your past. Perhaps both. I do not know. Think not on it; wyrd shall work as it will."

A shrill wind howled, and Daegar glanced up, a sullen look on his face. "The Guardian calls me," he said. "My time with you has ended, and I must return to your mother."

"So I'm not dying," Delgar stated.

Daegar shook his head. "When you come, it will not be me who greets you. You have much time left; use it well."

Tears flowed down Delgar's cheek as his father faded into the light mist. He looked around to see the field of ice itself vanishing, the mist destroying all before it.

"Goodbye, father," Delgar said. The words echoed around him as the world itself vanished.

He opened his eyes to find Jenara sitting before him. Her faced danced in the candlelight, her features coming alive as her loved one finally awoke.

"Jenara," he rasped. "Where am I?"

"You're in our quarters in Taerra," she said, embracing his limp form. "I thought you would never wake."

"I saw my father," he muttered. "And a field of ice. And I feel as though I've been asleep for years. How long have I slept?"

Jenara stroked his long hair. "A month and a half. Classes have already begun."

Delgar blinked. "That long?"

Jenara nodded sadly.

"Where's Velnan?"

"On sabbatical," she said. "He said he had some important things to do, and that you would be fine." She broke into tears. "Oh Delgar, there were times when I doubted him. I'm so glad you're here!"

"So am I," Delgar said. He tried to sit up, but he found he could barely move. "I feel so weak."

"Archmage Willam said it would be like that," Jenara said. "He said you probably won't be able to leave bed without help for another two weeks or so."

"Surely I'll be able to move around a bit," Delgar said.

Jenara shook her head. "You're not allowed to leave the bed at all."

"But how will I take care of...my business?" Delgar stammered. "I can't have you helping me with that; it would be indecent."

Jenara put her hands on her hips. "Who do you think has been taking care of that for you in the last month and a half?"

Delgar glanced away sheepishly. "I see. I guess I don't have any secrets from you, then."

Jenara shook her head and handed him a glass of water. "If it helps, I like what I saw."

Delgar nearly choked as he drank.

Jenara laughed, and for the first time in what felt like years, Delgar's heart soared.

"Is there anything I can get you?" Jenara asked, taking the empty glass from him.

Delgar nodded. "I should try to get some work done. Velnan must have left an assignment for me of some sort. Did he say what it is?"

She nodded. "He said: 'Make sure he gets well.'"

"So I'm just to rest, then," Delgar said.

Jenara nodded. "I'll bring you some soup and call Willam. Then, maybe you'll be able to eat solid foods again."

Delgar nodded and lay back. "Thank you." He yawned.

"You get some sleep. I'll take care of you."

Delgar tried to nod, but darkness overcame him.

Willam was a tall, thin figure with flaming red hair. He stood over Delgar like an angel of the Eternal One, clucking his tongue as he felt the young Mage's forehead. Finally, he sat back at Delgar's bedside and closed his eyes in thought.

Delgar lay uncomfortably for a moment before Willam finally opened his eyes. "How do you feel, Mage Delgar?" the Archmage finally asked.

"Weak, but otherwise fine," Delgar said. "I feel almost strong enough to get out of bed."

"I can see that," Willam said grimly. "You've passed through the worst of it and survived. Maybe this will serve as a lesson to you."

Delgar nodded. "Everybody's been telling me the moral of this little adventure. I wish they would stop."

Willam shook his head, stroking his bushy mustache. "There is a serious lesson to be learned. Many Mages do this sort of thing, and almost a quarter of them don't survive it when it is this severe. You are very lucky."

"I had a good teacher."

"I know. Velnan could have been the Chancellor or Vice-Chancellor if he had wanted it."

Delgar blinked.

"Yes Mage Delgar," Willam said. "You have quite the teacher. Now, you can probably take care of your own toilet business now, which will be a relief to your fiancé, if you'll pardon the expression. However, I want you to remain in bed for another two weeks, no matter what the Vice-Chancellor says."

Delgar frowned. "What does the Vice-Chancellor say? I haven't seen him since I left."

"Vice-Chancellor Vertanus has a task for you, but it will have to wait until you are better. I am going to leave now." He began to rise.

"Can I at least get out of bed to take care of my toilet business?"

Willam paused for a moment. "Yes, but have Jenara

near you at all times. The last thing you need to do is bump your head on the floor."

As Archmage Willam left, Delgar nodded and said: "Thank you." Then he leaned back and closed his eyes.

An hour later, Jenara returned from her classes and helped Delgar up so that he could urinate. Delgar wanted to protest her presence as he performed a very private act, but the nausea that engulfed him as soon as he was up removed all objections.

Soon, he promised himself. *Soon I'll be walking on my own.*

As the week passed, Delgar found himself becoming restless. He wanted to get out of bed and walk outside, watching the autumn leaves fall. But he was still too weak to walk without Jenara's help, and Velnan had left him nothing to do.

So Delgar made do with what he had, losing himself in long forgotten books of romances, where great warriors fought for the hands of fair maidens. He read of the last glories of Idonia and of the rise of Taerraland, of great heroes against incredible powers.

Sometimes he wondered if he was reading fantasy or merely a reflection of reality. "After all," he said to Jenara one night, "surely every myth has some truth behind it. And, in a thousand years, how will they remember us?"

"Maybe the Tuatha de Danaan could answer that," Jenara said. "Our lives are too short for us to ever find an answer."

Delgar nodded. "True. We are not immortals, nor are we made for immortality."

But it was the writings of the prophet Karana of Barsh which caught his eye. He had found some books on Barsh, and discovered that their worship of the Eternal One was markedly different than his own. But their holy writings were particularly fascinating, revealing a people both immensely learned and savage at the same time.

Karana had lived at the time of Idonia and written a translation of the Scriptures of the Eternal One from the Idonian before the Great Controversy that had schismed the two lands. Delgar had found his writing to be lucid and readable, but had paused when he came to the chapter where Karana described the end of the world:

> *And the Eternal One revealed to me that there will be a great surge, and the land will suffer. And Death will look upon the land with an icy gaze, and bring many of the Eternal One's creations into his grasp. And both the Damned One and the Eternal One will fall before a wall of ice, and the great lands will perish.*
>
> *And from the ice will come a savior, born to mortality but immortal, a destroyer and creator of worlds. And he will push back the darkness and the tower of ice will perish. Thus the land will be reborn and the cycle of the Eternal One will begin anew.*

As he closed the book, a chill crept down Delgar's spine, as though some dark force had walked over his grave. For a moment he felt his wyrd shifting around him, but then the sensation was gone, and he was alone in a darkening room as the sun set.

And as he lost himself in his romances, another week passed. Finally he was able to walk about with the aid of a staff, but never for long, and Jenara often had to help him back to bed.

And outside the leaves of autumn began to fall.

Delgar was sitting at his chair, reading a book on

elemental magic, when Vice-Chancellor Vertanus walked into his room. The Archmage looked at the books piled on every flat surface as Delgar stood slowly.

"Still not yet quite on your feet?" Vertanus asked with a smile. "Don't worry about it. Just about every Mage does this sort of thing to themselves; I was out for nearly three months."

"I can walk around a bit, just not for long," Delgar said. "But, I'm feeling much stronger now. I don't need the staff anymore. I was even able to cast something yesterday."

Vertanus raised an eyebrow. "What did you cast?"

"I helped a plant grow," Delgar replied. "Some simple magic to get me back into practice."

"A good idea," Vertanus said.

"Now I'm just waiting for Archmage Velnan to return so that I can start my studies in earnest again."

Vertanus sat on Delgar's bed. "Sit down, young Delgar. You look like you're about to collapse anyway."

Delgar nodded and sat back in his chair. "What can I do for you, Vice-Chancellor?"

"I have a task for you," Vertanus said. "You can leave as soon as you are ready, but I would counsel haste. I need you to go into the deserts of Barsh to find the Cave of Dreams. Inside is the Gem of Sidhe. Have you ever heard of it?"

Delgar shook his head. "I have heard of the Cave of Dreams, but only vague descriptions. I always thought it was just a myth."

"It exists," Vertanus said. "It is in the mountains on the border of Barsh and Pakaria, opening onto the desert. The Gem of Sidhe is an item we only just discovered by accident in our scrying. It is a powerful focusing gem for magic, and the Mageschool wants to study it."

"It is an interesting proposition," Delgar said. "But I

really have to worry about my studies. I've already lost a term, and Velnan will be back soon."

"If you go, the Mageschool will count it for a full year of credit at the Archmage level," Vertanus stated. "This is very important to us."

Delgar blinked. "I'll have to think about it. Why me, though? Couldn't an Archmage go?"

"First, you are the most impressive student in the Mageschool," Vertanus said. "Nobody else can claim to have defeated an Archmage on their own."

"But it wasn't-"

"Secondly, there is a personal stake in it for you."

Delgar blinked. "What do you mean?"

"Yours would not be the first expedition to find it. The first was sent while you were dealing with Ignar in Pakaria. We used the usual policy of sending a freelance wizard to find it with a payment in gold; half in advance, half on delivery. They were expected to take a month and a half, and they are now a month overdue."

Delgar felt a sudden unease, and some of his nausea returned. He leaned forward. "Who did you send?"

"Tomlin and Melina," Vertanus said sadly. "I'm sorry, Delgar."

Chapter XVI: Journeys

"I still don't understand why you have to go," Jenara said. "Why can't they send somebody else?"

"None of the other general Mages are qualified," Delgar replied, packing some clothes into a backpack. "And all the Archmages are either busy with classes or on sabbatical. This sort of thing does happen."

"And why can't I come with you?"

Delgar paused. "You have to see to your final year."

"But do you have to leave right now?"

Delgar nodded sadly. "It's been another two weeks, I can walk now, and if I hurry I'll make it down to the coast in time for the winter lull. If I miss it by so much as a week, I'll be caught in storms, and the overland route is closed because of the war."

"But why *you*?!" Jenara cried. Delgar turned to find her in tears. "Why do you have to go into danger again?"

He embraced her. "I owe it to Tomlin. He's my friend, after all."

She pressed herself closer. "He's my cousin, you know. He's probably dead. I can't bear the thought of losing both of you."

"I'll only be a month and a half," Delgar soothed. "Vice-Chancellor Vertanus says he's going to give me more detailed instructions and lots of supplies. I'll even have a horse so that I can make it to the coast in lots of time. And then I'll be back before the term's over."

She sobbed on his shoulder, holding him tightly. He closed his eyes, enjoying her warmth pressed against him. The moment seemed to last for eternity, and then it ended too quickly. She disengaged and sat on the bed, watching Delgar pack the last of his clothes into the rough hide backpack. Once he had done that, he pulled on a heavy woolen white cloak and black leather gloves. Finally, he tied the backpack and slung it over his shoulder, shifting it to get the weight centered properly.

Delgar sat beside her on the bed and held her for a moment. "I have to go now," he said.

Jenara nodded, her eyes deep and sad. "I love you. Come back to me."

"I love you too," Delgar said, kissing her long and hard. "And I will return in a month and a half. I promise."

With that, he stood and walked stiffly out the door, making his way down the corridor to the exit. He finally descended the steps of the residence to find the Vice-Chancellor standing beside a saddled grey mare, checking the almost overflowing leather saddlebags.

"Welcome, Mage Delgar," Vertanus called, looking up. "I have just been seeing to your provisions. You have enough for two months of travel, although you will want to transfer at least three weeks into your pack when you set sail. The meat has been enchanted, so it will provide you with more energy; keep that in mind lest you overuse it."

Delgar nodded, stepping down to the mare. "What is her name?"

"I'm afraid our master of horses is rather quaint," Vertanus said. "Her name is Daisy." He looked down at Delgar's feet. "How are the new riding boots?"

"They still need to be broken in," Delgar replied. "But, otherwise, they are fine. Thank you."

"It was the least we could do," Vertanus ginned, pulling out a large map. "Now, take the Queen's Road south to the sea-port of Maeritima; with Daisy the trip should take about a week. The scroll I am about to hand you will permit you to book passage to the Barshian port of Narek; that trip should take you approximately five days, if the wind is with you. That will give you just over a week to find the Cave of Dreams and return to Narek. The journey home should take the same amount of time as the journey there, the Eternal One willing."

Vertanus put the map aside and held out a small piece of parchment. "This is your note of credit. It is good for booking a ship at Maeritima; the harbor will see that Daisy is well cared for." As Delgar took the scroll and put it in one of the pockets of his robe, the Vice-Chancellor pulled out a large changepurse. "And this will buy you passage home, as well as provisions and a guide for the desert. Be very cautious with the nomads, Mage Delgar. Some tribes are very honorable and will serve you well. Others, however, will rob you blind and try to murder you. Most are somewhere in-between. They are not like us, and it is very dangerous to assume anything about them. I fear that may have been Tomlin and Melina's mistake."

Delgar nodded and took the changepurse, buckling it securely to his belt. "Will I get to take the map?"

Vertanus shook his head. "This map comes from our main archives; I promised Archmage Hurran that I would return it to him by sundown, and he can be rather obsessive about his library. However, I did have a smaller copy made for you." He passed Delgar another scroll, slightly larger than the first one.

Delgar nodded. "I will be back in six weeks," he said. "Until then, farewell sir."

"Farewell, Mage Delgar," Vertanus said. "Remember what you have learned here, and remember who you have to come back to. May the Eternal One shine on your venture."

Mounting the mare, Delgar nudged Daisy into a trot, and began to make his way out of Taerra, his mount's hooves crunching down the fresh snow.

The Queen's Road was a wide stone-paved path stretching from the northern coast of Taerraland to the Middle sea. Delgar had read once that it was originally created by an Idonian queen named Celera, who had made a successful bid to power, changing the capital to Stataria. To celebrate her regency, she ordered the construction of a great path from the northern expanses to the south. The work had been hampered by political unrest, however, and was completed by her successor two decades later. Taerraland had taken it as a point of pride to maintain the road, a fact Delgar found reassuring as he trotted through the snow.

It snowed heavily for the first two days, but on the third day the clouds threatened but later began to clear. He found inns conveniently placed along the road, and paid for his lodgings with minor conjuring tricks to amuse the locals. Delgar smiled at the drawbacks; he had somehow become a favorite for the children in the small villages scattered along the Queen's Road, and despite his speed his reputation somehow managed to precede him. By the fifth day he was drawing crowds whenever he took his rest, and often the children followed him as he left. He almost felt guilty for enjoying it so much.

On the sixth day, the sea rose over the horizon, the sparkling blue contrasting with the spotty white of the sparse, snow-covered forests. The road still stretched over the horizon, but he found himself smiling as he approached his destination. That night he stayed in an inn named *The Laughing Sea*, where a rotund innkeeper eagerly asked him to perform some magic.

Delgar chuckled, the sea air already invigorating him. "Of course, good sir, of course! I would be more than happy to!"

That evening, the crowd watched in amazement as Delgar first made a small tree grow from an acorn, and then began to weave translucent shapes in the air, forming Dragons and griffons and other magical beasts.

"That's REAL magic, daddy!" a little girl cried, a silly grin on her pudgy face.

Delgar smiled. If only she knew how powerful the *real* magic was. His smile widened as the crowd oohed and aahed at another trick. He already knew what the innkeeper was going to say when he drew the Mage aside after the show.

"Have you ever thought about becoming a stage wizard?" the innkeeper asked. "There's a lot of money in it."

Delgar smiled. "Perhaps some day. Today I would just settle for a room and board."

The innkeeper shook his head. "Well, if you ever change your mind, come to me. Galen Twigglesworth is the name!"

"I won't forget it," Delgar said. "Could I please see my room?"

The next morning Delgar arose from a comfortable bed, well rested and ready for the new day. He put on his riding clothes, bid his farewells, and rode toward

167

Maeritima.

Delgar found Maeritima to be a small town in comparison
to Taerra, but well supplied. Rather than the metropolis or
disorganized jumble of huts that he had expected, he found
the town to be an organized collection of stout wooden
buildings in a small, forested valley, some of the houses
covered with a light snow. Around them a rose stone wall,
in slight disrepair but still defensible.

He made his way quickly through the crowded streets
into the warehouse district, where several large, squat
structures stood, company names engraved on faded wood.
He stood for a moment, trying to work out who he would
have to talk to. Finally, he pulled aside a passer-by and
asked for directions.

"You'd want the *Middle Sea Shipping Company*," said
the slightly plump woman. She pointed down the road, the
way Delgar had originally come. "They'll take you
anywhere."

Delgar nodded. "Thank you, good madam."

"It's a good day to be out," the woman called, bustling
away on some errand. "It's not usually this sunny this
close to the sea in the winter."

Delgar led Daisy down the street until he found the
company name blazoned on a large warehouse sign with a
ship and sea serpent illustration. He stood outside for a
moment, deciding whether or not to knock. Finally, he left
Daisy outside tied to a post, moved most of the provisions
into his backpack, opened the door and walked in.

He found himself in a small wooden room, the only
illumination provided by a large window at the side,
although an unlit torch stood at each wall. A large man
wearing a leather tunic worked at an interior window. As
Delgar approached, the man looked up.

"Ah! A customer!" the man declared. "What can I do for you?"

"I need passage for myself and my belongings to Narek," Delgar said. "I'll also need to have my horse seen to while I am gone. Can you do this?"

"I can get you on a ship today, if you wish," the man said. "If you have the money. Narek is a long trip, and we don't make the journey very often."

Delgar removed his scroll of credit and handed it to the man. The man unrolled it and stared at it. Delgar stood still and waited.

"Haven't seen one of these in over two months," the man muttered. "A rather cute couple bore them. Going to the same place, too. Made it just before the winter storms. Looks like you have their timing." He looked up and quickly wrote out a scroll for Delgar. "This will do nicely. The ship leaves in about an hour on pier five. Leave your horse outside and hand this to the captain when you see him." With that, he handed the scroll to Delgar.

Delgar took the scroll and nodded. "Oh, by the way, where is pier five?"

The man pointed. "Just down the street; it's quite clearly marked."

"Thank you."

Delgar stepped outside, taking a deep breath of the fresh sea air. He suddenly remembered his childhood, when his father took him to one of the ports to sell some goods at a market. Somehow, the air there smelled much nicer than the air here. He shook his head and made his way down to the pier.

He found the pier to be a long wooden walkway over the shoreline, a tall sailing ship docked alongside, mooring ropes attached to several large poles driven through the dock and into the shallow water. The planks creaked under his boots as he made his way to the boarding ramp.

A short but stout man stood at the ramp, scratching his sandy beard. Delgar stepped over to him and motioned with his ticket. "Are you the captain?"

"Aye," the man growled. "I'm Captain Cuthbert of the *Swordfish*. What can I do for ye?"

Delgar handed over his ticket. Captain Cuthbert unrolled the scroll, glanced at it, then passed it back. "Welcome aboard. The passenger quarters are in the aft sections, just beside the cargo holds. If you have anything you need to stow, just speak to me first mate. He'll also tell you the rules."

Delgar nodded. "Thank you, sir." With that, he boarded the *Swordfish* and made his way towards the back. As he walked, he gazed up at the white furled sails. Already seamen were climbing up the rigging, agile as a spiders on a web. He looked down to find himself standing before the first mate.

The first mate was tall, athletic, dark haired man with a long moustache and midnight-black skin. He held out his hand to Delgar, which the Mage shook readily.

"Welcome aboard," he said. "I'll put you in room seven; that has a nice view, and you can close the window if the sea becomes too rough for you. The rules here are simple: you must be in your cabin by sundown, and for the entire trip you will have to stay off the rigging. As a rule, just keep out of our way, and the voyage will be nice and smooth. Any questions?"

Delgar nodded. "When are meals?"

"At noon and sundown. Any others?"

"Where is the outhouse?"

"A chamber pot will be provided. You will have to see to cleaning it yourself, however. This is mainly a cargo vessel. Any other questions?"

"No."

The first mate nodded. "Thank you. If you'll excuse

me, I have another passenger to see to now."

Delgar walked into the cabins to find his room, finally settling in a small, wood-paneled cabin with a bed, a candelabra, a desk and a chair. He set his pack under the desk, moving aside the clay chamber pot. Then he stepped back out on the deck.

All around him, he heard the shouts of the men as they threw off the mooring lines. He gazed at the dock where a small crowd had gathered to see the ship off. Probably family and friends of the sailors, Delgar reflected. For a moment, he felt a tug at his heart and wished that Jenara was here, but he quickly suppressed it.

"Set sail!" the captain roared, grinning as the seamen rushed to unfurl the sails. "We have the wind! Let's catch the bugger!"

Delgar chuckled at the colorful language and looked out over the side. The sails caught the slight wind, puffing out towards the sea. With little jarring, the ship began to move out onto the greenish-blue sea, the crowd waving at it.

"Tack it properly!" the captain commanded. "If we lose the wind, we could find ourselves caught before the mother of all storms."

Delgar watched the first mate rush up to the captain and salute. "All sails are set, sir," the mate reported. "We have the wind and are on course."

"Keep a good watch on the men," Captain Cuthbert said. "Some of 'em are new, and could get into trouble."

Delgar turned and glanced over the side, closing his eyes as the fresh sea wind rushed past him. He hoped that the rest of the voyage would be like this; it was a sort of bliss.

The voyage was smooth, but not without some minor

wrinkles. On the fourth day a gale rose up, and the captain ordered all the passengers into their cabins. What followed was a jarring experience for almost an hour as the ship swayed back and forth. Once or twice Delgar feared he would be sick, but the feeling passed as the seas became calmer. Finally, he opened his window to find the winds had died down and the ship was underway once more.

By the end of the fourth day, land was once again in sight before them. Delgar stood at the prow of the ship, watching the ribbon of brown appear on the horizon. He tried to see any sign of greenery, but without success; Barsh appeared to be exactly as he had expected it. It was a desert, and nothing more.

And on the fifth day, just as the Vice-Chancellor had predicted, the ship made port in the land of Barsh.

Chapter XVII: Barsh

Delgar pushed his way through the marketplace, sweat streaming down his back. He had changed into lighter clothes back on the ship shortly after they made port, but the warmth over the sea had done nothing to prepare him for the dry heat of the desert town. Unlike Maeritima, Narek was a disorganized jumble of dwellings, most of them made from mud-bricks. Delgar grimaced as more sand made its way into his boot; he had preferred the sea voyage to this.

A camel and its owner ambled past him, the camel fixing him with a malignant stare. Delgar tried not to inhale for a moment, but the stench still filled his lungs. Finally, he sputtered, attracting the laughter of a couple of bystanders.

Delgar glanced around in desperation. He had tried asking several people where he could find a guide, but nobody had spoken the common tongue. Delgar cursed under his breath; he had disembarked in the morning, but it was already just past noon. At this rate he wouldn't get out of Narek until the next day, and then he would be behind schedule.

Finally, he stepped out into the middle of the market square, past a small group of camels, and raised both his hands. "Does anybody speak common?" he shouted at the top of his lungs. The crowd stared at him for a moment, and then went back to what they were doing.

A tall, dark skinned man stepped out from the crowd. "It is not often we see foreigners!" he called, a strange accent ringing in his voice. "Most of them do not care anyway. But I do. I am Harun al-Baraq, and I am at your service."

Delgar nodded and shook the man's hand. "Delgar Daegar's son," he said. "I am looking for a guide to take me into the desert."

Harun smiled. "Then you have come to the right man! I will gather some good men, and along with them I myself will take you out."

Delgar shook his head. "You don't really have to do that much."

Harun stepped back, and for a moment Delgar feared he had offended the man. "But I insist! The Holy Book declares that we must be kind and helpful to strangers, for we were strangers in the desert when the Prophet came upon us. We are commanded to lead strangers with charity and kindness, so that they may find their path. They are words to live by." He motioned for Delgar to follow him.

Delgar fell into step, winding his way through the market, careful to keep up with Harun. "They are certainly words of wisdom."

Harun stopped for a moment. "Words of great wisdom. But look around!" He motioned at the crowd. "They have all forgotten. Most of them have to speak the common tongue; there are many languages in Barsh, but only one for commerce. But will they help a stranger? No! As soon as they see one who is not of their kind, they are quiet as a desert mouse. They all speak the words of the Prophet, but they have lost the meaning. I think that must be the fate of all religions. People hear what they want to hear; what the Prophet actually said has been lost."

"So you think there are no good men in the world?"

"Some, but few," Harun said. "Those clothes you wear, have you any others?"

Delgar blinked. "Some, but they're all for the weather back home. It's winter there, and there's a fair bit of snow. Why?"

"You are from Taerraland, yes? I can tell by the accent, although there is something a bit different about it. Perhaps you moved there, and have been there long enough for your accent to change. However, if you wear those clothes, you will find yourself losing much moisture. Water is very precious in the desert, and you will die if you lose too much of it. Have you money to buy what you need?"

Delgar held up his moneypurse. "I have enough for the guide and the trip back. I don't know about the clothes."

Harun laughed heartily. "It is good to see a foreigner who comes prepared! So many come here with nothing. I will see to your clothes, good Delgar! And then we will get you your guides. Where is it you want to go?"

"The Cave of Dreams," Delgar said.

Harun frowned. "That is a long way through dangerous land, my friend. The guides will be expensive."

"Do you know where it is, then?"

"Nobody is certain," Harun said. "There are legends that it lies at the base of Mount Asabe, but none have ever seen it! I fear you chase a ghost, my friend."

"And yet I must find it," Delgar said. "Two very good friends also sought it, and now they are missing. I seek them as well."

"I do not know of your friends, good Delgar. I myself just recently arrived; I am a trader as well as a good man! A combination not usually seen, I think!"

Delgar grinned in response, but wondered for a moment how long he could stand to be in the presence of this strange man. Most of the traders he had known had been kind family men. But, it was a different culture; perhaps that was the problem he was having. He had been warned by his teachers that he should take care when dealing with other cultures, lest he accidentally offend them.

Harun led him to a large tent, where after a brief conversation in one of the Barshian dialects, he handed him a long white robe, belt and veil. "Wear these always in the desert!" Harun said. "They will protect you from the sun in the daytime and the cold at night."

Delgar nodded in thanks. "Now what of the guides? I want to leave as quickly as possible."

"Patience is a virtue, my friend! We will come to them soon enough. First we must buy provisions, however."

"I already have some," Delgar said, patting his backpack. "I don't think it's necessary to buy more."

Harun shook his head. "The desert makes different demands on a body than the north, my friend! If you want to travel through a desert, it is best to eat desert food. Fear not; I will find you some of the best."

Delgar stood by and waited as Harun haggled with several merchants, purchasing dried meat and a sort of flat bread. Finally, as the sun sank in the sky, Harun led him to several small groups of robed figures. As he walked, he talked, motioning to several groups.

"You must choose your people well, yes? Take this tribe, for instance. They are the qal-Harii. They will rob you blind. And here are the qal-Baraq. They will kill you and then rob you blind. No loyalty except to themselves, you see? But that is desert life; the Prophet's words cannot always stand when survival is at stake."

A robed figure with silver lining on the robe leapt up and shouted something at Harun. Then the nomad turned to Delgar. "You no listen to this man! This is devil speaking with Prophet's voice! You come with us, we take you across desert. Only ten gold! You no listen to him!"

Harun pushed the man aside and spat some quick words at him which Delgar didn't understand. Then he turned back to Delgar. "You see what I mean? This man is qal-Harii. He would leave you stranded in the desert with no money or food. But as you see, I am different."

They came to a group of five men, sitting and playing a game with dice. "Now this is my people," Harun said. "They are qal-Qatar. The lions of the desert! They will protect you and guide you. And you will only have to pay five gold pieces, for we are the followers of the Prophet."

"How long will it take to get there?" Delgar asked.

"For where you want to go, never perhaps." Harun said. "But to get to Mount Asabe, that will take four days on camel-back. Remember what I have told you; you cannot last for more than three days in the desert without water, and that is if your clothes are intact!"

"Can we leave immediately?"

"We will go with the setting sun!" Harun barked something in his native tongue, and the five men walked toward the camel stalls. Harun turned to Delgar and smiled. "Once we have our camels, then we will set out by the setting sun. It is a good omen, you see! It means we will begin without the heat."

"And then?"

"And then it will be hotter than the domain of the Damned One, my friend," Harun chuckled. "He has no fury like the open desert."

Delgar awoke in one of the rough tents the qal-Qatar had planted, the morning sun streaming through a slight tear in the door-flap. He tried to count the number of days he had been on the desert so far, but without success. The days had begun to meld together, as unremarkable as the sand dunes.

He remembered that on the second night out there had been a sandstorm. Harun had ordered him into one of the tents, rushing in right after him as the rest of his people scrambled to get their tents pitched. As he closed it up on the inside, he told Delgar not to worry.

"How long will it last?" Delgar had asked.

"It could last for days," Harun had replied. "It could last for only hours. We must wait it out, my friend. Do not worry! The Prophet will see to us."

For hours Delgar listened to the howling of the sandstorm, watching the sides of the tent push menacingly towards him, blown by the wind and sand. "How safe is it to travel in that?" Delgar had asked.

Harun had shaken his head. "It is not safe at all! The sand will strip your flesh right off of your bones, if you stand outside in it. All you can do is take shelter and wait."

Delgar had shrugged and laid down, closing his eyes. But with the sandstorm howling outside, his sleep was fitful at best. Finally, the noise ceased. Harun poked his head out of the tent, then turned to Delgar, a large grin on his face.

"I told you the Prophet would see to us!" he exclaimed. "Now see the power of the desert!"

Delgar stepped outside, only to trip on a shelf of sand. He stood up, looking at the half-buried tent. Then he turned to gaze at the horizon. The landscape had completely changed, the sun floating low in the sky.

Harun had stepped out easily, smiling at the open

desert around him. "You see what I mean about the desert!" he declared. "It is the cradle of civilization! And now nature has reclaimed it. Once this was a fertile land, and mankind arose here. But you see how things change? The cities are buried under the sand. I saw one once, a long time ago, and then it vanished once more. We are no longer the masters here."

"Do you think we were ever the masters here?" Delgar had asked.

Harun had shaken his head. "I think it is a lesson of the Prophet that mastery is never forever. We now recognize that we are on sufferance here."

How many days ago had that been? Delgar tried to remember; it could not have been more than two. Yet the mountains remained below the horizon. He shook his head, trying to wake up. The incredible heat was making him slow again. He still couldn't understand the dichotomy of the place. In the days he could barely keep from swooning in the heat, yet at night he was forced to take shelter lest he freeze.

Harun poked his head into the tent. "I see you are up, my friend. Come! We have much traveling still to do!"

"How close are we?" Delgar asked. "I feel as though we've been traveling forever."

"We are not far," Harun replied. "The desert has slowed us, but the mountains should appear today. You must have patience! Come and claim your camel; we shall leave quickly."

Delgar put on his headdress and stepped outside. The sun had only just cleared the horizon, and already the nomads were beginning to stow their tents on the camels. Delgar began to roll up the tent, carefully storing it, and then turning to his camel. The beast glared at him for a moment, and Delgar wondered if camels ever truly looked happy about anything. Then he awkwardly mounted, resigning himself to another day with a sore body. He was still trying to master the skill of riding camels; the beast had thrown him once on the first day, and only with a great deal of coaching from Harun had he been able to finally begin to ride.

It was mid-morning by the time they set out across the sand dunes, Delgar fumbling for his canteen. Sweat ran down his back, and the glare of the sun off the sand began to hurt his eyes. He glanced at the western sky, noticing that there were no clouds. He blinked; he hadn't seen a single cloud since he had left Narek. Then he turned back to the head of the column, shading his eyes.

Harun rode up to him. "Are you all right, my friend?"

"Hot and tired, as usual," Delgar replied, trying to smile.

"You should drink more of your water."

"I don't want to waste it."

Harun shook his head. "You must know when to use it and when not to. Men have died from thirst here with a full waterskin at their belt. So drink! That is what it is there for."

Delgar took a long drink from the water, carefully stopping the waterskin once he had finished. "Thank you," he said. "You truly are a friend."

"The Prophet commands us to be kind," Harun said. "Have you ever read the Holy Book?"

Delgar shook his head. "My studies have usually taken me elsewhere."

"It is something you should investigate, if you should have the chance," Harun began. "It sometimes goes against conventional wisdom. The Prophet says we must treat strangers with kindness, but conventional wisdom tells us that strangers must be treated with reservation and not trusted. They are foreigners, and can only have their own interests at heart. There is some wisdom there, do you not agree?"

Delgar shook his head. "I have learned that we should embrace differences when we can. Perhaps there are some greedy men, but there are no truly evil ones. And two cultures can compliment one another instead of fighting."

"But that is wisdom of a place where survival is not an issue," Harun argued. "Would you not say that in a place like this, one must see to their survival before they can help another. And should one come across another, how can he know that the stranger is not seeing to his own needs then? Survival and civilized wisdom do not always agree my friend."

"Well, I don't think-"

"The Prophet teaches us that we must tend to ourselves, and while we must treat strangers with kindness, we must also be wary of infidels."

Delgar startled. "Now wait a moment-"

He felt a crushing blow to his head, and fell off his camel onto the hard sand. The impact knocked the wind out of him, and he struggled to stand, to get some focus. He searched for some life energy around him to draw on, but the sand was completely dead.

Boots crunched in the sand behind him. Another blow hit him, knocking him to the ground. He saw Harun above him for a moment, shaking his head. "Infidel," the man spat, and then Delgar saw only darkness.

181

Chapter XVIII: The Wanderer in the Desert

Delgar dreamt of Dragons. Huge, multicolored Dragons glided across a clear sky, spinning and weaving in a great, complex pattern. Then they began to land by him, cooing restlessly. He reached out to touch one of them, but when he came close to a red one the heat singed his hand. Every single Dragon made the area around it hotter. He tried to warn them, to make them understand, but they kept landing by him, and he got hotter and hotter and...

The world went dark.

He opened his eyes to see Jenara standing over him, a wet towel in her hands. She stroked him gently, telling him that it was all over. But the next time she stroked him, her hand was searing hot. He tried to push her away, but she lay on top of him, kissing and caressing him, and Delgar screamed as the heat burned him away.

He startled awake, rolling over as the sun exploded in his eyes. Blinking furiously, he felt something rough in his mouth. He spat, and wet sand fell to the ground. The hot sand singed his hand, and he quickly stood up.

The desert stretched out around him, as far as his eye could see. He fumbled for the waterskin at his belt, but his hand only met fabric. He looked down in horror.

His waterskin, moneypurse and backpack were gone. The only things he had were the tattered clothes he wore.

The midday sun beat down on him. He staggered forward, trying to find any sign of where his assailants might have gone. But the desert wind had obscured any tracks that might have been there. He swallowed, wincing in pain as the hard saliva dropped down his parched throat.

"Help me!" he shouted, his voice hoarse. "Somebody please help me!"

His cry for help echoed across the dunes, and then faded. Delgar glanced around in desperation, trying to see something new, anything that could help him.

There was absolutely nothing.

He began to walk, trying to work his way northwards, but uncertain of his direction in the midday sun. If he continued north, he would run into the coastline, and he would be saved. Along the sea there would be some villages of some sort, somebody who would help him. There had to be; it was his only hope.

He corrected his direction as the sun began to sink in the sky. He cursed softly; he had been going south, into the heart of the desert, rather than north. He found himself following his tracks, but soon they also vanished, covered by the blowing sand.

He continued to walk north, the sun creeping toward the horizon at a painfully slow rate.

For a while, Delgar tried to work out some way he could produce some water with his magic. He looked around at the forces in the air and in the ground, but there was nothing useful. Many forces wove around him, but there was no water anywhere.

His shadow began to lengthen.

Out of the corner of his eye, Delgar saw water. He turned, barely believing his eyes. Just by the next dune a small pool of water waited, a beautiful sparkling blue paradise. He ran towards it, watching as it grew before him, the water distorted as the heat rose off the sand. He tripped and rolled down the dune, spitting sand out of his mouth as he came to a halt. Then he looked around in shock.

The water was gone. Once again he was surrounded by the rolling dunes of the open desert. He shook his head, nearly in tears. There had to be water somewhere! There had to be!

He turned back and began to head north once more. The sun beat down on him relentlessly, and Delgar's walk became a stagger.

And the sun set.

Delgar kept walking in the night, trying to keep himself warm. The stars shone over him, but there was no heat. His teeth chattered endlessly, but he kept going. He had to. He had promised Jenara he'd be back.

He tripped and fell, rolling in the sand for a moment. The darkness threatened to close on him, but he forced himself to stay awake. *If you fall asleep you'll die*, he told himself. He stood back up and staggered onwards, wrapping his robes tightly around himself in an effort to keep out the cold.

The sun rose, and the chill of night was replaced by searing heat. Delgar staggered on, desperate to reach the sea. It was so wonderful and blue, and if he could reach it, he could go swimming! And there would be lots of water, that was the wonderful thing about the sea, and it would be so amazing and such a nice change...

The morning became midday.

Delgar tripped and fell, lying on the ground for a moment. He tried to rise, pushing himself up with his hands, but his strength faltered and he lay on the sand once more. It burned his face, startling him, and he struggled painfully to stand. Finally he stood once more, the desert around him, beckoning to him like a lover or mortal enemy.

From the corner of his eye, he noticed something sticking out of one of the dunes, just a bit lighter than the sand itself. He staggered over to it, touching it to make sure it was real. His eyes widened in amazement.

It was the corner of a building. He began to brush away the sand around it, ignoring the burning sensation on his hands. An inscription in some ancient tongue glared at him, its letters curved and elegant. He saw a bit of faded green beside the writing, and began to brush some more sand away. The green became a tree, and Delgar's heart beat with excitement. He cleared away more of the mural to find a depiction of some ancient garden, trees and shrubs leaning over a stepped pyramid.

And then he looked at the sun and grimaced. It was beginning to set. He wrapped his robes around him once more, waiting for the cold to come.

I'm going to have to keep moving, Delgar realized. Otherwise he would freeze to death. He began to walk northwards, leaving the ancient building behind. As he heard the sand blowing, he could almost feel the structure being covered again, the garden lost to human memory once again.

A biting wind swept over him, trying to blast him into oblivion, but he wouldn't let it. He began to sing rhymes in his head, to remember anything he could, anything to pass the time and help him survive the cold.

A voice from the past came to his mind. *I name you Dragonfriend, Delgar of Nordland. Should you ever be in need, all you need do is call upon us.*

Delgar blinked, stopping in his tracks. The cold penetrated his robes, chilling him to the bone. He could call upon the Dragons, but how would they hear him? He was in the middle of the desert, and he didn't even know where he was.

He shook his head; there were no other options. He could already feel death closing in on him. He looked up at the sky and screamed as loud as he could. "Dragons! I am Delgar of Nordland, and I need your help! Please help..."

But as he finished speaking, his shout became a croak, and a single tear slid down his cheek. They would never be able to hear that. There would be no rescue.

Dejected, he began to wander again, no longer caring where. The sun rose, pushing aside the cold with an intense heat.

The last of Delgar's energy left him.

He fell to the ground, rolling over so that he could see the sun. The sand burned his skin, but he no longer had enough energy to care. He just wanted to see Jenara one last time. He tried to raise his hand, to reach out and grab the sun, but the limb wouldn't move.

A shadow fell over the sun, a shadow of some great, graceful bird. Delgar began to laugh weakly. So death had come to him in the form of a bird! He had always expected some sort of cloaked figure.

The shadow swept over him, and once again there was darkness.

Chapter XIX: The Cave of Dreams

The sound of running water rushed through the darkness, and Delgar startled awake. He found himself lying on the floor of a large cavern, a shallow stream running beside him. He looked above to see several stalactites reaching down from the ceiling, and for a brief moment he feared one would fall on him. Then he shook his head, bringing himself back to reality.

The sun blazed in his eyes when he knelt down to take a drink, and he blinked furiously. The water soothed as it poured down his throat, and he began to wonder why it hurt so much. He stepped closer to the entrance of the cavern and looked outside. His gaze was met by a vista of snow-capped mountains cast in shadow as the sun rose over them.

I'm in the mountains, Delgar realized. *Why am I in the mountains?*

He tried to think back to what had been before. He had been on a quest of some sort. He had promised Jenara that he would be back, and then they had kissed and he had left. He had taken a ship to the desert, and then...

He shook his head. He knew that his situation had something to do with the desert, but he couldn't say what. Nor could he say what he had been in the desert searching for in the first place.

His thirst returned, and he turned back to the stream, taking a deep drink. The water had a metallic taint, but it was still the best tasting water Delgar had ever drank. Why was that? How could he have become so thirsty?

He settled down by one of the walls of the cavern, watching the sun rise over the mountains. As the sun crept across the sky, the shadow lifted from the great peaks, revealing light grey rock capped by blinding white snow. A chill wind swept through the cavern, and Delgar pulled his rags closer to him, trying to wrap himself up.

Something sparked in his memory, and a bit more of the picture filled itself in. He had been betrayed. Some nomad had led him out into the desert and struck him down. He tried to feel angry, but he couldn't even remember the man's name or face. Just a shadow standing over him and a harsh voice cursing him. And then he had wandered in the desert, but for how long? And what had he been after?

He shook his head sadly. Jenara would know, if she were here. And so would Vice-Chancellor Vertanus; he was sure Vertanus had given him the assignment. But he really missed Jenara. A soft moan escaped his lips. "Oh, my love," he rasped. "I'm lost and I don't know the way home. I just want to see you again."

A horrible thought crossed his mind. *Could I be dead?* He glanced around, but everything seemed incredibly real. He pinched himself on the arm, wincing as it stung. So, he wasn't sleeping, at least. And all indications were that he wasn't dead either.

A shadow flickered in the corner of his eye, and he turned to look outside of the cavern. The mountain scape was brighter, but otherwise nothing had changed. Then he saw it again: a slight shadow, almost like a large bird, streaming over one of the mountains. He watched with a strange detachment as the shadow grew closer and larger, and then the bird itself came into his view.

Finally Delgar could make out some details, and he startled. It was no bird that was coming towards him — it was a Great Dragon. The Dragon flew closer and closer, until it finally touched down on a ledge just outside of the cavern. Folding its enormous wings, it strode into the cave, its green eyes glowing in the darkness. Delgar's gaze slid down its long ebony length, covered with the shining black scales.

"I see you are awake, Dragonfriend," the Dragon rumbled. "I feared that I had come too late."

"Where did you find me?" Delgar rasped. He blinked. What had the desert done to him?

"In the deserts of the land you mortals call 'Barsh'," the Dragon replied, its head snaking down to gaze at Delgar. "But we have an older name for it, of course. We remember it when it was still a great and fertile land, before the great drought. But that all has passed now."

"How did you know to look?" Delgar croaked. "I was alone and helpless."

The Dragon's eyes appeared puzzled for a moment. "You are a Dragonfriend, and you called for aid. We all heard you. But I was the closest, so I came."

"My name is Delgar." He swallowed. At least his voice seemed to be returning.

"My name is Leoht'heortan, child of Fleot'heortan," the Dragon declared. "If you tell me where you wish to go, I will take you there."

Delgar shook his head. "I was supposed to bring

189

something back to the Mageschool with me, but I can't remember what it was. I just remember I was in the desert, my guide struck me, I wandered for a bit, and then I woke up here, wherever here is."

"You are in the mountains at the border of the land you call Pakaria, by the shores of the Dark Sea. Could this guide have stolen the thing from you?"

Delgar shook his head. "I was on my way to find it when I was betrayed. It was a gem of some sort, but I don't remember what exactly. A green gem? A blue gem?"

Leoht'heortan stood thoughtfully for a moment, and then his head snaked down to face Delgar. "Where is this gem?"

Delgar pulled at his memory, trying to find some clue of what he was looking for. It was in the mountains somewhere, in a cave of...

"The Cave of Dreams!" Delgar exclaimed. "The gem is in the Cave of Dreams! But what is it?"

An alarmed look came into the Dragon's eyes, and he pulled back. "Do you seek the Gem of Sidhe?"

Delgar snapped his fingers. "That's it! The Gem of Sidhe! But what is it, and where is the Cave of Dreams? I still don't remember those parts."

"The Gem of Sidhe was created by the Tuatha de Danaan shortly before the Dragon Masters were driven to the great beyond," Leoht'heortan said. "They created it out of the essence of this world, and stored it in the Cave of Dreams for all eternity. It is ancient and very powerful, and should stay where it lies. Why do you seek it, Delgar Dragonfriend?"

Delgar scratched his head. "The Mageschool wants to study it. I don't know why; usually it's to learn something for the better, or just for the sake of knowledge. Will you take me to it?"

Leoht'heortan paused, his head arching towards the

high ceiling. Then it came down again, intense green eyes blazing. "You are a Dragonfriend, and therefore worthy of our trust. Although it is against my judgement, I will take you to the Cave of Dreams. You must be very careful, however; the Cave is not safe."

"What is the matter with it?"

"It is the Cave of Dreams," Leoht'heortan said. "It is a place where dreams and reality mix and collide. Some things are real and some are not, and you must be cautious to realize what is reality. Some have been lost for all eternity, feasting on phantom food until they starve to death. Some have been driven screaming by the horrors they have seen."

"Driven by dreams?"

"By nightmares. They are dreams too."

Delgar blinked. "What can I expect to find in there?"

"Only what you take with you. Rest a while, and I will take you there."

They set out at daybreak, Delgar clinging onto Leoht'heortan's back for dear life as the Dragon glided gracefully above the mountains. The sun burst over one of the higher peaks, forcing Delgar to squint and turn away.

"How do you like it in the clouds, Delgar Dragonfriend?" Leoht'heortan roared joyfully.

"It will take some getting used to," Delgar replied, trying to not get sick.

"When we Dragons are young, we fly much higher than this," the Dragon declared. "But it is harder to breathe, so we do not stay up for long."

"Why would it be harder to breathe?" Delgar inquired.

Leoht'heortan banked and turned, and Delgar held on tighter, praying that he would survive the trip. "No Dragon knows for certain. It just is."

The Dragon began to slow down and lose altitude, Delgar gulping as a mountain rose before him, majestic and intimidating. The peak and then the slope rushed past him, and Delgar closed his eyes until he felt the Great Dragon set his feet on the ground. He opened his eyes to see the serpentine neck stretching out towards the ground. He climbed down the neck and stood on the earth once more, sand crunching under his boots.

A wave of heat passed over him, and then a chill breeze. He turned in the direction of the wind to see a large cave opening into the mountain, mist streaming out of the entrance.

"That is the Cave of Dreams," Leoht'heortan intoned. "Are you still certain you wish to do this?"

Delgar nodded. "I have to complete my mission."

Leoht'heortan looked at Delgar sagely for a moment. "Remember what I have told you. All your dreams and nightmares will await you in there. Remember that the dreams are as substantial as the mist, but many will be as real as you allow them to be. If you think it is real, a nightmare can kill you."

"Can you guide me?"

The Dragon shook his head. "We Dragons are too close to that which dreams are made of. This place is more dangerous to me than it is to you. I see your wyrd, and despite it you are still the dreamer, rather than the dream. But you are about to claim a talisman of great power. Can you assure us that it will be used wisely?"

Delgar nodded. "The Gem will be used honorably, I am sure of it. Where will I find it in there?"

"It will be on an obsidian pedestal in the center of the Cave," Leoht'heortan said. "Remember that it is also that which dreams are made of. I can tell you no more; you must enter now, or leave."

"Will you wait for me?" Delgar asked.

"Of course. I will wait as long as I have to."

Delgar turned to face the Cave's entrance, the huge cavern gaping open, filled with swirling mist. He took a deep breath, then stepped in.

The mist closed around him, and he lost all sense of direction as he walked. Blinking, he shook his head. He had been going towards the center of the cave, and he had not turned, therefore it stood to reason that he was still facing in the correct direction. But he needed a marker of some sort.

He tore a strip off his white sleeve and lay it on the ground, a corner folded towards the exit. Then he began to walk forward.

"Delgar, come here and help your mother," a familiar voice called. Delgar spun to find his father regarding him, his mother standing close by. The mist had gone, and he was on the hill leading to the old farm in Nordland.

He yearned to join them, to hold his mother in his arms once more. Even as he began to step toward them, the Dragon's warning filled his mind. He shook his head. "I can't. You're not real."

"Of course we're real," his mother said. "Why, I'm standing right here."

Delgar shook his head again. As he watched, the scene dissolved into the mist, and he was alone once more. He looked back to see where his marker was, and then he stepped forward again.

And somebody leapt into his arms and kissed him.

He jerked back to see a beautiful face under a wave of beautiful, blonde hair. For a moment he stood by the body of his beloved once more. But then he looked up, and Lera stood there, her arms inviting him. Tears rolled down his cheek.

"I've missed you so much," Delgar nearly sobbed. "But you're not real."

"Here I'm as real as you want me to be," her shade said. "We can stay here forever."

Delgar paused. Then he recalled Jenara's raven beauty, and he looked back up at Lera.

"No," he said, his voice almost a whisper. "You are my past, and I will always remember you. But I must live in the present. Goodbye, my love. I will always cherish my time with you."

He leaned forward to embrace her, but his arms only passed through the mist. He glanced around to find his marker barely visible behind him, but otherwise he was alone. For a moment, he could only stand still and weep. Finally, he took a deep breath and wiped the tears from his face. He tore another strip from his robe and lay it on the ground, folding over one edge so that it pointed back to where he had come from.

He took several steps forward, then a deafening rumbling surrounded him. He spun to find a great wall of ice bearing down on him, demonic power radiating from the huge glacier. He held up his arms in warding, and as the ice approached him he closed his eyes. "It's not real," he cried. "None of it is real!" He opened his eyes as the ice passed through him, as insubstantial as the mist.

He shook his head. "I have to get the Gem and leave," he muttered. "This place will drive me insane." Once again, he tore off a strip of his sleeve and left it as a marker. Then he continued onward.

He nearly tripped over the bodies.

The two corpses lay before him, hand in hand, the skin withered and desiccated. From the clothes, he could tell that one was a man and the other a woman, but the hair had become grey and brittle, while the faces were so drawn he couldn't tell who they once were. He knelt down by the bodies to take a closer look. The man's face looked horrified, while the woman's face merely had an expression of shock. Then something glinted in the mist, drawing Delgar's gaze.

His heart fell. He reached down to the man's hand and pulled off an ornate gold ring. He would have known that ring anywhere; it was Tomlin's family signet. He clasped it in his hand, willing it to be just a dream, but it remained, pressing hard and firm into his palm. Finally, he put the ring in a pocket of his robe and moved on.

A large obsidian pedestal rose before him. On it lay a multi-faceted blue gem, shining in the mist. Delgar gasped at its beauty. As he looked upon it, he saw great deserts and lush forests reflected in its facets. This had to be the Gem of Sidhe; it could be nothing else. He reached out to grasp it and closed his fist around it.

But there was nothing but empty air. He recoiled in shock. The Gem still stared at him, filling him with longing, but when he tried to touch it again, his hand passed right through it. Then he remembered what Leoht'heortan had said. *"It is also that which dreams are made of."* And if a dream was made real by his willing it to be so...

He closed his eyes, wishing with all his heart that the gem would be real. Then he reached out and grabbed it. Its cold surface nearly burned when he touched it, but still he held it in his hand. He took one last look at it, and then wrapped it under his robe. Then he turned around and made his way back to the bodies.

As he came to the bodies and caught sight of one of his markers, he heard a great roar behind him. He turned back to see a horde of goblins bearing down on him, primitive axes raised.

His nightmares had arrived.

He barreled towards his marker, reminding himself that the goblins weren't real as he went. Two goblins caught up with him, swinging their axes. The blades passed right through him, but his heart still pounded. In that moment his concentration lapsed, and another goblin crashed into him, knocking him down.

"You're not real!" Delgar shouted as the goblin raised its axe. The blade came down, only to pass through him as though it was mist. He staggered up and raced to his next marker. Then he stopped short.

The huge glacier rumbled towards him at an impossible speed, blocking the entrance. Delgar tried to tell himself that it wasn't real, but his nightmares had been so vivid it was hard to believe. He closed his eyes, willing it to go away, and ran right into it. He felt nothing, and then he felt heat as he tripped and fell, rolling in the sand. He opened his eyes to see Leoht'heortan over him, a concerned look in his glowing green eyes.

Delgar looked back at the cave. The mist still flowed out of the entrance, but it was just as before. Nothing had followed him out. Then he reached into his robe. He felt a rush of happiness as he felt the Gem of Sidhe resting at his side, but then his heart fell.

He pulled out an ornate gold ring, as substantial as it had always been. A tear streaked down his cheek.

"It is true," Delgar moaned. "My friends are dead."

Chapter XX: Return

Delgar sat in the sand and wept, Tomlin's ring grasped in his hand. Above him, Leoht'heortan stood a quiet watch. Finally, the Dragon turned to him and leaned his head forward.

"We must go soon," he said. "The heat of the day is coming, and you are still weak."

Delgar nodded and sniffled. "They were very good friends. I'm sorry, but this is very difficult for me."

Leoht'heortan nodded sagely. "I too have lost friends, and it is difficult. But they have gone beyond, and all you can do now is honor their memories."

Delgar stood and brushed himself off, trying to stifle the tears still running down his cheeks. He put the ring in his robe and turned to the Dragon. "Can you take me to Taerra?"

Leoht'heortan lowered his neck, allowing Delgar to climb on. "I believe I know that place. It is in the nation called Taerraland?"

"Yes."

"Then we will be there before the sun sets," the Dragon declared, taking flight. Once again Delgar clung to the neck for dear life, watching as the ground drew away and the mountains raced by. But his thoughts kept returning to Tomlin and Melina. He had once promised Tomlin that he would take him north to see Nordland. And Tomlin had sworn by his family signet that he would take Delgar to see the forests of his home. But neither of these promises would be fulfilled now. Tomlin and his wife were gone, and only the signet remained as proof that they had ever been.

He broke down into tears, leaning against the smooth scales. Through his blurred eyes he saw the sea passing beneath him, sparkling like some great magical creature. And then more memories returned. He remembered Tomlin first seeing Melina in the middle of class, declaring with a grin that he liked her. Delgar looking at him and asking if she liked him back, and Tomlin saying: "I'll find out this Friday." Delgar smiled despite his grief. Tomlin had always been a rogue, and many of the girls had tried to catch his eye. Melina had been the first who succeeded, though.

He also remembered their wedding, Tomlin suffering through the entire affair in a heavy white formal robe while the summer sun blazed overhead. And when Brother Gelban of the Order of the Eternal had asked if Tomlin would marry Melina, Tomlin had suddenly startled out of a trance and asked him to repeat the question. The entire episode had evoked a laugh from the audience, a stern look from the monk, and a warm blush from Melina.

Delgar shook his head. That marriage had seemed blessed, as though absolutely nothing could ever happen to destroy it. And yet something had occurred in the Cave of Dreams, something which had stolen both their lives.

Delgar blinked sadly. He would never see them again, no matter what happened. A final tear fell from his eye.

"Hold on tightly!" Leoht'heortan declared. "We are going to pass over a storm."

Delgar gazed down to see the storm fly past. Brilliant white lightning leaped between the inky clouds, and even high above the storm the winds picked up, blowing through Delgar's clothes and forcing him to shiver. The crashing thunder echoed up as another bolt flashed beneath them.

"How large is the storm?" Delgar shouted, rubbing his sore eyes with his right hand.

"I do not know," the Dragon replied. "It is the storm season, however, and it may be very large."

A gust of wind burst up from the clouds, nearly blowing Delgar off his mount. Delgar held on even more tightly, closing his eyes as the winds battered them. When he opened them he found them passing a large platform of the dark clouds, almost as high as they were.

And then, abruptly, the storm passed under them and they were flying beside milky white clouds. Far beneath them Delgar saw farmland, covered with a thin layer of snow, so that the ground appeared speckled.

"I do not see any more storms, Delgar Dragonfriend," Leoht'heortan stated. "I believe that it will be an easy trip from here."

"How fast are we flying?" Delgar asked. "It took me almost two weeks to cover this distance."

"I am flying at a fairly fast speed, but it is still moderate," the Dragon replied. "But we have been flying for almost five hours. The sun is beginning to set."

Delgar glanced up with a start to see that Leoht'heortan was speaking the truth. The sky was darkening around them as the sun sank down to the horizon, bathing the ground in a crimson glow.

A river snaked before him, stretching far into the distance. Around it lay snow-covered farmland, giving the appearance of a rough white blanket. A city began to appear before him, growing larger as each minute passed. The Dragon banked and set down short of the town walls.

Leoht'heortan lowered his neck. "I fear that too many of your kind still fear us, and I cannot take you any farther. If you walk for a few hours, you will reach your city without incident."

Delgar dismounted, discovering to his dismay that all his muscles ached. "Thank you for your help. I owe you my life."

"You may repay me in kind some day," Leoht'heortan said. "Wyrd shall work as it will."

Delgar nodded and turned, stretching his aching legs and arms. He heard a flapping behind him and looked back to see the Dragon flying back to the southeast. As a slight chill began to penetrate his robes, he walked towards the city just over the horizon, rubbing his hands together to keep them warm.

His first sight of Taerra was by the crescent moon, the towers creeping over the horizon like shadowy needles. He considered doubling his pace, but finally decided against it. It was hard enough to see in the moonlight; there was no need to run a greater risk of tripping and hurting himself.

As he walked, the towers came closer and the moon rose higher in the sky. Delgar found himself smiling, the prospect of Jenara in his arms bringing a wistful smile. Despite himself, he found his stride becoming a slow jog. He was coming home.

And, finally, after what seemed like hours of walking, Delgar reached the gates of Taerra.

Vice-Chancellor Vertanus gazed at the Gem of Sidhe with

an analytical eye. "So that's what it looks like," he muttered. "Doesn't look like much, does it?"

Vertanus had met Delgar as soon as he had come to the gates of the Mageschool, appearing almost as tired as Delgar felt. "I was watching your progress home with a scrying glass," Vertanus had said. "It is a good thing that you landed outside of the city; the war has people rather more paranoid than usual."

"The war is still on?" Delgar had yawned. "Why hasn't it stopped yet?"

"It is a war of raids," Vertanus had replied. "They raid us, we raid them, and there hasn't been enough communication to end it yet. But come, Chancellor Berran is also waiting for you."

Berran wasn't the only one waiting in the office Vertanus brought him too. Velnan stood in a corner by an oak desk, a stern look on his face. He just had enough time to see his mentor when Jenara swept him up in a hug, kissing him passionately. He returned the kiss and held her close for a moment, only returning to reality when he heard Vertanus clear his throat.

"I decided she should be here to meet you," Velnan said, then shot an acid look at Vertanus. "Just about the only decision I had in the matter."

"You were not here to consult, Archmage Velnan," Vertanus stated. "And I acted with the full sanction of the Mageschool." He turned to Delgar and Jenara. "So let's see this Gem of Sidhe which has caused us so much trouble."

Delgar handed over the Gem, and then Berran took him aside for a moment as Vertanus appraised it. "What about Tomlin and Melina?"

Delgar passed the Chancellor Tomlin's ring. "They died in the Cave of Dreams." His voice cracked. "They were so close to it too..."

"I'm sorry, Mage Delgar," Berran said. "If we had known, we would have sent somebody more experienced."

Delgar looked at Jenara, still cradled in his arms. Then he cuddled her fiercely. He thought she was holding up well, but still her eyes were red and glistened with tears.

She ran her finger down his rough face. "You look as though you almost died."

"I'll tell you about it later. But I'm back now, and home before I was expected."

"Well, we have to discuss this," Vertanus declared. "Mage Delgar may as well have some say in this matter, as he did recover it for us. We now have a problem."

"It is the Gem of Sidhe, is it not?" Berran said, his eyebrow raised.

"It is indeed," Vertanus stated. "But even a preliminary examination indicates that it is a talisman of great power. It may affect the magic practiced by the students and Mages, as well as any faculty experiments." He handed the gem to Berran, who examined it closely. "Do you see what I mean?"

"That explains why I felt something coming during the earlier part of the night," Berran said. "This could amplify magic a hundred fold, at the very least."

"Probably much more, if the literature is correct," Vertanus said. "This could make it dangerous."

"If I may cut in, sirs," Delgar interrupted. "If it is so dangerous, why did you have me find it?"

"Focusing crystals," Velnan answered. "Many students have difficulties with the early part of the practical curriculum. If we had some proper focusing crystals, then these pupils would find it easier to learn the basics of magic. Then we could simply hand out the crystals to the next class, and so on. We thought that this was merely a large focusing crystal, and that we could copy the design."

"It isn't," Berran said, placing it on the desk. "It may be much more than that. Only further study will tell."

"But if it is dangerous in the way you describe, then we cannot study it here," Velnan commented. "It will have to be studied at a great distance, preferably where there are no other Mages."

Berran looked at Vertanus for a moment. "You have a tower in the far north, don't you Vice-Chancellor?"

Vertanus blinked. "Yes, I do, but I don't really think..."

"It's an idea," Velnan said. "It's remote, and the gem will be safe in the hands of such a powerful Archmage as yourself."

Vertanus swallowed. "But I'm getting married at the end of the term, and I was planning to take a vacation. And I've got to get the tower ready for her, and..."

"You may study the Gem of Sidhe at your leisure, if I am not mistaken," Velnan pressed. Delgar smiled; it was just like Velnan's to get even with the Vice-Chancellor for sending his student away without permission.

Berran clasped Vertanus on the shoulder. "Will you do this for us? You may work at whatever pace you wish. Besides, you're going up to your tower in the next couple of days anyway; you can take it with you and store it until you've finished your work and your honeymoon."

Vertanus' face fell. "I guess I'll take it. But I'm going to give it back to you as soon as I can."

Berran nodded. "That is not a problem."

Velnan turned to face Delgar and Jenara. "As for you two: Mistress Jenara, I believe you have a test tomorrow morning, and you should rest for it. Mage Delgar, you have done well, and we shall determine what your level of study should be in the morning; get some rest and I will see you then."

Delgar and Jenara nodded, bade their farewells, and

walked out of the office, arm in arm. Jenara stopped and kissed him. "I'm so glad you're home."

Delgar kissed her back and grinned. "So am I, my love. So am I."

Chapter XXI: Consequences

Velnan watched Delgar cast the spell, and then sat back, his eyes thoughtful. Leaning back, Delgar gazed across the table at his mentor. A large pine tree stood on the table, poking out of a small brown pot and scraping the cciling of the Archmage's office.

"How much did that drain you, Magc Delgar?" Velnan asked. "Do you feel tired at all?"

Delgar shook his head. "I feel fine. I feel a bit drained, but not much. I could easily do this again, if you wish."

Velnan leaned back and scratched his beard. "Well, your powers have grown, although whether it is from close exposure to the Gem of Sidhe or just the effect the gem has had on the Mageschool is in question. Did you find your magic amplified by the gem while it was in your possession?"

Delgar shook his head. "I didn't have an opportunity to make use of my powers. I walked in, picked up the gem, and made my way out. The only thing it took was willpower."

He glanced out the window, watching as a banner was raised from half-mast. Delgar had heard that Vertanus had left last week, shortly after Tomlin and Melina's funeral, but some students were still finding their spells to be stronger than usual. Jenara was taking it quite well, throwing herself into her work as much as Delgar was. But, they still gathered every night, sharing in each other's warmth as they grieved for their lost friends.

"Mage Delgar," Velnan interrupted, snapping him back to the present. "Please keep your attention on the moment. You will be free to go shortly. Now, I want you to shrink this pine tree back to the size of a sapling before it breaks the table."

Delgar concentrated, watching the streams of life swirl around the tree. He made a quick alteration and watched as the tree began to shrink, the branches shriveling and disappearing, until its sapling sat in the pot. He felt as though his powers had been drained slightly, but the feeling quickly passed.

Delgar blinked. "I felt drained for a moment, but then the power just came back."

"Are you certain?"

"Yes," Delgar said. "It was almost as if I was calling upon some hidden reserve."

Velnan looked down and grumbled something under his breath, then looked up again. "I wish I knew exactly what is going on. You have a level of power equal to an Archmage, even if you still have a great deal to learn. However, it may be temporary or permanent; only the Eternal One knows for certain. I will teach you based on your having half of these powers, I guess."

There was a knock at the door, and Velnan grumbled once again. "Who is it?"

"Mage Catrina," a female voice called. "I have a

message from the Chancellor."

Velnan rolled his eyes. "Oh, come in." The young woman poked her head through the door, flinching at Velnan's hostile gaze. "Well, be quick. I am trying to teach my student."

"I was told I should deliver this in confidence," Catrina said.

Velnan waved his hand dismissively. "This is my Archmage student, and you may say anything in front of him that you may in front of me. So speak, quickly. I have a lesson to finish."

"Archmage Tartarus has been seen following Vice-Chancellor Vertanus," Catrina reported, shooting a brief, but friendly look at Delgar. "Chancellor Berran has sent a messenger to warn him, but wishes to know if you have any further ideas."

Velnan shook his head. "I never should have accepted the position of acting Vice-Chancellor," he grumbled, then gazed at the young Mage. "Tell the Chancellor that I have every confidence that Vertanus can take care of himself, and that there is nothing else we can do that will help in time. All of this is my opinion, of course."

Mage Catrina nodded and slipped out of the office, closing the door quietly behind her. Velnan shook his head and turned back to Delgar.

"Who is Archmage Tartarus?" Delgar asked. "And why is he following the Vice-Chancellor, if I may ask?"

"You may ask," Velnan replied. "Archmage Tartarus was found to be worshiping the Damned One, and was expelled from the order of Archmages. I think he might have been one of Archmage Ignar's instructors, which may explain why Ignar came out the way he did. More importantly, it is possible that Tartarus wants the Gem of Sidhe."

"Is the Vice-Chancellor in danger?"

Velnan shook his head. "I doubt it. Tartarus may be dedicated to evil, but that does not make him very powerful. Vertanus is far more powerful, and could easily handle him. In fact, you could probably easily handle him. However, where the Gem of Sidhe is concerned, there is a concern, so we have done what we can."

The Archmage checked a sundial by his office window, then cursed under his breath. "I fear that our lesson must come to a close now; I have a novice class to teach in about ten minutes." He rose and stepped over to a bookshelf at the side of the office, pulling out several volumes. "I want you to learn the spells in each of these. We will review one spell per session, so this should take us until the end of term. And then we shall see if you are ready for Archmage status."

Delgar stood and took the books, nodding. "Thank you, sir." As he turned to leave, Velnan suddenly cleared his throat. Delgar spun, wondering what he had forgotten.

"And please give my regards to that young lady of yours," Velnan smiled. "Both of you seem to be wandering around the school looking rather glum."

Delgar smiled and nodded. Then he walked down the corridors, balancing the stack of books in his arms. He finally came to the door of Vice-Chancellor's Hall, and shouldered it open, taking a deep breath as the chill wind of late winter blew against him. Stopping at the top of the stone stairs for a moment, he tried to work out a way to bundle up without dropping any of his books, finally deciding to put them down. He placed them on the ground, just by the line of snow, and tightened his woolen robes.

"Dragonmage!" a voice called. Delgar startled and glanced around. A young man watched him from the bottom of the steps, snow matting his dark hair. Delgar leaned down and picked up the books, casting a small spell over them to keep them dry. Then he walked down the steps to where the young man stood.

"Excuse me," Delgar said. "Do I know you?"

"I'm new here," the man said. Delgar looked at him for a moment. Yes, he was definitely a novice. "You're the Dragonmage."

"I don't know what you mean," Delgar said, and then began to walk away. He heard the crunching of snow behind him, and the novice jogged up.

"You came here on a Dragon," the boy said. "A friend of mine in one of the outer villages saw you. That makes you a Dragonmage. The Dragonmage. I've never met somebody who rode Dragons before."

Delgar shook his head. "You probably never will. Everybody knows that Dragons keep away from people."

"Not from you. I'm Novice Gerant. May I shake your hand?"

Delgar stopped and looked at the boy. "My hands are rather full right now. Why are you bothering me?"

"There's a group of us," Gerant said. "We all love Dragons. And since you can ride them, you should join us. You'd fit right in!"

"No," Delgar declared, regarding the novice. "First of all, I have just lost one of my best friends, and my fiancé is waiting for me. Secondly, as you can see, I have a lot of work to do. Thirdly, even if I did ride a Dragon, do you really think I would let everybody know about it?"

The novice stared at Delgar for a moment, his eyes wide. "Go study," Delgar said. "Leave me be."

As the boy ran off, Delgar shook his head. He shouldn't have been so rude, but he really didn't have a lot of time. Jenara was waiting for him, and the pain of Tomlin's death still ached, piercing his heart as painfully as a crossbow bolt.

"What is happening to me?" Delgar wondered out loud. The novice had tried to burst into his personal life, but still, he had been rather rude to him. There had probably been some easier way of getting the boy to leave him alone, but he just hadn't had time for it. That seemed to be happening more often, Delgar realized. The only things he had time for anymore were Jenara and his studies; everything else had become unimportant.

He shrugged his shoulders. No permanent harm had been done, and he was already late for his meeting with Jenara. He bustled into his dormitory room to find that she was already there.

"Where were you?" she asked. Delgar noticed her eyes were bloodshot.

He put the books onto his study table. "I was delayed. Velnan was interrupted, and then some novice wanted me to join a Dragon club."

Suddenly, she hugged him passionately, and he held her close. "I thought I saw Tomlin and Melina today, walking hand in hand," she said. "It was just out of the corner of my eye, and when I turned to take a closer look, it was only some young couple. But it still hurt."

"I know," he said.

"Is it any easier for you?"

Delgar shook his head. "I try so hard not to think of them, but every time I close my eyes to go to sleep, I see their bodies in the Cave of Dreams. I can remember every little detail, and I wish by the Eternal One I couldn't."

She sniffled and pulled away from him. "Well, at least I had a good day before that. I passed my test."

Delgar smiled. "Almost a full Mage."

"I'll always be your Mistress," she said, a smile overcoming her sad features. Then she embraced him again.

He kissed her. "I was hoping you'd say that."

The weeks began to pass, but not nearly as quickly as they once had. Somehow, without Tomlin and Melina, something was missing, and Delgar found the work becoming dull. Still, there were some interesting things happening in his life.

The nickname of "Dragonmage" began to spread, until even Velnan chuckled over it. "You won't be able to shake it," the Archmage laughed. "Even if it wasn't true, you'll always be larger than life."

"I don't want to be larger than life," Delgar protested, crossing the floor to gaze out Velnan's office window.

"You were larger than life after you killed Ignar," Velnan said. "That got around quickly enough. And, given the choices, I think 'Dragonmage' is a better nickname than 'Magekiller'."

Delgar chuckled. "I guess you're right."

And then they began to get on with the lesson. To both Delgar's and Velnan's surprise, Delgar's power did not weaken with the loss of the Gem of Sidhe. Velnan could only conclude that Delgar's exposure to the gem had caused his powers to grow somehow, and that further study would be necessary.

But, in retrospect, it was on the first day of spring that everything changed. Delgar woke up in the morning, got dressed, and ambled across to Jenara's room. They had been sharing quarters since his encounter with Ignar, and Velnan had found a two bedroom suite for them. In light of Delgar's upbringing and Jenara's morals, they didn't share a bed yet, but Delgar looked forward to the day when they would.

He woke Jenara with a kiss on the cheek, and she embraced him, pulling him to the bed. They held each other for a moment, and then Delgar stepped out to let her get dressed. He sat down at his working desk, leaned back for a moment to enjoy the Saturday morning, and then began to read.

And then it hit him.

He suddenly felt his power drawn out of him, and he gasped for breath. The earth began to shake under his feet. He fell to the floor, and then he felt Jenara's arms around him. And then it all ceased.

He lay in her arms for a moment, his face white with shock. Slowly, his power began to return to him, but he still felt strongly overextended; with a start he realized that it would be at least a day before he was strong enough to cast any spell whatsoever.

"What happened?" Jenara asked, still in her night-robe. "I was getting out of bed, and then I suddenly felt drained, and then the earth started to shake. And then I rushed in, and you were on the floor..."

Delgar reached up and held her, using her warmth to steady himself. "I don't know, my love. I just don't know."

He struggled to his feet, pulling on a cloak. "I'm going to consult with Archmage Velnan," he said. "I shouldn't be long."

He hurried outside, where several students and Mages staggered around the grounds, their eyes dazed. Finally, he dashed into Vice-Chancellor's Hall, seeking Velnan's office. When he found the Archmage's office, he found Chancellor Berran already present.

"Come in, Delgar," Velnan puffed, his visage pale. "From the look on your face I see you felt it too."

"My office is filled with Archmages demanding to know what has happened," Berran said. "Three of our new Archmage graduates are overextended to the point where they may die."

Delgar raised his hand. "Does anybody know what happened?"

Velnan shook his head. "All we know is that somebody cast a spell. It was more powerful than anything we have ever seen, and it was so strong that we cannot even determine who cast it and where they are."

Delgar suddenly felt dizzy, and he leaned back against the door-frame. A memory popped into his mind, of what the Great Dragon had said after he had fought Ignar.

"Great events are coming, and we will need a protector."

A chill ran down Delgar's spine as the realization struck him. It had begun.

Chapter XXII: The Beginning of the End

Like the majority of the Mages in Taerra, Delgar's power returned to him slowly, a day at a time. Whatever the great spell had been, it had affected almost everybody. Classes had to be delayed as the instructors regained their strength, and those few Archmages who were able to regain their power quickly found themselves trying unsuccessfully to scry out the spell.

For Delgar, it had become a matter of waiting. Velnan still taught him as much theory as he could, but there were no practical experiments. Even making a small plant grow taxed his energy.

"Odd," Velnan observed one morning, watching the morning sun peak through the clouds. "You seem to be recovering at the same rate as an Archmage. Most of my undergraduate students have fully recovered."

"Why could that be?" Delgar said.

Velnan scratched his beard. "It could simply be a matter of how much power you have. Most Archmages have much more power than a Mage, and thus take longer to recover their power. However, I find your slow recovery quite odd."

"But I do have a lot of power," Delgar said.

Velnan shook his head. "It should not be taxing you to make a potted plant grow by two inches. At any rate, we will see how long it takes you to recover. Now, onto our lesson."

And so it went. The weeks began to pass, and Delgar's power gradually returned under Velnan's watchful eye. Jenara's classes resumed, and she began to live a furious life in their rooms, more often out than in. Delgar found himself frustrated, as more and more he wanted her soothing presence, but she was too busy. Often, their only time together was in the late evenings, when they held each other and talked about their days before retiring to their rooms to prepare for early mornings.

As the spring began to pass into summer, Delgar finally felt his full powers return. This prompted an afternoon meeting with Archmage Velnan and Chancellor Berran, and Delgar found himself in the Chancellor's office answering questions Velnan had already asked several times.

"Considering the power of the spell and Delgar's reaction, I think we can assume the Gem of Sidhe is involved," Berran declared, scratching his beard.

Delgar blinked. "I don't understand."

"This spell was powerful," Berran stated. "Powerful enough that we still cannot penetrate its shield, although it is possible that it is simply so large that we cannot see all of it."

"But I don't understand what that has to do with my powers," Delgar said.

Velnan leaned forward, the leather padding on his chair creaking. "Your increased powers suggests that in your close proximity to the Gem of Sidhe, you became linked to it somehow. Now, the gem bolstered your powers, but when the spell hit, all of us were drained. However, you recovered much more slowly than any of us, suggesting that you are still being drained somehow, even now."

"And the only way we can see of such a spell coming into being," Berran cut in, "is if it was created using the Gem of Sidhe. Not even a circle of Archmages working in tandem could cast a spell like this."

"Have we been able to contact Vice-Chancellor Vertanus?" Velnan asked, turning to Berran.

The Chancellor shook his head. "The messenger we sent to warn him about Tartarus discovered Vertanus' baggage destroyed. There were several scorch marks, but not enough to be able to ascertain exactly what happened. We had been hoping that Vertanus would send a messenger to check in, but that hasn't happened yet."

"Then it is possible that Tartarus has taken the Gem of Sidhe," Velnan said. "If so, Vertanus may be dead. Have some of our scryes been able to locate the gem?"

Berran shook his head once again. "It is shielded along with the spell."

"If Delgar is linked to the gem, then perhaps he can be a conduit to locating it," Velnan suggested. "Would you be willing to do this, Delgar?"

Delgar nodded. "Of course. When should we begin?"

"If you can wait five minutes, I'll fetch Archmage Perrina," Berran said, rising. "I'll be right back."

Delgar waited, watching Velnan fidget with his thumbs. Finally, Berran came back into the office, followed by a slim, dark skinned woman with greying hair.

"Delgar, this is Archmage Perrina," Berran said, motioning to the woman. "Just follow her instructions."

Perrina pulled a chair from the wall and sat, facing

Delgar and staring into his eyes for a moment. She blinked in shock, then turned to the Chancellor. "He has the most remarkable wyrd," she said. "I'm not sure how to get around it."

"If Delgar concentrates, it should move aside for you," Berran said. "This is rare, but cases have been recorded before."

Perrina nodded and turned to Delgar. "Mage Delgar," she said, taking his hands. "I want you to hold my hands and concentrate. I want you to clear your mind, and then to think only of the Gem of Sidhe."

"Do I have to close my eyes?" Delgar asked.

She shook her head. "You can if you want to, but most Mages don't have to."

Delgar shut his eyes, framing Jenara and his lost friends in his mind's eye, and then pressing them aside. His lessons sprung up in his memory, and then his encounters with the Dragons, but he pushed them away too. Finally, his mind was clear. He began to visualize the Gem of Sidhe, every facet, the way that a part of the world was reflected in every surface. Then he opened his eyes.

"I'm ready," he said.

She closed her eyes. Suddenly he felt her inside his mind, probing around the image of the gem. She muttered something and magical lines began to form in his intellect, tracing around the image of the Gem of Sidhe. They came to a link, a thin thread of magical power, and then her presence began to slide down it, passing through his being as though he was merely a shade.

Suddenly, the thread snapped, his head pounding as he felt the link recoil in his mind. Archmage Perrina's eyes shot open in shock, and Delgar startled in fear. Her hands began to wither before him, her smooth skin wrinkling with age. Her mouth gaped open like a landed fish, gasping for air.

217

"Ice," she gasped, and then fell over, a withered old crone. Delgar stared in shock at the wrinkled corpse. He looked to his mentor to see Velnan's mouth hanging open.

Chancellor Berran was the first to recover. "What did she mean, 'ice'? Did she need it, did she see it?"

Delgar shook his head. "I felt her go down the connection to the gem, but suddenly it snapped. Then she began to...age."

Berran cursed under his breath. "That makes two confirmed fatalities from this spell."

"What?" Delgar said, glancing from one Archmage to the other.

"One of the overextended Archmages died last week," Velnan replied. "We've tried to keep it from becoming public knowledge."

"You say that the connection has snapped?" Berran asked.

Delgar nodded. "I can't feel it anymore. My powers also feel slightly weaker."

Berran frowned. "Then we must continue trying with our old methods. You may as well rest, Mage Delgar. Your studies call you, and I doubt there is much you can do to help us for some time."

Delgar nodded and left. As he closed the door, he heard Velnan and Berran talking quietly.

"And if this spell is both large and hidden?" Velnan asked.

"Then we may be in very serious trouble very soon," came the reply.

That weekend, Delgar managed to convince Jenara to take some time off and rest with him. The sun rose early in the morning to reveal a cloudless sky, a perfect day for a picnic.

They spent the morning packing their lunch, placing sandwiches and fresh fruit into a wicker basket. Then they wandered out of the city, Delgar ignoring several shouts of "Dragonmage!" as some novices tried to get his attention. After all, as he had said to Jenara earlier, it would be their day off, and some time for both of them to be together alone.

They walked arm in arm through the market, Delgar holding the basket in his left hand and Jenara in his right. Several merchants tried to call them over, brandishing cloth or fruit, but Delgar and Jenara merely strode on, making their way for the hills outside of town.

By the time they got out of town and made their way to an isolated hill, the midday sun was high in the sky, framed by wispy white clouds. They spread a blanket on the ground and then settled into it, alternating between eating their lunch and holding each other close. Finally, as they began to work on the last of their lunch, they started talking about magic.

"So what is Archmage Velnan teaching you right now?" Jenara asked.

Delgar crunched down on an apple. "Healing magic," he said as clearly as he could. Then he swallowed. "For example, if somebody is wounded or poisoned, how to heal them."

Jenara blinked, swallowing a piece of her own apple. "Does this mean you could bring people back to life, or just heal them?"

"Just heal," Delgar said, shivering as a chill wind washed over him. "No Archmage can create life by magical means; it's impossible. Nor can an Archmage restore life. There must be a certain amount of life left in a body for healing magic to work."

"How do you mean?" Jenara asked, placing her apple core in the basket.

Delgar shrugged. "Well, Archmage Velnan described it like trying to fan the embers of a fire. If the embers are not strong enough, then the fire will die, regardless of how hard you fan them. The same with healing magic."

"What about disease?" Jenara said, pulling out another apple and biting into its lush green skin.

"I haven't finished learning that section, but from what I've seen, it depends on the disease. If it is chronic, like cancer or leprosy, then there is nothing I can do except make the patient comfortable and perhaps slow the disease. If it is something contagious, such as plague, then it can be cured."

A low growl sounded towards the bottom of the hill. Delgar and Jenara startled, Delgar dropping the apple and rising.

"Did you hear that?" he asked.

She nodded.

The growl became a roar, and a large creature raced up the hill. Delgar and Jenara gasped when they saw its gaunt frame, the skull-like face, the glowing green eyes. They had heard of it many times before, but never seen one: it was a lesser demon.

Jenara recovered first, raising her magical guard with a quick gesture. Delgar shook his head free of fear and raised his hands, preparing a spell. The demon bounded toward them and leapt forward.

Jenara's bolt of energy smashed into it, driving it backwards. She followed up with a ball of fire, knocking the monster down. The creature stood up again and bellowed in rage.

"How do you kill it?" Jenara shouted, sweat matting her robes.

Delgar shook his head, trying desperately to remember Velnan's brief lesson on demons. Delgar finally began to weave a cage out of the currents in the air, hoping to contain it. At the very least, it would buy them some time.

The Demon crashed through the cage, only to be struck by another of Jenara's energy bolts. It staggered back and howled, baring razor teeth and claws.

"Can we outrun it?" Jenara asked, her voice trembling.

"I don't think so," Delgar said, trying to keep his own words steady.

Suddenly, the memory snapped back into place. "Any demon's link to life is its heart," Velnan had said. "Even cutting off its head will only slow it down. If you can destroy its heart, however, you can kill it or send it back to where it came."

"Strike for its chest!" Delgar declared. "If we can burn out its heart, we can destroy it!"

They began to fire balls of energy and flame at the creature, striking it directly in the chest. The creature howled as they kept firing, clutching at its body in anguish as its skin peeled back to reveal its rib cage. With a snap, the bones shattered. Delgar gazed upon its beating heart, slowly covering up as the demon healed itself. The creature roared and began to charge, claws outstretched.

Delgar and Jenara both fired at once. The creature stopped in its tracks, falling to its knees as it pawed at the charred hole in its chest where its heart once lay. Its eyes went wide and then dimmed, the creature falling to the ground less than three feet away from Delgar and Jenara. Delgar leaned forward, but then leapt back as the demon's body erupted into white hot flame.

Finally, the fire died, leaving only ashes. Delgar and Jenara stared at it in shock, holding each other for comfort. He turned to look at her, only to find sweat matting her face and clothes. "I feel so tired," she moaned.

Delgar nodded. "Me too." Concerned, he looked her over; the battle hadn't drained too many of his own powers, but she had clearly overextended herself. "Do you feel up to walking, my love?"

She nodded. "I think I can make it."

She leaned against him as they made their way back into the city. A couple of people whistled, obviously thinking that he had gotten her drunk, but he ignored them. Jenara had to rest, or she could find herself in serious trouble. She shuddered for a moment as he remembered when he had overextended himself almost to death.

Archmage Velnan was waiting for them at the iron gates of the Mageschool, his eyes stern. The look vanished when he saw the state they were in. "By the Eternal One!" he exclaimed. "Whatever happened to you two?"

"We were attacked by a lesser demon," Delgar said, noting the look of surprise on Velnan's face. "We managed to kill it, but Jenara overextended herself."

"Let me see her," Velnan directed, stepping close to Jenara. He gazed into her eyes, then held her hand. "You're right, Mage Delgar. Mistress Jenara, you have overextended yourself, and I hope you never do it again. Happily, you have not overextended yourself badly, and you should feel fine in a day or two."

Delgar shook his head. "I don't know where it came from. I just don't. One minute we were relaxing and eating our lunch, the next thing we knew we were under attack."

"And you destroyed its heart?"

Delgar nodded.

"Well, I fear that I must add misery to your day by delivering a summons," Velnan said. "Chancellor Berran wishes to speak to you in the courtyard outside Vice-Chancellor's Hall immediately."

Delgar blinked. "What's the problem?"

"Well," Velnan said, pausing as if he was trying to find the words. "He would like you to explain precisely why a Great Dragon has landed in the middle of the courtyard asking for you by name."

Chapter XXIII: A Call to Arms

The first thing Delgar realized when he saw the Dragon sitting sagely outside Vice-Chancellor's hall was just how much of a disruption it was. A large crowd had gathered around the wyrm, and the Chancellor paced back and forth in front of it with an impatient look on his face. Delgar stepped down into the courtyard, helping Jenara as they wound their way through the crowd. Several of the younger students looked at Delgar and nodded, only receiving a dismissive gesture in return.

They finally came to Chancellor Berran, who stopped pacing as they approached. The Archmage waved Delgar over, his face red with frustration. "I hope you can explain yourself, Mage Delgar!" he nearly shouted. "Just about every class scheduled for today has been completely disrupted. And examinations are approaching in the next month; this is not something we need."

"I'm sorry," Delgar said carefully. "But I didn't expect to be visited like this. We were just relaxing outside of town, and..."

Berran shook his head and turned to Velnan. "Vice-Chancellor Velnan, would you please disperse this crowd? Perhaps we can salvage what little is left of today."

Jenara suddenly clutched Delgar, squeezing him tightly. "It's a Dragon," she said. "A real Dragon! I had no idea."

As the murmurs of the crowd dimmed and finally ceased, Velnan bustled back before the Chancellor and Delgar. "I've been able to convince most of them that they will be able to look at the Dragon later," he said. "That should hold them off long enough for us to determine what is happening here."

Delgar stared at the Dragon, realizing with a start that he recognized it. "Leoht'heortan!" he exclaimed. "What has brought you here?"

"I have come seeking you, Delgar Dragonfriend," the Dragon declared. "We are in need of you."

Jenara startled at his side. "You know this Dragon?"

Delgar nodded. "He saved me in the desert when I was stranded. I owe him my life."

Chancellor Berran stepped forward. "Excuse me, but I believe that I am entitled to some sort of explanation. What has happened that has made it necessary for you to reveal yourself to us, Great One?"

Delgar blinked and turned to Berran. "Do you mean that the Mageschool knows the Dragons?"

"Of course we know the Dragons," Berran said. "From the earliest days of magic the Archmages of Mideorth have had contact with the Great Dragons. However, it has been a closely kept secret among the ranks of the Archmages, until now. After this landing we will be lucky to keep the news contained within the country."

"We are threatened," Leoht'heortan stated. "A great wall of ice has swept down from the north, destroying all before it. Many of us have been forced to leave our homes and flee south. But some of us are unable to flee, for they are small and relatively weak. And soon they will be in grave danger."

Delgar shuddered at the news, a plethora of old dreams and nightmares flashing through his mind. "Which Dragons are threatened?"

Leoht'heortan turned to regard Delgar. "You aided their kind once, and for that you were declared Dragonfriend."

"The Teraeni Dragons," Delgar realized.

"They are small, and cannot flee the ice. Nor can they survive in the only places they could flee too. Therefore we must call you to battle."

Jenara shook her head. "Why him? Why can't somebody else go?"

"Who are you?" the Dragon demanded.

"She's my, er, mate," Delgar replied.

"Then she has some claim on you," Leoht'heortan said.

"Yes," Jenara stated. "He's my love, and I don't want to lose him again."

"Then you must understand that he is a Dragonfriend," the wyrm said. "And while all Dragonkind have an obligation to him, he also has an obligation to us. We have never before called a mortal to battle with us, but we have never before been in such peril."

"What is this danger you speak of?" Berran demanded.

The Dragon turned his head to regard the Archmage. "The ice drinks all life it touches. I have personally seen trees wither and break, watched as countless animals and mortals were ground under it. It is not natural."

"This is linked to the great spell," Velnan realized. "It has to be."

Berran nodded. "So now we know what it does."

"It is moving quickly, as though it wishes to consume the world," Leoht'heortan said. "All Dragonkind is at risk, for none may touch it and live."

"How large is the glacier now?" Berran asked.

"It has consumed almost all of the land you call 'Nordland'," the Dragon replied.

Delgar swallowed in horror, a tear rolling down his cheek. If Nordland was gone, then he could never return to his homeland. The loss felt like a crushing weight, nearly so large as to be undefinable. Jenara held him for a moment as he sobbed, lost as the Dragon and Archmages held council.

"That confirms it, then," Berran stated. "Even if he was not killed when the Gem was stolen, Vertanus is dead. His tower was in the north of Nordland."

"If that is the case then it cannot be too long until Taerraland is also in danger," Velnan said. "We should send as many Archmages as we can."

Berran shook his head. "Half our number are on sabbatical, and we don't know exactly what this wall of ice is yet. We should recall our Archmages, and then attack this problem with our full strength, rather than half of it."

"So we use Delgar as a scout," Velnan said.

"Yes."

Delgar cleared his throat and raised himself to his full height, facing the Dragon. "I will go with you."

Jenara held him tightly. "But I don't want to lose you! Every time you go away like this you return hurt. How long will it be before something kills you or worse?"

Chancellor Berran turned to face her. "Mistress Jenara, I cannot think of any safer company than the company of Dragons."

Delgar kissed her. "This thing has destroyed my homeland. I have to at least see what it is. And

Leoht'heortan is right: I do have an obligation." He turned to the Dragon. "How many of the Great Dragons will be there?"

"All."

Delgar blinked. "All?"

"Yes, all. All of Dragonkind is at risk, and all of us must fight. Not since the time of the Dragon Masters has there been such a threat to our kind."

"Mage Delgar, we need to know what this threat is," Berran said. "Discover all you can, and report it back to us. If the Dragon is correct, then all of Mideorth is threatened. If the Dragons fail, then we will take our own measures. Do you understand?"

Delgar nodded. "Yes, I understand." Then he embraced Jenara. "My love, when I return, I will not leave you again."

She pressed herself close to him. "I'll hold you to that promise. Take care of yourself."

He pulled back from her and faced the Dragon. "How long will it take us to get to the ice?"

"A matter of hours only. The others are almost assembled, and will be by the time we get there."

Delgar nodded. "Then we should depart now."

The Dragon lowered its neck, and Delgar began to climb on. As he did, Velnan grasped him by the sleeve of his robe. "Be careful, Mage Delgar," the Archmage said. "We'll need your help when you return to us."

"I will be back as soon as I can," Delgar declared as Leoht'heortan lifted his neck and flexed his wings. "With luck, I will be able to tell you that this wall of ice has been destroyed."

At that moment, the Dragon took flight, soaring over the Mageschool. Delgar gazed back to see Jenara standing in the courtyard, tears streaming down her eyes. He grimaced, a solitary tear joining hers. Then he stared ahead as the land raced beneath them, his gut feeling as though it was coiling itself in a knot.

"You love her a great deal, don't you?" Leoht'heortan said, beating his powerful wings.

"I hadn't thought you noticed," Delgar shouted, trying to talk above the howling of the wind as they picked up speed.

"Any who cared to look could see it," the Dragon said. "You feel some pain right now. It is in your voice."

"Yes," Delgar replied. "I hate having to leave her like this."

"Even for immortals parting is never easy. It would not be love if it was."

Delgar merely nodded and looked ahead. Trees passed below him, and after a while they crossed the long wall marking the frontier between Taerraland and Pakaria.

"Where are we going?" Delgar finally asked.

"To the north of the land you call Pakaria," Leoht'heortan replied. "There we will find the Teraeni Dragons and the wall of ice. I only hope we are not too late."

Delgar gazed ahead once again. The trees had given way to plains, and once again turned to forest. Then he saw a strange glow on the horizon, almost as if a blue sun was rising.

"What is that?" he called.

"What?"

"That odd glow."

"That is the wall of ice," the Dragon replied. "We will stop before we reach it."

As they approached, the glow on the horizon grew, becoming a malignant blue strip overshadowing the trees. Several specks appeared in the air before it, dodging and weaving with incredible grace. As they came closer, Delgar managed to make out what they were.

Dragons. Hundreds of Dragons.

Leoht'heortan flew through them, the great wyrms soaring past them in the sky. Finally, the Great Dragon set down in the trees, allowing Delgar to get down and stretch. Once again, he found his back and legs aching from the long trip.

Several Teraeni Dragons settled in the trees around him. Delgar bowed, hoping that it was a polite way to introduce himself.

"We have heard of you," one chirped. "Relara has told us of your aid in the past."

"I hope to aid again shortly," Delgar said. "I will do everything I can."

The Teraeni Dragon gazed at him for a moment. "We know you will," it said, and then took wing.

"This is the home of the Teraeni Dragons," Leoht'heortan stated. "This is where we shall make our stand. A great evil has come upon us, and called us all to battle. I fear the fate of the world may be decided on this day."

Delgar looked around. To the north he saw the ribbon of the ice bearing steadily down on him. A cold wind ruffled his robes. He shuddered for a moment, full of dread. Then he looked up, and his heart soared.

The sky was filled with thousands of Dragons.

Chapter XXIV: The Glacier

Leoht'heortan took him to a mountain at the very southern end of the range leading into Pakaria. Several Great Dragons perched on the peak, watching the oncoming wall of ice. The others filled the sky, so great in number that they nearly blocked out the sun. Without a word Delgar dismounted and stood at the edge of a large cliff, gazing at the glacier as it towered over the landscape. He shook his head; it had to be at least three thousand feet tall, if only that little.

From the glacier came a strange pull, almost as if it was drawing him in. With a start, he realized that if he so much as touched it, the ice would absorb his life. He looked down at where the ice met the earth, watching as several trees withered and shattered as the glacier touched them. He glanced to the south to see the valley of the Teraeni Dragons, laid open to the onslaught of the ice.

"It will only be a matter of hours before it is upon our smaller cousins," Leoht'heortan said. "We must act quickly."

"How many can be evacuated?" Delgar asked.

"None," the Great Dragon replied. "They cannot fly high enough to get away, nor are they willing to leave their homes. We have tried for some time to convince them."

"It's huge," Delgar stammered. "How do we stop something that big?"

"We fight," Leoht'heortan said. "With all of our strength, we strike until it is destroyed. Will you lead us, Delgar Dragonfriend?"

Delgar blinked. "Me?"

"The only leader of our kind was my father, Fleot'heortan," the Dragon explained. "The ice drank his life and soul; we all felt his passing. None of us now are strong enough to dominate over the others. However, all will follow a Dragonfriend. You have performed great service for us, and we all know of you. Will you lead us in this fight?"

Delgar stared at the glacier, watching as it crushed through the forest, just as it had his homeland. He nodded. "I will lead you. I need a moment, though."

"Take as long as you need, but be quick," Leoht'heortan said. "Our time is running short."

Delgar knelt on the cold rock, the chill biting into his legs. He ignored it, turning his mind toward a god he had rarely worshiped. "Eternal One," he prayed. "You have given me so much, and now it is threatened. My homeland has been destroyed, and I can feel the evil behind the ice. I must go into a battle I barely know how to fight, and I must beg for your protection. So much is now at stake, for this abomination drinks life itself. Please grant me protection and victory. Grant me vengeance for my homeland, protection for my loved ones and friends, and victory for the world. For I fear that if this fight is lost, then it is the end of Mideorth."

As he opened his eyes, a power surrounded him. With a shock, he realized his wyrd was coiling around him, providing a strength he wouldn't have had otherwise. He gritted his teeth as cold anger flowed through his heart. With a leap, he mounted Leoht'heortan.

"Great Dragons!" he bellowed, his voice amplified by magic, his words echoing across the landscape. "In the name of Garasus the Greater One, in the name of the Teraeni Dragons, and in the name of all Mideorth and the Great Road, attack!"

There was a great roar. As if they were part of one enormous cloud, the Dragons all leapt into the air, bearing down on the glacier. Delgar felt the cold wind racing past his face as Leoht'heortan dove down upon the ice, a deafening battle-cry roaring from his mouth.

The Dragon swept down, breathing a long jet of flame onto the ice. As he glided back out for another pass, Delgar spun around to see giant cracks appearing in the glacier, but almost immediately closing again. At least two Dragons brushed past the ice, falling dead to the ground as the glacier's pulsing glow grew.

Leoht'heortan made another pass, striking at the ice with a great roar. As flame exploded from his mouth, breaking chunks of ice off the glacier, Delgar began to fire bolts of energy, the spells splashing off the rough hewn blue-white cliff, small pieces of ice breaking and falling to the ground. Leoht'heortan broke off, gliding over the surface of the glacier to come around once again for another strike. As he did, Delgar watched in horror as several Dragons fell slain to the ground, struck by flying pieces of ice.

"Don't let any of the ice touch you!" Delgar shouted, magically amplifying his voice. And then his mount charged into the fray once again.

Leoht'heortan dove towards the glacier once again,

white-hot flame streaming from his maw, the heat causing large chunks of the ice to erupt from the side of the glacier. Delgar shot several spells at it, but to his dismay the glow of the ice had not faded at all throughout the onslaught. It had grown much brighter.

As his mount banked away to make another pass, Delgar suddenly saw a large crack break through the surface of the glacier, splitting the cliff almost to the ground. Delgar pointed. "Concentrate your fire there! Concentrate your fire there! We have it!"

As he watched, several Dragons broke away from the cliff to bear on the crack. The crack became a vent of flame as the wyrms each flew in, fire streaming from their mouths. Suddenly, to Delgar's horror, the crack began to close, the ice groaning under the pressure as it moved.

"Get out of there!" Delgar screamed. "It's a trap! Get out of there!"

The chasm shut, only a couple of the Great Dragons escaping. A single wing lay forlorn on the surface of the ice, the only remains of a Dragon unable to escape the closure. The ice blazed even brighter, fed by the life of so many Dragons.

The cliff suddenly erupted, enormous chunks of ice spraying out into the mass of Dragons. Delgar felt a pull on his life energy as a block of ice sailed past his head, impacting on a Dragon behind him. A great scream erupted from the Dragons as they were pelted with the deadly missiles, the wyrms falling to the earth in pain and death.

Delgar shook his head, desperate to clear the ringing in his ears. Somehow, the Dragon's roaring hadn't bothered him, but the crashing of the glacier had momentarily deafened him. He glanced around to see the sky almost clear, most of the remaining Dragons keeping a careful distance from the ice. Finally, the ringing stopped

233

and Leoht'heortan's voice crashed into his ears.

"-ragonfriend, are you hurt?" the wyrm was asking. "We cannot stand against it now! More than three quarters of us are dead! We must flee!"

Delgar shook his head once again, trying to sort out what he was hearing. "What of the Teraeni?" he asked, hoping he hadn't heard correctly.

"We cannot help them now," Leoht'heortan fumed. "The ice has absorbed the life of so many of the best of us that we cannot stand against it. The Teraeni are lost. But we will have revenge! By the blood of Garasus I swear it!"

Delgar shook his head, barely comprehending what was going on. It had to be a setback; that's all it could be. For if they had truly lost, then the whole of the world could be destroyed. Finally, his shoulders slouched in defeat. "Let's go. We will fight another day."

He was barely conscious of the ground passing under him, until Leoht'heortan landed with a large portion of the surviving Dragons around him. Delgar dismounted and gazed around in dismay.

He stood on a large hill overlooking the distant valley of the Teraeni Dragons. As he watched, the glacier began to crush through the trees, eliciting a chorus of draconic screams. The ice pulsed bright blue, and then the screams stopped. The glacier continued pushing through the valley, moving even faster than before.

And on the hill, all was silence.

Leoht'heortan was the first to speak. "We have lost some of the best of us. They have gone, never to return."

Another Dragon stepped forward, its rough voice grating to Delgar's ear. "We will always remember them, even after we have left. But the time has come for our protector."

Leoht'heortan shook his head. "I had hoped to delay it as much as possible."

"You have seen his wyrd," the other Dragon declared. "He is the one."

"We all know it is not easy for mortals. He should have as much time as one as he can."

"It may already be too late. He has much to learn."

"What are you talking about?" Delgar demanded. "Are you talking about me?"

Leoht'heortan turned to him, a sad glint in his eyes. "Yes. Your wyrd has overcome you, I fear. Dragonkind has now entered a time of great need, and we require a protector. This has only been bestowed on two individuals before, back when the cycle was young."

"Is it an honor?" Delgar asked. "What is it?"

"Perhaps," the Dragon said. "I think it more likely to be a curse. You must now make a decision. We need a protector for the dark years ahead. One who will not falter on our behalf. One who will endure immortality for as long as he must. One who will accept great power for little or no reward. One who has your wyrd." His neck craned so that he looked at Delgar eye to eye. "Will you accept this task, Delgar Dragonfriend?"

Delgar looked down into the silent valley, watching as the lethal ice continued its slow voyage across the earth. "Will I be able to save the world?"

"In the end, yes," came the reply. "But it may take a very long time."

"And will I be able to stay with Jenara?"

"Your mate?"

"Yes."

"So long as she will come with you, yes."

"Then I will accept this gift," Delgar said. "What must I do?"

"Hold out your hand," Leoht'heortan said.

Delgar did what he was told, taking a deep breath to steady himself. With a quick motion the Dragon caught the

Mage's hand in his huge talon, cutting deeply into Delgar's palm. Delgar grunted as the blood began to flow. "What are you doing?!"

With his hind leg, Leoht'heortan sliced open his own wrist, holding it over Delgar's hand. Several large drops of his blood fell onto Delgar's hand, mixing with the fleshy wound. He was suddenly aware of the Dragons standing around him, staring expectantly.

And then the pain came. The burning started in his wound, searing up his arm. He gasped as he watched the skin char and crack, the wounds bleeding in a crimson rain. As he fell to the ground, he heard Leoht'heortan chanting.

"Facio te Magum Draconum, defensor omni draconum. Immortalis oritus est mortalitas. Viator in via fabularum. Is qui videbit per centurias ad opus eius perfectus est. Is qui unum ex nobis non est. Is qui optimum ex nobis est. Is qui Melium Draconem est, qui sanguen Garasi ferit. Facio te Delgar, Magus Draconum."

The pain became overpowering. Delgar curled into a ball, his insides burning, consumed by an incredible fire. He felt his skin changing, the old charred wreckage flaking off to be replaced by something new. His gasp became a scream. Then the burning entered his head, flowing behind his eyes, and his world went red.

The meaning of Leoht'heortan's chant flowed into his mind, accompanied by memories of places long passed. *I name you Magus Draconum, protector of all Dragonkind. The immortal born of mortality. The traveller on the Road of Legends. He who will see through the centuries until his task is done. He who is not one of us. He who is the greatest of us. He who is the Greater Dragon, who bears the blood of Garasus. I name you Delgar, the Dragonmage.* A great battle sprung into his head, and he was at the head of a mighty army of Dragons and beings of all sizes, fighting against an invincible foe in a rebellion across a thousand worlds. But he won, of course, for he was Garasus, the greatest of Dragonkind. And then he was declining and a new identity consumed him. A huge force of demons stood before him, and the Dragons charged around him. Blood splattered the earth, and he felt his wyrd coiling around him. He drew a great sword, raising it in his talons and roaring in laughter as his enemies quaked in fear. For he was Vetarius, the Greater Dragon, the one who was Garasus. But then he too declined, waning as he became old and lonely.

The pain ceased. Delgar opened his eyes and stood, feeling his charred clothing rasping against his tender new skin. He startled in shock. He looked around to see the glacier stretching far beyond the horizon. To the west he saw the long border fortifications of Taerraland snaking off into the distance, while a small raiding army tried to approach it from the far south. As he gazed around, he became aware of something pulsing just behind his eyes, promising power greater than anything he had ever experienced. And it was a part of him, inside him. He concentrated and saw the currents of air passing before him, more obvious than they had ever been. He glanced down to see the power of the earth, just waiting for him to seize and manipulate it. Then he blinked, and the currents were gone.

He turned to look at Leoht'heortan and the other Dragons gathered around him. "What has happened to me?" he rasped, blinking as he realized how sore his throat was.

"You have become one of us," the Dragon replied. "You bear our blood in your veins now. You are immortal and powerful. It will take you years to learn your full potential, but you have time. You are the most powerful creature on all of Mideorth, and perhaps on the Great Road itself. You are Magus Draconum, the protector of all Dragonkind. You are the Dragonmage."

As the rest of the Dragons took flight, leaving Leoht'heortan and Delgar alone on the hill, one question lingered in Delgar's mind.

And what of my humanity?

Part II
Delgar Dragonmage

Chapter I: Aftermath

Delgar stared down from his mount, watching the ground race by underneath him. For the tenth time he tried to tap into the strange new presence lingering in the back of his consciousness, but without success. He felt the Dragon blood pulsing behind his eyes, but when he tried to touch it with his mind it became distant.

He looked behind to where the fight had been. Without the strange change which had come over him, he would never have been able to see that far away. However, with the new powers of sight, he watched as the glacier slowed to a crawl once more, only slightly faster than it had once been. The blue-white ribbon dwindled on the horizon, finally disappearing under the new clouds.

"There will be rain," Delgar observed dispassionately. "The battle released a lot of vapor into the air." He tried to feel something, something other than shock at this transformation. Somehow, he couldn't. He knew that he would never be the same again, that he would live forever.

But the full impact he had expected never arrived.

Had he grown used to it already? Or was he just trying not to, holding back in case there was some way to never deal with it?

He shook his head, noticing the long grey ribbon of the border wall between Taerraland and Pakaria stretch beneath him. He breathed a sigh of relief. Leoht'heortan was taking him home, or at least to the last home he had left.

"What will become of me?" Delgar asked. "What will your kind need of me?"

"Our kind," the Dragon corrected, flapping his wings. "You must grow into your powers. It will take years, and you must learn on your own. We will come for you when we need you again."

"When will that be?"

"We can no longer stay here," Leoht'heortan stated. "This ice threatens the last of our kind. So, when the time comes, we will all leave. And you will lead us."

"I don't understand. Where will we go?"

He could swear the Dragon was smiling. "You will understand when the time is right. Until then, you should enjoy what remains of your life. Great events have come, and you must play a large part in them. When we need you, we will come for you."

Delgar gazed ahead to see the city of Taerra stretching across the plain, quiet and peaceful. He shook his head, marveling at the innocence. But he knew it would not last now; it was unlikely that all the Archmages in Mideorth could do anything about the glacier now; the realization twisted his stomach into a cold knot.

Leoht'heortan set down in the courtyard in front of Vice-Chancellor's Hall. Both Archmage Velnan and Jenara were waiting for him. As he stepped down from his mount, Jenara leapt into his arms, holding him tight.

"I was worried about you," she murmured, pressing her head against his breast.

"I told you I'd be back," Delgar said, trying to smile. Somehow, he couldn't bring himself to do it.

"Mage Delgar, you are required," Velnan declared. "Chancellor Berran awaits you in his office."

Delgar nodded and wrapped an arm around Jenara's waist. "Come, my love. We have a meeting."

Velnan held up his hand. "This meeting is for you alone."

Delgar stopped. "This involves her too."

"Not right now it doesn't."

"I'm not going in without her."

"I'll wait outside," Jenara said.

Delgar looked at her. "Are you certain?"

"You'll tell me everything I need to know anyway," she said. "And the sooner you're out of there, the sooner we can be together. I'm holding you to your promise."

Delgar nodded. "Okay. We'll have to talk once I'm out of the meeting."

She smiled and kissed him, her eyes softening in concern when he didn't kiss back. "You be well."

"I will."

"We couldn't do a thing," Delgar fumed. Velnan and Chancellor Berran had listened patiently as he had recounted the battle, leaving out his transformation at the end. Some things they didn't need to know about. "It destroyed the Teraeni Dragons without even slowing down. It slowed down a bit once the destruction was complete, but not much."

Velnan nodded. "Then we have a definite problem. This glacier is stronger than before."

"Archmage Velnan, I want you to see to it that the

scryes discover how long we have," Berran ordered. "I want to know if it is weeks, months, or years."

"Yes, Chancellor."

"And place an urgent priority on the recall to all the Archmages."

"Can an army of Archmages accomplish what Dragonfire can't?" Delgar asked.

Velnan shook his head. "I don't know, Mage Delgar. I don't think anybody does. Nobody has ever encountered anything like this before."

"We have to try," Berran said. "We have an obligation to our host city, if nothing else. And if we fail, then we may have to hide."

Delgar shook his head sadly. "You can't hide from this thing. We ran away after it killed most of the Dragons, but it is still coming after us."

"If we can't stop this ice, then we will have to salvage what knowledge of the world remains," Berran said. "To do that, we may have to hide. Perhaps for a long time."

"Can we seek the Dragons' help in leaving Mideorth?" Velnan asked. "Mage Delgar said that they are planning to leave."

"The Dragons have tolerated our inquiries, but they have never given us any true secrets," Berran replied. "We can try to ask their aid, but I doubt they will lend it."

"I am a Dragonfriend," Delgar said. "Perhaps I can help there."

"You are much more than that," the Chancellor stated. "You've kept something from us. What is it?"

"I don't understand what you mean."

"Any Archmage is a creature of power," Velnan said, stepping forward. "And one creature of power can always sense another. You have become so powerful that we both sensed your coming from almost ten miles away."

"And even that felt like somebody shouting in our

ears," the Chancellor added. "So what has happened to you?"

Delgar swallowed. "They changed me. They put Dragon blood into me, and...that changed me. I don't really understand what has happened to me myself."

He saw Velnan's eyes widen in surprise. "You've become a true Dragonmage. I never thought I would ever see something like that happen."

"I don't understand."

"Our most ancient books record legends of two others called Dragonmages," Velnan explained. "Very little is known about them for certain. The only thing which is truly known is that they shared Dragon blood, and that they were more powerful than any other creature in the world."

"What happened to them?" Delgar asked.

Velnan shrugged. "There are so many different legends it is impossible to say. We also only have one name: Garasus. And that figure has been transformed to fit characters in any number of stories or myths."

Delgar pulled over a chair and sat on it. "So what do I tell Jenara? That I might not even be human anymore?"

Velnan shrugged again. "That is for you to decide. There has not been anybody like you in at least thirty thousand years. You must explore yourself and your new abilities on your own."

"Can you help me?"

Velnan glanced at the Chancellor for a moment, and then turned back to Delgar. "With the power you now have, there is nothing more I can teach you. I can't even begin to help you. Perhaps the only person who can help you is Jenara, because of your love, but I do not know for certain."

Berran shrugged. "Well, there is very little to do with you now. Mage Delgar, I confer upon you the rank of

Archmage, with all the privileges and responsibilities accorded to that rank and fellowship. The papers certifying this will be delivered to you shortly. You may as well go and be with your loved one."

"What of the glacier?" Delgar asked.

"We still have very little information, and the messengers are still being sent to the other Archmages," Berran replied. "Once they arrive there will be a great council, which you will be required to attend. It will take a couple of months."

"We may not have a couple of months," Delgar pointed out.

Chancellor Berran eyed him coldly. "If that is the case, so be it."

Jenara listened to him in silence, a tear rolling down her eye. They sat in their quarters as he explained the battle and what had happened to him.

"I don't even know if I'm human anymore," Delgar said, trying to keep his voice from cracking. "And I don't know what I can offer you while I'm like this."

"Which will be for all eternity," Jenara said, her voice unsteady.

Delgar nodded. "And with all of this happening, I think we should call off the engagement."

Jenara started to cry. "I don't understand! I love you, and I want to be with you! I don't care if you've got Dragon blood in you!"

"I love you too, and that's why I'm saying this," Delgar said, a tear trickling down his cheek. "What if we get married and we can't have children because of me? What happens if I accidentally hurt you while we're trying? I don't know what I am anymore, and I don't know what I can do."

"And what if everything is okay?" Jenara sobbed. "What then? How can you know?"

Delgar swallowed. "I can't. But I don't want to put you at risk."

"I'm already at risk, you fool!" Jenara stormed, leaping out of her chair. "Everybody's going to have to fight this glacier, so I'm at risk from that. Even without the glacier, there's a war going on, so there's danger from that! Many women don't survive childbirth, so I'm at risk from that too! The only thing we have in life is risk! But I've decided to risk all this for you, and only you! Do you really think it matters to me if you now have hotter blood?!"

Delgar shook his head. "But what if I'm not me anymore? What if I've become somebody else?"

She dragged him up to her, placing his head between her breasts. He felt the rhythmic pounding of her heart through her soft dress. "This beats for you," she said. "And if you've changed, it will know. And it doesn't see any change yet."

He broke down into tears. "I'm sorry," he sobbed. "I'm so sorry. I just didn't want you to get hurt, and I don't know what's happening to me, and..."

He heard her weep, holding him even closer. "You can't hurt me," she said, her voice cracking. "Nothing you could do could hurt me. Just don't leave me! Please don't leave me! I can't imagine my life without you, it would be unbearable!"

"I won't ever leave you," Delgar swore. "I'll never ever leave you."

"I want you to marry me," Jenara said, allowing him to rise and embrace her. "I don't want to wait any longer. I want you to marry me as soon as you can."

"I'll see Chancellor Berran about it in the morning," Delgar promised. "We'll be together, always."

Chapter II: A Lightening of Days

Chancellor Berran sat quietly, lost in thought. Delgar turned his attention to the morning sun rising through the sky outside the office window.

"The timing of your request is exceptionally poor," the Chancellor said. "We are in a state of crisis. You cannot be allowed a honeymoon, as you are now a member of the Council of Archmages, and therefore subject to the recall. To make matters worse, you are the only Archmage to have faced this glacier and lived. We need you."

"She needs me too," Delgar stated. "And I need her. And we don't have to take our honeymoon until the crisis is over."

"None of us may survive this crisis," Berran pointed out. "Have you thought of that? And what if she dies fighting the glacier? What will you do then? The law does not allow you to remarry, especially if you are an Archmage. For that matter, what if you die? The law is just as strict for her. Will you deny her the right to bear a child should you pass beyond in this crisis?"

Delgar swallowed. "Neither of us would ever love another. And it may be months before we must face the glacier. We have waited too long, and been separated too many times. We both want some peace, even if it is only for a while."

Berran sighed. "You are being silly, and you have not thought this through. You won't have a great deal of time for peace anyway; all of the Archmages here are working on the crisis. It's getting to the point that classes have been canceled indefinitely. What will she do while you work? She's not even a Mage yet. And if she's married to you, she won't be able to go home."

"She wouldn't go home anyway," Delgar retorted. "I know her. I've loved her for four years now, and by now I should know her well enough to understand how she thinks. She'll help out any way she can. Sir, we won't be talked out of this."

Berran grimaced. "That is painfully obvious. Very well, I will give you another day to think about it, and if you are still determined to make this mistake, then I will marry the two of you."

Delgar grinned. "Thank you sir!"

He was rewarded with a soft, thin smile. "Don't thank me until the end of your life, young Archmage. Only then will you know if I've done you a favor."

As Delgar gazed at Jenara once again, his heart soared. She had dressed in a long, white gown, the soft fabric revealing her slim figure. She glanced at him and smiled radiantly, then looked back towards Vice-Chancellor's Hall. Chancellor Berran and Archmage Velnan strode down the steps, dressed in formal black robes. Delgar straightened his own robes, suddenly hyper-aware of even tiny creases. He looked around to see a small crowd had gathered, most of them students who would be close to graduation if the classes hadn't been canceled.

Chancellor Berran cleared his throat and raised his hand, the shadow of his figure stretched long against the ground in the morning sun. "We are gathered here today to join this man, Delgar, Daegar's son, and this woman, Jenara, Paladin's daughter, in the bonds of matrimony. It is perhaps the most joyous of services that one in my position can fulfill, for it is the binding of two souls together in life and wyrd.

"It is also a bond of love, which can never be breached. A bond of caring and fertility, for it is a union which is by nature fertile. It is a bond of hopes and dreams, for both man and woman pledge themselves and their dreams to one another. It is in the mutual giving of all to the other that these dreams are made possible, for it is easier for two to pursue a dream than one alone. And as both partners give themselves to the other, their souls are bound as well.

"And in this day of crisis, it is a bond of hope for all. For if these two may find happiness in one another for all eternity, perhaps the same may happen to the rest of us. They are a reminder that no matter what, life will go on. It is only up to us to remember to live it. To fight for what we believe, and to pursue our loves, passions and dreams no matter the cost. Some will do this alone, but these two will do it together. Please raise your hands to be fastened."

Delgar and Jenara raised their hands, and Velnan tied a white ribbon around their wrists, linking them. Delgar looked at her and smiled, his heart pounding as she beamed back at him.

The Chancellor turned towards Jenara. "Do you, Jenara, Paladin's daughter, take this man, Delgar, Daegar's son, to be your wedded husband? To have and to hold, in sickness and in health? To share in his dreams, and to share all of yours? To bind your lives together for all eternity in the name of your love and the Eternal One?"

Jenara took a deep breath and nodded. "I do."

Berran faced Delgar. "And do you, Delgar, Daegar's son, take this woman, Jenara, Paladin's daughter, to be your wedded wife? To have and to hold, in sickness and in health? To share in her dreams, and to share all of yours? To bind your lives together for all eternity in the name of your love and the Eternal One?"

Delgar swallowed. A drop of sweat ran down his brow, and his throat seemed painfully sore. He nodded and opened his mouth to speak. "I do," he said, surprised at how clear it came out.

Berran nodded. "Then by the power vested in me by the Order of Archmages, the School of Mages, the city of Taerra and the will of the Eternal One, I now pronounce you husband and wife, and bid you to cherish each another for all your lives. I now bind your souls and your love for all eternity. You will experience happiness and tragedy, for that is the nature of life. But, no matter what happens, you will experience these things together. You may kiss the bride."

Delgar reached over and kissed Jenara, twisting his hand in the bond. As he pulled away, he saw a happy tear running down her cheek.

Velnan cleared his throat. "I, Archmage Velnan, Vice-Chancellor of the School of Mages, in the name of the Order of Archmages and the Eternal One, witness and bless this union. May it be fruitful and joyous for all eternity."

The crowd roared, Delgar grinning widely as Velnan reached down and undid the ribbon, handing it to Jenara. "These are gifts from the Mageschool," the Archmage said, handing Delgar two gold rings. Delgar placed one on

Jenara's finger and then the other on his own.

"Thank you, all of you," Jenara gushed.

"Yes, thank you," Delgar blurted. "You've made us both so very happy."

"It was nothing," Velnan said. "We have so little joy now; yours is a blessing to us too. Now, the ceremony is concluded. You two may as well go and do whatever it is you want to do."

Delgar smiled and picked Jenara up, bearing her off to their quarters. They finally reached the entrance to the dormitory, and he let her down to open the door for her. A quick walk down the hall, and they came to their rooms.

She opened the door, an impish smile on her face. "I think it's traditional for you to bear me over the threshold," she said.

He picked her up, enjoying the feeling as her arms wrapped around him. "You're right," he smiled, and stepped in. With a nonchalant motion, he kicked the door closed behind him and bore her to his bedroom. He placed her on the mattress, and she settled down, shrugging to become more comfortable. He sat beside her for a moment, gazing into her eyes, her face somehow framed perfectly by the blue linen sheets.

"I love you, my husband," she said, pulling open the laces to his robe. "Come to me."

He fiddled with the tie at the front of her gown, finally undoing it and opening the flap. As she pulled his upper body free of the robe, he opened the dress with a gentle touch, revealing her perfect breasts, watching as her nipples became hard and erect.

He stood, the rest of his robe falling to the ground. He slid his loincloth off and placed it with the rest of his clothes. Then he pulled her dress off her, kissing every inch of her body, until they lay naked together. A thought rose unbidden to his mind, a horrible fear that if anything did come of their lovemaking, it would destroy her. But one look in her eyes, the exquisite grey orbs becoming black pools, and all his fears melted away.

He slid on top of her, kissing her body again as he went back up. She yelped briefly in pain when he entered her, and then her body became soft and yielding. Her legs wrapped around him, and he began to thrust into her, a part of him listening in detachment as both of their voices became moans of passion.

He felt his seed coming, and suddenly the fear returned, stronger than before. He pulled out, milky fluid splattering on her leg and the sheets. Her eyes widened in shock, and he rolled beside her, suddenly unwilling to meet her eyes.

"Why did you do that?" she asked, her voice hoarse. "What is wrong?"

"I'm afraid," Delgar panted. "I'm afraid that if I give you a child, it will hurt you, or something worse."

They lay for a long moment, and then she pulled him back to her. "Don't be afraid," she said, stroking him back to life. "Nothing you could do now can harm me."

He nodded, letting her straddle him, trapping his sex inside her. She began to gyrate until he grasped her by the waist, both of them moaning in passion. Then he came, spilling his seed deep inside of her. She lay down, absently stroking his chest, as spent as he was.

He gazed at her, running his eyes down her smooth, slick skin. What little sunlight trickled through the window drapes reflected off the sweat from their passion. "I love you," she murmured contentedly, cuddling up beside him.

"I love you too," he said, holding her gently. Somehow, he knew that the seed he had planted was taking root at that very moment. But instead of happiness or relief, all he felt in the very center of his being was cold terror.

But by mid-afternoon, the fear had faded, and they spent an hour exploring each other's bodies. That night, he dreamt of his hands on her flesh, the wonderful look in her eyes, her soft moans as he caressed her. He woke up, the afternoon sun high in the sky, to find her already awake, and they made long, tender love once again.

In his bliss, the days began to stretch into weeks. When they weren't in their passion, they watched as the students began to trickle out of the Mageschool, waiting for the crisis to pass. Even as the students left, Archmage after Archmage returned, most with large wagons of baggage.

They watched one rotund, red-bearded Archmage amble through the gateway towards Vice-Chancellor's Hall, gesturing at several of the dormitories along the way. Delgar held Jenara, his chin resting on the top of her head, his hands caressing her breasts through her light gown.

"How long will it be before you're needed?" she asked, pressing his hands closer.

Delgar shook his head. "I wish I knew. When they want me, they'll send for me."

"I hope they don't send for you too soon," she said.

"Why?"

"You're mine," Jenara replied, turning and grinning at him impishly. "And I have a surprise for you."

He cuddled her. "Really? What is it?"

"A surprise," she laughed. "I'll tell you when I'm ready."

He laughed and kissed her passionately, his hands running all over her. And then they made love once again.

But their bliss ended the next day. Delgar was awakened by a knocking at the door early in the morning. He gave a brief shout and slid out of bed, throwing on a loose robe. He opened the door to find Velnan standing before him, circles under his eyes.

"The Council of Archmages meets this afternoon, Archmage Delgar," Velnan intoned. "All of us are here, and we have the information we need."

"Is it good or bad?" Delgar asked.

Velnan handed him a piece of parchment, sealed with the arcane sigil of the Order of Archmages. "Bad, I fear. You'd better come at once."

Chapter III: The Darkening of Days

Delgar had never seen the council chamber of the Order of Archmages before. Velnan led him into a large, circular room in the heart of Chancellor's Hall, which Delgar had always thought of as just having faculty offices.

Chancellor Berran nodded to Delgar as he entered, motioning towards an empty seat. The room had filled with men and women in long, dark formal robes, and Delgar felt out of place wearing the light blue robes he had tossed on right after being summoned. He shook his head; now he knew why Velnan had been chuckling on the way to the hall.

Delgar sat beside a tall and rotund Archmage with a long grey beard. To his right sat a young Archmage, her sandy hair cut short and her robes not quite able to hide a distracting figure. The older man glanced at Delgar's robes and grunted, leaving Delgar trying to sit down and not to be noticed.

Once he was seated, he surveyed the room. Velnan and Berran stood behind a large table, while the rest of the Archmages sat on a raised semi-circular platform surrounding it. Large torches at regular intervals lit the room, and a skylight revealed a cloudy day. Delgar forced back a grin; he had always thought that the weather only ever matched the mood of a place in stories.

"This had better be important," the older Archmage grumbled. "I was conducting some vital experiments, and I must get back to them."

The young Archmage tapped Delgar on the shoulder. He turned to gaze into her bright blue eyes. "You're new here?" she asked.

Delgar nodded. "I just made Archmage about a month ago."

"The first thing you'll find is that they take themselves too seriously," she said.

"And what's the second thing?"

"They usually think they're right."

Delgar nodded sagely. "Ah."

"This council is called to order," Berran declared, and all eyes fell upon the Chancellor. "I now convene this emergency session of the Order of Archmages. I'm sorry I had to recall all of you, but we have a crisis that could destroy us all. For some time, we have all noticed odd events occurring. Now there is a glacier descending upon us from the north, and we can finally determine what has happened."

Delgar leaned forward, stroking his goatee.

"I will ask Delgar Daegar's son to step forward," Berran said. "He has had the most direct contact with the glacier, and can tell us the majority of its properties."

Delgar swallowed and stood, suddenly aware that all eyes rested on him. Once again, he wished he had taken the time to change his robe into something more formal.

He stepped down from his seat until he stood before Berran and Velnan.

"Just tell them the important bits," Velnan whispered. "You don't need to tell them the personal ones."

Delgar nodded and faced the council. He recounted as much as he could remember, often filling in gaps whenever he remembered them. Although he feared his story had come out incoherently, he found most of the Archmages nodding sagely and whispering among themselves.

"Not bad," Velnan whispered. "A bit more practice and you'll be good at it."

The grey-haired, rotund wizard stood up. "Mage Delgar," he said.

"Archmage," Berran corrected. "Despite his unfortunate choice of dress today, he was confirmed in our order last month."

"Archmage Delgar," the wizard continued. "Do you mean to tell us that Dragonfire was unable to harm it?"

Delgar cleared his throat, wishing for nothing other than a drink of water. "The Dragonfire was able to do some damage, but the ice advanced so quickly Dragonfire didn't even slow it down."

As the wizard nodded and sat, another Archmage stood, this one dark haired and clean-shaven. "Did you see it absorb life in any other fashion than physical contact?"

Delgar shook his head. "Not that I saw. But that does not mean it can't."

The Archmage remained standing. "And are you certain that the great spell created it?"

Delgar shrugged. "I'm afraid I don't know enough about it. I wish I knew where it came from, but I don't."

"I have a question," Berran cut in. "Archmage Delgar, were you not attacked by a lesser demon after your return from Barsh and the casting of the great spell?"

Delgar nodded. "Yes, I was. But I don't see what-"

"Thank you, Archmage Delgar, you may sit down."

Delgar walked back to his seat, wiping the sweat from his brow. He shook his head in relief. At least that was over.

Berran raised his hands. "I will now turn the floor over to Vice-Chancellor Velnan."

Velnan stepped forward. "Our scryes have been able to determine some facts about the glacier, although even the scrying has cost lives. The glacier was created by the great spell, and we believe that the Gem of Sidhe was the focusing crystal used. This gem was stolen from Vice-Chancellor Vertanus when he was attacked and killed, we believe by Archmage Tartarus.

"When the spell was cast, it had two effects. The first was to create the glacier from the northern ice and begin its advance. The second was to open several portals to the netherworld. As you have heard, the glacier drinks life itself, and that provides its power. We have approximately three months before it reaches Taerra."

The young Archmage beside Delgar stood and raised her hand. "Why would anybody want to open portals to the netherworld? I mean, how could summoning demons help advance a glacier?"

"The portals were not opened to summon demons," Velnan replied, "although that has been a result. As everybody here knows, the netherworld is extremely cold. The intent of the portals, as far as we can discover, was to make our realm colder so that the glacier can advance with greater speed."

As she sat, another Archmage, this one with long, dark hair draping over her slim form, stood and began to speak. "How do we know that Vertanus is dead? Have we seen a body?"

Berran nodded, taking a place beside Velnan. "There

were remains where Vertanus was ambushed, but they were so badly burnt that an identification was impossible. However, it has always been the Vice-Chancellor's habit to send a messenger to assure us of his safety in cases like this, and no such courier has arrived. Furthermore, every message we have sent to his tower has been unable to reach him. Therefore, the only possible assumption is that he was murdered in the attack."

"Then Archmage Tartarus has the Gem and control of the glacier."

"Archmage Tartarus is likely dead as well," Berran stated. "He has never been a powerful Archmage, although he has a grasp of the element of surprise, as the murder of Vertanus indicates. But, even with the Gem of Sidhe, this spell would have overextended him far beyond the point of death. Therefore, the crisis lies in the spell, not the man.

"The decision for us is simple. If this glacier is not stopped, it could destroy all of Mideorth. Even if it doesn't, it will still destroy the world as we know it. Therefore, it must be stopped. The question before us is whether we attack now, or marshal our forces and attack later."

Velnan stepped forward. "Are there any other questions?"

There was a moment of silence, and then Berran nodded. "We will put the matter to debate now."

Delgar swallowed, the bile rough against his throat, and then he stood for a moment, trying to work out what to say.

"Archmage Delgar, you are recognized," Velnan said. "Please feel free to speak, rather than keeping us in suspense."

"I think we should attack now," Delgar finally blurted. "I mean, it will only get worse, won't it?" Then he sat down, hoping he hadn't somehow alienated the entire order.

"There is merit to what our newest member says," an Archmage behind him rumbled. Delgar turned to see who it was, but there were too many people between them. "However, he is young and inexperienced. It would be better for us to marshal our forces and attack when we are truly strong. Should we attack now, we would not have time to prepare."

"But it grows stronger than us faster than us," Delgar protested. "I've seen it! We are already at a disadvantage. The longer we wait the more that disadvantage grows."

"Archmage Sarius is correct," a raspy voice called from the right side of the council. "If we do not prepare, our battle will be in vain. However, Archmage Delgar is also correct. If we wait too long, we will not be able to fight. I suggest we wait only a couple of weeks, and then attack."

There was a muttering of agreement throughout the council. Finally, Chancellor Berran nodded and spoke. "Then it is decided. We will attack in two weeks time. Archmage Vilnia will lead a scouting party of five Archmages to the glacier. There, they will observe the advance and report it to us, but they will not attack until we get there. Vice-Chancellor Velnan I hereby formally confirm as the Vice-Chancellor of the School of Mages, until such time as he chooses to seek a replacement. He will remain with ten Archmages in Taerra to provide a last defense of the Mageschool should we fail, and to oversee the evacuation of the city if it becomes necessary.

"As for the rest of us, we will leave in two weeks time. Archmage Delgar, because of his previous experience, will lead the attack with me, and help us plan our strategy. That will be all. Archmages Vilnia and Velnan, you should stay and choose your people now."

Delgar nearly stumbled on his way out of the council

room, lost in thought and fear. He tried to walk calmly back to his quarters, but the reality of the situation kept intruding on his mind. He was going back into danger. And there was no way he could see this assault succeeding.

Seeing the look of concern on his face as soon as he came into the apartment, Jenara embraced him. He sat for several long moments in her arms, trying to find the words to explain what was going to happen.

"I'm going to have to go back into danger again," he finally said.

"When?"

"Two weeks," Delgar answered, his sorrow seeping through his voice. "The Order of Archmages is going to attack the glacier in two weeks. And they've told me to lead them."

"You don't think they can win," Jenara stated.

Delgar nodded. "I've seen it defeat all of the Great Dragons and nearly drive them into extinction. If Dragonfire can't do it, what can a hundred and fifty Archmages do?"

"They can try," Jenara said. "And they might succeed. Stranger things have happened, my love."

"Only in stories."

"Every story has some truth," she stated, holding him tight. "At least, that's what you told me."

"When I leave for the attack, I want you to go south," Delgar said. "It should be safe there for a while, and I'll find you."

Jenara shook her head. "I'm coming with you."

Delgar blinked. "What?"

"Even in the condition I'm in, I'm not a fragile doll," she admonished. "And I need you. I'm going to come with and do whatever I can. If I can only help pack the lunches for the attack and watch the light show, I'll be there."

"But there will be a lot of danger," Delgar protested. "You could be killed."

"I could die anyway in about nine months," Jenara said. "Delgar, my love, my husband, I'm carrying your child."

Delgar choked back a sob of joy. "Somehow, I knew it would happen, but I had no idea I was right..."

"I'm going to be there," Jenara declared. "I'll be at your side, and at the least you'll have incentive to survive."

They held each other, lightly caressing until their touches became passionate. And then they made slow, tender love, as though they would never have the chance again.

Delgar leaned over the map, examining the minute markings. A long wavy line had been drawn in an attempt to approximate the border of the glacier, but he didn't think it would be that accurate. Several other markings had been placed along the line, representing groups of Archmages.

He rubbed his eyes. The letters on the map wavered in the candlelight. He glanced out the window, watching the full moon in the inky night.

"So," Chancellor Berran said. "What do you think?"

Delgar shook his head, trying to clear away some of his fatigue. "I don't really know. I think they're too close, though. Definitely too close."

"How do you mean?"

"This glacier does not simply roll over things," Delgar explained. "It can attack as well. And every single piece of thrown ice can drain one's life. Everybody will need to be at least twice as far back as you have them here."

Berran frowned. "Anything else?"

"There might not be enough of a concentration of fire," Delgar yawned. "I'm just not sure."

"We leave in two days," Berran snapped. "You had better be certain by then."

Vice Chancellor Velnan stepped forward from where he had been seated. "I think it is time to retire for the night," he said. "Obviously Archmage Delgar is in no shape to think any further tonight, and you, Chancellor, respectfully, are becoming quite irritable."

"I am not irritable!" Berran grumbled, glaring. "We are merely running out of time."

"Another reason why you should both retire," Velnan said. "If you are running out of time, then you will require sleep to plan the assault properly. Otherwise, it will fail because of something you missed. At any rate, you have been planning this for almost two weeks; there is little point in going over the same material another four times tonight."

Delgar rubbed his eyes. "Velnan's right. Besides, my wife was expecting me at least an hour ago."

Berran waved his hand. "Very well. Go, both of you. We will reconvene at dawn."

Delgar nodded and walked out of the office, stumbling a couple of times as he made his way out of Chancellor's Hall. Finally, he reached his quarters, where he fumbled with his key.

He opened the door, stepped in, then closed it softly, hearing a slight click as it locked. With a brief flick of his power, he ignited a candle and began to undress. He snuck into the bedroom, stopping briefly to snuff out the candle, and slipped into bed.

He felt Jenara turn around to hold him, and he hugged her to him.

"I couldn't sleep," she said.

"Worried about me?" he asked, a smile on his face. He

kissed her forehead.

"Worried about both of us," she replied sleepily. "In two days we have to go and fight."

"You can stay here."

She shook her head. "I'm staying with you for the rest of my life."

He smiled. "I can't think of better company."

She snuggled closer to him, and he lay there, enjoying her warmth against him. "I love you," she murmured. "No matter what happens, no matter what the danger, I want you to always know that I love you."

"I love you too," he said. After a while, her breathing became slow and regular against him, but he remained awake, staring up into the darkness. The coming battle played through his mind, possible defenses, attacks. Every time, he came to the realization that they still had to plan one last thing. Should they fail, they needed a way to escape.

As that unsettling thought fell up on him, a light sleep took him, filled with dark dreams.

Chapter IV: Revelations of Power

Although it was still late summer, it felt like Autumn. Even the trees seemed to be withering as Delgar rode past them, shivering in the chill breeze. Delgar basked in Jenara's warmth as she clung to his back, pleased, despite the danger, to have her present.

He gazed down the column, watching the long line of Archmages make their way along the road. They had been riding for a week, stopping early in the evening to wait for the baggage train to arrive. Delgar and Chancellor Berran had plotted the route to the glacier carefully: not only was it relatively quick, but it also provided an easy route for escape if things turned for the worse.

Delgar suddenly spotted a flash of light from one of the hills and spun to give it a closer look. A figure on horseback in the robes of an Archmage trotted towards the column.

"Chancellor Berran!" Delgar called. From farther along the column the wizard broke step and trotted

266

forward.

"Our scout?"

Delgar nodded. "It looks like Archmage Vilnia herself."

Delgar turned back to the red-haired beauty riding towards them. "Greetings, Archmage!"

Vilnia held up an arm in greeting. "I am glad to see all of you, Dragonmage. The glacier will be within our range in two days time."

Delgar winced at the nickname, but didn't say anything about it. He turned to see Berran scratching his beard.

"How quickly is it moving?" the Chancellor asked.

"Slowly," Vilnia replied. "It covers perhaps three miles in a day. We watched it for several days. Even from a distance, though, we could feel it trying to sap our power. It is like some sort of living thing."

Jenara tugged at Delgar's robe. "How big is it?" she whispered.

Delgar stroked her hand. "Extremely big."

"Why is it so slow?" Berran asked. "According to Archmage Delgar, the glacier has already absorbed several Dragons."

Vilnia shook her head. "I can't explain it. Have you ever encountered true evil, Chancellor?"

"I have encountered some I could call evil, but there was always something redeemable about them."

"When you're in the presence of the ice, it feels like you're in the presence of utter evil," Vilnia said. "You feel as though it knows it is going to kill you, and is just biding its time."

Delgar nodded. "It felt that way when the Dragons fought it as well. It even seemed to have some notion of tactics."

"Were you able to evacuate the people from its path?"

Berran asked.

"Some," Vilnia said. "Some wouldn't leave. Some wouldn't believe me. But most left. I sent them down the two parallel roads to us so that they wouldn't encumber the column."

"Even if Taerra is swamped with refugees, I'm sure Vice-Chancellor Velnan can handle them," Berran declared. "Unless Archmage Delgar has anything else he needs you to do, I guess you should get back with your Archmages and keep a watch on it. Make sure you send runners to keep us informed."

Delgar turned to look at the horizon. To the north he could see the thin ribbon of ice stretching across the world, and a chill went down his spine as he thought of how it would loom over them in a couple of days. A small barrow stood to the east, and a sudden memory of a cold night in a storm flashed through his head. Yet it was only a flash, a single recollection. He shook his head, trying to remember more, but it fled his mind, tantalizing him with forgotten knowledge.

"What is it, my love?" Jenara asked.

He turned to see her staring at the barrow. "I think I spent a night there once. I'm not sure, though."

"Archmage Delgar," Chancellor Berran called. "We still have some distance to go before we may stop tonight."

Delgar nodded. "I'm coming!" With a quick kick, he sent the horse into a gallop, riding back to lead the column. They rode until the sun was beginning to set, and then Delgar called a halt. He rode forward for a moment to survey the area, seeing only a deserted village and some slightly overgrown fields.

"Some of them must have left earlier," Jenara observed, letting go of his waist and dismounting. "I just need to stretch for a moment."

Delgar climbed down to join her. As he stretched his

arms, Chancellor Berran rode up to him from the column. "I gather we stay here for the night?"

Delgar nodded. "It's as good a place as any. If we need some cover we can use that village there. Otherwise, we'll need our rest for the battle ahead."

Berran dismounted, grimacing as his joints cracked. "I must be getting old," he muttered. "This sort of thing never used to bother me."

Delgar chuckled. "Don't worry about it. Everybody is sore after a hard day's march."

"Unlike the rest of us, Archmage Delgar, you and I aren't allowed to be. We're in charge, after all."

"So they've told me," Delgar said, grinning. "But I've always thought that this was more of a pleasure outing for the wife."

At that moment, Jenara hit him and Berran burst out laughing.

"I'll give the orders for the wards to be cast and the tents pitched," Berran said. "Hopefully, you'll survive until tomorrow. Or at least be in one piece."

After their lovemaking, Delgar rolled over and Jenara caressed his chest absently. Suddenly, she stopped and looked at him carefully, casting her shadow over him and the tent wall.

"Something's on your mind," she said. "I could sense it."

"Was I that clear?" Delgar asked.

"You're always clear to me," Jenara said. "That's one of the reasons I love you."

"In a couple of days we're going into battle, and I just don't think we can win," Delgar said. "I'm afraid that all of us will be lost, and our child won't have a world to grow up in."

269

"There's always a way to survive," Jenara said. "That's something my father used to tell me. He was once stranded in the great war in Barsh, and it looked like there was no way to get out alive."

"What did he do?"

"He managed to bribe a nomad to hide him, and he left the country in the next caravan."

"I guess we just have to find a way out here," Delgar mused. "But who knows how far this ice will go?"

"If we lose here and it comes after us, we'll move," Jenara said. "We'll call on the Dragons for help; you can do that. We'll find a way out."

"I guess you're right," Delgar said, cuddling her. "But I want you in the rear of the battle, away from all the fighting."

"Delgar, I-"

"I need you to survive, no matter what."

"But I have to help somehow."

Delgar shrugged. "You can help out with the supply line. But I know what we're facing, and you don't stand a chance against it. So I want you out of danger."

"And you do stand a chance against it?"

Delgar shook his head. "I don't know. I don't know if any of us do. But if something happens to me, at least you and our child will be safe."

Jenara buried her face in his neck. "Just hold me."

As he held her, sleep overcame him.

He found himself soaring above the camp, the grand vista of the plains stretching out before him. On the northern horizon a strip of blue-white lay waiting, slowly advancing as it drew the life out of the very ground.

He flew toward the ice, watching as it came into sharp relief. He heard the groaning of the earth, the sudden crackling as a stone shattered under the weight of the glacier. He saw the minute cracks on the rough surface, the powdered ice as fine as snow sweeping along the glowing landscape.

He gasped in horror as it began to move forward more quickly, advancing without mercy. It crushed the city of Taerra as those few who remained fled in terror. Without slowing, it swept down on the southern coast towards Barsh, turning the ancient desert into chill wasteland.

He watched as the time passed, as the glacier slowed and stopped. Before him a few people living in a strip of land by the glacier's edge tried to survive, bringing in harvests that even a beggar would pity.

Then he saw himself, his face lined with sorrow, trudging across the ice.

He woke with a start, Jenara curled up beside him. He blinked, trying to remember the dream, but all that remained were vague images. As he lay back beside his wife, waiting for the dawn, he felt the Dragon blood pulsing behind his eyes.

The glacier stretched out before them as the battle-line of Archmages began to form. Delgar stared at the massive blue-white ribbon, a chill running down his spine, but he could not tell if it was from fear or the cold. Crunching gravel sounded behind him, and he turned to find Chancellor Berran standing beside him, a long wooden staff in his hand.

"Everybody's almost in position," Berran said. "Are you certain you want it done this way?"

Delgar nodded and looked down the line. Each Archmage was standing with at least four feet of empty ground around him. "So long as everybody keeps their distance, one of the glacier's attacks won't do as much damage. Can everybody focus and draw from each other at that distance?"

"I think so," Berran said. "But it will be difficult. And if the line is broken, our plan will fail. As a matter of curiosity, where is Jenara?"

"In the back," Delgar replied. "She's organizing the supply line. She can't link with us anyway; she's not powerful enough."

A runner came dashing up, his red robes billowing in the wind. "Vilnia is in position," he panted. "The line is ready."

"Rest for a moment," Berran said. "When you're ready join the line and link with us." He turned to Delgar. "It is time."

Delgar stepped forward, gazing first at the long line of Archmages, defiant against the blue ribbon of ice that awaited their onslaught. Then he looked at the ice, felt the Dragon blood pulsing in his veins.

"I am Delgar, Daegar's son!" he declared. "I am Magus Draconum, protector of all Dragonkind! And in the name of Garasus, THIS ENDS HERE! Link and attack!"

He reached out with his mind, feeling his power join with Berran. He reached out further to find an entire network of minds, their powers linked, waiting. They all began to strike out, forming the forces of the elements into a great web, working together to forge a spell that none of them alone would have been powerful enough to cast.

He lent his strength as they created a wall of fire, watching it turn from red to white hot. The flames stretched farther than his eye could see, scouring the horizon, reaching up high into the sky.

With a push from all of them, the wall began to move forward, pushing against the ice. They felt the ice break and shatter, huge holes appearing as the face of the glacier cracked. Delgar's heart soared: despite his fears, they would succeed! The ice would be stopped.

And then, the link was broken.

Delgar spun to the west, his eyes widening in horror. Several of the Archmages were reeling and falling, their eyes empty of life. He glanced to the east to see the same thing. When he looked forward, he saw the flames die and the glacier advance, its glowing face smooth and undamaged.

"What happened?" Berran cried, his voice frantic. "I thought we had it!"

"It misled us!" Delgar replied. "It used the spell to get to us! Quick, tell everybody to do as much damage as possible with fireballs and then to run!"

Berran nodded and called for a runner. Delgar began to cast fireballs, watching them splash against the face of the ice with barely a bit of steam. The Dragon blood pulsed behind his eyes, more insistent, as though it was trying to escape.

And then the glacier erupted. Blocks of ice fell on and around the Archmages, crushing and bruising many of them. Even those that were bruised fell dead almost immediately, their life drained by the foul ice.

The Dragon blood exploded inside him, and Delgar's world became red.

Delgar felt his face lengthening, great wings bursting from his back, his skin turning to scales. He felt the power surging up inside him, and his humanity submerging and joining with something greater. With a great roar, he took flight, his powerful wings catching and holding the breeze.

In a brief moment, his human side realized what had happened. He had become the Dragon.

Delgar sped across the glacier, sending his white-hot breath splashing against it, burning large holes in it. The glacier erupted, trying to catch him, but he swung away from it, and the ice fell on empty ground.

He turned back to fly over the Archmages, and his human side recoiled in horror. Jenara was shaking

Chancellor Berran, a block of ice beside them, urging him to get up. A large red welt spread across Berran's pale forehead. The line of Archmages had vanished, and the ground was littered with bodies as the ice bore down on them, moving faster than before.

The battle was lost. There was nothing that could stop it.

Delgar gazed back at Jenara, suddenly realizing that the ice was bearing down on her. She stood up and began to run, but the ice was gaining. With a roar, Delgar swept down, picking her up in a talon and sweeping her off the battlefield. For a moment he feared that he had seen a look of surprise and terror on her face when he had grabbed her, but he wasn't certain.

He flew as quickly as he could away from the glacier, leaving the ice behind. As he retreated, he felt the glacier slow once more, as though it was trying to conserve energy. Despite his Draconic form, Delgar felt sick to his stomach.

He finally set down when Taerra was in sight, placing Jenara on the ground. He gazed down at her tiny form, but there was no movement. His heart pounding, he wished with all his might that he could hold her again.

He felt the Dragon blood receding, and his form begin to change. The wings retracted and the talons became hands, the scales turning back into skin. And then the Dragon was in his blood once more, waiting just behind his eyes to come out.

"Jenara?" Delgar asked, dropping to his knees to hold her limp form. With relief, he realized she was breathing. "My love?"

Jenara's eyes fluttered open, and she grasped Delgar to her. "My love, I thought you were lost!"

"What did you see?" Delgar asked, a sudden nausea overtaking him as the realization struck. They had lost; the world was doomed.

"There was a wall of fire," Jenara said. "And it pushed into the ice, but it did nothing. Then some of the Archmages suddenly fell down, and the ice exploded. And then there was this roar and suddenly you were gone and this Dragon was..." Her eyes widened. "By the Eternal One, it was you, wasn't it?"

Delgar nodded. "I don't know how I did it, it just happened."

"We've lost, haven't we?"

Delgar nodded. "I think we're the only ones that made it out."

She rolled out of his arms and knelt on the ground, retching. Delgar swallowed hard, the sound of her vomiting making him even more nauseated. She spat and gazed up at him, her face pale.

"So what do we do now?" she asked.

"What you said we should do earlier," Delgar replied. "We survive. First, though, we have to go to Taerra and warn Velnan."

"And what then?"

"I guess we should pray," Delgar said. "I don't know what else there is to be done."

Chapter V: Movements of Life

It took two days for Delgar and Jenara to stagger into Taerra, weak and hungry. To Delgar's disappointment, a pickpocket had struck when they stopped at an inn on the first night, and they were forced to put on a small magic show for their room. Almost penniless and with barely any food, they made their way south in the morning, watching the walls of Taerra grow before them as they approached.

At the end of the second day they managed to get into the city, where Vice-Chancellor Velnan ushered them quickly into his offices in the Mageschool. As Velnan offered them their first proper meal in two days, Delgar told him of the battle. When Delgar had finished, Velnan leaned back in his chair, stroking his beard.

"So they're all dead," Velnan finally said. "Even Chancellor Berran."

"We both saw his body," Jenara stated.

"And how did you two survive?"

"I rescued her," Delgar replied. "I'm still not sure how

I did it. I think I suddenly turned into a Dragon, if that means anything to you."

Velnan nodded. "As a matter of fact, it does. Most myths of Garasus have him dying as a Dragon, but he was supposedly born human. I wish I knew more, but your transformation does not come as a surprise. Tell me, could you control it?"

Delgar shook his head. "It all seemed to happen on its own. One moment I was part of the link, then the link was broken, and then I changed."

"How long do we have, do you think?" Velnan said.

"Perhaps a few months," Delgar replied. "It isn't moving more than a couple of miles per day, but I wouldn't hope for more than two years."

"So what are we going to do?" Jenara said. "We can't fight again."

Velnan nodded. "I will contact the city council and begin the evacuation. As for you two, I want you both to take what you can and leave."

"But we can help out!" Delgar protested. "Surely you can use every hand you've got."

"No," Velnan declared. "The libraries can be transported magically to some southern towers, and the people can be moved out easily by the city guard. I have enough for an evacuation now, and any more would only hinder it. You two should leave, and I'll find you when I can."

"But where will we go?" Jenara asked. "I've seen this thing too. You can't hide from it."

"Just keep heading south, I guess," Velnan said. "Take the Queen's Road south to Maeritima, and then the King's Road east to the Pakarian border. You should be able to cross easily enough. From there, try to find some protected town."

"What about the warlords?" Delgar asked.

"You'll have to take your chances," Velnan replied. "Not all of them have a hatred of Taerraland, but some do. At least with them there is a chance of survival."

Delgar nodded. "We'll need some money."

"That won't be a problem," Velnan said. "The Mageschool is nothing if not well funded. Rest for a day, pack what belongings you'll take with you, and I'll see you off with some gold. But travel lightly; if I'm not mistaken, the roads will soon be flooded with refugees, if they aren't already."

With that, Velnan showed them out the door. Delgar and Jenara made their way to their rooms, where Jenara sat down on the bed and Delgar paced.

"I thought we could win," Jenara muttered. "All that time I was saying we could survive, I thought we'd never have to run. I don't even know what I should take."

"Clothes and books, I guess," Delgar said. "Enough for a long journey."

"We'll need a wagon," Jenara pointed out. "And horses."

Delgar nodded. "It seems that once again I'm a refugee. At least this time I can take the woman I love with me." As he spoke, there was a flash of painful memory, but then it was gone.

He sat down on the bed and they embraced for a while, sheltering each other from the world they would have to face in the morning.

It was easy for Delgar to find a wagon; word was only just spreading about the evacuation and he managed to buy one before the prices rose. Horses were a bit more difficult, and he used the last of his savings to buy them, hoping that Velnan would provide enough for the trip.

As he returned to the Mageschool in the soft morning

light, he was struck with a feeling of change, as though he had once again finished one part of his life and moved on to the next. He only hoped that there would be some light at the end of the horrific tunnel he seemed to be trapped in.

Jenara was waiting for him when he got to the door. He tethered the horses to a post and helped her put the few belongings they were taking into the cart. It was a quick job; they had spent the previous evening gathering their most valuable books and clothes, leaving almost everything else behind.

Jenara placed the last chest onto the wagon and kissed Delgar. "I'll stay here with our belongings. You go get the money from Vice-Chancellor Velnan."

Delgar nodded. "I'll be back shortly."

He walked across the campus, noticing for the first time how desolate it seemed. Where once there had been Mages and students playing games and studying on the gentle fields, they were now empty. It seemed that to Delgar that if he just closed his eyes he'd see Tomlin and Melina sharing a picnic outside Vice-Chancellor's Hall, surrounded by students long gone. He choked back a tear as he thought of all the Mages that would never come to this school, a school that would soon be trapped under thousands of feet of ice.

He was so lost in thought that he nearly walked right into Velnan, who was striding towards him. Velnan smiled. "I take it you're thinking the same thoughts I am."

"What makes you think that?"

"Your eyes," Velnan replied. "I was thinking about how I'll never teach another class here, never have another group of promising students to guide. I never thought I'd leave this place for good, much less outlive most of my friends."

Delgar grimaced. "How do you handle it? This is just so much greater than I am that I'm not quite sure what to think."

"I remind myself that everything must pass," Velnan stated. "And then I think of all the work I still have to do."

"Does it help?"

"Only a bit," Velnan admitted. "The only way to truly deal with grief is to accept it. Suppressing or denying it will only poison your soul."

"How many of us are left here?" Delgar asked.

"Of Archmages, only those twelve left alive. All the Mages have left. Once the last Archmages have left, I will lock the gate."

"What good will that do?" Delgar asked. "The ice won't stop for a gate."

"This is not an average gate," Velnan said. "Once the gate is locked, the key will be hidden somewhere in the deserts of Barsh. Only I will know exactly where. And once the gate is locked, the Mageschool will disappear until the key is found again. Thus, the knowledge we can't move will be preserved until the time is right and the key is found."

"How do you know it will be found?"

Velnan shrugged. "I don't. But I have come to believe that even a world has wyrd. And even if it doesn't, the key is an object of power, and objects of power have a habit of being found."

"Then this place will survive us," Delgar mused. "That is comforting, at least."

"I take it that you are ready to leave," Velnan said. "I have your money for you."

"Will you see us to the gate?" Delgar asked.

Velnan nodded. "Of course."

The two walked back to the wagon, finding Jenara sitting on the driver's seat, idly playing with the reins. She smiled once she saw Velnan and Delgar. She hopped down from the wagon and embraced Delgar.

Her smile faded. "I guess we have to go now. I suddenly wish I could send a message to my parents, to warn them."

"I'll see to that, Lady Jenara," Velnan said. "I still have a few things to take care of before I leave, and I'll make sure I send a courier to your parents."

"Do you know where they are?" she asked. "I can tell you if you don't."

Velnan held up his hand. "There is no need for that. Even if I forget where they are, you are still in our files, and the Mageschool has always kept excellent records. I rather wonder what people will make of them in a few millennia, once the ice has passed."

Jenara raised an eyebrow.

"I'll explain it on the road," Delgar said, stepping onto the cart and holding out his hand. She accepted it with a sad smile and sat beside him. With a quick pull on the reins, the horses began to trot forward, Velnan easily keeping pace beside them. Before long, they reached the ancient doors of the Mageschool.

"As I told Archmage Delgar, I will join you two as soon as I am able," Velnan announced. "I don't know how long that will be, but I don't think it will be too long."

"We'll be waiting," Jenara promised.

Velnan held up a small pouch, offering it to her. "Here are three thousand gold crowns. May it aid you on your journey."

"May the Eternal One guide and protect you," Jenara said.

"Do not tarry," Velnan said. "The evacuation may have already started. I will see you two when the time is right."

"Goodbye Velnan," Delgar said, holding up his hand. "I will miss you!"

And with that, Delgar turned forward, knowing that

Velnan was watching them leave. He held Jenara close as he guided the wagon to the city walls, and for a while he watched people beginning to pack up their belongings. Velnan was right; the evacuation was beginning, the word spreading as quickly by mouth as by the city guard.

Nobody challenged them at the gate. Delgar and Jenara simply rode their wagon through, trying to look anywhere but behind them. Finally, Delgar glanced back to see the city for one last time. The white stone walls presented a fortress that seemed as though it could never be breached, but that fantasy was quickly dispelled in Delgar's mind by the reality of the glacier. For a moment the sun was partially covered by a cloud, framing the city with a soft, perfect light.

With a sinking heart, Delgar turned back to the road, and never again laid eyes on the city of Taerra.

For the first week they traveled mainly in silence, passed by the occasional courier. At one point Jenara wondered out loud if one of the couriers had been sent to her parents, but Delgar could only shrug and turn back to the road. Around them they saw the summer turning to autumn, perhaps for the last time.

They sheltered in inns whenever they could, using Velnan's money as sparingly as possible. To protect their belongings Delgar cast a warding spell over them every night before he went back to join Jenara. Although neither of them wanted to talk about it, Delgar knew that they were both mourning the imminent loss of the city they had both come to love.

Finally they came to the port of Maeritima, and they spent a day resupplying. True to Velnan's advice, they didn't tarry, for even in that port they could see signs of a future evacuation. The prices were high, but Delgar discovered an aptitude for haggling, and the costs didn't end up affecting them too much. As the sun rose the next morning, they headed east on the King's Road.

The weather began to change in the second week, a chill wind blowing through the leaves as they blossomed into a rainbow of color. The sky clouded over, and Delgar found himself wondering continuously if there would be rain. Just in case, Jenara reached into the back of the wagon and pulled out some warm clothes.

It was that night, in the middle of the second week, that Delgar noticed that Jenara's belly had a slight curve that he could swear hadn't been there before. They were snuggled tightly that night, camped at the side of the road as they were unable to reach an inn. As they fell asleep, they caressed lightly.

"What's that?" Delgar asked.

"Our daughter," Jenara replied.

Delgar grinned, caressing the soft curve. "How do you know it's a daughter?"

"I just know."

And then, under the moonlit clouds, they made love. Somehow, after that night, the rest of the voyage seemed much brighter to Delgar, and he spent most of his time holding Jenara when it was her time to drive the wagon.

As the third week began, they reached the border of Pakaria. The great wall was still crumbling from the recent war, and they passed through one of the gaps onto the vast plains. The sun finally broke through the clouds as their first day in Pakaria came to a close, and he turned to find Jenara smiling at him and pointing at the sky.

"A good omen, don't you think?" she asked, an impish grin on her face.

Delgar embraced her. "Definitely, my love."

They camped under the stars that night, holding each other and gazing at the constellations. That evening,

Delgar found he was able to forget the glacier, the lost battles, and his forced flight from Taerra. He had the woman he loved and the stars; in that all-too-brief night, it was all he needed.

The next morning they awoke and began moving again, hoping to find some small village they could settle down in. As they traveled, Delgar used his Dragon's sight to gaze around the countryside, but all he saw were the rolling plains of the Pakarian midlands. Then, around midday, he saw the soldiers.

A small group of them, clad in leather and mail, rode towards them from the east. Delgar felt Jenara tug at his arm. He turned to see a concerned look in her eyes.

"What's wrong?" she asked.

"Soldiers," Delgar replied. "Don't worry, though. If they're hostile, I can handle them."

"So what do we do?" Jenara said.

He shrugged. "Ask for directions? They shouldn't be too hostile; we're not at war right now, at least to my knowledge."

"How far away are they?"

"About an hour, I think."

Delgar was off by about ten minutes. The six soldiers came to a halt at the side of the wagon. Delgar took a moment to take stock of them. For the most part they were well groomed and equipped, which Delgar took to be a good sign. Their weapons, however, also showed signs of recent use, which he thought might be a bad omen.

"Can I help you, sirs?" Delgar asked.

"What is your name and business?" a blond-haired soldier demanded, his voice rolling with a strange, musical accent.

"I am Delgar Daegar's son, and this is my wife Jenara," Delgar replied. "We're refugees seeking a new home."

"This is Lord Cennyth's land," the soldier said. "No man, woman or child may settle on it without his permission. What is your profession?"

Delgar paused for a moment, debating whether to tell the truth. "I'm an Archmage of the Mageschool of Taerra," he finally said. "My wife is a former student."

"And how does an Archmage of Taerra become a refugee?" the soldier asked, his voice skeptical. "I thought you all were invincible."

Delgar shook his head. "Sadly, no, we're not. However, the reason for our flight should be taken up with your Lord Cennyth."

"Why don't you want me to know?"

"You can't do anything about it," Delgar said. "Lord Cennyth might."

The soldier sat on his horse for a moment, gazing at the horizon. Finally, he turned to Delgar and Jenara. "You two will come with us to see Lord Cennyth. Follow us."

As Delgar guided the horses to follow where the soldiers led them, he gave Jenara a hopeful smile. "I guess we have our directions."

It took them another two days to reach the fortress of Lord Cennyth. The fortress sat on a hill overlooking a small town and a large river. The soldiers led Delgar and Jenara to a stable inside the fortress where they left the wagon, Delgar placing a quick warding spell on it. Then they were brought before Lord Cennyth.

Lord Cennyth was a tall, dark haired man of regal stature. He clad himself in velvet robes over a plain leather tunic and breeches. The robes seemed to be his only concession to his position; the audience room was Spartan at best, and his throne was a simple wooden chair.

Delgar bowed and Jenara curtsied. There was a

moment of silence, and then Lord Cennyth directed them to rise.

"I understand you are Delgar, Daegar's son," Lord Cennyth stated. "Is this correct?"

"Yes, lord," Delgar replied, hoping he had used the correct term of respect.

"Your name sounds Nordish. Is that where you are from?"

"Yes, lord."

"And your wife has a Taerran name, Jenara is it?"

"Yes, lord," Jenara said.

Lord Cennyth shot her a harsh look, and then turned back to Delgar. "Is it your custom not to teach women their place before nobility?"

Delgar wet his lips, trying to decide the best way to reply. "Lord, in Taerra the customs appear to be different than here. We have only been here for a very short time, and do not know your customs."

"We are not so different than Taerra," Lord Cennyth stated. "However, since you appear not to know, it is considered impolite to speak to a noble unless you are directly addressed, even if you are a warrior maiden or sorceress." He turned to Jenara. "Do you understand?"

Jenara nodded. "I apologize, lord."

Lord Cennyth nodded. "Gladly accepted. I fear my hospitality may not be the best right now. I have heard disturbing rumors from the north and west. And now, an Archmage of Taerra and his wife appear at my door as refugees." He turned to Delgar. "Why are you running?"

As clearly as he could, Delgar told him about the glacier and the struggle against it. He left out the personal parts and the battle with the Dragons, but tried to paint a picture of what the ice was capable of.

When Delgar was finished, Lord Cennyth leaned back in his chair, his hand absently stroking his beard. "What do you suggest we do?"

"You must prepare your people to leave," Delgar replied. "You cannot fight this with steel, and all attempts with magic have failed."

"Lord Gwynnyn to the south is not very friendly right now," Lord Cennyth said. "It will take some time before he will let my people pass on his land. But I think it can be done. And you, Delgar Daegar's son, what do you seek?"

"Lord?"

"You haven't come all this way just to spread the word," Lord Cennyth said. "The Mageschool has messengers for that."

"We seek a place to live, for a time," Delgar replied.

"Until you must flee again."

"Yes."

Lord Cennyth nodded. "You may stay here, under one condition. I could use an Archmage as an advisor, but how do I know you are really what you say you are? If you can prove that you are truly an Archmage, you may live here with my household."

Delgar held up his hand, manipulating the element of air around it. There was a burst of light, and a pillar of flame stretched from his palm towards the wooden ceiling. Then he closed his fist, and the flame vanished.

Lord Cennyth stood and applauded. "I'm convinced. I will talk to the Captain of the Guard, Archmage Delgar. You and your wife may stay here, at least until we must all flee."

Delgar grinned and turned to Jenara, who threw herself into his harms and kissed him. Once again, they had a home.

Chapter VI: The End of Light

The Captain of the Guard turned out to be the same soldier who had questioned Delgar on the road. He escorted Delgar and Jenara to one of the stone towers inside the wall of the fortress.

"If you need anything, Archmage Delgar, Lady Jenara," he said. "Just ask for me. My name is Captain Caerwyth."

Delgar nodded. "Thank you for your time, Captain. If we need anything we will call you."

"Lord Cennyth is having a feast in your honor tonight," Caerwyth said. "If you do not have the proper dress for the occasion, I am instructed to find it for you."

Delgar smiled. "We brought the proper apparel. If you'll excuse us, right now we just need to get everything unpacked."

"Then I will fetch both of you when it is time for the feast," Caerwyth declared. "Until then, good day." With that, he spun on his heel and left.

Jenara poked around the small tower, finally settling on the feather mattress in their sleeping chamber. "Not quite what I thought a wizard's tower would be," she said.

"Always figured it would be larger?" Delgar asked, grinning as he brought in some of their clothes.

Jenara nodded, rising to walk back to the wagon. "So, will this do?"

Delgar surveyed the tower. "For as long as we have here, yes, it will."

They had finished unpacking and stored almost all their belongings when Caerwyth returned to fetch them to the feast. Delgar told the soldier that he would be along shortly, and then he and Jenara quickly changed, leaving Caerwyth waiting outside the tower. Finally, once they were properly attired, Caerwyth escorted them to the keep, the hoary stone bathed red in the sunset.

The feast had already started when they arrived. Delgar nearly startled when he saw the packed hall. Lord Cennyth must have invited every single villager within twenty miles, for every table was filled to capacity, with the exception of two places beside the warlord at the high table. Lord Cennyth rose from his seat and motioned to the two Mages. "We are pleased you finally decided to join us! Please, join me at my table of honor."

Delgar bowed. "We would be delighted to, my lord." He took Jenara's hand and led her to the table in as stately a fashion as he could manage. Once he had seated her, he took a place beside her to the right of Lord Cennyth. As he sat, a servant placed a plate with a steaming cutlet of lamb before each of them and poured them both some wine.

"This is our special wine," Lord Cennyth declared. "It is made only once a year with the best of our grapes. Very few lords of Pakaria have the facilities for this, and of those who do, ours is the finest."

Delgar took a sip, smiling when the wondrous flavor

exploded in his mouth. For a moment, he thought he would be lost in the remarkable aroma of the drink. "It is excellent," he said. "What is it called?"

"Fillian," Lord Cennyth replied. "We bring it out only on special occasions, such as the arrival of you and your wife."

"I do not mean any offense, Lord Cennyth," Jenara said, "but I would prefer to have water, if possible."

Lord Cennyth frowned. "Are you certain?"

"I am with child, lord," Jenara said. "I must be more cautious with myself now."

Lord Cennyth beamed at Delgar. "I had no idea you were so lucky a man! This is definitely cause for celebration! More wine for everybody, excepting, of course, your wife, Archmage Delgar."

Delgar nodded and smiled. "Thank you, my lord."

"There is no need to be so formal now," Lord Cennyth stated. "You are a valued member of my council, and I would like to consider you a friend. With the dark news from the north, my people have not had cause to celebrate very often in the recent past. The war against Taerraland also took a toll."

"I do not understand," Delgar said. "I was under the impression that you were friendly to Taerrans."

"I am," Lord Cennyth said. "Unfortunately, in the war the Taerrans did not usually distinguish between friendly lords of Pakaria and hostile ones, and we all ended up fighting. I am only pleased the war is over now."

Lord Cennyth paused to take a drink of wine, and then turned to Jenara. "Tell me, my lady: are the accommodations to your liking?"

Jenara put down the mutton she had been eating and nodded. "Not quite what I am used to, but very decent. Thank you for your hospitality, lord."

"It is the least I can do," Lord Cennyth said.

"However, Delgar and I will be spending a great deal of time in council about refugees. I fear that you are only the beginning of a flood, and I cannot afford to give everybody the same hospitality."

"These are harsh times, lord," Jenara said.

"Indeed," Lord Cennyth said, standing up. "But tonight, at least, we celebrate!"

As the cheering wore down, Delgar looked at Jenara, wondering why she suddenly seemed so distant.

Delgar watched Jenara that night as they lay in bed, his fingers idly tracing over the soft curve of her belly. Her skin was bathed with a soft glow from the full moon shining through their window.

"What is wrong, my love?" Delgar asked.

"Sorry?"

"You seemed very distant tonight," Delgar stated. "You're not usually like that."

"When we got into the feast hall, I suddenly felt like this was the wrong place for me," Jenara said. "I'm not sure how to explain it."

"Do you think we're in danger?" Delgar asked.

Jenara shook her head. "Lord Cennyth seems to be one of the most decent men I've ever met. I don't think we're in any danger from him. But there is something, and it doesn't feel quite right."

"Do you want us to leave?"

Jenara shook her head vigorously. "We would be foolish to. Besides, once again we're needed here. We can help these people, and I want to."

"But something still seems wrong."

Jenara nodded. "And I have absolutely no idea what it is."

With that, they fell silent, cradling each other in the

moonlight as they waited for daybreak.

Lord Cennyth might have been a friendly lord, but Delgar quickly discovered that he was also a very busy one. The day after they arrived he found himself summoned to discuss the refugee situation, and they spent the day making plans to house the flood of refugees that would come from Taerraland. The next day followed in the same suit, and the day after that, and soon Delgar found weeks passing by and the autumn breezes changing into the chill snows of winter.

He came to admire Lord Cennyth. The man was very eager to assist in the crisis, and soon Delgar found himself helping to arrange for meetings between Lord Cennyth and the other lords of Pakaria. There was a strange sadness in Lord Cennyth, though, and every now and then Delgar wondered why he was so eager to welcome Jenara and himself into his household.

Jenara, on the other hand, spent her time organizing and managing their tower. Delgar offered to help several times, but she always turned him down, telling him: "You have your tasks, and I will see to mine." He thought she was mostly content, but every now and then he would catch her looking out from the battlements with a disapproving gaze, and he knew that while she might be content, that did not mean she was happy.

Delgar wondered what he could do, and as the weeks went by, and she began to show her condition more and more, he finally decided to bring the matter up after a council.

"Lord Cennyth," Delgar said, carefully choosing his words. "Would I be free to leave, if I absolutely had to?"

Lord Cennyth leaned back in his chair, a curious and sad look in his eyes. "Certainly. I hold you under no contract of service. Why do you ask?"

"My wife isn't quite happy here," Delgar said, and then paused, uncertain of what to say next.

Lord Cennyth smiled. "And you want her to be. I understand; I was married once myself. It could be many things, though. Her pregnancy is showing more and more; women can become slightly odd as their condition progresses. It could be that she is unhappy having settled in a place that she knows she is going to have to leave soon. I must admit that I am not perfectly happy here either, knowing that. If you feel you must leave, however, I will not stop you. I would warn you against traveling at this time of year, however. Our Pakarian winters can be much harsher than what you have experienced in Taerraland."

Delgar nodded. "Thank you for your insight. I was just worried about her. I think I understand a bit more, now."

Lord Cennyth chuckled. "Now I know this is a serious crisis."

"Sorry?"

Lord Cennyth grinned. "An Archmage of Taerra just thanked me for my advice. The world can't possibly be working properly when that happens."

Both Delgar and Lord Cennyth burst out into laughter, and for the first time in days Delgar felt some relief.

The refugees began to arrive as the winter was ending. Lord Cennyth housed the first refugees in the village, using an old barracks to hold them until better facilities could be built. Those who were well enough to travel were sent southwards as soon as possible, but many were exhausted.

Jenara began spending her days helping to nurse the sick and injured, even though she herself was heavy with

293

child. Delgar assisted her whenever he could, but during the winter he had become Lord Cennyth's most trusted advisor, and Lord Cennyth had him in attendance for most of the daylight hours. The stories Delgar heard from Taerra chilled his blood, however.

"I saw the ice," an old man told him just before he was moved south. "I saw it crumble the walls of Taerra. It was horrible. I can still hear the screaming."

"When did it happen?" Delgar asked.

"The day I left, maybe three weeks ago," the old man said. "I got out as quickly as I could, but most of us still there couldn't. We all wanted to stay, Damned One take our souls, we all didn't believe what they were telling us and wanted to stay!"

Delgar decided that night to give Jenara the news. She rocked awkwardly on her chair, cradling her swollen belly, a shocked look in her eye. "Then it really is gone," she finally said, and wouldn't say anything else about it. But both of them knew what the news meant: time was running out.

Almost as if the Eternal One wanted to show them that there was still some hope in the world, the winter snows began to melt, and the spring sunlight shone through the clouds. Delgar and Jenara enjoyed the freedom from the biting cold, and began to spend time sitting on the battlements, watching the east and trying to pretend that no refugees were coming from the west.

"At least we have another spring," Jenara said one day, gazing at some farmland. "I'm glad we can see the spring again before we have to move on."

Delgar mumbled an agreement and held her. As they sat together, he felt a sudden kick from her belly.

"You're glowing, you know," Delgar said.

"I have a new life inside me," Jenara said, smiling. "I only wish you could experience this wonder for yourself."

He put his hand on her stomach, hoping to feel another kick. "Our child," he said.

"Our daughter," Jenara corrected. "Don't deny a mother's instincts."

"And what about a father's instincts?"

"They don't count."

Delgar laughed. "I see."

Jenara stiffened, her eyes wide in shock. "Oh my!"

Delgar leapt to his feet. "What is it? Are you okay?"

"My water just broke," Jenara said. "Call a wet-nurse."

Delgar took a step towards the battlement stairs, but Jenara gripped his robes with an iron grasp.

"Don't leave me!" she gasped, her breathing heavy.

"But how will I find a wet-nurse?"

"Have Caerwyth do it!"

Delgar nodded. "CAERWYTH!" he shouted. "We need some help!"

He heard somebody pounding up the stairs, and then Caerwyth was there. "Are you under attack?" the soldier asked. "What is it?"

"She's going into labor," Delgar said. "Find us a wet-nurse, and quickly!"

"Right away!" Caerwyth said, and dashed down the stairs into the courtyard.

"You'll be alright," Delgar said.

"I don't feel well," Jenara muttered. "It doesn't feel right."

Caerwyth returned, a plump woman behind him. "Caetlyn delivered my son a year ago," he said. "She's very good."

Caetlyn looked Jenara over, her eyes widening in alarm. "We need to get her inside immediately."

Delgar wasn't entirely sure how it happened, but there was a flurry of shouting, he heard Lord Cennyth giving some orders, he remembered helping Jenara across the courtyard, and then he found himself holding her hand as she lay on a bed, some ancient charms at her feet as she moaned in pain.

"Push!" Caetlyn ordered, and Jenara gritted her teeth in pain. Delgar tried to think of something helpful to say, but he couldn't. Instead, he just held her hand as she tightened her grasp.

"Push!"

"I love you," Delgar said, watching his wife's features distort in agony. He looked to the wet-nurse, only to find a very concerned look on Caetlyn's face.

"Push!"

Jenara's back arched, and suddenly she relaxed, her limp fingers in Delgar's hand. He heard something wet slide onto the bed, which he could only assume was the afterbirth.

"My baby?" Jenara whispered. "What's happened to my baby?"

"Is it a son or a daughter?" Delgar asked. "Is she okay?"

Tears running down her cheeks, Caetlyn held the child up. Delgar's heart plummeted as he saw the large baby, its head turned at an unnatural angle from the umbilical cord wrapped around its neck.

"I'm sorry," Caetlyn said, cutting the cord. "There was nothing I could do for her. It was a daughter."

Delgar could only hold Jenara as she began to cry, and then her weeping was joined by his own.

That night Delgar sat on the battlements, his eyes teary. He tried to think of what his daughter would have been like if she had survived, a beautiful raven-haired beauty standing out in his mind. She would have been just like Jenara; he knew it. He wished he could cry for her some more, but he had no tears left.

"Do you mind if I join you?" a familiar voice said. Delgar turned to find Lord Cennyth by the top of the battlement stairs. When Delgar didn't answer, Lord Cennyth approached. "I didn't think I'd find you up here. It's quite a view, though."

"I needed some fresh air."

Lord Cennyth looked over the battlements, gazing to the hills in the north. "You're in mourning," he said. "Even though you didn't really know her, you still feel as though you've lost a part of yourself."

"Just before I came here I looked at Jenara," Delgar said. "And for a brief moment, I saw her in the shadows, looking as though she was still pregnant. But it was just a trick of the light."

"That won't end soon," Lord Cennyth said. "I wish I could tell you otherwise. I wish I could tell you that you'll forget it all tomorrow. But you won't. All I can tell you is that you are still lucky."

Delgar stared at him. "How could you possibly say that?"

"You still have your wife," Lord Cennyth said. "When my son was stillborn, my wife only survived him by a day."

Delgar blinked. "I had no idea."

"I don't like to talk about it," Lord Cennyth said. "But, I know that right now Jenara needs you, probably more than she's ever needed you before. You should go to her."

Delgar stood and nodded. He stayed to look over the hills once more, gazing out with his Dragon sight. And then his blood chilled. Almost beyond his sight, behind one of the hills, he saw a glowing blue-white ribbon of ice creeping toward him.

Chapter VII: The Dawning of Darkness

The approach of the glacier was marked by an increase in activity at Lord Cennyth's fortress. Lord Cennyth finished his negotiations with the lords at his borders and began to move his people, joining a flood of refugees heading southwards. What had once been a relaxed air at the castle became one of apprehension.

"I wish we could all just get up and leave!" Lord Cennyth sputtered after one long meeting. "But my people number in the tens of thousands, and they aren't soldiers. We still need to see to food and lodgings along the way, and it is just a mess."

Delgar, however, had problems of his own. Jenara was not well. Instead of getting better after the stillbirth, she was constantly feeling weak, as though the child had taken some part of her life essence with it. Delgar found himself spending half his time nursing Jenara and the other half trying to help Lord Cennyth make heads or tails of the mess the evacuation had become.

And every time he looked out to the north, the glacier was closer. It was coming for them, slowly but surely.

Lord Cennyth found him on the battlements with Jenara in his arms a couple of weeks after the stillbirth, watching the north.

"I thought I'd find you two here," Lord Cennyth stated. "I still can't see it, though."

"You don't have my sight," Delgar said. "I can see it coming. We only have a few weeks, if that."

"Can you see anything, Lady Jenara?" Lord Cennyth asked kindly.

Jenara only shivered against Delgar's chest and held him tighter. Delgar turned away from the north and stared down at the courtyard, watching some of the villagers leaving on the southern road with what few belongings they could take.

He took a moment to look at Jenara, and then he held her more tightly than before. Her skin had become pale and cold to the touch. He had tried several times to heal her with magic, but to no effect; he still wasn't certain what was ailing her.

Delgar was summoned the next morning to Lord Cennyth's side. He walked through the courtyard, shuddering in the chill wind from the north. The once sunny sky was covered with clouds, and Delgar wondered why it hadn't started snowing yet.

He found Lord Cennyth sitting on his throne, stroking his beard. His court, usually Spartan at best, was completely empty.

"The spring is turning back into winter," Lord Cennyth stated. "I fear you were right all along, Archmage Delgar."

Delgar only nodded sadly.

"Is there anything you can do against this glacier?"

Delgar shook his head. "The entire council of Archmages, with a couple of exceptions left to take care of the Mageschool, tried to destroy it. Jenara and I were the only survivors. All you can do is run and hope it doesn't have the power to follow you."

"I remember there were once these little Dragons to the north," Lord Cennyth mused. "Tiny things, really. Every now and then you would glimpse one in the forests when you were hunting. Nobody's seen them for months."

"They're all gone, my lord," Delgar said, his voice cracking as he remembered the last moments of the Teraeni Dragons. "I was there when it happened."

"And soon the lords of Pakaria and the kingdom of Taerraland will be no more," Lord Cennyth said. "We are in the last age, I think."

"Perhaps. I don't know."

"I will be the last one to leave," Lord Cennyth declared. "However, your wife is ill, and she needs to be safe. If she is well enough to travel, I want you to go south tomorrow morning."

"Do you have no further need of me?" Delgar asked.

"I have much need of you," Lord Cennyth said. "But Lady Jenara needs you more. See her out of here, and I'll meet you in the south."

Delgar bowed and turned to leave. With a heavy heart, he walked towards the door. Just as he was about to exit, Lord Cennyth called out to him.

Delgar turned. "My lord?"

"If I don't see you again," Lord Cennyth said, "I want you to know that I have been honored by your presence."

"Thank you, my lord," Delgar said, and then left.

He made his way back to his tower, his mind running through all the things he would need in order to leave. They would have to pack their clothes again, and they would have to reclaim their wagon. He shook his head.

300

Once again they would be refugees, trying to escape the end of the world, if it was at all possible.

When he got into the tower, he called for Jenara, but there was no answer. He stopped into the anteroom, his mind racing. Surely she had just gone out for a moment, it had to be that. After all, she had said that there were a couple of things she wanted to do the previous night.

"Jenara?" he shouted, walking up the stairs into the library. "Are you there?"

He climbed another flight of stairs into the bedroom, and rushed to the bed in panic. Jenara lay there, her face waxy, her breathing labored.

"Jenara, my love?" Delgar said, trying to keep his voice calm. "Are you alright?"

"I tried to get up," Jenara rasped. "But then I felt dizzy and I had to lie down again, and then I felt cold, and..."

He placed his hand gently on her forehead, grimacing as he felt the intense heat. He knew that no doctor would be able to do any more good than his magic had; during his time in Pakaria he had seen the local doctors, and he was much less than impressed.

"I need you to rest, okay?" Delgar said. "I'm going to get you some nice warm soup, and I want you to rest. You're going to be fine, I swear it."

With that, he dashed out to get some soup.

For a couple of days, he nursed her on bread, butter, soup and water. Lord Cennyth stopped in every day to ask as to her condition, but Delgar never had anything promising to report to him. Every morning and night he tried to use his magic to heal her, but to no effect.

On the third day, she could no longer hold down the bread and butter. That night, Delgar prayed to the Eternal One for her life, that by some miracle she would recover.

He found himself unable to sleep, wandering the battlements like a ghost in the early hours of the morning when he knew that Jenara was sleeping as comfortably as she could.

Lord Cennyth called a doctor the next day, but after his examination the man declared that nothing could be done. Delgar continued to nurse Jenara as best he could, hoping that he could somehow make her whole again. He spent that entire night watching her in candlelight, trying to remember better days only to be brought back into the present by her shallow breathing.

By the fifth day, snow had begun to fall in the courtyard. Delgar awoke from a brief slumber to see the morning light streaking through the clouds, illuminating the snow so that every flake appeared magical. He turned to Jenara, and whatever joy had been in his heart perished at the sight of her. Her once vibrant skin was a pale grey, and her breathing was shallow and quick.

"Hello, Delgar," she rasped, and he leaned forward to hear her more clearly. "I feel strange today."

"What do you mean?" Delgar asked, trying to keep his voice under control.

"My body feels numb, and I feel sleepy," she said. "I wonder if this is how the end feels."

Delgar shook his head. "You'll get better, I swear. Lord Cennyth said he'd bring you some flowers today. You know how much you like flowers..."

Jenara shook her head, a sad smile on her face. "I can't stay, my love."

Delgar began to cry. "But you have to stay. I don't know what I'd do without you. You're the only thing that made this world bearable to me."

"I can't," Jenara said, a tear rolling down her cheek. "My time has come. I've led a blessed life: I've had you to love me."

"I don't want you to go," Delgar sobbed.

"You're beginning to fade," Jenara whispered. "When it is your time, I'll see you again. Until then, I love you."

"I love you too..." Delgar began, but the light in her eyes was gone. With trembling fingers, he closed her eyelids. Then he tucked her sheets in, so that she'd be nice and comfortable with the snow falling. And then he walked out of the tower.

He collapsed at the foot of the tower, weeping. As the sat, the snow fell around him and on him, covering the world in a white blanket. She never minded snow, Delgar recalled, remembering some happy winters in Taerra. The memory only brought more tears.

"I've come too late," somebody said, and Delgar looked up to see Lord Cennyth standing over him, a pot of flowers cradled in his arm.

Delgar only had the strength to nod.

"By the luck of the Damned One," Lord Cennyth cursed, sitting in the snow beside him. "It was probably the damned ice approaching that did it."

"It was the child," Delgar said.

"Sorry?"

"I felt it every time I tried to heal her," Delgar stated. "The child was special, and when it died it took too much of her life energy with it."

"Now I understand the old Barshian curse," Lord Cennyth said. "'May you live in interesting times.' Just our luck that we had to be born in time for the end of the world."

At any other moment, Delgar would have laughed. Instead, he stared sullenly forward, remembering Jenara's easy sense of humor. It was all gone now.

"I'll arrange for her burial," Lord Cennyth said.

Delgar shook his head. "She should be burned. I won't give her bones to the ice. She deserves better than that."

"Burning is not our custom."

"It's mine," Delgar said. "If the smoke rises quickly upwards, her soul has gone to the Eternal One. If the smoke lingers, the soul has gone to the Damned One."

Lord Cennyth nodded. "As you wish."

The funeral pyre was set that night, the chill wind and blanket of snow somehow making the occasion even more morose. Delgar held Jenara for the last time as she lay on the pyre, and as he did he was tempted to join her. But somehow, he gathered the strength or the cowardice to step back and take the lit torch Lord Cennyth held out for him.

"Goodbye, my love," Delgar said. "I will see you again when my time has come to join you."

He lit the embers at the bottom of the pyre and stepped aside, watching as the flames rose up to claim his beloved's body. Once again, he felt an urge to leap onto the pyre and join her, but instead he stood still, feeling lonely and sad. Somehow, he knew that the empty place in his heart her passing had left would never be filled.

A poem suddenly came to mind, something he had read back in the Mageschool in his second year. He had never truly understood it until this moment. Softly, under his breath, he began to recite:

> "I walk down the road-side,
> The memory of friends long passed as my company.
> I look into time and see no answers.
> The future has not been written,
> The past is set in stone,
> And I am but a lonely wanderer,
> With time as my only home."

To his small relief, despite the chill wind, the smoke

rose quickly upwards in a long column stretching into the sky. He smiled, tears rolling down his cheeks, knowing that she truly had gone to a better place. As the pyre burned down, his last thoughts were of her, and he wondered when he would be able to join her.

The tower seemed especially empty without her, perfectly matching his heart. Delgar found himself in a dreamlike state, seeing Jenara out of the corner of his eye wherever he turned, but there was only ever empty space. He spent a day wandering aimlessly through his tower, noticing all the things she used to like. Then he lay down on what was once their bed and wept.

He startled awake with the sunrise, and for a moment he wasn't sure where or when he was. Then the memory of the last night returned, and he wept again for his lost love. He felt empty inside, as though the best of him had been cut out with her death.

He was awakened from his thoughts by a pounding at the door. For a couple of minutes he ignored it, not really caring what it was. But when the knocking didn't cease, he finally walked down the tower steps and opened the door.

Caerwyth stood before him, a frenzied look on his face. "Lord Cennyth wants you to come immediately," he gasped. "It's an emergency."

"What is it?" Delgar asked.

"We are surrounded by Dragons!" Caerwyth cried. "Great big ones! They're flying around us and landing in the courtyard!"

"Let me get my Archmage robe on," Delgar said. "I'll be there in a minute."

"But we don't have a minute-" Caerwyth protested as Delgar closed the door. Delgar's mind raced as he pulled on his robes. What could the Dragons want from him now?

His oath as Magus Draconum suddenly came to mind, and he hoped that they didn't want something too difficult; he really didn't feel up to anything large.

Delgar stepped out of his tower to see Lord Cennyth pounding through the courtyard, trying to keep a distance from the several Great Dragons that had landed. Delgar stepped out with a measured pace, looking for a Dragon he recognized.

"Archmage Delgar!" Lord Cennyth shouted. "There must be hundreds of them! What do they want?"

"They want me," Delgar said. "I'm sworn to them."

"What?" Lord Cennyth sputtered, his eyes wide in shock.

"I am Magus Draconum, the Dragonmage," Delgar said. "In a very real way, I am one of them as well. Now that you know my secret, you'll also know that they've come for me. If you'll excuse me, I have some business to attend to."

Delgar looked around. "Leoht'heortan!" he shouted. "Are you here? Who speaks for all of you?"

"I am here," Leoht'heortan boomed in the Dragon-language, landing in front of Delgar. "You are not looking well, my friend."

"I have lost my mate," Delgar said, speaking in the Dragon tongue. "My heart is broken."

"I grieve for you, Delgar," the Dragon said. "We all do. We will sing a song of beauty to take her soul to the heavens. But I fear you do not know how lucky you are."

"I don't understand," Delgar said. "My soul is empty. She was the best part of me."

"You experienced mortal love," Leoht'heortan declared. "We Dragons have watched you mortals for millennia, and there is nothing more powerful than mortal love. None of us have ever experienced it, and we can only marvel at what you must have felt."

"Surely you know love."

"We do," the Dragon said. "But our love could never be as intense as mortal love. We will live forever; mortals will not."

"What is happening here?" Lord Cennyth cut in. "What are you saying? Are these your friends?"

Delgar turned to him and nodded. "They are my friends, comrades, and in a way my only family. I have fought beside them and I owe them my life. This here is Leoht'heortan, who saved my life in the deserts of Barsh."

"I am honored to meet you," Leoht'heortan said in the human tongue, snaking his head down in a sort of bow. "We have watched you carefully, and you have treated our friend well. You have nothing to fear from us. But now we must have council with Delgar alone."

"I guess I'll be going, then," Lord Cennyth said, backing away. "I will see you later, Delgar."

"The time has come, and we need you, Delgar Dragonmage," Leoht'heortan stated, switching back to the Dragon tongue.

"The council of Archmages tried," Delgar said. "We tried to destroy the glacier, but we couldn't. It defeated us."

"This world is lost, at least for now. We must make our home elsewhere."

"I do not know how I am to help you with that," Delgar said. "I'm not even sure what I am anymore."

"You are one of us, and you are greater than us," Leoht'heortan said. "It is time for you to walk the Road of Legends."

Delgar blinked. "What is that?"

"It is the great Road, the Road that links all worlds together," the Dragon replied. "On it you will find every world ever imagined, and like us you can walk upon it."

"How do I do that?"

"We will teach you, just as we will teach you to unlock your true powers," Leoht'heortan said, his head snaking down so that he gazed directly into Delgar's eyes. "Delgar, my friend, the time has come for Dragonkind to leave Mideorth, and it is your task to lead us."

Chapter VIII: The Road of Legends

Delgar plunged himself into his Draconic training, half hoping it would drive his grief away. He was certain that Lord Cennyth, still swamped with the task of moving the last of the refugees southwards, was not entirely happy with the Dragons surrounding his fortress. But, as with the glacier, there was nothing anybody could do about it.

His efforts to hold back the pain of Jenara's death were to no avail. He spent his nights weeping as he tried to sleep alone in his bed. As soon as he got up in the morning, Leoht'heortan began to instruct him, drilling him on how to use his powers.

"The Dragon is inside you," Leoht'heortan told him after a long day practicing the transformation. "It is a part of you. You must never deny it, or it can drive you mad. Embrace it and your true nature will serve you well."

"But I'm not a true Dragon," Delgar said. "I was born a mortal."

"And that is why you are greater than us,"

Leoht'heortan stated. "You have experienced all the things we never could. You understand what it is to live in the moment. You are the best of both worlds, and you can draw power from that."

"So I won't lose my humanity?" Delgar asked.

Leoht'heortan shook his head. "It is one of your greatest strengths. And soon you will learn to use your other great strength."

"But the ice will be here soon."

Leoht'heortan laugh boomed across the courtyard. "You are still thinking like a mortal! You will still be learning for centuries after the ice comes."

Delgar blinked, a tear running down his cheek. "Centuries."

The Dragon nodded. "Do not fear; you will find life quite bearable, once you know how. And the Road is filled with wonders."

"When will you teach me about the Road?" Delgar asked.

"I think you will be ready tomorrow," Leoht'heortan said. "I will be your guide for your first journey. You should go and rest."

Delgar walked onto the battlements and stared north. The ice loomed before him, always approaching and finally within mortal sight. If he was right, they only had about two weeks left.

"I see you are up here again," a voice said, and Delgar turned to find Lord Cennyth regarding him. "I find myself spending a great deal of time here as well."

"Can you see the ice?" Delgar asked.

Lord Cennyth nodded. "I never thought it would look that big. Somehow your description never did it justice."

"How are the refugees?"

"Only a few remain," Lord Cennyth said. "I will be leading them to the south tomorrow morning. I always thought I would be the last to leave. I guess I was mistaken."

Delgar gazed out over the landscape, watching the blue-white ribbon tower over the snow-blanketed hills. "You're saying farewell, then."

Lord Cennyth nodded. "My place is with my people. We Pakarians are a hearty folk; we'll survive easily enough in the south. I guess I have to wonder if you will be as well where you're headed."

Delgar shrugged. "I do not know. I feel as though I am living out some horrible dream."

"That is grief," Lord Cennyth said. "It will pass, and then there will just be the memories. I think, in your case, they will be good ones."

"Jenara knew," Delgar said. "Right after we arrived, she said that this place felt wrong to her. She knew something bad would happen. I should have listened."

"Delgar, I want you to remember this," Lord Cennyth began. "You cannot be responsible for her choices. I know that if she had wanted to leave, she would have, you at her side. You must never forget her, but do not blame yourself for what happened. Right now, the best way to honor her is to live your life as well as you can. And while she no longer needs you, there are several Dragons that do."

"I'll remember that."

"I only wish I understood what your task is," Lord Cennyth said, shaking his head. "You certainly keep interesting company. They've done me one favor, at least."

"What?"

"No new refugees will come near them. So long as they are here, I don't have to worry about any newcomers."

In spite of his pain and grief, Delgar chuckled.

"I should go and rest," Lord Cennyth said. "Somehow, I doubt I'll see you again in my lifetime. Farewell, Delgar

Dragonmage. While our paths crossed, it was an honor to have known you."

Delgar nodded and embraced his former lord. "Farewell, Cennyth. I will always remember you with honor."

Lord Cennyth smiled. "What more can a man ask for? I'll see you in the next life." With that, he stepped down from the battlements and walked into the keep. Delgar watched him go, and then stayed on the wall to watch the stars rise.

The morning sun shone in Delgar's eyes as he faced Leoht'heortan. He had been uncertain of what to wear, and had settled on some light robes with a warm cloak. If he came to a hot place, he would only have to remove the cloak.

The Dragon's head snaked down to face him. "A bit overdressed, aren't you?"

"It's best to be prepared," Delgar said.

Leoht'heortan nodded. "True enough."

"So how do I walk on this Road?" Delgar asked.

"Do you believe in the Road?" Leoht'heortan demanded.

"Of course I do," Delgar said. "What does it matter."

"It matters more than anything else," Leoht'heortan declared. "To walk on the Road of Legends, you must believe in it. Otherwise, you will never be able to go where it can take you."

"I don't understand."

"How can you every truly go somewhere you don't believe in?" Leoht'heortan said. "Even if a place is real, if you do not believe in it you can never see it for what it truly is."

"True, I guess."

"The Road is the sum of your dreams and beliefs," the Dragon stated. "It is made of the very stuff of the universe, and it is the very stuff of dreams."

"Like the Cave of Dreams?" Delgar asked.

"The Cave of Dreams is a part of the Road," Leoht'heortan replied. "But most people do not realize it."

"So how do we get to it?" Delgar asked.

"The way we get to any road," the Dragon replied. "We walk or we fly, whatever is our pleasure. Walk with me, Delgar."

As Leoht'heortan strode out of the castle, Delgar jogged to keep up. The Dragon led him down into the once vibrant village, but the thatched roofs had begun to crack with decay. As they stepped through the abandoned village Delgar reflected that Lord Cennyth had spoken truly; the last of his people had left with him.

"Keep your mind on the Road," Leoht'heortan said, never breaking stride.

"I remember," Delgar replied.

Delgar suddenly stopped and glanced around. He was surrounded by a dense mist, the faint form of the Dragon before him.

"Why have you stopped, Delgar?" Leoht'heortan asked. "Are you well?"

"I don't know where I am," Delgar said. "I can't see through the mist."

"You are on the Road of Legends now," Leoht'heortan said. "The mist is the stuff of the Road, that which dreams are made of. Keep pace with me, for I do not want you to be without a guide."

Delgar hurried to the Dragon's side, trying to peer out of the mist without success. When he looked down at his feet, he found that the ground was as grey as the fog itself. A cold shiver went down his spine.

"Where are we?" Delgar asked.

"We are between worlds," Leoht'heortan answered.

"Do you know where we are going?"

"Yes. Please follow."

As Leoht'heortan padded into the mists again, Delgar followed, trying to keep the faint outline of the Dragon in sight. It seemed to him that they had walked for hours, the grey fog coiling around them so that they walked together in limbo.

"How long will we walk?" Delgar finally asked, wondering why he wasn't growing tired.

"For some, forever," the Dragon replied. "And for others, only a few minutes. Time does not exist on the Road as it does on other worlds."

"That's not much of an answer," Delgar said.

"There are some things that cannot be easily explained," Leoht'heortan declared. "This is one of them. Once you have experienced it for a few millennia, then you will understand the Road. Until then, you must take it on faith."

They walked in silence for what seemed like a few more hours, and then the mists began to clear. Delgar found himself stepping onto a harsh desert, a searing sun beating down on him. He shielded his eyes with a sweaty hand, looking around for any sign of water or life.

"What is this place?" Delgar asked.

"None of us know," the Dragon replied. "It has been here for as long as the Road itself, and even when we first saw it we found it to be a dead world. Perhaps it was one of the casualties of the wars between the Dragon Masters."

"Who were the Dragon Masters?" Delgar asked.

"They were the creatures of power who enslaved us," Leoht'heortan said. "Few of us alive now know where they came from, only that we were their slaves. They warred between themselves for eons, and then we and the other creatures of the Road were freed in the Great

Rebellion."

A flicker of ancient memory flashed into Delgar's mind. "Led by Garasus."

"Yes. And we have traveled the Road ever since."

"Why do you need me?" Delgar asked. "Surely you can find your own world."

Leoht'heortan shook his serpentine head. "You forget what I told you. We were slaves; we were never meant to lead. While we were on Mideorth, we sought our solitude. Only the Great Dragonlords, who stood with us against the Dragon Masters, were meant to lead, and they left long ago. None of us knows where they are now."

"Were the Great Dragonlords Dragons like you?"

"They were greater than us. And after the rebellion they took a few who were willing to follow them and left."

"Why didn't the rest go with them?"

"Because those of us who remain will never again be slaves, and we will never again have masters," Leoht'heortan declared. "Now you are our protector, and you will lead us to a new home. When you have found a way to destroy the ice and restore Mideorth, you will lead us back. But you will not be our master, just as the Great Dragonlords will not be our masters."

"Am I a slave, then?" Delgar asked.

"No," the Dragon said. "You are free to do whatever you wish while you complete your task. But you have an obligation to us until it is done."

"So what now?" Delgar asked. "If you already know that this place is dead, why are we here?"

"It is a good place for you to learn about the Road," Leoht'heortan said. "Here you may walk on and off the Road without anybody seeing."

"How did we get onto it?" Delgar asked.

"We walked," the Dragon replied. "While you believed, I willed us onto it."

"Willpower is all it takes, then?"

Leoht'heortan shook his head. "There is more than that. There is belief, and there is focus."

"I still don't quite understand."

Delgar heard a chuckling behind him, and he spun to see a grey figure regarding them from a sand dune.

"Leave it to a Dragon to make something perfectly simple into something incredibly difficult," the figure said. "I fear too much wisdom ill suits a teacher."

Leoht'heortan bowed his head. "Greetings, Daelyn."

Daelyn smiled and approached. "Greetings, Delgar. I hope you have been well."

"Daelyn," Delgar breathed. "I never thought I would see you again."

"I knew we would meet here," Daelyn stated. "It was in both our wyrds. Will you have me as a teacher?"

"I would be a willing student," Delgar said. "Assuming Leoht'heortan has no objections."

"I will leave Delgar in your care, Daelyn," Leoht'heortan said. "The ice is coming shortly, so you must teach him quickly."

"Return to Mideorth," Daelyn said. "I marked the path you took. We will be there soon."

With a great leap, Leoht'heortan took flight, leaving Delgar and Daelyn alone in the sands. Delgar looked at his former sponsor, looking for some sign of the time which had passed and finding none.

"You look older, Delgar," Daelyn said. "You have some grey in your beard now."

"I have lost my wife and I am losing my world," Delgar said. "I feel very old."

Daelyn smiled. "You have discovered the most horrible aspect of life, then."

"And what is that?"

"Life is not kind, nor cruel. It is completely

316

indifferent. All we can do is live it."

Delgar nodded. "That sounds about right."

"I grieve for your loss," Daelyn said. "I remember Jenara; she was a very good woman."

"Yes, she was."

"Well, we must go," Daelyn said. "We have a long journey, and we are almost out of time."

Chapter IX: Travels Through Distant Worlds

Delgar followed Daelyn back onto the Road, marking how they simply began walking and the mist followed. It curled around them, and even though the Tuatha de Danaan was very close, he still appeared to be only an outline to Delgar.

"How did you do that?" Delgar asked. "When Leoht'heortan took me onto the Road, we walked for some time before we got there."

"The Road is everywhere," Daelyn said. "You can enter it from any point, so long as you have the will."

"So it is really just a matter of will," Delgar said.

"Essentially, yes," Daelyn said. "But that act of will that allows you to walk on the Road only works if you believe in it and can focus on it."

"But how will we know where it is taking us?" Delgar asked. "I see no markers."

Daelyn stopped and smiled. "If you look, you will find

them. We are not the only travelers on this Road, and those who came before us left signs."

"What should I look for?" Delgar asked.

"You will feel the markers as you pass, if you are looking for them," Daelyn explained. "The signs are just as the Road itself, made of beliefs and dreams. I guess you should extend your senses and look for magic." He began walking again. "But right now we are too far between worlds to see a sign. We must walk further."

"Where are you taking me, anyway?" Delgar asked.

Daelyn glanced back, but kept walking. "We are going to a world I found that would be perfect for the Dragons."

"You know my mission?"

"I have been watching you," Daelyn said. "And it was written in your wyrd."

"So all of this was pre-ordained?" Delgar demanded. "The ice, losing Jenara, all of it?"

"Yes," Daelyn said. "But while wyrd is your destiny, in the end it is made of your choices. Everything that occurred was bound to happen, but it was you that made it so."

"But how can I have any choices if it is all pre-ordained?" Delgar asked.

"That is an ancient question," Daelyn said. "And people have been asking it for millennia. All I can tell you is that you did have the choice to do otherwise at every moment of your life. But some events are greater than you are. Had you not married Jenara, the ice would still have come and she would still have died. But, since you did, she had the happiness of being with you in her final moments, rather than being alone and afraid."

Delgar grimaced. "Perhaps we are in the shadow of our wyrd, then."

"Perhaps," Daelyn conceded, and then fell silent. They walked through the mists, Delgar mulling over the question, but failing to think of anything helpful or comforting.

It felt as though more hours had passed, and then the image exploded in his mind. Delgar reeled as he suddenly saw vast green fields, high mountains, and clear lakes. For a moment he was soaring as high as an eagle, gazing over a virgin landscape. He glided over the green forests, the wind whistling through his hair and clothes. And then, as suddenly as the image began, it faded, leaving him in the mists of the Road.

"What was that?" Delgar asked, trying to regain his balance.

"That is a landmark," Daelyn said, his form a mere outline in the fog. "That is how we know where we are going."

"Who could have left something like that there?" Delgar asked. "I've never experienced anything like it in my life."

Delgar thought he saw the Tuatha de Danaan shrug through the mist. "Nobody knows. I suppose that before the Dragons and the Tuatha de Danaan, there were others who traveled this road. But these roadmarks are all that remains of them."

"So how does it tell us which direction to go?" Delgar said.

Daelyn approached and smiled. "In time, you'll learn how to read that too. However, you have much to learn, and I will teach it to you later. For now, we must walk."

Delgar followed Daelyn through the fog, and finally the mist began to part, revealing the green, fertile world Delgar had seen earlier. He stood in awe at the untouched landscape, watching what appeared to be a herd of cow-like animals grazing in the plains of a great valley.

"What is this place?" Delgar breathed.

"I do not know," Daelyn said. "I have only been here

a couple of times, and all I know is that it has never been touched by the hands of civilization. It is an untouched world, Delgar. It is perfect."

"There is nothing to threaten the Dragons here?" Delgar asked.

"Nothing at all," Daelyn stated. "Here they may live in peace, at least until the time comes for them to return to their home."

"Paradise," Delgar said.

"Yes."

"Leoht'heortan will be very pleased," Delgar stated.

"They all will."

"Come, Delgar," Daelyn said, waving towards the Road. "We have an exodus to lead."

"You're coming with me?" Delgar asked.

Daelyn chuckled. "Of course! How else do you expect to be able to return here?"

Delgar conceded the point as he followed Daelyn back onto the Road of Legends.

The glacier was within a couple of miles of the fortress by the time Delgar and Daelyn arrived. Delgar watched the Dragons pacing nervously around the abandoned courtyard, and then looked up at the wall of blue-white ice.

"We really are almost out of time," Delgar muttered. "My world is lost."

"For now," Daelyn said. "Your wyrd says you will reclaim it some day."

"How is it that everybody knows my wyrd but me?" Delgar asked. "It really is getting annoying."

Daelyn smiled. "How can you see all of a land when you are standing on it? You are surrounded by wyrd. Do not worry; soon you'll learn how to read the wyrd of others."

"Delgar, my friend!" Leoht'heortan called, landing before him. "You have returned! We had begun to worry."

Delgar scratched his beard. "How long were we gone?"

"Three days," Leoht'heortan declared. "The ice is moving faster now."

"I'm not hungry," Delgar mused. "How can that be?"

"When you travel on the Road, it sustains you," Daelyn said. "If you stay here for long, however, you will grow hungry."

"Have you found us a new home?" Leoht'heortan asked, his head snaking down to gaze at Delgar.

Delgar nodded. "It is an untouched world. You can live there in peace for as long as you wish."

Leoht'heortan grinned. "You were a good choice for the powers of the Greater Dragon. When you are ready, you will lead us there. We are ready to leave whenever you wish."

Delgar turned as he heard a stir in the assembled Dragons. Finally, a figure stepped out from between two of the serpentine forms.

"Delgar!" a man in long robes called. "I've found you at last!"

Delgar blinked. "Velnan!" The two embraced. "I thought I would never see you again."

"I hid the key in a safe place, and then I came back to find you and Jenara," Velnan said. "It was not easy, but then I started hearing rumors about a warlord of Pakaria who had an Archmage of Taerra as his counselor. I went from fortress to fortress looking for you, but without success."

"And then you came here," Delgar said.

Velnan smiled. "When I saw this many Dragons in one place at one time, I decided you had to be involved. I was hoping to give my regards to your wife, but I couldn't find her."

When Velnan looked into Delgar's eyes, his face fell. "Oh no," Velnan said. "It can't be."

Delgar nodded. "The child took too much out of her. I lost them both."

Velnan sat on the ground, shaking his head. "I should have come here sooner."

"Nothing could have been done," Delgar said. "Not even by you."

Velnan looked up at Delgar. "I just hope you believe that as well some day. I can see you don't now."

"Delgar," Daelyn said. "We should go."

"Daelyn!" Velnan cried. "I hadn't noticed you there. So you're here too."

"I'm Delgar's new mentor," Daelyn said. "He has a great deal to learn."

"He has a good teacher, then. So what is all this about?"

"The Dragons are leaving Mideorth," Delgar explained. "As their guardian, I have to lead them."

"So the world really is lost," Velnan stated, looking out to the ice. "I had never thought I'd see this day."

"Will you follow us?" Delgar asked.

Velnan shook his head. "I don't know the road you will take. Besides, there are many people in the south who could use the help of an Archmage. I think I will go to them and do what I can to preserve what is left."

Delgar heard a rumbling, and when he looked up he saw the face of the glacier explode, pieces of ice falling against the fortress walls. The blue-white wall surged forward, and Delgar could feel its power pulling at him, trying to drink his life and essence.

"Almost as if it knows," Daelyn muttered. "Incredible."

"You're out of time," Velnan shouted, casting spells

of protection. He winced as the ice exploded out again, the shards crashing against an invisible barrier. "Go! I'll hold it off!"

"Delgar, we have to leave," Daelyn said. "Follow me."

Delgar cursed under his breath. He took one last look at the world around him, the snowy plains to the south, the ribbon of ice to the north, and said his farewells. Then he called out to the Dragons and followed Daelyn onto the Road, leaving his world and all the beauty it had once shared behind. The last sound he heard was Velnan's shouts as he held off the assault of the ice.

He could barely look up as he walked, following Daelyn's form through the shadowy mist. When he glanced back, he saw the Dragons behind him, some walking and some flying. He gazed forward, making certain he still had Daelyn in sight.

His world was gone. He rolled the thought through his mind again and again. The forests and fjords of his homeland were gone. The lovely plains of Taerraland had passed too, never to be seen again. He remembered the harsh desert of Barsh, no doubt the next thing to be claimed by the ice. All of them existed now only in his mind.

The image of a desert world flashed through his mind, and he realized with a start that in what had felt like a short time he had already come to the first new world he visited. Daelyn led him past it, but he could feel the gateway looming before him as he passed by it.

I am a traveler, Delgar realized. *But what have I become to be one?*

As they walked, the Dragons began to sing, the melody filling the air. Delgar was reduced to tears by its beauty. The song was mournful and sad, speaking of lost hopes and new beginnings.

Delgar turned to find Leoht'heortan beside him,

crooning his part of the song.

"Why do you sing?" Delgar asked.

"We mourn," the Dragon said. "We mourn for our home, and for all those who have been lost. We are singing their souls into the heavens."

A tear ran down Delgar's cheek. "I think you have done them all justice."

Leoht'heortan shook his head. "We have only just begun. It will take us centuries to finish our grieving."

The green world flashed through Delgar's mind, and he suddenly realized that their trip had almost finished. As he looked forward, the mists parted, and the valley opened up before them.

"Is this our new home?" Leoht'heortan asked.

Delgar nodded. "Here you can live in safety."

"What is its name?"

Delgar shrugged. "Nobody knows."

"Then we shall name it," Leoht'heortan declared. "We shall discover the very spirit of this world and name it accordingly. It will take us centuries, but we should do this if it is to be our home."

"What now?" Delgar asked.

Leoht'heortan shook his head. "Our flight has ended, but your task has only just begun. Now you must free Mideorth from the ice."

"It could take forever," Delgar said.

"You are immortal," Leoht'heortan pointed out. "You have all the time you need."

Chapter X: The Beginning of Immortality

"You should come with me," Daelyn said, offering Delgar a ration of beef jerky. "You still have a great deal to learn."

They sat on the grass, watching the Dragons gliding through the air, exploring their new home. The song of sorrow had been joined by a chorus of joy.

"I don't understand," Delgar said.

"You will," Daelyn stated. "But first you must learn how to survive immortality."

"I thought that was easy," Delgar said. "I just don't have to get killed."

Daelyn shook his head. "It will be very difficult for you to lose your life. But if you are not properly trained, you can lose your sanity, and your soul."

"Where will we go?" Delgar asked, standing up.

Daelyn stood and smiled. "I will take you to my home. I think you'll like it there."

"Will it be a home?"

Daelyn nodded. "For a while, at least."

Delgar held out his hand. "Lead and I will follow."

He followed Daelyn back onto the Road, wandering through the mist. For a while, it seemed as though they would walk forever. Every few hours Delgar felt the flash of a world pass through his head. One world was filled with water, and life flourished under the vast oceans. Another held cities in the sky, where great thinkers gathered and discussed the universe.

Delgar walked as though he was in a dream, hardly believing what he was seeing. He had once thought that the world was something simple, but already he had seen that the universe itself contained infinite variety. He shook his head. He would have as much time to discover these worlds as he wished. For a moment, he wasn't sure if his immortality was a blessing or a curse.

There was the flash of another world, a world of great variety. To the north were great fertile valleys and islands, while to the south lay great deserts and savannas. For a moment he felt homesick, as though he had returned to Mideorth before the ice.

"We are almost at my home," Daelyn said. "You will stay with us for a few centuries."

"What is it called?" Delgar asked.

"Just 'Earth,'" Daelyn replied. "The land we are going to is named 'Ireland.' We have lived there for millennia."

"How many of you are there?" Delgar said.

Daelyn grinned. "Thousands in Ireland. But we are also on many other worlds. The Tuatha de Danaan have traveled and settled all over the Road. But we call Ireland our home, at least for now."

"What do you mean?" Delgar asked.

"It has been prophesied that one day we will be forced to leave," Daelyn said. "I don't know when that will

327

happen, but these prophecies tend to come true in the end."

The mist cleared around them, and Delgar found himself walking through a green forest, small birds chirping in the trees.

Daelyn held out his arms. "Welcome to Ireland! My home, at least for now."

"And I'll learn how to be immortal here?" Delgar asked.

Daelyn dropped his arms and nodded. "Do not fear. We have trained many before you. You are not the first mortal turned to immortality, and you will not be the last."

"And then?" Delgar asked.

"After you've been trained, that is up to you. I can only tell you that you will return to Mideorth more than once; that is written in your wyrd."

Daelyn began to walk forward, beckoning for Delgar to follow. He led Delgar through the trees, winding deeper and deeper into the ancient forest. Delgar felt as though there were others watching him, but whenever he turned to look, he only saw the foliage and a couple of small animals scurrying away from his gaze.

"Are we being followed?" Delgar asked.

"Of course," Daelyn said. "This is our land. But you are safe whenever you are with me."

They came to a large mound surrounded by trees. On the mound was a great castle, the spires reaching up into the heavens. Delgar's eyes widened at the sight.

"This is the hall of our king, Manannan," Daelyn said. "He will help you in your training."

"Are you not training me?" Delgar asked.

"I am," Daelyn said. "But I will not do it alone."

Daelyn led Delgar into an entrance in the mound, and Delgar found himself in a large corridor, the wood carved into elegant spires and visages of animals. Several tapestries lined the walls.

"King Manannan's court is this way," Daelyn said. "He is expecting us."

Delgar followed Daelyn through a small maze of corridors until they came to a large hall. Delgar swallowed, wondering how the ceiling could possibly be as high as it appeared. He looked down to see a throne at the end of the room, and a tall, powerful man seated in it. The man stood and stepped forward with a catlike grace.

"Greetings Daelyn," he said. "Greetings, Delgar, Magus Draconum, son of Daegar. I am King Manannan."

Delgar fell to one knee and bowed. "I am at your service, lord."

"Stand, please," Manannan said, and as he approached Delgar felt as though he was in the presence of a being of great power. "I have heard a great deal about you. Why have you come?"

"To learn to be immortal," Delgar replied, rising to his feet.

"And what do you already know?"

Delgar paused. "Almost nothing."

Manannan smiled. "Good. You are ready to learn." He motioned to the few Tuatha de Danaan lingering around the court. "Prepare for the feast! We have a guest who would stay for a while."

Daelyn turned to Delgar. "We will retire to the feast hall now."

Delgar nodded. "I hope I have not offended."

Daelyn shook his head. "We are all immortal, Delgar. We have little need for ritual, with the exception of our druids. We will eat, we will relax, and in the morning you will begin your training."

"How long will it last?" Delgar asked.

Daelyn shrugged. "Ten centuries should do rather nicely. Do not worry; as your Dragon friends said, you have all the time you could ever need."

The feast of lamb settled pleasantly in Delgar's stomach. He looked around the hall, watching Manannan speaking softly to one of the Tuatha de Danaan ladies.

Daelyn prodded him on the shoulder. "Save some room, Delgar. The hunters brought back a stag, and it will be the next course."

"We've already had three courses," Delgar protested. "How many more are there?"

"Only seven or eight," Daelyn said. "Remember, we are in no hurry. Here we will sit, linger and enjoy."

"What about my training?" Delgar asked.

"Your training is important, but it will come at the proper time. One thing you will learn is that your mortal priorities must change for you to survive. What you used to consider a crisis will often be a mere annoyance for an immortal. For example, what do you consider the most important thing in life?"

Jenara's face flashed before Delgar's eyes and he wiped away a tear. "Love."

Daelyn smiled. "For a mortal, that is quite true. But for an immortal, life itself is the most important. In many cases, love is transitory. For immortals, it is slow and gentle, rather than quick and passionate. For us, love must last for eternity. For mortals, it must only last a little while."

"So I will have to live without love," Delgar said.

"Without mortal love," Daelyn corrected. "You will find many brothers and sisters here. But you will find no lovers; I can see that in your wyrd. Your heart was taken once before by your wife, and she will hold it for the rest of time."

"Are all mortals who are forced to immortality like me?" Delgar asked.

Daelyn shook his head. "Not all," he said. "But most.

I can see into your heart, and you will carry your Jenara with you until your dying day."

There was a brief pause as the plate of lamb was replaced by a helping of venison.

"Can you see all men so clearly?" Delgar asked.

Daelyn smiled. "Most. Mortals tend to wear their souls on their sleeves. That is something else you will learn not to do."

"What else must I learn?" Delgar said, taking a morsel of the meat and placing it on his plate. He stared at it for a moment, and finally began to eat.

"You will learn true patience," Daelyn said. "You will learn how to be one with the world. You will learn how to be one with the Road of Legends. Those are just a few of the things you must learn; there are too many to count. I guess you could say that you are going to learn how to live."

"I still don't quite understand."

Daelyn smiled, placing some venison on his plate. "You will. You can start by savoring that food. Understand, above all else, that you have become truly special, now that you are becoming a part of the Road."

"How do you mean?"

"Some people are dreamers," Daelyn said. "They wish to see more, but are unable to. Some, such as the Great Dragons and the Tuatha de Danaan, are the dream. You started as one and became the other. You are both the dreamer and the dream."

"I suppose I'll understand later."

"In time," Daelyn said. "Now enjoy your dinner."

That night, Delgar lay down in the feather bed provided to him and fell into a fast sleep. He dreamt first of Jenara, feeling her skin against his once more. He held her to him as though he would never see her again. But he found no peace, for when he opened his arms to kiss her, she had gone. Then he saw the glacier, a malevolent blanket covering his world, waiting for his return.

He woke up with the morning sun, strangely rested. He stood in his nightclothes and stared out the window at the forests around him. *I will travel*, he decided. *I will see all the worlds the Road has to offer. I will travel until I can find my peace, and my soul can rest.*

And then he got dressed and walked out into the hall of the Tuatha de Danaan, ready to learn to be an immortal.

Part III
The Destroyer of Worlds

Chapter I: The Fugitive on the Ice

Delgar blinked, the memories of six thousand years receding. Once again he became aware of the snow swirling around his boots, the dull chill climbing up his legs. The Dragon blood throbbed behind his eyes, urging him to soar, but he pushed it down. Instead, he walked forward, listening as the light snow crunched under his boots.

Daelyn was right, he thought. *Immortality is difficult for those not born to it.* He tried to remember even a single point in time, a point where he was completely and utterly happy. Only one moment came to him: he was sitting on a hill, Jenara in his arms, the two of them watching the sunset. He had not yet graduated, and they were taking shelter in each other from their mutual stress of exams.

But Jenara had been dead for six millennia. The Mageschool and Taerra were no more than cherished memories. He felt completely alone.

Utterly ancient.

He shook his head. His world was still dead, the age of ice still remained, and he was still trapped in the past by his own memories.

Delgar drew his cloak and robe closer. He would have to leave soon; there was still nothing he could do here. Perhaps in another century or two he would be able to lead the Dragons back, but it would not be today. It was time to return to his wanderings across the Great Road. He turned, taking a deep breath as he prepared to step onto the Road of Legends.

And then he sensed life, just over the horizon. Life where there should be no life. Not even the great bears ventured this far onto the glacier. He closed his eyes, extending his senses. He felt a small human running across the glacier, filled with distress. Almost a mile behind the human was something otherworldly, emanating evil from its core. A nomad, perhaps? What mortal man would ever want to walk on the ice in the first place, much less with something chasing him?

Delgar opened his eyes to see a small speck on the horizon before him, perhaps two miles away. He opened his mind to the Dragon within, the warm blood throbbing in his veins. He began to stride forward, his legs carrying him faster than any mortal man's ever could. As he walked, he saw the small figure collapse in exhaustion.

And the evil *something* was behind him. Delgar picked up his pace, his senses stretching out to touch whatever was chasing the man. Still the identity of the attacker eluded him. Finally, Delgar came to the strange man, now a crumpled figure on the thin layer of snow. The man was clothed in grey furs, and bore a long bone-handled knife and a quiver with two wooden arrows secured in it. Whatever bow the man had once carried seemed to be long since lost.

With the slightest touch of his powers, Delgar erected

an invisible shield around the strange man. Then he turned as the attacker raced towards him.

Delgar grimaced. Whatever it was, it was unnatural. The creature had a horned head with a face that was almost human. Dirty yellow fangs protruded from its thick lips, and its skin held an unhealthy greenish tint. The beast stopped short at Delgar, looking unsure of what to do against somebody who simply stood his ground.

"This man is under my protection," Delgar stated. "Leave now."

The creature snarled and motioned with hairy, clawed hands. Delgar's eyes narrowed, his gaze running over the beast. It looked almost like a cross-breed between a man and the basest of apes, with some reptilian features. It wore only the simplest of smocks, but Delgar was unsure about the fabric. Possibly a tanned skin of some kind.

Before Delgar could observe any further, the creature lunged, fangs bared. Delgar felt the Dragon blood flow through him, almost scalding in intensity, and the heat behind his eyes grew. With a quick motion, Delgar grabbed the beast in mid-lunge. He saw a look of horror pass over the creature's face, and then Delgar struck at the thing's throat with his other hand. It fell back, blood spurting from severed arteries. The beast writhed in agony, but Delgar raised his hand, ending the creature's life with a burst of flame.

Delgar glanced at his hand. The razor sharp claws retracted, flowing and reforming into fingernails. The heat of the Dragon blood faded to a comfortable warmth. Then he turned to the strange man he had just defended.

His inspection revealed two things. The first was that the man was still alive, but suffering from the extreme cold. Delgar extended his power, creating a small, controlled fire on the ice, using the glacier's own energy for fuel. Then he pulled the figure as close to the flame as he dared, at which point he confirmed the second thing.

He thought on it as he watched the color slowly return to the person's cheeks: the man was really a young woman.

Delgar was warming his hands by the fire when she awoke. She startled, staring at him with wild blue eyes, and then she seemed to relax a bit. With a quick glance, he examined her from a distance. She was small but athletic, frazzled dark hair draping over a ragged fur cloak and robes.

"You are welcome at my fire," Delgar said.

"What are you doing this far on the ice?" she demanded with a rough voice. She scurried back, keeping a careful distance from him.

"I could ask the same question about you. Let me just say that I am a wanderer."

"We don't have many visitors in my village," she said. "And the next village is several days journey. I've never seen one like you."

"My home is very far away," Delgar said. "More than you could ever imagine."

"Everything is very far away," she mumbled. "Even food."

"What is your name?" Delgar asked.

She only stared at him for a moment, and then turned to the fire. She warmed herself for an instant, and then startled away in fear.

"Wizard!" she screamed, drawing her knife. "You keep away from me, wizard!"

Delgar raised his hands. "I mean you no harm."

"Your fire has no wood," she said, trembling with fear. "You are the wizard."

Delgar frowned. Standing up slowly, he said, "If I had

wanted you dead, I would have killed you when you were unconscious."

"Why are you here?" she demanded.

"I am wandering," Delgar explained. "I mean you no harm."

She approached, the knife still drawn. "Who are you?"

"My name is Delgar, Daegar's son," he said. "That is my true name. And yes, I am a wizard."

"The only wizard I know of is the Dark Wizard in the Tower of Ice."

Delgar blinked. "I can assure you that I'm not him. But who is this Dark Wizard? I thought I was the last of my kind on this world."

She sat down, but the knife edge remained pointed towards Delgar's chest. "He sends monsters to collect tribute. If we don't give him most of our food, he takes what we have and burns part of the village."

"Is that what sent you running across the ice?" Delgar asked.

She nodded. "We tried to fight them this year, only a couple of months ago. They killed ten of us before they left. I was in a hunting party looking for snow elk when they attacked. We tried to drive them off, but they kept coming, and they overcame us in the night."

Delgar pointed at the charred corpse of the monster. "Those things."

She nodded, tears in her eyes. "I woke up tied to a pole. They had moved us during the night across the ice. They took Leeta down and they..." She dropped her knife and began to sob.   Delgar sat for a moment, unsure of what to do. Then he carefully stepped over to her and took her in his arms. "It's all right," he soothed. "They can't hurt you now. Not while I'm here."

"Oh Great One," she cried. "They skinned her after they took her. I can still hear her screaming. Then they

339

cooked her and made us..."

"It's over now," he said, holding her as she cried on his shoulder. With a burst of sheer horror, he realized what kind of hide the creature had been wearing.

Her sobbing stopped, and then she looked at Delgar with haunted eyes. "I killed one and escaped during the night. And I ran and ran, but I knew that they were behind me. And they won't stop coming, I know they just won't..."

"How many of them were there?" Delgar asked.

"At least ten."

Delgar closed his eyes and strengthened the wards around them. As he opened his eyes again, he heard the woman gasp. Around them a circle blazed in the ice, glowing bright blue.

"Anything that tries to cross the circle will die," Delgar said. "That will keep them away tonight. Tomorrow I will take you home."

"It's so far away," she said.

"I have enough food for both of us. Now, sleep and rest."

As she closed her eyes and fell into a slumber, Delgar gazed across the ice, watching as the red sun dropped below the horizon.

They would come tonight. He knew it. He could already sense them just out of sight, waiting for their moment. And when they came, he would be ready for them. He took off his cloak and draped it over the woman, careful to lay a spell across her to keep her warm and restful. Then he stood and waited for them to come.

They attacked sooner than he expected. It was only two hours after the sun had set that they made their way over the horizon, using the night to cloak their movements.

Delgar scratched his goatee as they approached, loping over the light snow with inhuman ease.

They are Mage-made, he realized. That was why the first one felt so unnatural. Another Mage survived the glacier. But who is it? It couldn't be Velnan; Delgar had all but seen him die. Most of the Archmages had been killed fighting the glacier. Or was it some wizard who had come after the ice; a wild Mage gone mad?

The first creature tried to cross the circle. A sudden scream tore through the darkness as the intense heat burned the beast to ashes before it even had a chance to step away. The four other creatures backed away, weapons at the ready.

"Who created you?" Delgar demanded quietly.

The beasts growled. One took out a bow, knocking a rough-hewn arrow to it. Delgar raised his hand and a bolt of fire slammed into the creature, throwing it to the ground and turning it into a living torch. The creature wailed in pain, struggling to put itself out as it was consumed.

Delgar turned to the others, his arm raised, the Dragon blood throbbing through his veins. "Do not think I will spare any of your lives. I know what you are and what you have done. But, if you answer my questions, you will have a quick death."

The creatures only snarled. Delgar struck another down with a bolt of fire, and as its screams faded he glared at the last two.

"Who created you?" he demanded.

"Wizard," the one to the left spat, its voice guttural.

"I already knew that," Delgar said, and struck the creature down. As it writhed in agony, he turned to the last creature. "What is the wizard's name?"

The creature spat something incomprehensible and hateful. Delgar only shook his head and killed it. Then he sat down to think.

Delgar was sitting on an outcropping of ice watching the horizon when she awoke. He turned to see her rubbing her eyes and staring at him. He smiled kindly. "Did you sleep well?"

She nodded. "They didn't come for me?"

"They did," Delgar said. "I stopped them."

"I wish I had been awake for it."

Delgar shook his head. "I was harsh and brutal. I wish I hadn't had to do it."

"It was justice."

"Yes. But true justice is never satisfying; people tend to want more than they are entitled to."

She stood for a moment. "Are you going to watch me piss, or do you want to turn away?"

Delgar shook his head and turned his back to her. "My apologies. I've gotten used to traveling alone."

There was the rustling of clothing behind him. "How long have you been traveling?"

"It seems like forever," Delgar said. "And I suppose it is almost that long."

He heard her laugh, but it sounded hollow, as though she couldn't truly mean it yet. Then he heard water running. "Are all wizards prone to exaggeration?"

He smiled, but with little true mirth. "Most of us, I think. Part of the mystique."

The water stopped. "So why do you wander? Why don't you have some arcane tower or something like that?"

"My home was destroyed," Delgar replied. "And my wife followed shortly after. So now I wander, seeking some solace."

Clothes rustled again. "I'm sorry. You can turn around now."

Delgar turned to see her straightening out her furs. "Do you still miss her?" she asked.

Delgar nodded, blinking back a tear. "Every moment of every day. In many ways, it is her memory that keeps me going."

"I wish I loved somebody like that."

Delgar smiled sadly. "Some day you will. All you have to do is realize that the love is there when it comes."

"You said you would take me home," she said.

Delgar nodded. "Which way is it?"

She pointed. "I think it is that way. I can't be sure any more."

"Then that way we will go," Delgar said. "You never told me your name."

"I am Freela, Guthfrid's daughter, of the Elk People."

Delgar nodded. "A pleasure to meet you, Freela, Guthfrid's daughter. Let's take you home now."

They set out towards the south, two solitary figures on an ocean of ice.

Chapter II: The Elk People

It took Delgar and Freela two weeks of hard travel to reach the edge of the glacier. The land fell beneath them, a patch of brownish-green with a thin line of white at the farthest horizon. Delgar glanced across the edge of the ice, trying to find some way that would allow them to climb off it.

"There is a path down this way," Freela said, her eyes beginning to sparkle at last. She led Delgar along the edge of the glacier until they came to a collapsed slope of ice and rock. They carefully made their way down the path, Delgar steadying himself a couple of times as they came to the narrow parts of the path. Freela moved like a gazelle, picking her footfalls with an easy caution. Finally, after what seemed like hours, Delgar stepped off the ice onto the hard ground, inhaling softly as the chill left his feet. Then he looked around.

The glacier had not been kind to the land nearest to it. Although there was some grass, it was unhealthy and rooted in hard, unfertile soil. Large patches of earth protruded from the uneven covering, and an extremely sparse forest cropped up on the horizon. To the north and west, the glacier loomed over the land like a great white demon, constantly threatening to consume all that was left. Although Delgar couldn't see it, he knew that another glacier was only a week's journey to the south.

The Dark Sea used to be north of here, Delgar realized. Even the Cave of Dreams was to the north, buried under the ice. He shook his head as the memories began to intrude. It was time to stay in the present.

"Do you recognize this place?" Delgar asked.

Freela nodded. "This is where our hunters begin to hunt the snow elk. The elk dance along the ice, looking for something of sustenance that they can't get here. We don't know why they do it."

"They look for salt, I think," he said. "The ice comes from the salt-water oceans of the far north." It was truly amazing how nature had adapted to the ice. Where before the glacier had destroyed all life it touched, now it was merely part of what little habitat remained.

Freela stared at him, awe plain on her face.

"Where is your village?" Delgar asked.

She pointed to the south-west. "Two days that way."

Delgar nodded. "Let us go then."

As they walked, Freela drew close to Delgar. "Do you still want to question the elders?"

"Yes," Delgar said, never breaking stride. "I want to learn as much about this 'Dark Wizard' as possible."

"What will you do once they tell you?"

"I don't know yet," Delgar replied. "I suppose I will have to confront him about seeking tribute, but other than that...I just don't know. Hopefully there will be no need for violence."

"Do you think you can do something about him?"

"I hope so."

"Are you really powerful?"

"More than most."

"But not the most powerful in the world."

Delgar paused. "Probably not. No matter who you are and what you do, there is always somebody better than you."

"Who is the most powerful wizard in the world, then?"

Delgar started walking again. "I don't know."

"I wish I could be a wizard."

Delgar smiled. "It is not an easy life, and too much knowledge has been lost. I do not think there will be new wizards for quite some time yet."

"You're a wizard. Will you teach me?"

Delgar shook his head. "I am merely a wanderer. I am not a teacher. If you want to learn magic, you must be mindful of what is around you and how it works. Once you understand that, then you can understand magic."

"But magic is so wondrous and mystical and supernatural..."

Delgar smiled sadly. "No, actually it isn't. Magic has always been all around you. It is the most natural thing in the world, so long as it is not abused. When you can see it around you, then you can begin to manipulate it."

"How long would it take me to learn?"

"You entire lifetime," Delgar said. "Far too much wisdom has been lost."

Freela tried to ask more, but Delgar waved her to silence. For the rest of the day they passed through a sparse forest of evergreens. That night they made camp under one of the trees, Delgar collecting deadwood and lighting a small fire.

"How did you learn magic?" Freela asked as Delgar passed her some dried meat.

"I went to a special school," Delgar replied. "I studied

very hard for many years, and then I was declared to be a Mage."

"Can I go to that school?"

Delgar shook his head. "It was destroyed a long time ago."

"You must be very old, then."

"Yes."

"How old?"

"Old enough."

"Why can't you teach me?"

Delgar smiled. "I have my share of secrets, and very few could ever understand them." He paused for a moment. "Do you really want to learn magic? With all your heart?"

Freela nodded furiously.

"Okay," Delgar said. "This is what you will have to do. Watch the world around you. See how the grass grows, how the water flows, and how the birds fly. Understand why it happens. And then, after years of study, if you have learned the truth, the doorway to magic will have been opened to you. The rest will follow naturally."

"And will I some day be as powerful as you?"

Delgar shook his head. "You will be a beginning. When you have learned what you can, teach it to others, and they will continue your work once you have passed to the Eternal One."

"The Eternal One?"

"The Great One, I think you called Him," Delgar said. "You should rest now. We will reach your people tomorrow, and I fear we will both be asked many questions."

As she curled up by the fire, Delgar watched her with sad eyes. Even after a truly horrifying experience, she still had her optimism and enthusiasm. He remembered having those qualities once. As he settled down to sleep, he felt older than ever.

They reached the village around midday. Delgar wasn't surprised to find that it was a collection of wooden, fur-covered huts; most villages he had visited since the coming of the glacier had taken that form. They approached slowly enough that the entire village had time to come out to greet them, and Delgar found himself facing a large crowd of men, women and children, all garbed in leather and furs.

Freela threw herself into the arms of a large, grey-haired man. "Father!" she cried. The man simply held her and wept. As he watched, Delgar realized that part of the crowd had grown curious and surrounded him, some of the younger children poking at his garments. He glanced around, trying to find the headman of the tribe.

Freela's father stepped forward. "I am Ealdorman Guthfrid, the leader of the People of the Elk. I had feared my eldest daughter to be dead, but you have restored my hope. How can I repay you?"

Delgar bowed politely. "I am Delgar, Daegar's son. I only did what any other man would do. I only wish that I had come in time to save the others with her."

A pained look crossed Guthfrid's face. "Then my youngest daughter is dead," he said, a tear running down his cheek. "She has joined our ancestors with the Great One and the spirit of the Elk."

"I took what vengeance I could," Delgar said. "Most of the monsters who did this were killed. At least you will have justice."

Guthfrid looked at Delgar with glassy eyes. "I would rather have both my daughters back. But what is done is done. We will dance Leeta's spirit to the sky tonight. Please accept our hospitality this night. It is the least we can do."

Delgar bowed again. "I would be honored."

"Beogar will show you to my home," the Ealdorman said, motioning to a short but muscular warrior. "Please stay as long as you like."

Delgar nodded and followed the warrior into the village.

Delgar watched the figures dancing around the fire, their voices chanting a song for the dead as the smoke drifted high into the night sky. He sat at a large table in the village square, seated beside Ealdorman Guthfrid and his daughter. Guthfrid had offered what food he could, which amounted to some dried venison. Regardless, Delgar accepted it with the gravest of thanks; to do otherwise would have been an insult. He noticed Guthfrid's eyes were red and glassy, but otherwise the Ealdorman was hiding his grief well. He also noticed Freela stealing several glances at him, but decided not to react.

"My daughter tells me that you are a wizard," Guthfrid said. "Is this true?"

Delgar paused for a moment, and then nodded. He already had their gratitude, so they were unlikely to be fearful of him so long as he didn't tell them too much. "I had thought myself to be the last Mage in the world, until your daughter told me of the Dark Wizard."

"We have tried to send messengers to the People of the Snow Bear to ask for help, but they have never returned," Guthfrid said sadly. "The Dark Wizard seeks to destroy us. I do not believe we can stand against him alone."

"Can you tell me of this wizard?" Delgar asked. "I may be able to do something about him."

"He came to us in my grandfather's time," Guthfrid said. "A demon came at his side, and he demanded tribute

349

for his protection against the great demons. He said that if we didn't give him what he wanted, he would make us slaves of the Tower of Ice. He asked only for what food we could afford, and we were too weak to fight him then. So, my grandfather gave the wizard what he wanted."

"How often did you pay this tribute?" Delgar asked.

"Once a year, after every harvest. But lately the great ice has begun to move again. Very slowly it creeps towards us, and every year the land becomes less fertile. Last year we had no grain or food to give him. So, when the demon came to collect the tribute, we refused. He burned several houses and murdered ten people without giving us a blood price for them. Then he said that he would come back soon and take everything we had.

"Now we must fight, but we are weak against him. What little grain we have left we will plant in the second harvest this coming moon, but I fear the demon will come to take everything before then. Can you help us against him?"

Delgar nodded. "I will try my best. This does not make sense, however. It is almost as if this wizard wants your people to die. If he still wanted tribute from you, he would know that he would have to leave you to grow your crops. So why would he suddenly want you dead?"

"He is evil," Freela piped up. "What other reason is there?"

Delgar shook his head. "I have had more experience with evil than I have ever wanted. Evil does not simply destroy without a purpose. It takes without giving back, it serves only itself, it betrays its servants, but it does not destroy arbitrarily. Tell me, do you know the Dark Wizard's name?"

Guthfrid shook his head. "We do not know his true name, friend Delgar. We only know that he has a demon at his side, and he lives in the Tower of Ice."

"Do you know where the Tower of Ice is?"

"It is somewhere on the ice. Some have sought it, but none that have returned have ever found it. Perhaps some have found it, but were killed by the Daruks."

"Daruks?"

"The monsters of the Tower of Ice," Guthfrid explained. "Unnatural creatures almost like men. It is said they eat those they kill, and they wear the skins of the slain. I do not know what spirit they serve, but it could never be pure, like the spirit of the Elk."

Delgar nodded. "I think I've met them."

Guthfrid motioned Delgar towards him. "My daughter likes you," he whispered. "And I think you would make a good husband for her. Would you be willing to join the people and spirit of the Elk?"

Delgar shook his head. "I have been married before, and I still mourn for my lost wife. Also, I am far older than I look, and I am only fit for wandering now. I'm sorry, but I do not think it would be right to accept your offer."

Guthfrid nodded. "She had asked me to try. I hope I have not offended you, friend wizard."

Delgar shook his head. "I have taken no offence; I have been in love, and I understand entirely."

A tall, lithe man broke through the small road between two of the houses and motioned for Guthfrid. The Ealdorman politely excused himself and walked over to the man.

Delgar leaned over to Freela. "Who is that?"

"That is Eamund," she said. "The fastest man in the village. He is our scout."

"You like him," Delgar noted.

Freela nodded. "But he is not nearly as interesting as you."

"Put me out of your mind, young Freela," Delgar said. "I am far older than I look, and merely a traveler. Your

351

future does not lie with me."

Guthfrid returned to the table, an urgent look in his eyes. "Friend Delgar, I must ask your help sooner than I had hoped," he said.

"Some Daruks are coming," Delgar stated. "I can see it in your eyes."

"Eamund thinks they will be here by tomorrow afternoon. And there are so many of them!"

"How many warriors do you have?" Delgar asked.

"Too many have died recently," Guthfrid replied. "We have less than fifty warriors now."

"And how many are coming?"

"At least twenty," Guthfrid said. "But one Daruk can destroy five warriors easily! We cannot stand against them."

"We can and we will," Delgar stated. "Now you have a wizard on your side. And once this battle is over, we will see who this 'Dark Wizard' is and what has to say for himself."

Chapter III: Battle

Delgar watched the preparations with unease, the midday sun shining in his eyes. Although he had seen several battles in his time, he never relished the open bloodshed. Where some men found that combat made them feel more alive, he had only found that it made him sick. Unfortunately, sometimes it had to be done, and when that was the case, it had to be done quickly.

Guthfrid stood beside Delgar, his daughter close behind. "Almost all of the spears are in place, friend wizard," he said. "But I do not understand why we will not completely surround the village."

Delgar looked down the main road. To the right and left of the street he saw long sharpened stakes driven into the ground, so close together that barely a child could pass through them, much less a full-grown man. If Guthfrid was correct, then in a matter of an hour the only entrance into the village would be the main road.

"We have to control where they can come in," Delgar

said. "We must destroy this small army, not merely fend them off. To do that, we have to make certain that they can only enter where we want them to, and only meet who we want them to meet."

"Who do we want them to meet?" Freela asked.

"Me," Delgar replied. "Anybody with me will only get in the way."

"Can you destroy thirty Daruks?" Guthfrid demanded. "You may be powerful, friend wizard, but I do not believe you are a god. We will attack when you do."

Delgar took a deep breath. If this was to work, he had to be able to work alone. But if they didn't trust him, they wouldn't let him, and the entire effort would be wasted. And if he told them the truth...

Delgar sighed. "I was born six thousand years ago, before the ice came," he said. "And I have Dragon blood in my veins. They will not be able to stand against me."

Both Guthfrid and Freela stood in a state of shock, their mouths wide open, just as Delgar had expected. Guthfrid recovered first.

"Then we will place our lives in your hands," the Ealdorman said. "I will see to the last of the stakes."

Delgar watched him leave. It had not taken long to convince him that using some wood from the forest for stakes was a good idea, but Guthfrid had also thought that his people would be doing more in their defense than just building a wall. Delgar shook his head. If there had been another way, he would have found it; Guthfrid was a good man, and Delgar hated to disappoint him like that.

Only after her father had left did Freela finally speak. "How did you survive so long?"

"Dragon's blood," Delgar replied.

"But the loneliness..."

Delgar held up his hand. "The solitude and long years are bearable if you know how to live without mortal love;

how to cherish past loves without seeking new ones. It took me a very long time to learn how, and it is why I am not your future. I cannot love, Freela; it was a price of my immortality. Seek your path without me."

Something tickled at the edge of Delgar's consciousness. He closed his eyes, stretching his senses beyond the village. He felt the last of the sharpened poles being driven into the ground, the villagers retreating into their meeting hall. Further afield he felt a couple of snow elk startle and run as something approached them from the north. He stretched farther, finally sensing the Daruks riding towards the village. He counted twenty-seven of them, but there was one other presence, a creature of little power, but a creature of power regardless. This must be the demon, Delgar thought, opening his eyes to stare down the main street. He took several steps forward, his boots crunching down on the hard earth. As he walked forward, the riders became visible on the horizon, mere specks against the white of the glacier and the greenish-brown grassland.

Freela stepped up beside him. "Are they coming?"

Delgar nodded. "Tell your father that I will need two weeks of provisions as soon as the battle is over. Now, go; there is nothing you can do here."

"What are you going to do?"

Delgar crossed his arms thoughtfully. "I am going to wait until the moment is right, and then I will do what needs to be done. Leave me now; you must tell your father what I need."

Freela backed away into one of the sidestreets. Delgar felt her go, but didn't watch. He was too busy remembering what Daelyn had once told him about battles. "You must never concentrate on anything except the moment," the Tuatha de Danaan had said. "If your thoughts stray to the future or the past, the moment will be lost, and your enemies will overcome you. Let the past remain in your memories and the future in your dreams; there is time for both afterwards. Concentrate on the moment, and you will survive, even if you don't win."

He saw the riders break into two groups in the distance, each group circling the village in an opposite direction. After a few moments, he sensed them meet behind the village and reform into a single formation. Then they began to make their way back to the entrance by the main street, once again coming into sight just beyond the ring of spears. He saw all but two of them draw crude cudgels and axes, and then the group charged, the two unarmed creatures holding back beyond the ring.

And Delgar's Dragon's blood began to take hold, so hot in his veins that it was nearly burning.

Freela remained in the shadows of the alley long after Delgar had turned away. She had watched him thoughtfully as he stood as still as an oak, his arms crossed, his eyes dead set on the main road ahead of him.

So he had Dragon's blood, she thought. And he thought he could live without love. But she knew differently. She had longed for a true love for so long that she knew that nobody could ever live without somebody to love them. And he was the most exciting man she had ever met. He had saved her life, and told her something about magic, and there were lots of other things he could teach her if she could just make him love her.

And it wouldn't be too hard, would it? After all, he was obviously lonely, and his age merely gave him experience. And he would give her all the love that she had lost when her sister...

She choked back a sob. Her sister was gone, she told herself. But Delgar was here now. And she would follow him until the day she died, because she loved him, and she was sure she could make him love her, and...

Delgar's stance changed slightly, and for a moment Freela was afraid that he could read her mind. But he didn't look at her; instead he kept his eyes directly ahead. She heard the sound of the horrible horses the Daruks rode into battle, and then her gaze fell back on Delgar.

She gasped in shock. His eyes were glowing a bright crimson, and he was beginning to kneel, one leg on the ground while he lowered his hand to the earth. And then the riders stormed into view, their weapons raised and ready to strike.

A wall of fire leapt up in front of Delgar and began to advance on the riders. She heard one of the riders give a sickening scream as he tried to ride through the wall, managing only to fall off his horse and stagger around, a living torch. The smell of burning flesh filled the air, and then the rider was still, the fire reducing him to ashes. The riders slowed, their eyes wide, but the wall began to advance more quickly, destroying the first line of Daruks before they even had a chance to turn.

Some of the Daruks managed to dodge into side streets, waiting until the deadly flames passed by them, and then charging back onto the main street. Delgar easily picked them off, bolts of fire leaping from his hands, burning the creatures to death. The stench of dead and burning flesh began to overpower her, and she turned away, swallowing hard. All she could do was hold her hand to her mouth, praying for the shrieks of pain to end. Finally, once the screams of agony had died down, she looked out again.

Delgar stood in the center of the street, his hands crossed once again, the red glow remaining in his eyes. All around him lay the charred corpses of the Daruks, but his gaze never strayed down to them. She heard something approaching, the soft crunching of feet on soil. Then she turned away, unwilling to watch any more. Besides, she still had to deliver Delgar's message.

She managed to make it almost all the way to the village meeting hall before she fell to the ground, vomiting the contents of her stomach onto the ground. She spat for a moment, trying to remove the bitter taste from her mouth. Then she got back up, walking unsteadily towards her father. She had a message to deliver.

Delgar stood in the field of corpses, watching the last two riders. The Dragon blood throbbed in his veins, the heat almost painful. The stench of death rose all around him, but he was not sick; he had seen battle too many times to be sickened by its results. He felt remorse, however. He never enjoyed bloodletting, although some warriors seemed to, and all he could see around him were lives he had taken.

The two riders consulted for a moment, and then the larger of the two spurred his mount forward. As he trotted into sight, Delgar could see what he had already suspected; the thing was a demon. Its eyes glowed bright yellow, and its skin was stretched over its face, giving the impression that its head was some sort of alien skull.

The demon cleared the stakes and came to a halt in front of Delgar. For a moment, it just stared at him. Delgar met its gaze, the Dragon blood pulsing behind his eyes.

"You are a creature of power," the demon finally said.

Delgar nodded.

"You are in a conflict that does not involve you," the demon said. "This village owes us tribute, and we are here to take it."

"You are here to kill them," Delgar stated. "You know that if you take what you want, they will starve. Why do

358

you want them dead?"

"They have displeased my master."

Delgar shook his head. "Do not bother lying to me. Any fool could see that there is much more than that."

The demon hissed, drawing a blood-stained curved blade from its belt. Delgar stood his ground.

"I have no time for petty posturing," he finally said. "Tell me who your master is and what he wants, or I will kill you."

The demon recoiled as though he had been struck. "I will have your head on a plate!"

Delgar shook his head. "If you thought you could kill me, you would have tried already. Who is your master and what does he want?"

"My master is the Dark Wizard," the demon spat.

"What is his name?"

"He has never told me."

"And what does he want?"

"Death," the demon spat.

"Death for whom?"

"Death for everything! Death for the world!"

Delgar raised an eyebrow. "Does he command the glacier?"

The demon raised his sword and struck. The blade bounced harmlessly off Delgar's cloak. Delgar shook his head.

"That was a mistake," he said, and raised his hand. With a quick burst of power, he blasted the demon off its horse, the mount skittering away as soon as the creature's iron control had left it. The demon tried to rise, but Delgar struck too quickly. The Dragon blood pulsing behind his eyes, his fingers became talons, ripping into the demon's inky-black chest. The creature screamed as Delgar tore out its heart, the pulpy organ still beating as he dropped it to the ground.

"Return to the netherworld, where you belong," Delgar commanded, crushing the heart under his heel. The demon screamed as it erupted into fire. As Delgar watched, the flames burned hotter and hotter, finally becoming a searing white, until only a charred outline on the earth remained where the demon once was. Taking a deep breath, Delgar's talons became fingers once again.

He looked up to see the last rider retreating as quickly as it could. Delgar nodded; everything had gone perfectly. He waved his arm in a sweeping arc, and the bodies of the Daruks burst into a final, white-hot flame. He strode toward the meeting hall, letting the Dragon blood recede into the background of his being. After a couple of minutes, he came to the wooden longhouse, two warriors standing guard at the doorway.

"Tell Guthfrid the battle is over," Delgar said. "And I need my provisions."

The guard whispered something to a dark figure inside, and then Guthfrid came out, followed by Freela. The Ealdorman looked at Delgar for a moment, and then his gaze turned downwards.

"Your hand is bloody, friend wizard," he said. "Have you been hurt?"

Delgar shook his head. "It is the blood of a demon. Your people are safe now, Guthfrid. But I need some supplies."

"Did any escape?"

Delgar nodded. "One escaped, and he has gone to call for help."

Guthfrid's face fell. "Then more will come, and we are doomed."

Delgar shook his head. "The Daruk escaped because I let him. He will lead me to the Dark Wizard and the Tower of Ice. That is why I must leave now."

"Can you not stay?" Guthfrid asked. "The Great One

360

and the Spirit of the Elk must be honored for today's deeds."

"No," Delgar said. "But I wish I could. But where your task is finished, I still have much work to do. Reclaim your wood and put it to its proper use, friend Guthfrid. Have your celebration; your people have all helped win this victory. I must have my supplies; the longer I wait, the colder the trail becomes."

Guthfrid turned to face the inside of the meeting hall, and gave a couple of orders. Then he turned to face Delgar. "You will have your supplies immediately, friend wizard. Does this mean that today was not a final battle?"

Delgar grimaced. "The final battle is yet to come. And I must fight it alone."

Chapter IV: The Tower of Ice

Delgar walked across the glacier, careful to keep his distance from the Daruk he was following. He was beginning to get nervous; he had been on the ice for almost eight weeks, and there had been no attempt on his life. He had no illusions that the Dark Wizard was ignorant of his presence; one creature of power can always sense another, and the sorcerer would certainly have felt the destruction of his demon. But the Daruk still moved at a steady pace northward, leading him towards what had to be the heart of the glacier.

He had left the village without looking back, even though he had wanted to stay for just a bit longer. But, in the end, perhaps it was all for the best. Delgar knew it was unlikely he would return to the People of the Elk, especially if the Dark Wizard was the creator of the glacier. For the first time in his life as an immortal, he began to hold hope that his mission would soon be over. But only time would tell.

He glanced up at the sky as he continued his journey. The sun remained high, as it had for the last two days. With a start, he realized that he had come farther north than even Nordland had been. Had he passed his father's grave, buried deep beneath the ice? He brushed the thought aside. His mission was all that mattered now. He had to find the Dark Wizard, discover who he was, and destroy him if necessary.

He extended his senses, seeking any sign of life behind him. Once again, his stalker was present. Delgar groaned. He had first sensed Freela following him a couple of days after he had left her village, but he hadn't had time to warn her off or send her away. He wasn't entirely certain how she was following him, either, but the fact remained that she was present, alone on a field of ice following a trail that was faint at best. He had hoped that as the weeks passed she would grow weary and give up; once he got to the Tower of Ice, he would have to deal with her.

Delgar pulled some dried meat out of his robe and began to nibble. His Dragon blood could sustain him for years if necessary, but it would be no good to waste the power. Only the Eternal One knew what he would find.

He felt the Daruk stop and make camp, and sat down to rest. The endurance of the creature had been astounding; it had only made camp once every three days, and even then it had only rested for a couple of hours. Delgar chuckled for a moment, thinking of his pursuer. She was falling behind, but not quickly, and she might still catch up. When she finally decided to marry a mortal man, she would probably keep him very busy.

After a few hours, he sensed the Daruk begin to move again, and he stood up and stretched. Only a couple of times did Delgar worry that he was walking into a trap, but when he thought about it, it seemed unreasonable. The demon had been the commander, not the Daruk; Delgar had felt that when he crushed the demon's heart, its power flashing through him on its way to the underworld. The Daruk's mission would simply be to find help, and the only logical place for that would be a Daruk village or the Tower of Ice. If it was a Daruk village, then Delgar would deal with that when he came to it. Otherwise...

Two days passed, the cold sun beating down on the ice. Still Delgar walked, keeping his pace with the Daruk soldier. Still Freela followed, a couple of days distance behind him. The ice before him grew hilly and uneven, and Delgar was forced to watch his step as he climbed the occasional steep slope. Finally, he felt another power flickering before him. He grinned. He had found the Dark Wizard and the Tower of Ice at last.

He still kept pace with the Daruk, even when the Daruk was lost in a mass of other creatures. The Dark Wizard might feel him coming, but there was no need to let him know the extent of Delgar's senses. When Delgar finally crested a hill that overlooked the Tower of Ice, his mouth hung open in awe.

It was the most beautiful thing he had ever seen.

The tower lay in a deep valley, the spires reaching up into the heavens. Every spire was a shimmering blue-white, and they twisted and joined like a living thing. Every now and then Delgar thought he could see some part of the tower shift and grow, but he could not be certain it wasn't just an effect of the light. Below the tower lay a city of ice houses, their spires similar to the Ice Tower itself, but much smaller. Several different kinds of creature milled about the city, many of which Delgar had never seen before.

Delgar shook his head. Despite the beauty of the place, he still had work to do. He wandered down to the city, waiting for some armed guards to appear. He smiled grimly. It was one of the first times in his life that he actually wanted to be caught.

Five Daruks rushed towards him, axes in hand. Grimacing, Delgar hardened his skin, just in case they decided to attack. As they came within range, he held up his hand in greeting.

"I have come to see your master, the Dark Wizard," Delgar said. "You will take me to him."

"You come with us!" one of the Daruks demanded.

Delgar smiled and met his gaze. "Certainly. Understand, however, that I am a very powerful Archmage, and I will not treat treachery kindly." He let some of the Dragon's blood pulse behind his eyes, and the Daruk flinched back. "Take me to see the Dark Wizard."

The Daruk nodded quickly, and motioned with his axe. Delgar began to walk, careful to keep himself in stride beside his Daruk escort. He found himself before a large wall of ice, shining almost blindingly in the sunlight. Nailed to the wall was another Daruk, its eyes glazed over in pain, blood still running from its mouth. Delgar stopped and swallowed hard; the Daruk had literally been disemboweled and left to die.

He pointed at the suffering creature. "What do you call this?"

"Justice," a Daruk guard grunted.

Delgar raised his hand, and a bolt of energy struck the crucified creature. The Daruk's body jerked, the life bleeding from its eyes. Delgar turned to his Daruk escorts. "I have no patience for watching others suffer. Now take me to the Dark Wizard."

The Daruk grunted and led the Mage through the gate. As he passed under the glassy arch, Delgar suddenly snapped his fingers and turned to the guard beside him. "I almost forgot. There is a human following me, a woman. She is about two days walk from here. See to it that she is brought here to me unharmed. If she suffers so much as a scratch, I will see to it that it takes you and every one of your companions months to die."

The Daruk guard tried to meet Delgar's gaze, but quickly looked away. He called one of the other Daruks and grunted some orders in a language Delgar had never heard, and then it turned back to face the Mage. "It done now. You come with us."

Delgar nodded. "Lead the way."

The Daruks took him through a maze of glassy streets, paved with a sort of rough ice. As they wound their way through the labyrinth, the Tower of Ice grew larger and larger, until Delgar could only see the base. With a start, he realized that he had been walking for several hours; the city stretched out around him as far as the eye could see.

"Gate this way," one of the Daruks grunted. The icy path they led Delgar on sloped uphill, but the roughness of the ice prevented him from slipping. For what seemed like hours, they skirted the base of the tower, the path widing up and around it, the Daruk city stretching out below them. Finally, Delgar was led to a large gate in the side of the tower. The Daruk motioned for him to enter, and he stepped inside.

Delgar found himself in an immense hall of ice. The arched ceiling stretched up almost a hundred feet, and several sculptures lined the walls. Some were mythical beasts, while glassy wizards in powerful stances stared from other pedestals. Delgar passed at least two statues of powerful warriors, each from a different part of Mideorth.

Delgar swallowed, halting to stare at one of the statues for a moment. A warrior of Nordland gazed on him with icy eyes, and memories of Delgar's childhood flashed before him. He shook his head; all that had passed with the glacier. At least he now knew that whoever this Dark Wizard was, he was as much a part of the past as Delgar was.

"Come," the Daruk guard said. "Wizard waiting."

Delgar turned to find himself and the guard alone in the hall. "Where are the others?"

"I send them away. You no trouble."

Delgar raised an eyebrow. "Very well. Lead the way."

The guard led Delgar out of the hall onto a massive, luminous, glassy staircase. Delgar stared up for a moment, awed by the size of it. Then he began to ascend the steps, carefully at first, lest he slip. The steps were as rough as the floor, not nearly as difficult to walk on as the glacier had been. They climbed for what seemed like an hour, passing several doorways. Finally, they came to the top of the staircase, the guard breathing heavily. Before them was a large door of ice, slightly ajar.

Delgar smiled and patted the Daruk on the back. "You need to get in shape," he said, pushing the door open. Then he stepped past the Daruk and entered the heart of the Tower of Ice.

He found himself in a large circular chamber, the icy walls offering a distorted view of the massive city outside. On the wall opposite the door a glowing blue orb stood in a brass stand. To the side he saw what looked like a large table, covered with a huge sheet of blue linen that stretched to the floor. Several bookcases littered the room, and in the center was a large wooden writing desk. The Dark Wizard sat at the desk, dressed in black robes, scribbling something on a large piece of parchment. Then he looked up.

Delgar inhaled, his eyes wide.. There was no way he could ever forget the tall, thin man before him with the fair complexion and blue-green eyes.

"Are you the Dark Wizard?" he asked.

The man nodded. "Yes, Mage Delgar. I never believed I would see you again, except in my memories."

"I thought you were dead, Vice-Chancellor Vertanus,"

Delgar said. "We all did."

Vertanus nodded, a sad smile coming to his lips. "The illusion was necessary, I fear. I have had my mission for far too long, but I am almost finished. So, how have you survived the years?"

Delgar smiled wryly. "Magic."

"You're certainly more powerful than any Archmage I've ever seen. I felt you appear on the glacier. So it was you who kept visiting every couple of centuries."

Delgar nodded. "So all of this is your doing?"

Vertanus stood and gave a small bow. "With the power I now have, it was quite easy. And this is much more grand than my old wizard's tower. All I needed to do was keep the Tower supplied and prevent the people outside the glacier from unifying and trying to kill me."

"And the Daruk nailed to the wall?"

Vertanus frowned. "A necessary death, I'm afraid. But one does have to set an example."

"Against failure?"

Vertanus shook his head. "Against stupidity. Everybody has their bad days; it is the way of the world. But to lead a powerful enemy to the gates of what is supposed to be a secret base demonstrates a terminal dose of idiocy. If I wasn't certain I could handle you, I would have destroyed him on the ice. But, now I have him as an example, and you are in my hands."

"And you think you can handle me."

"My dear Delgar," Vertanus chuckled. "I am more powerful than you could ever imagine, even with your power. I was able to destroy the greatest civilizations in the world with one fell blow. What makes you think I can't destroy you?"

Vertanus closed his eyes. "Ah, I see my Daruks have found the girl who was following you. Just one moment, please." There was a sudden flash of light in the corner of the chamber, and then Freela stood, a spear held warily in her hand.

"Thank you," Delgar said, turning to the girl. "You stand by that wall and stay out of the way. I will collect you when I am finished."

Freela raised her weapon. "But I-"

"No buts," Delgar snapped. "You should not have followed me, and now you are only in the way. Stand there and be silent."

Vertanus chuckled. "She's in love with you. I can see it in her eyes."

Delgar turned. "In her case, it is an unhealthy infatuation. But, while she is under my protection, I must tolerate her."

"So why have you sought me out?" Vertanus asked. "Why have you come here century after century, interfered with my plans, killed a demon who was very difficult to summon and control, and destroyed one of my battalions?"

"I promised the village my protection," Delgar stated, his hands moving to his hips. "And now that I know you brought the glacier, I want to know why."

Vertanus smiled. "For love. Why else would I do such a thing?"

Chapter V: The Final Battle

Delgar blinked. "I don't understand."

"I find that doubtful," Vertanus said. "I remember how you loved that Jenara girl. Didn't you ever get around to marrying her?"

"That was a long time ago."

"I see," Vertanus said, sitting down behind his desk. "You know what it is to have enemies, do you not?"

Delgar nodded. "Of course. It comes with any sort of power."

"One of my enemies was particularly powerful," Vertanus explained. "His name was Gerinth. I had defeated him in a contest of magic for the position of Vice-Chancellor, and for that he never forgave me. Oh, he did everything he could to make me believe that he had forgiven me, but while I thought that amends had been made, he slowly formulated his revenge.

"He visited me on the day of my wedding. Marissa and I had just retired to my tower, and he wished to offer his best wishes. Like a fool, I let him in, past the rings of protection around my tower, into my inner sanctum. And then he took his revenge."

Vertanus stood and stepped over to the covered table. "Before I knew what had happened, he had cast a spell around Marissa. She fell to the ground and began to...change. And then she became this." Choking away a sob, Vertanus threw off the linen. Beneath was a block of ice, a beautiful woman with golden hair lying inside, her features preternaturally still. Her once-fair skin held a bluish tinge, and Delgar could feel the magic around the block.

Vertanus stepped away. "Gerinth said that the world would have to be covered in ice before I would ever see her stir again. In my rage, I cast a spell that utterly destroyed him. But his curse remains, and no matter what, I was unable to break his spell. Finally, I decided to fulfill his curse; I decided to cover the world in ice. And I am almost finished."

"That's why you wanted to starve the villages," Delgar realized. "You wanted to give their lives to the glacier, so that you can finish your work."

"Glaciers," Vertanus corrected. "My power was such that I could create two of them, and fill the world with ice in half the time. But that power was just not enough. So I have waited, gathered my strength, and now I can finally finish my work. And then I can be happy again."

Delgar gritted his teeth. "You destroyed the world for the love of a woman," he stated. "How can you possibly justify yourself?"

Vertanus laughed. "You aren't the innocent here, Mage Delgar. You made it all possible. You're the one who found the Gem of Sidhe for me; with that I was able to focus all the magic in the world on my task. And that helped more than I could ever thank you."

371

Delgar shook his head, trying to deny it to himself. But yet, he had found the Gem of Sidhe. He had given it to Vertanus. He had made the destruction of his world possible. He looked to the glowing orb, realizing what had to be in it; it was all true.

He took a deep breath. He couldn't allow himself to feel guilt; he had not given the gem to Vertanus with the intent of harm, and Vertanus had abused what should have been simple research.

A prophecy he had once read leapt into his mind. *And from the ice will come a savior, born to mortality but immortal, a destroyer and creator of worlds.* Delgar nodded to himself; he was beginning to understand. He felt wyrd shifting around him once again, but this time he had some idea of where it would take him.

Delgar stepped over to the block of ice, letting his Dragon sight flicker over the woman inside. He saw the strands of the spell all around her, strong but simple.

"What are you doing?" Vertanus demanded.

"Seeing if what I helped create was worth it," Delgar replied, continuing to look into the spell. The nature of the spell finally revealed itself to him. A wave of sorrow washed over him. He shook his head, a tear flowing down his cheek. "My world died for nothing," he muttered.

"What do you mean?" Vertanus demanded.

Delgar turned to look at the wizard. "Your enemy's revenge was more complete than you realize. He didn't just want you to mourn, he wanted you to wait for years in false hope, breaking your spirit to the point that you could never recover."

"False hope?"

"Yes," Delgar declared. "False hope! You spent so much time trying to break and overpower the spell that you never bothered to find out what it was! The spell made her body appear as though it was still sleeping, but even if you had succeeded in covering the world with ice, she would have never awakened. Vertanus, your bride has been dead for six thousand years, and you destroyed the world for her!"

Vertanus shook his head, his eyes wild. "No," he sobbed. "It can't be true. You're lying!"

With a wave of his hand, Delgar swept away the spell. The beautiful figure in the ice melted and shifted, finally becoming a shriveled, desiccated corpse. "The spell is gone," Delgar said sadly. "Do the right thing now, Vertanus. Remove the glaciers. Let the world live once again."

Vertanus fell to his knees and screamed. The Dark Wizard was still for a long moment, and then he looked up. Delgar let the Dragon blood begin to take hold, feeling heat behind his eyes; where there had once been cold, determined sanity behind Vertanus' eyes, now there was only madness.

"I am Delgar, Magus Draconum," Delgar declared. "The Dragonmage, last of the Greater Dragons, and blood-child of Garasus. I command you to destroy the glacier, or I will use my strength to destroy you."

Vertanus raised his hand, sending a bolt of energy hurtling towards Delgar. Delgar extended his power and blocked it, but the impact sent him tumbling into a bookcase. He replied with three fire-bolts, only to see Vertanus easily disperse them.

"Power," the Dark Wizard laughed. "You have no conception of power, little Mage. I have the power of almost all the life in Mideorth at my fingertips. How ironic that you gave it to me!" With that, Vertanus sent another bolt of energy towards Delgar.

Delgar rolled out of the way as the bolt flew past him, the heat searing his shoulder. He quickly used the forces of air to send several of the books from one of the bookshelves flying towards Vertanus, and then shot another fire-bolt at him. One of the books hit Vertanus on the head, but he blocked the rest and dodged the fire-bolt.

"Inventive," Vertanus sneered. "But you failed." He raised his hands, and Delgar was thrown against the wall, pinned in place. Vertanus sent a bolt of power at the pinned Mage, but at the last minute, Delgar managed to break free of the binding. The bolt crashed through the wall, sending shards of ice flying down toward the city below. A chill wind howled through the gaping hole.

Delgar skirted around the rim of the room, sending several fiery missiles at Vertanus. The mad wizard easily blocked each one of them and laughed.

"You have no conception of what you gave me," Vertanus declared. "The Gem of the Sidhe is the source of all magic on Mideorth. It is what made it possible to manipulate the natural forces in the first place! And I have had it for six thousand years! Your Dragon power may be great, Dragonmage, but it is puny compared to the power of an entire world!"

At that moment Freela leapt out from behind a bookcase, spear in hand. Screaming in rage, she struck out at Vertanus, only to have him stop the weapon in place with a mere gesture. Vertanus plucked the spear from her hand and pulled her close, one hand around her throat. Delgar raised his hands as the Dark Wizard pulled her in front of him. Freela's eyes went wide with fright, her mouth moving in what appeared to be a silent prayer or call for help.

"The little girl comes out at last," Vertanus mocked, tightening his grip. "I guess I'm vulnerable now, little Mage, but will you kill her to destroy me? Or will you just watch as I strangle her? She'll make a very good shield, I think. Or maybe I should take her first, have a bit of fun. I'll be sure to make you watch, just so-" his voice cut off in a scream.

Vertanus' taunting had given Delgar just the time he needed. As he had been talking, Delgar struck out one last time with his power; with a bolt of fire and energy, he shattered the blue orb and the gem inside. Vertanus bellowed in horror and agony, dropping Freela. As the girl staggered away, the wizard erupted in white-hot flame, his screams echoing around the room as he was reduced to ashes.

"What is happening?" Freela cried.

"I have destroyed the Gem of Sidhe," Delgar said, rising to his full height and taking a deep breath. "Since he was linked to it for millennia, when it was destroyed all its power was channeled into him. We have to go now; we won't have much time."

The room began to shake. A block of ice fell from the ceiling, barely missing Delgar and Freela. Delgar glanced outside to find steam gushing from huge vents in the glacier. He gazed down to see the city of ice below the tower rocked with explosions as the steam erupted from the ice. The room shifted, several blocks falling down into the doorway. As he spun to look, part of the wall collapsed, exposing even more of the chamber into the open air.

Delgar turned to Freela. "The tower is dying, and the glacier with it!" he declared. "I can get us out of this, but you have to trust me. Stay here, and no matter what you see, don't be afraid!" With that, he dove out of the tower and let the Dragon blood completely take hold.

Freela staggered in fear as the floor trembled beneath her. Not only had she seen Delgar destroy the Dark Wizard, but she had also seen what true magic could do. It terrified her.

As the tower shook itself apart, Delgar turned to her and told her not to be afraid. She thought that he was going to magically transport her away back to her village, but he only walked towards the collapsed wall. And then he threw himself over.

She screamed in terror, not believing what she had just seen. He couldn't be about to kill himself and leave her to die, he couldn't! He might be strange and scary, but he couldn't be evil! Could he?

She ran over to the precipice and looked down. She saw Delgar falling, but something strange was happening to him. His shape began to shift and grow, giant wings sprouting out of his back, his robes becoming a mottled combination of red and green scales. She gasped in fright.

The Dragon turned in a graceful arc, its wings propelling it back towards her. With a start she realized that it had to be a hundred and fifty feet long. The Dragon sped toward her, its glowing red eyes strangely human. Its shadow covered her, and a huge talon reached out and plucked her from the tower. She saw the ground drop away from her, moving at an impossible speed, and then she was surrounded by blissful darkness.

Chapter VI: Endings and Beginnings

Delgar landed just outside the village of the People of the Elk, craning his Draconic head. He watched the villagers pour out of the village, weapons in hand. Delgar grinned; it was no surprise that they would be frightened by their first sight of a Dragon.

He placed Freela on the ground, running his gaze over her to ensure that she was undamaged. The villagers drew closer, forming a ring around the two of them. Delgar furled his wings and let the Dragon blood lose its hold. He felt the wings retracting, his head shortening, and the ground becoming much closer. Finally he stood in human form again, straightening his robes.

Guthfrid stared at him, his mouth agape in shock and awe. Delgar smiled and turned to address the entire village. "I have defeated the Dark Wizard," he declared. "The glacier is dying."

Freela stirred beside him, slowly standing up, her legs unsteady. Guthfrid rushed to meet her, holding her closely in his arms. "My daughter," he cried. "I thought I would never see you again!"

"She followed me," Delgar said. "It was a very poor idea. I was only just able to save her."

"He turned into a Dragon," Freela stammered. "And he picked me up and flew me away. And before that, there was this great big fight, and he..."

Delgar held up his hand. "There will be plenty of time to tell stories about me later. Right now, however, I must speak to Freela for a moment." With that, he drew the young woman aside and whispered in her ear. "This infatuation of yours ends now."

"But I love you," Freela protested.

Delgar shook his head. "You love your sister, and you miss her. But I cannot provide the love that she could, as you believe I can. If you do not mourn for your sister's passing, it will poison your life. I have seen this before, and I speak from experience. Grieve now, and then you will truly be able to live."

"But I want to learn magic," Freela said, her eyes glassy.

"The magic that I once knew is gone; I destroyed it to kill Vertanus. It has left this world, and nobody can restore it. However, there are many kinds of magic, and it must now be your task to discover them. I envy you; you will be taking the first steps in creating a new wizardry."

"You aren't staying?" Freela nearly sobbed.

Delgar shook his head once more. "I have my own tasks to carry out. Now go to your father; he needs you as much as you need him right now. You may have lost a sister, but he lost a daughter."

Freela backed off, turning and embracing her father. The two stood silently for a moment, just holding one another. Delgar smiled; they had finally begun to heal. Then he turned to address everybody.

"I have destroyed the old magic," Delgar announced. "And while it will take several months, the glacier will melt and recede. So now I give all of you a new world. This land used to have great and ancient civilizations, a proud legacy. But now it is virgin soil, waiting for you to claim it. I wish I could join you, taking these first steps on a new world, but I must go."

Guthfrid looked up. "Will you not stay with us, friend wizard? There is much you could teach us."

Delgar shook his head. "I still have much to do. I have destroyed magic, but now I must restore wonder. There will soon be Dragons in the sky once more, most of them wise, ancient and powerful. If you treat them well, they could teach you a great deal."

"What will you do after that?" Freela asked, her voice hopeful.

"I do not know," Delgar replied. "I am the protector of all Dragonkind, and perhaps I will have to continue in that role. Or, perhaps I will finally be able to rest. I just don't know."

"Will we ever see you again, friend Delgar?" Guthfrid asked.

Delgar shook his head once more. "I do not think so. There are always possibilities, but I do not believe this one to be likely. I bid you all farewell. Remember what I have done for you, and make this new world worthy of my deeds."

As Delgar began to turn, he heard Guthfrid's voice once more. "We will rebuild the ancient civilizations!" the Ealdorman declared. "We will make the land worthy of you!"

Delgar stopped. "Make your own great civilizations," he said, looking behind him at the hopeful group of villagers. "Build the future rather than rebuilding the past. It's healthier."

With that, he took two steps forward, mist curling around his boots, and strode onto the Road of Legends. He walked in silence towards the world of the Dragons, trying to decide what he would say. He felt his wyrd wrapping around him, thinning, and finally vanishing.

I have fulfilled my destiny, Delgar realized with a start. *The rest of my future is mine to determine.* As he walked, the burden of wyrd free from his shoulders, he felt almost naked. He shook his head; his first true freedom, and he felt better without it. Then he smiled; the feeling was already beginning to pass.

With each step, he remembered a face from his past. His father and mother, gentle Lera, his beloved Jenara. Chancellor Berran and Archmage Velnan. Somehow, they had all helped to bring him here. If only they could have seen him now, at the end of his task, the world saved. But they were gone, dead for six thousand years, and he was all that was left, the last survivor of a civilization long since crumbled to dust. A tear ran down his cheek.

He finally stepped off the road onto the grass of a familiar world, the mist thinning into nonexistence. He watched as two Dragons arched gracefully in the sky towards him, approaching and finally landing before him. The one which landed to his right was small, only twice as tall as Delgar, with light-green scales, while the other was an ebony Dragon at least thirty feet long.

"We have awaited you for centuries, Magus Draconum," the green one said. "Have you any news?"

"Summon the others," Delgar commanded. "Mideorth is free. It is time to return home."

The black Dragon flared its nostrils in excitement. "Is this true? Is the great ice finally destroyed?"

Delgar nodded. "It is in its death throes. We can all finally go home."

With a great leap, the ebony Dragon took flight,

soaring up into the sky with a joyous cry. Delgar smiled and sat down to wait. As he watched, the sky began to fill with Dragons of every size and color.

Leoht'heortan landed beside him, his green eyes glowing in joy. "It is true," he bellowed. "You have come to lead us home."

Delgar nodded. "Are we all here?"

"We have all come."

"Then follow," Delgar said, stepping onto the Road of Legends one last time.

The Dragons appeared on Mideorth under the shadow of the glacier. As Delgar watched, the ice crumbled, fell to the ground, and melted.

He turned to find tears flowing down Leoht'heortan's face, the Great Dragon gazing upon the receding ice. "I only wish the Teraeni Dragons could be here to witness this."

"They will hold a place of honor until the end of the cycle and beyond," Delgar declared. "But I have something to ask of you."

"What do you wish, Magus Draconum?" Leoht'heortan asked.

"Mankind has suffered here as much as we have, if not more," Delgar began. "They have watched their civilization crumble, and, unlike us, they have not been able to escape. And now magic has left the world; I had to destroy the Gem of Sidhe to free Mideorth."

Delgar turned to face the Great Dragon. "Help them to build a new world. Teach them the paths of wisdom. Help them to find a new magic. That is what I must ask."

Leoht'heortan nodded. "We shall consider them our children. With luck, in only three millennia or so, they will no longer need us."

Delgar nodded. "Thank you."

"How do you feel, Delgar?" the Dragon asked.

Delgar blinked. "Sorry?"

"How do you feel?"

"Tired," Delgar finally replied. "Very, very tired. And very, very old."

He felt a talon rest gently on his shoulder. "Then perhaps you should finally rest."

Delgar nodded. "At least for a while."

Epilogue: The Passing of a Legend

Delgar sat by the lake, watching the Dragons soar across the clear blue sky as he idly plucked at the new grass. He watched the great wyrms twist and turn gracefully in the air, their very movies a celebration of the return to their long lost homeland.

The glaciers were retreating to the north and south with remarkable speed, and wherever they passed, the land was revitalized. It was almost as if all the life the evil in them had destroyed was being returned to the earth, a payment for six millennia of hardships.

"You've done well," came a familiar voice. "They're already singing of your deeds around campfires."

Delgar nodded. "Hello, Daelyn."

Delgar turned to see the Tuatha de Danaan standing over him, his green double-breasted overcoat flapping in the breeze. For a moment, they stood in silence, basking in the nature. "Has there been any sign of your people?" Delgar finally asked.

Daelyn shook his head. "They could be anywhere on the Road. I just wish I had arrived in time." The Tuatha de Danaan had summoned Daelyn a thousand years ago, but he had been late in arriving, and found his ancient home deserted. Now he wandered the Road of Legends in search of them. "I'll find them eventually," Daelyn said. "It may take millennia, but I have all eternity." He knelt by Delgar. "And what of you? Are you happy to be home at last?"

Delgar shook his head. "This isn't my world anymore. My Mideorth passed with the coming of the glaciers. I do not know this new land." He motioned at the surroundings. "This used to be the desert of Barsh, and the Cave of Dreams was south of here." He pointed northwards. "The Mageschool in Taerraland used to be that way, and so did Nordland. But all of that is gone; it was ground to dust under the glacier six millennia ago."

"It will return some time," Daelyn said. "The cycle is far from over, but it will end. And then Mideorth will be reborn, and your world will live again."

"I am so weary of it all," Delgar sighed.

"Your task is over," Daelyn pointed out. "You can rest now."

"I am Magus Draconum, the protector of all Dragonkind," Delgar said. "I cannot simply abandon my duty."

"Your task is finished, and you have done well," Daelyn stated. "Centuries and millennia from now, they will still be telling stories of Delgar Dragonmage, and how he freed the land from the ice. But the Dragons no longer need a protector."

"They need to survive in this new world. The struggle isn't over yet."

"There is no end to that," Daelyn said. "Survival is not a gift, or a right, but a struggle. If it ceases to become a struggle for somebody, than that one has died. Your part of the struggle has ended."

"And what of contentment?" Delgar asked.

"Contentment is a form of death," Daelyn stated. "Didn't you know?"

Delgar looked Daelyn in the eye. "So I can rest now?"

Daelyn nodded, and then stood up. "I fear that I must bid you farewell, Delgar. There are no Tuatha de Danaan here, and I must continue my search. I just wanted to see you one last time."

Delgar chuckled. "You've become a wanderer on the Road of Legends. I think your wyrd must be similar to mine."

"Perhaps. Wyrd will work as it will." Daelyn turned and began to walk away. "Farewell, Delgar Dragonmage. I do not think we will not meet again."

"Farewell, Daelyn!" Delgar called. Then he lay back on the ground, watching the first flower of a new spring blossom. The petals began to open softly, tenderly, a rebirth of life long forgotten.

Delgar's memories came to haunt him again, and he thought of his life, his brittle moments of happiness and peace, the great glacier, and his travels on the Road. As he remembered, a tear began to slide down his cheek, and he longed for a happiness that had long since passed.

"Hello, Delgar, my love," he heard, and he looked up to see Jenara silhouetted in the sunlight. He stood up unsteadily, a flood of tears blurring his vision. Still, he could see her, and she was as radiant as the day they wed so many thousands of years ago.

"My love," Delgar cried. "I've waited so long!"

"Come to me," Jenara said softly. "I have waited for an eternity."

Delgar took her in his arms and held her close, tears pouring down his cheeks, rejoicing in every touch, every sensation. "We'll never be apart again," he promised.

"Never."

As he held her, the world around him darkened, and he knew only her. And after six millennia, Delgar Dragonmage finally knew peace.

And as he found his peace, the land around him continued its rebirth.

About the Author

Robert B. Marks wears many hats, only one of which is a Stetson – he is a writer, editor, researcher, publisher, independent historian, and teacher. He has degrees in Mediaeval Studies, English Literature, and War Studies. He is the author of *Diablo: Demonsbane*, *The EverQuest Companion*, *Garwulf's Corner*, *An Odyssey into Video Games and Pop Culture*, and co-author of *A Funny Thing Happened on the Way to the Agora*. In his spare time, he has done everything from make mead to historical swordfighting to rockhounding.

He lives in the area of Kingston, Ontario, with his wife and two children.

www.ingramcontent.com/pod-product-compliance
Lightning Source LLC
Chambersburg PA
CBHW050122030726
47505CB00007B/1992